DAMNED
YANKEES

RAY DEPTULA

ISBN: xxx (hardcover)
ISBN: 979-8-89079-168-9 (paperback)
ISBN: 979-8-89079-169-6 (ebook)

Those who fight their nation's wars are typically those least able to avoid it.

Professor Charles P. Niemeyer,
U.S. Naval War College

Be it known to the present,
And to all future generations,
That the Sons of Liberty in Taunton
Fired with a zeal for the preservation of
Their rights as men, and as American Englishmen,
And prompted by a just resentment of
The wrongs and injuries offered to the
English colonies in general, and to
This Province in particular,
Through the unjust claims of
A British Parliament and the Machiavellian policy of a British ministry,
Have erected this monument of Liberty standard,
As a testimony of their fixed resolution
To preserve sacred and inviolate
Their birthrights and charter rights,
And to resist even unto blood
All attempts for their subversion or abridgement.
Born to be free, we spurn the knaves who dare
For us the chains of slavery to prepare:
Steadfast in freedom's cause, we'll live and die,
Unawed by statement; foes to tyranny,
But if oppression brings us to our graves,
And marks us dead, she ne'er shall mark us slaves.

October 21, 1774: Declaration in Massachusetts upon the erection of a liberty pole with the saying, CRESCIT AMOR PATRIAE QUE CUPIDO (The love of Country and the Desire for Freedom)

Yankee Doodle came to town
For to buy a firelock
We will tar and feather him
And so we will John Hancock
When old Georgie took the field
He proved an arrant coward
He wouldn't fight the British there
For fear of being devoured
Then old Georgie grew so bold
He said there is no greater
But he will sing a mournful tune
When he's hanged as a traitor

Alternate British version of *Yankee Doodle*

PROLOGUE

For if any be a hearer of the word, and not a doer,
he is like unto a man beholding his natural face in a glass:
For he beholdeth himself, and goeth his way, and straightway
forgetteth what manner of man he was. But those whoso looketh
into the perfect law of liberty, and continueth therein, he being
not a forgetful hearer, but a doer of the work, this man shall be
blessed in his deed.

James 1:23-25 KJV

BLUE HILL, MAINE, NOVEMBER 1829

The man stared in the distance as he bobbed evenly atop his horse, peering past the nearby bend in the road for what he had been told would be a break in the forest. Arriving at a clearing he paused briefly and took a deep breath as his eyes meandered through an orchard up toward a simple house on a small hill. He said a prayer out loud before turning onto the rutted lane that wound through the apple trees. Well past the autumn harvest the sticky odor of pine quickly gave way to the pungent scent of rotting fruit left on the ground, mixed with sweet hardwood smoke blowing down from the house. With the sky turning grey as the morning progressed, he faced directly into an increasing southwest wind, not so cold as it was

1

raw and damp. Tightening his scarf as he cinched up his coat and continued up the hill toward the house, hearing only the sounds of muffled hooves clomping on the worn grass path.

His journey had started in Annapolis well back in the spring and had required more effort and finances than most would have considered equitable, or even sane. But he was a man of considerable means and perhaps more stubborn than prudent. Leaving his native Maryland for the first time ever, he traveled north to Philadelphia then over through New Jersey eventually crossing the Hudson River onto Manhattan Island. The transition to New York had been surprisingly easy, both in climate and civic temperament as the lingering influence of the Dutch had rendered those surroundings somewhat familiar to his mid-Atlantic Quaker home. He had remained in Manhattan longer than needed through the summer and into autumn, conducting business and enjoying the hospitality of the affluent class to which he belonged.

But if his travels to New York had proven relatively seamless, his transition into New England had decidedly not. With the summer now replaced by an increasingly volatile climate, gone were the easy rolling farmlands along the mid-Atlantic fed by wide, slow rivers, gentle and generous in countenance to their dependents as a mother with a favorite child. Before him lay now hard-scrabble countryside covered with dense forests and steep hills, strewn with rocks more plentiful than the stars themselves. Gone also was the friendly tolerance of mankind, replaced instead by suspicion and distrust of any person who did not emanate from whatever hamlet he approached. He soon learned, however, that the one New England value that superseded even the wariness of strangers was the absolute reverence of hard currency, of which he possessed in sufficient quantities. The ruggedness of the landscape and its inhabitants only increased as he moved farther north until now, here in the Penobscot region of Maine, formerly a region itself of Massachusetts but having gained statehood less than a decade prior, where he found himself in the outer reaches of the known world.

Reaching the house, he dismounted his horse and tied it to a nearby tree within sight of a gravestone not far from the side of the building; before the orchid gave way to a copse of old maples. The structure itself looked sturdy and functional in a rough fashion, much in keeping with the rest of his surroundings, with wooden shingles so beaten and weathered that it gave the impression of a middle-aged spinster no longer concerned with upkeep and appearance. He waited in the yard for several minutes and, when no one appeared, he approached the front entrance, a faded red windowless wooden door that sat crooked on its hinges. He made the sign of the cross, then raised his hand to knock, pausing momentarily before mustering three small raps. Wringing his hands, he waited, eyeing his oblivious horse as it sniffed the ground for something to chew. Several moments later he knocked again, this time with more authority.

Shuffling sounds now emanated from inside and eventually, tediously, the entry opened, but just a crack. He stood in silence as he waited, peering into the thin dark space that gave nothing away.

"Can I help you?" a male voice asked flatly from behind the door.

The man gathered himself. "Excuse me for bothering you, sir. I mean you no harm. I am looking for a Mister *John Halliday*. I believe that he goes by *Jack*."

"I am Jack Halliday. Are you with the government?"

"No, sir, I am not with the government. I am...." The man hesitated, hanging his head as he took a deep breath. "I am Roger Coleman Stuyvesant from Annapolis, Maryland. My mother was Priscilla Coleman Stuyvesant, daughter of Arthur Coleman, a prominent landowner. If you are Jack Halliday from Liverpool, England, then I believe I am your son."

There was now a long silence as the man stood frozen in place before the entry. Finally, the door crack opened slightly more but not enough to see inside. The voice in the dark spoke again. "Come a little closer so I can see you."

The man shuffled right to position himself in full view of whoever was beyond the crack. He waited a full minute, not moving again. The door now opened full to reveal an elderly man of medium height with the wiry build of a laborer, brown eyes and a full head of shoulder-length grey hair pulled back neatly into a ponytail. The pair stared at each other in silence.

The elderly man now motioned with his hand. "Come in, please," he directed softly.

The younger man followed down a short hallway that split the house in half and into a main living area on the right that was sparsely furnished save for a table and large chair that faced an ample fireplace that crackled with embers of hardwood logs. The elderly man retrieved a smaller chair and set it on the other side of table. "Please, sit," he gestured as he took a seat across in the large chair.

They looked at each other again for a long moment. The elderly man attempted to speak several times but stopped. Finally, he managed to mutter, "My *son*, you say?"

The younger man nodded. "If you are the Jack Halliday that knew my mother and grandfather, then I believe so."

"Yes, I did. A long time ago. And your mother, how is she?"

The younger man hesitated, as he gazed down at the floor and clasped his hands together before looking back up. "She died in the winter. She had been sick with a fever and not well last year." He looked down again, his eyes beginning to tear up.

The elderly man nodded. "You have your mother's look about you. I saw it at the door. What is your given name, again?"

"Roger," the younger man replied softly. "My name is Roger."

"Roger," the elderly man repeated. "It is a strong name. You came to look for me now? Why?"

"Mother told me about you the day before she passed. I had no idea. She said that she wanted me to know. Grandfather died some time ago. Also, my father, several years back. My wife is gone as well. I have no children. Mother said that if you were still alive you would be my only living relative."

The elderly man nodded. "All the way from Annapolis. How could you have known where I was?"

4

"I remember when I was a child the slaves spoke of a strange white man who had come to work for Grandfather. He lived and worked with them, and they liked him very much. Then he left and they didn't see him again. But somehow, they had knowledge, had received some correspondence, that the white man was somewhere north of Boston with an apple orchid. That's all I had to go on."

"That's not much to go on to make such a journey. What else did your mother tell you if she wanted you to find me?"

"She said that you were a soldier. She said that you were a soldier who went away and didn't come back. She said that she cared for you very much but that you didn't come back."

The elderly man stiffened as he looked away. "She told you that, did she?" he asked curtly now, folding his arms and leaning back toward the table. "I'm sorry to hear about your mother as I loved her more than you could know. Because of that I'm here where you find me. Because of that I've learned to be content with what little I have. I've learned not to want as those who always want are also always disappointed. Because the one thing in life that I wanted, the only thing I ever truly wanted, the one thing that I was willing to trade my life for, was to come back to your mother. And that was the last time I ever let myself want anything."

1

Six hundred niggers I bought dirt cheap
Where the Senegal river is flowing;
Their flesh is firm and their sinews tough
As the finest iron going.
I got them by barter, and gave in exchange
Glass beads, steel goods, and some brandy;
I shall make at least eight hundred per cent
With but half of them living and handy.

Excerpt from the poem,
The Slave Ship, Henrich Heine

ELMINA, WEST AFRICA, DECEMBER 25, 1772

John *Jack* Halliday stood on the foredeck of the slave ship, *Pigeon*, leaning on the starboard gunwale, the upper-most edge of the hull that rose about waist high from the deck. He brushed back his shoulder-length dark hair pulled neatly into a ponytail with a hand far too callused for a lad of sixteen as his brown eyes stared onto the crescent-shaped shoreline of the anchorage that served as a harbor. Inland from the rocky coastline several hundred yards to the north sat a large castle, distinct both in its European style and bleached white seashell construction. Several hundred yards behind that structure farther north on a hill stood yet another fortress, drabber and less dramatic, perched above the first like a bird of prey. On either side of the harbor farther along the coastline as far as the eye could see lay more such edifices, each within cannon shot of the next like a giant European chain much out of place along this primitive Guinea Coast. To the right of the white castle sprawled a ramshackle village of huts that seemed built by children in a game of sticks and in front of that, rows of brightly colored large canoes lined a steeply pitched beach. All of this appeared against a backdrop of deep green vegetation so dense that it threatened to swallow anyone who entered. Yet, the most unusual sight of all were the inhabitants themselves with which nature had chosen to populate this alien land.

"Are those the last ones?" Jack asked as he turned to Georgey.

"Aye, lad," Georgey answered in his raspy voice. "Can't hardly fit no more in the hold. We'll be weighin' anchor soon as these are stowed. Wind's blowin' right. Get yer last look at this jewel of a place, lad, 'cause soon yer'll be seein' nothin' but ocean."

In contrast to Jack's average, lean stature, Georgey stood tall and bulky with thinning red hair on a large square head out of which shone bright blue eyes and held maybe half his teeth, with a weather-beaten frame so crooked he looked like a question mark. His sunburnt skin covered with faded tattoos, he seemed as if he had been melted down, then reconstituted back into something not quite the same. Except for the mate, he stood the biggest man on board and, depending on his mood, could be kinder than a saint or meaner than a sore-headed dog. Somewhere north of forty years in age, the vast majority of that *before the mast*, he claimed to have poked out a man's eye with his thumb just for shorting him on a ration of rum. No one on board seemed to doubt him.

The *Pigeon* had been loading a cargo of Negroes since arriving in late November and now was nearly finished with the task. Another half-dozen ships lay anchored in the vicinity, each adding to the hustle and bustle of the small but busy port as the canoes from the beach crisscrossed the harbor, hauling human payload and other supplies. Two such canoes made their way toward the *Pigeon*, each carrying a couple dozen black men bound together by the hands with rope.

"Seems a hell of a place to be on Christmas Day," Jack offered as he watched the laden vessels strain to approach.

"Aye, lad," Georgey chuckled, "one 'ell of a place to be on any day. Time to count yer blessings that God made ya a Christian and not one a the likes of them."

Jack nodded and focused on the approaching vessels, beginning to make out faces. "Did you ever wonder why He did that, Georgey?"

"Jesus, lad," Georgey swore as he shook his head, "I'm a sailor, not a goddamn reverend. But take my advice and don't trouble yerself 'bout it. We've a whole ocean to cross yet and yer'll need to be on yer toes, ya will. Compassion is a virtue to be sure, but not out 'ere. From 'ere to Curacao, fear is yer best friend, lad – fear'll keep ya alive. Those devils in the hold'll just as soon slit yer throat as look at ya. Make no mistake on that account, lad, if ya want to see the other side of the ocean."

Jack nodded silently as Georgey continued.

"We all have our station in life, lad, and there is nothin' we can do about it. If God didn't want this lot for such a purpose, then 'E wouldn't 'ave made them such as 'E did, now would 'E 'ave? We're not at liberty to know why."

"Liberty," Jack repeated softly.

"Aye, lad – a precious thing, eh? Not much liberty to go 'round 'ere, least not for the likes a us. Even less fer those poor buggars. What liberty we 'ave we better guard like gold."

"Plenty of work, meager liberty, but no freedom," Jack joked.

"Aye, lad," Georgey answered with a good bit of seriousness. "There is yer portion on the good ship *Pigeon*. But nobody's free anyways 'less they're dead, so just concern yerself with the first two. Now quit yer lollygaggin' 'cause there's work to be done. Don't want the mate up our arse, now do we?"

The *Pigeon* was a three-masted bark out of Liverpool, seventy-three feet long, about a third of that wide and nearly thirteen feet deep with a displacement of almost ninety-seven tons. Built as a grain ship a decade before in the Brittany region of France, she had since been modified for other uses and, on this trip, carried a general cargo of metal ware, knives, firearms and gunpowder, wool, cotton cloth and various textiles, fine linens, jewelry, brandy, rum, and most importantly, cowry shells to be used as currency. Her master, a stern small-statured Scotsman named Captain Ross, ruled with an iron fist with his communication as frugal as his finances. The rest of the officers were Scottish as well and of them, the First Mate, Bailey, kept a willing reputation as a bully – a monster, actually – quite necessary to rule a mainly English crew comprised of the dregs of society who functioned little better than a pack of jackals.

They had departed Liverpool that September with a charter to trade the general cargo for Negroes in Guinea West Africa, then haul them across the Atlantic Ocean to the West Indies in exchange for sugar, molasses, tobacco, and indigo for transport back to Liverpool. The expedition was financed by a consortium of Dutch investors who understood that for a relatively meager investment of common items readily found on the European continent, a massive potential profit lay not in selling the Negroes themselves – on that account they would be lucky to break even – but rather by importing those Caribbean commodities acquired in trade to an addicted Europe.

Trade and enterprise in mineral-rich Guinea had been originally established by the Africans themselves long before any European had even an inkling of their existence. Portuguese explorers in the 15th century were amazed to discover a massive indigenous mining industry and aptly named this stretch of West Africa the *Gold Coast*. As a matter of practicality, the Portuguese built a fortress to protect and facilitate their new and growing gold trade, naming their prized facility *Elmina*, meaning *the mine*. Such a monopolistic situation could not be tolerated by other European powers and eventually this stretch of coastline contained more concentrated firepower than anywhere in the known world. Blows were traded both locally and in Europe itself to establish coastal African dominance and eventually the Portuguese were pushed out by the better armed and organized Dutch and English. But no sooner had the situation somewhat stabilized, than the discovery of the New World with better quality gold and a massive need for labor to support agricultural industries suddenly changed Guinea's most valuable commodity from minerals to humans. Now long-established outfits such as the Dutch West Indies Company profited not from the harvesting of gold but rather the natives themselves.

Quite conveniently, a robust slave trade already existed as part of the West African fabric since long before the Europeans arrived, as competing tribes conquered whomever they could to conduct commerce with each other and also with northern Arabs, who would transport various quantities by foot over the Sahara Desert. The paradigm shift to provide humans for profit to the ravenous New World proved not a hard one to make, particularly for the likes of the dominant *Akan* tribe that were only too happy to exploit their weaker neighbors and trade them for advanced weaponry and other manufactured items that would increase their ability to keep their stock full. Monopolizing and leveraging European technology into a massive capture machine, the Akan kingdom of *Asante* grew to an area larger than Europe itself with Elmina remaining, as originally intended, one of the key economic portals. As long as European traders were willing to pay to fill their wooden vessels with human cargo, powerful tribes such as the Akan were willing to supply them in a virtually unlimited and mutually advantageous fashion.

"Damn yer eyes, lad." Georgey scowled at Jack with his characteristic feigned angry expression and an orange face that looked from exertion in the wet heat like a warped pumpkin. "Give us a little a that fid."

Jack fetched a nearby fid – nothing more than a wooden club with a narrow, tapered end – and placed the point onto a thick rope hawser at the spot where Georgey pointed. As he held the fid firm, Georgey hammered the opposite wide end with a mallet, quickly opening the three main strands that twisted together to form the line. The craftsman carefully began to weave the unraveled strands at the line's end back through the newly created openings to form a loop, or *eye*, as if it had existed to begin with.

"Don't be makin' yerself scarce, lad, 'cause yer'll be weavin' the rest a these," he scowled again before leaving Jack with nearly a dozen such lines. As the old sailor strode off in search of other projects, Jack watched as he lowered himself down the nearby main hatch, his red head disappearing like a sunset. All around, the deck bustled with commotion as the crew busied themselves with general housekeeping duties in preparation to depart. It could take a ship several months to load a full hold of Negroes and normally required stops at numerous outposts; however, the *Pigeon* had managed it in a single port visit with the terms negotiated and general cargo offloaded in less than three weeks. Purely by chance, Captain Ross and his ship had arrived at a buyer's market as the castle storerooms were bursting due to recent aggressive activity of the Akan. The Dutch company factor in charge of the castle had been only too happy to relieve his surplus at a favorable price, in large part to preserve the health of his overcrowded storerooms.

As the general cargo was emptied, the entire ship underwent a significant alteration to convert to storage for humans instead. In the hold below the main deck carpenters built shelf-like platforms along the inside of the hull as well as creating an athwartship bulkhead that divided the hold in two sections, fore and aft. A similar barricade was erected on the main deck above just aft of the main mast, a wall that rose up and outward on both sides of the ship to ensure that no man could climb around to the quarterdeck that loomed above from behind. From the initial onload through the entire voyage the men in the forward hold were isolated from the women and children aft. All the way aft topside at the stern on the quarterdeck, the control station of the ship, the crew organized an armed rally point in case of rebellion. Even in the ideal situation the loading process proved tedious, with several Negroes lost over the side, some by accident during the transfer from the canoes and others that chose suicide over captivity. Each disappeared in a matter of moments, not even having time to drown before they were devoured by sharks that swarmed around the hull like moths to a candle. The men were loaded first, shackled by the ankles in pairs in the forward hold with the women and children loaded after, remaining unshackled and merely locked below in the aft section until out of sight of land. In all, Captain Ross had traded every last bit of the general cargo he brought for one hundred forty-eight men, eighty-two women, nineteen boys, and five girls – two hundred fifty-four total, which filled his hold to capacity.

With the entire cargo now on board the tension among the crew increased with the common knowledge that most rebellions took place at this point, immediately after the loading, with the ship still within sight of land – the chief concern not a staged uprising but rather a contagious act of individual desperation that would spark a cascading, panicked riot. The sailors walked on the deck like skittish cats as the throng of disorientated and frightened captives huddled below. Captain Ross ordered a chest of small arms, readied and primed, to be kept on quarterdeck, and the swivel guns loaded with case shot to be sighted at the main deck directly at the single hatchway that represented the lone egress from the hold. The most veteran deckhands acted as guards with strict orders to shoot on sight – man, woman, or child – any Negro who managed to even poke their head on deck or otherwise show signs of stirring the mob.

The air hung heavy like a damp, hot curtain as the final canoe headed for shore. With final negotiations finished, accounts settled, and the cargo transferred, Jack helped man the forward windlass as the crew turned the mechanical device that winched several tons of iron chain and anchor up from the muddy bottom back inside the ship. Setting her sails to the northwest breeze that would blow the ship on an east-southeast course, Elmina slowly disappeared in the *Pigeon's* wake, along with any hopes of those trapped below.

As counterproductive as it would seem, the quickest way, in fact the *only* way, for the *Pigeon* to head west from Guinea to the Caribbean was to continue further *east* toward the Bight of Benin, where the African coast turned south. Leaving Elmina, the ship was forced southeast by both the Guinea Current and prevailing northwest winds until it arrived in two weeks at São Tomé Island, barely north of the Equator. Here the enterprise stopped to re-provision with food and water, with the crew all the while keeping guard on the hold full of Negroes as they had at Elmina. Upon leaving São Tomé the ship encountered a weak southerly current and with the winds light and variable, drifted like a bottle a couple hundred miles below the Equator until finally catching the southeast trade winds that would drive it all the way to the Caribbean.

By February and nearly halfway across the Atlantic, the trip had proceeded relatively smoothly with the crew and cargo well-settled into a daily routine. Every mid-morning the Negro men would be brought topside two at a time and kept near the forecastle, the raised deck at the very forward part of the ship more commonly called the *fo'c'sle*. Their shackles were checked by one of the carpenters and an officer after which they were allowed to relieve themselves over the side on a specially built platform and then wash themselves with seawater. The women and children were brought up next and kept aft near the quarterdeck, usually unshackled as they were not considered a threat. After came the first meal, normally a gruel of fava beans, millet, manioc flour, and sometimes peas, along with a drink of water, served in buckets with ten captives squatting around, each with a wooden spoon. Next was the morning session of dancing, intended for health and exercise, with music provided by crewmen playing bagpipes. Both groups were prodded into motion – whipped, if necessary – even the men who remained shackled to a partner. The Negroes then worked under supervision to scrape clean the night's accumulated filth from the hold, after which was perfumed by passing through a vinegar-soaked sponge and the deck scrubbed with cold vinegar or sometimes seawater. At noon the

Negroes were given a second drink and allowed to relax topside. In the early evening came the second and final meal, followed by a third drink and dancing as before. After festivities the hold was inspected for hidden tools or weapons and the Negroes reloaded below for the night. The crew then washed down the upper deck and inspected for leftover contraband.

This monotonous but stable routine had continued for nearly two months since leaving Elmina as the ship and crew had experienced nothing but fine weather. However, as was bound to happen eventually, they now encountered an atmospheric disturbance with seas too rough to bring the Negroes topside. What began as an inconvenience deepened into a stubborn blow that carried on for nearly a week. The terrified captives below were fed as best as could be managed, but worse, had been forced to ride out the storm lying in their own vomit, urine, blood, and excrement, as the hold could not be cleaned. On the fifth morning the weather finally broke enough for the crew to inspect the hold as the seas remained rough with large, dark, southeast swells rolling in from their quarter astern. Lead by Mate Bailey himself, they immediately found two Negroes dead, several near dead, and a number afflicted with fever and rash on their face and chest. Shortly thereafter the officers huddled on the quarterdeck in conference with Captain Ross and Mister Ruud, the agent for the Dutch investors. Meanwhile, Mate Bailey organized a team that would make a second foray into the cargo hold, this time with the ship's doctor, to make a more detailed determination of the situation and to segregate the sick from the relatively healthy. Following closely on the heels of rebellion the second greatest fear was disease and as was predictable, this prolonged squall had produced an inevitable sickness. With the success of the enterprise now in jeopardy, the situation needed to be stabilized quickly before the illness could overtake the entire investment and even spread to the crew.

Finishing his early-morning watch, Jack had gone to the fo'c'sle for an attempt to rest in his hammock in the still rough seas. But before he could fall asleep a familiar hand rolled him by the shoulder out onto the deck.

"Come, lad. We've a job to do."

"Are we in for a rough one this morning, Georgey?" Jack asked as Georgey's face betrayed not a small amount of anxiety.

"I'm afraid so, lad. But unlike a good bottle a wine the situation's not goin' to improve with age."

Jack followed Georgey topside where others had gathered when Mate Bailey approached with a determined stride and more than his usual growling bellow. Bailey was taller even than Georgey, though not quite as broad with long angular features and a drawn face dominated by a large, crooked nose that had obviously been broken at least once. Poised above the main hatchway, they eyed one another like two large dogs that had come to a territorial understanding.

"What the Christ are you waiting for? I gave you a job, didn't I? Take the bloody crew and get down there!"

"No worries, Mister Mate," Georgey answered with a practiced smile that he seemed to save only for Bailey, "just discussin' a bit a strat'gy."

"What bloody *strategy*?" Bailey sneered. "You go down into the hold with the others and haul the Negroes topside. There's your bloody *strategy* right there. Now move, goddamn it!"

"Aye, Mister Mate," Georgey answered evenly. "We are a movin'."

Out on deck Jack watched as several of the crew descended the main hatchway then soon reemerged carrying two dead Negro men by the wrists and ankles. They half-shuffled, half-dragged the black lumps to the starboard gunwale amidships, moving carefully across the pitching and rolling deck as if on a tightrope. Here they paused to catch their breath and balance, then unceremoniously heaved the bodies over the side as if common refuse. Bailey then ordered Georgey to follow the doctor back down into the forward hold where the main problem seemed to exist, apparently not much affecting the women and children aft. Georgey hesitated as Bailey eyed him with a look that left no room for negotiation. Georgey stared back, not so much in defiance but as if to make a point that he could.

Georgey turned to the others of the crew. "Come now, lads. A tough bit of work this mornin' but we must get it over with. Don't touch nothin' 'cept what the doctor tells ya. There's a pint in it fer us all afterward." He grabbed Jack by the arm. "Stay with me, lad. Do like I say and yer'll be right as rain."

Georgey followed the doctor and carpenter down the main hatchway, leading several of the crew behind him like a mother duck. Entering the cargo hold an indescribable stench hit them like a wall as each began to alternately cough, gag, and swear. Jack instinctively turned to leave but Georgey pulled him back sternly by the arm and did not let go. Once fully inside they paused to allow their eyes to adjust to the darkness, adding to their misery by actually seeing the origins of the odor. One of the men behind Jack vomited, the product of which was not even noticeable amid the disgusting mixture of filth that coated the deck and human cargo alike.

"We start over here." The doctor pointed to a section of the hold close to the entrance and began to work his way around in a clockwise fashion. He paused briefly at each shackled man, stooping forward to check their face and chest. Georgey and the rest followed slightly behind, stepping over or on top of as necessary the disoriented Negroes wedged together into the deck. The doctor suddenly motioned with his hand. "Bring this one topside. And this one as well. Lay them out near the main mast."

As the doctor continued Georgey pointed to two pairs of sailors as the carpenter carefully unshackled the indicated Negroes. These crewmen removed the men from their places and carried them as best they could across the hold. "Make sure the swivel gun can reach 'em," Georgey ordered as they neared the main hatchway, "just in case."

"This one's gone," the doctor stated flatly then stepped over to the next. The carpenter methodically removed the shackles from a young man that looked to be about the same age as Jack, still alive but barely responsive.

"This is you and me, lad." Georgey turned to Jack. "Grab 'im by the ankles."

Jack complied as Georgey got behind the youth and lifted him from under the armpits, dragging him across the sea of bodies fixed to the still heavily pitching deck. Reaching the hatchway the pair grunted and strained, alternately pulling and pushing the limp dead weight up the ladder. Emerging onto the main deck they laid the boy down, pausing briefly to take a large helping of fresh air.

"Come now, lad, almost there." Georgey motioned to resume, "over to the gun'ale."

Jack hesitated but grabbed the boy's ankles again, starting toward the other two Negroes laid out by the main mast.

"No, lad," Georgey shook his head, "to the gun'ale I said. This 'ere's going over the side."

Jack hesitated again. He attempted to speak but no words came.

"Yeah, that's right – 'e's still alive." Georgey looked Jack directly in the eye and lowered his voice. "This enterprise don't collect insurance on cargo that dies of sickness, but it does if they drown. The ones the doctor says are dying go over the side, just like the ones already dead. Our good Mister Ruud is watchin' like a hawk to make sure the tally is correct so, the sooner we get these over the side, the better. Now move. There's sure to be more where this came from."

Jack lifted reluctantly and followed Georgey toward the starboard side amidships, only several steps away, stopping at the gunwale.

"Ready? We'll swing 'im inboard toward the main mast then back up and over then let go." Georgey waited for a response but received none. "What are ya waiting for?" he asked impatiently.

Jack looked away as he instead lowered the boy's feet to the deck. The young man gazed up at the sky in an apathetic manner, seemingly not cognizant of his surroundings.

"Listen to me, lad," Georgey implored, lowering his voice even further, "I know this isn't pleasant. But ya 'eard the doctor.

This one's going to die fer sure. Believe me, lad, we're doin' 'im a favor. Now move."

Jack remained still as an exasperated Georgey stared at him.

"What the Christ is going on over here?" Mate Bailey approached from the stern, waving his stretched arms excitedly. "Georgey, what the bloody hell are you two waiting for? We have work to do, for Christ's sakes!"

"No problems, Mister Mate," Georgey answered cheerfully, "all's well 'ere."

"All is *not* well here, goddamn it! I've been watching you two scupper trouts from the quarterdeck – lollygagging and all the while the cargo's spoiling! Now do your job!"

Georgey looked back at Jack and motioned with his head toward the ocean. "Come, lad."

Jack remained frozen still.

"I see," Mate Bailey stated, now more irritated than excited, "we have us a *doubter*." He produced a pistol from his belt and placed the muzzle against the back of Jack's head. "You throw that nigger overboard, lad, or your brains will be on the deck! Tell him, Georgey!"

Georgey nodded. "Do it, lad. Otherwise, I'll be throwin' yer carcass overboard next."

Jack looked at Georgey, who wore an uncharacteristic expression of worry, then swapped his gaze to the boy that continued to stare listlessly at the sky. Bailey pushed the pistol harder into the base of Jack's skull and cocked it.

"I'll not say it again, lad," Bailey sneered. "I'm running out of patience."

Still holding the youth by the ankles, Jack shook as he swallowed hard and nodded to Georgey, his arms straining as they took the weight. In one motion they lifted together, swinging the boy inward, then up and over the gunwale, where they released him. He dropped from sight below the horizon making a flat *thud* as he hit the water before floating back into the scores of sharks that had trailed the ship from the African continent. Jack turned away and followed Georgey back toward the main hatchway.

Bailey's cruel stare accompanied the pair as the giant replaced the weapon in his belt. "Good lad," he muttered with a rare chuckle. "We've no need of anymore of that then. There are more niggers to fetch, I imagine – eh Georgey?"

"Aye, Mister Mate, ya imagine correct, ya do."

A pair of crewmen passed by carrying another live Negro, pausing briefly at the gunwale to steady themselves against the still-heavy swells before discharging their burden over the side. Jack looked aft to the quarterdeck where Captain Ross and Mister Ruud stood, surveying the proceedings. The Dutch agent fidgeted, alternately pacing and writing in a large book. In contrast the captain remained motionless, seemingly a statue that peered down stoically with eyes that could only be described as cold as the bottom of a winter lake. Jack took one last large breath of fresh air and followed Georgey again down the main hatchway. For a good bit of the morning the crew brought more live Negroes up from below and threw them over the side with the remainder of the day spent cleaning the hold as the weather steadily subsided.

By the end of the day the wind subsided, and the seas lessened substantially. The surviving Negroes had been brought on deck for the afternoon and now were stowed for the night with the sick but hopeful segregated. Jack stared at the blue horizon fading with the setting sun as schools of flying fish skipped before him across the darkening blue blanket. As was the evening ritual the crew not standing watch gathered on deck near the foremast. On this night the normal lively chatter was replaced by an awkward calm broken by quiet murmurs and the musical chatter of the sails whistling in the light breeze. Jack found a place on a coil of line and sat.

"'Ere's a cup, lad." Georgey appeared above, smiling as if in relief.

Jack accepted the crude tin vessel with a silent nod.

"Ya earned it," Georgey said as he filled both his and Jack's with rum from a larger tin bucket and then took a seat nearby on the deck. "We all bloody well did."

Jack nodded and coughed, having taken a healthier sip than he should have.

"Slow down there, lad," Georgey chuckled, "'alf a pint extra is all ya get. Lucky fer us the cap'n's still in a good mood. 'E did not lose as many as he feared. Considerin' the day's events, I figure we come out ahead." Georgey raised his cup. "'Ere's to us. Bit a tough business that, eh?"

Jack simply nodded as he stared at the horizon.

"Fifteen," Georgey offered flatly. "Seventeen if ya count the two already dead. All in all, we've not fared badly, even with that lot. Bound to 'appen sooner or later – always does."

They fell silent for a while, watching the flying fish that continued to skip like stones across the now nearly flat ocean, which the day before had been a tempest.

"How much longer till we make Curacao?" Jack finally asked.

"Three or four weeks, I figure, long as the weather holds – long as we don't get 'nother blow like that one."

Jack surveyed the deck and the surrounding crew and nodded. "Tough way to make a living." He paused and turned to Georgey. "Why do you do it?"

"Aye, lad, now there's a good question. There's easier ways to be sure. I could be workin' a coaster out of Liverpool and not 'ave to sleep with one eye open every night – and I used to. Trouble is, that's all I would be doin' fer the rest of m'life. Here, at least, on a ship such as this, there's a certain *opportunity*."

"Opportunity?" Jack looked around the deck as if to find the answer there. "What opportunity?"

"Let me tell ya how this works, lad. The Dutchmen that financed this trip surely gave the officers permission to buy a few slaves fer themselves. That's a bit of incentive the company allows the ship's management to do a good job and protect the company's interest. Probably a couple of the officers, in particular the cap'n, might 'ave even bought a few extra. Because the price for these Negroes was negotiated in bulk by the company that means the officers bought their Negroes fer the same price as did the company. No doubt they picked out the strongest fer themselves. The important thing is they do not 'ave the cost of the ship to worry about and their Negroes are eatin' food already paid for by the company. So, when the cap'n and officers sell their Negroes on the other end along with the rest, fer them, it's pure profit. You do that 'nough times and yer can make plenty of money to do what ya want. I've been sailin' with Cap'n Ross fer some years now. 'E's a 'ard man to be sure but 'e always makes a profit, fer the investors and fer himself."

Jack merely nodded and sipped as Georgey continued.

"This 'ere's a family operation and most of the officers on board are relations or might as well be. Nobody in their right mind would be doin' this 'less there was opportunity fer 'em. Me, I'll never be a cap'n – can't neither read nor write. But I'm hopin' to move up to one of the mates first chance I get. Bailey's not goin' to last forever – too much of a 'othead 'e is. Someday, someone'll make 'im disappear just like those Negroes we threw overboard. Trouble is, 'e 'as been 'round long enough to know it. In any case, I saved up 'nough money to buy one of those Negroes fer m'self this time out. Did it through the cap'n, fer a small commission, of course. 'Ad to settle for one of the women. They don't fetch as much profit, but they 'old up better with nearly no chance of makin' trouble.

Georgey paused to take a healthy swallow. "What about yerself, lad? What are yer grand plans?"

Jack looked down between his knees at the deck. "I do not really have any."

"What are you doin' out 'ere to begin with – a young lad like you? Don't ya 'ave a family?"

Jack did not answer but rather continued to stare at the deck.

"I see," Georgey nodded, "yer an orphan, like me. I first went to sea when I was yer age. 'Ave not stopped since. 'Ad me a wife fer a time but could not keep 'er. This 'ere is the only family that sees fit to want me so I 'ave to make the best of it."

"I have a family," Jack finally mumbled.

"Ya do?" Georgey paused, viewing Jack with surprise. "Then what in God's name are ya doin' out 'ere? Yer a runaway?"

22

Jack raised his head. "I'm not a runaway."

Georgey chuckled. "Oh, no? At yer age yer either with yer family or yer a runaway."

Jack looked back at the deck again in silence.

"Listen to me, lad." Georgey's tone turned sharp. "There are days I wish I would just go over the side like those Negroes today – just pack it in and get it over with quick like. The rest of us 'ere are just dyin' more slowly, but we are all dyin' just the same. I went to sea as a lad like yerself 'cause I 'ad nowhere else to go. Do ya want to be an old man like me – still feedin' dead niggers to sharks and prayin' that one of 'em is not yers? 'Avin' a family is a damn gift and any man that's got one ought not to turn 'is back on it. Go 'ome, lad. When we unload this lot and 'ead back to England – *go 'ome*. Yer a damn fool if ya don't. And if I see ya back out 'ere again when we next sail from Liverpool I won't stand fer it."

Jack said nothing as he drained his cup. Georgey refilled it and looked back toward the horizon, now vanishing in the waning light.

2

"The gods love a bastard."

The Gates of Fire, Steven Pressfield

LIVERPOOL, ENGLAND, SEPTEMBER 1773

J ack stood on the main deck and took a final look around.
The *Pigeon* had pulled into the busy port city the day before
with all the fanfare of putting on a pair of old socks. Having
reached Curacao several months prior with the majority of the
cargo intact, Captain Ross had traded every last Negro for a hold
full of sugar and then some – a successful voyage by all accounts.
With a pocket full of wages Jack took a deep breath and started
for the brow, but not before Georgey appeared in his path.

"Ihought you would spare yerself the trouble of sayin' good-
bye, did ya?" Georgey said with a wide grin. "I would walk with
ya a bit, but this is as far as I can go, lad. Too many eyes fer ol'
Georgey in this 'ere town." He extended a hand that slipped a
leather sheath into Jack's grasp. "Made this m'self when I knew
ya weren't lookin'," he said with a wink and a slap on Jack's back.
"It's a good one – best I ever made. Do not use 'er unless ya 'ave
to. But if ya 'ave to, use 'er like I taught ya."

Jack removed a six-inch blade from the sheath with its hand-carved ivory handle. They had spent hours sparring on deck with a fid as Georgey revealed the fine art of knife play – how to wear it, how to remove it in stealth, how to conceal it against the inside of his arm, how to position oneself and move efficiently, how and when to transition the blade forward and, above all, just where to place it in a man's chest to stop his heart. Every time he received the same lecture. "*A man that can 'andle a blade can survive in this 'ere world. Killin' a man with a firearm's easy – that's what a firearm's made fer. But killin' a man with a blade – that takes quite a bit more – speed, skill and, above all, courage and commitment. Ya 'ave to get close enough to smell what 'e ate fer breakfast. If ya do it right, yer'll get one clean shot. Don't ever look to start a fight, lad, but if you 'ave to fight, never fail to finish it.*"

Jack replaced the knife, opening his coat to let Georgey fit and tie the leather strap over his right shoulder and around his torso so that the sheath fit neatly against his stomach near the waist. He looked into Georgey's tired eyes as his own started to well.

"But 'ere's one last thing I 'aven't told ya, lad," Georgey continued as he lowered his voice. "A man that can master a blade can also become a slave to it. Just remember that." Jack nodded as Georgey shook his hand firmly. "Do ol' Georgey a favor, lad," he added with a smile, "when you walk down that brow – just keep goin' and don't look back. Just don't look back. Do that fer 'ol Georgey, would ya?"

Jack hoisted his sea bag onto his shoulder and did as Georgey bade, moving nimbly on the wide but shaky plank to reach dry land as the familiar raspy voice called behind him. "When ya find yerself in a tight spot, lad, just think of ol' Georgey and yer'll be right as rain. Yer'll be right as rain, lad – right as rain."

Jack strode quickly with purpose, keeping his eyes forward until he cleared the port facility, nervously alternating the one free hand inside his coat from Georgey's knife to his bulging purse. It had rained the night before and the cool morning air produced puffs of condensation as he exhaled, working to avoid the endless puddles in the streets as he entered the city, the same trek he had made in reverse nearly three years prior. He soon reached his own district, a dilapidated slum filled with the unmistakable smell of roasting chestnuts and raw sewage. Little, if anything, had changed since his departure with filthy streets, rundown buildings, and the poorly clad working class – mostly unemployed – still painting a portrait of a place prosperity avoided like a plague. Nearly all of the inhabitants had never traveled more than a few blocks from their birthplace and never would, seemingly content to wallow like pigs in their own filth rather than risk what little they had to an unknown world. He continued like a ghost unnoticed through the alleyways filled with refuse before arriving at an all-too-familiar structure no less squalid and decrepit than the surrounding rest. Pausing briefly, with a deep breath he stepped through a crooked doorway into a dim foyer laced with the musty odor of an old cellar. Kicking several unidentifiable objects out of his path he moved up the stairway, constructed from old tea boxes that creaked and groaned as they bore the weight as if sorry for his return. Reaching the hallway at the top, he pushed through a door and entered the main living area of a four-room flat.

"Who's that?"

Jack looked around him, not seeing the person attached to the familiar voice.

"I said *WHO IS THAT*?" A younger teenage boy stepped from behind a corner holding a wooden club casually concealed behind a leg. "State your business, sir," the boy said coolly. "If you're here for my mother, she's busy at present, but you can wait if you'd like. If you're here to collect on a debt, then you ought to leave. We don't owe anything."

They stood silently for a moment, staring at one another as the boy gradually allowed the club to drift into plain sight. "Are you deaf or mute?" He now spoke with a decided edge. "State your bloody business or get out!"

"Luke, it's me – Jack." Jack answered calmly as he inched forward.

The boy raised the club as he backed a step or two. He squinted, then swallowed hard, lowering his arm as his eyes went wide. "Bloody hell. It is indeed. MATTHEW! COME QUICK!"

Jack studied his brother, closest to him in age, with a strong resemblance except for lighter hair that could almost be taken for red. Jack extended a hand but Luke backed away, his eyes and mouth stuck open. A younger boy suddenly appeared in a rush brandishing an iron rod in both hands. Luke caught him by the back of the collar as he attempted to thrust it into Jack's ribs.

"No need for that today, Matty," Luke shook the smaller boy as he explained. "Look – it's Jack."

The younger boy stared at Jack with a similar bewildered expression then turned back to Luke. Almost two years' younger than Luke, thickly built with light blond hair and hazel eyes, he resembled neither of his older brothers. "Bloody hell," Matthew murmured, remaining still as a statue. "We figured you dead."

Jack extended a hand to Matthew, who also refused to accept it. Jack forced a smile. "A fine welcome indeed for your older brother," he said evenly. "Took me for a bill collector or worse, did you?"

"And why wouldn't we?" Luke answered sharply. "Sneaking in here like a bloody thief? Damn near scared the daylights out of Matty and me. You're damn lucky, you are, that we didn't give you a bloody good beating."

"Can I not walk into my own home?" Jack asked.

"Excuse us, but we didn't exactly expect you," Luke continued. "It's been damn near two years."

"Three, actually. How are your sisters?"

"Bloody fine, they are," Luke answered indignantly.

"Bloody fine," Matthew added.

"At school, I imagine?"

"School's not an option these days," Luke stated as he folded his arms. "Everyone has to pitch in to earn wages."

"I see," Jack answered with irritation. "And what are *you two* doing on that account?"

"None of your bloody business," Luke retorted indignantly. "It's bad enough that you left like you did. But I'm in charge now and I won't have you order us about."

"Still a little twit, you are. I am not *ordering you about*. I just asked you a simple question." Jack eyed his brother crossly. "And where is Mother?" he demanded.

Luke did not answer as Matthew turned away.

"Did you not hear me?" Jack continued. "All of a sudden that sharp tongue of yours does not work?"

Luke looked down toward his feet and mumbled, "She's busy."

Jack stared hard at both, neither of whom chose to return his gaze.

Suddenly, a man appeared from the doorway in the next room. Pausing to adjust his trousers, straighten his shirt, and button his jacket, he placed a hat on his head as he brushed past them without the slightest acknowledgement of their presence. The hallway stairs creaked with the staccato rhythm of his hurried departure as Jack walked to the window in time to see him exit the alley and melt into the street. Jack turned to fix an angry glare at both his brothers, the two of them remaining frozen in place. He dropped his sea bag and flew back across the room in an instant, pushing Matthew out of the way to grab Luke with both hands by the shirt collar and brace him against the wall. Luke attempted to kick his way free, but Jack bounced him back into the brick.

"Goddamn you! Goddamn the both of you!" Jack's eyes welled as he dropped Luke to his feet, keeping him fast against the wall. "In charge are you now? Our home as a brothel?"

Luke growled and managed to push himself forward several feet, but Jack returned him hard again to the wall as if this time he would put the younger boy through it. Both of their eyes teared as Luke quivered. "You've no right to come back here now and make judgment. You bloody well left us years ago. If you had any backbone, you would've stayed and helped us – helped our mother! Instead, you ran away like a bloody coward. Don't scold us as if you're somehow better! You left us, Jack! If you want to scold somebody then start with yourself!"

Jack let go of Luke and stepped back as his brother continued, now sobbing. "Take a good look around, Jack. Work's not exactly plentiful, at least for the likes of us. Matthew and I do what we can, but it's not enough. At least this way we can eat and maybe someday the girls can return to school. With any luck they'll not grow up to be...."

"To be what?" Jack asked angrily.

"You know bloody damn well what I mean."

"But you can't say it, can you?" Jack continued. "You can't say it but you bloody well promote it!"

"Whores," Matthew contributed flatly from a distance.

Jack wiped his eyes with a sleeve and shook his head. He took a deep breath and addressed Luke through gritted teeth. "Where is he?"

Luke wiped his eyes as well. "Where do you bloody think he is?" he answered. "Where is he ever?"

Jack stared hard at both. "You are not my brothers. You are two miserable sots that choose to live your lives in mindless poverty, not capable of believing there's a better way. Nothing has changed here – absolutely nothing.

"I don't know what you think you're doing to come back here, Jack," Luke answered, raising a shaking finger, "but I'll tell you one thing: We depended on you, and you left us. Lord knows we cannot depend on *him*. We depended on *you,* and *you* left us. Now we must depend on ourselves. I don't know why you came back."

"I don't know why either," Jack retorted, "but don't worry – that won't happen again." He reached into his coat for his purse and handed it to Luke. "Take this," he said. "It's damn near three years' wages."

Luke's eyes grew wide as he felt the weight of the sack. He hesitated, then handed back the coins. "We don't need your charity."

Jack stepped forward and shoved the purse into Luke's chest. "Take it, goddamn it. Take it before I beat you with it."

Jack took a last look around the room and again at his brothers, both of whom stared back teary-eyed and silent. He picked up his sea bag and, turning abruptly, strode back through the door and down the stairs out of the building. With just enough time to wipe the tears from his eyes he reached the *Black Sheep* pub, the old sign above the door in need of mending as badly as the day he left. Entering the crude establishment, he stopped momentarily to allow his eyes to adjust to the smoky dark. Not even midday and already the place was littered with men having nothing better to do than to spend money they did not have. In the corner where the long bar met the wall sat a rumpled figure hunched and silent. Jack approached the man, stopping several paces behind and to the side, dropping his sea bag on a floor in need of a good sweep. The bartender, Fat Steven, more portly and balder than ever, shuffled over toward them both, with an ever-widening grin.

"Well, lad, it's been a while," he said with a smile. "Last I saw you were just another street rat in here scrounging loose change. Heard you ran off. Where've you been?"

Jack ignored Fat Steven, fixing his attention instead at the man hunched on a stool in the corner. After several awkward moments the figure slowly twisted around toward Jack, inspecting him with an expressionless gaze from yellowed eyes set deep into a weathered face. They stared at one another until Jack finally spoke. "It's me, Father."

The answer was merely an unintelligible grunt as the man resumed his original position, staring back in the opposite direction. Jack remained silent as he swapped nervous glances between the floor and the man in the corner.

Fat Steven turned to the man and retrieved his empty glass to wipe it out. "Got to be three years or so hasn't it, John? Looks like he's grown into a fine lad."

The man merely shrugged as he took a long draw from the new pint glass Fat Steven placed in front of him.

"I've been to sea for a spell," Jack offered, "mostly coastal trade. Lately to Africa and the Caribbean on a slaver. The work's hard, but the pay's steady."

"That's more than can be said for the likes of this city," Fat Steven scoffed. "What brings you back then?"

Jack did not answer but instead returned his attention to the man in the corner. He spoke in a stern but wavering voice. "Father, I want to have a word with you. I want to talk to you about Mother and the rest."

The man still did not answer as he tensed like a coiled spring. Fat Steven quickly moved toward the other end of the bar. After a couple silent moments Jack began again. "Father, I said...."

The man pounded his pint on the bar. "I heard you, god-damn it!"

Jack began to sputter. "It's just that...."

"It's just *what*, lad?" the man answered in a condescending tone.

Jack reached across and pushed the half-empty pint off the bar where it landed on the floor with a loud crash. He raised both a shaky voice and finger. "You are in the same place as when I left, drinking the family's hard-earned wages! You don't treat our mother with respect! This is why I left. Can you not start to be a father, at least to the others? Can you not start to be a man?"

The statue-like figure suddenly turned and leapt off the stool like a bolt of lightning. Before Jack could react, the man grabbed him by the coat lapels and drove his forehead hard into Jack's nose. Jack yelped in pain as his knees buckled and warm blood streamed down to his chin, covering his mouth. Still holding Jack by the coat, the man half-carried, half-dragged him back across the room. Jack tried in vain to find a purchase on the floor as his feet pedaled furiously. Reaching the door, the man plowed it open using Jack as a battering ram, spilling both of them into the street as if in a violent dance. Jack landed face down in a shallow puddle, coughing and sputtering his way to coherency as he managed to raise his head.

The man perched himself above with a wide stance, stooping slightly and waving an angry finger in rhythm with his words.

31

"Don't lecture me about being a man, lad, because you don't know the first bloody thing about it! I'll show you how to be a man and the first bloody thing I'll show you is that I won't take bloody instruction from the likes of you! You don't agree with the way I conduct my business, then to hell with you! I neither want nor need your bloody affection and that goes for the others as well, including your bloody mother!"

"Mother..." Jack managed to spit out the word, "she is... too good...for you."

"Let me tell you something about your mother, lad, that maybe you ought to know," the man answered, lowering his voice to a growl. "Or maybe you know it already and think it's my doing. Your mother's a bloody whore! She's always been a whore and no doubt she'll die a whore. She was a whore when I met her and, in fact, that's *how* I met her. Lucky for her I'm the only man in her life bloody foolish enough to stick around and help her out. Lord knows why the bloody hell I do it. You and the others think we're supposed to be some kind of bloody *family*? You call me *father* and come back after three years to lecture me because I'm not living up to my *responsibilities*? What the bloody hell do you know? The truth is I'm not your bloody father. You're not one of mine and neither are the others. I don't know who you belong to, and I don't really give a goddamn. You're a bloody bastard, lad. You're all bloody bastards, every damn one of you." He gave Jack a kick in the side as if to punctuate that point. "Take my *fatherly* advice and go back to wherever it is you just came from. You did the right thing when you left the first time. Do yourself a favor and next time don't bloody come back!"

Jack tried to answer but instead dropped his face back into the puddle where his tears mixed with the water and mud. After several failed attempts to stand he managed to roll himself out of the puddle to the side of the street, where he passed out beneath the sign of the *Black Sheep* that hung above like a guillotine.

* * *

Jack awoke in a mixture of disorientation and throbbing pain to his face and ribs as he attempted to sit up, no longer in the street but rather on the floor of a small room covered with burlap over straw. With much concentration and effort, he slowly lifted himself by the elbows and propped his back against the wall, the cool stones a small relief to the back of his head.

"Well, lad, you're alive after all." The strange voice startled Jack as he scanned his dim environment to find the speaker. "For a while there, we thought you might sleep the day away."

Behind an iron bar grating that served as a partition stood a man in a red uniform, a soldier of some sort, dressed crisp and neat with nary a button or crease out of place, not even one of his thinning silver hairs brushed back just so.

"Mind if I come in, lad? Fancy a bit of water?" The soldier waited politely for an answer and when Jack did not give one, he turned to a second man, a sloppily, unkempt individual, who unlocked the door in the grating with a set of large keys. Fetching a nearby bucket and ladle the soldier stepped through the door and assumed a seat on a wooden stool in the corner. He dipped the ladle in the bucket and handed it to Jack, who took the ladle greedily, drinking two more in addition.

"Looks like you took quite a knock, lad," the soldier said as he sat stiffly on the stool and studied Jack more closely. "Don't worry – young as you are you'll be on your feet in no time. Fancy fighting, do you?"

"Thank you for the water, sir," Jack finally answered, "but if you don't mind, I'm not in the habit of explaining myself to strangers."

"Quite right you are, lad." The soldier smiled politely. "Almost forgot my manners. I am Sergeant Reginald Grimes of the 4th Foot Royal Regiment of Lancaster – the *King's Own*. And you would be?"

"John Halliday from Liverpool."

The sergeant leaned forward and extended his hand which, with some effort, Jack cautiously accepted.

"Pleased to meet you, John from Liverpool. Can I ask what brings you to this fine establishment?"

"I go by *Jack*, sir. Where am I?"

"Well, Jack" the sergeant chuckled, "in the city jail, you are. The constable found you lying face down in the street, he did. Want to tell me what you were doing there?"

"No, I don't, sir," Jack answered flatly. "Am I in some sort of trouble?"

"Of course not, lad," the sergeant chuckled again. "It's not a crime to spend your time lying about in the street at midday. But you've the look of a strong, hardworking lad. You don't seem a vagrant. My guess is you're not the normal type that frequents the king's hotel. More water?"

Jack nodded and eagerly accepted another ladle. "Sir," he began, "I'm no vagrant. I earn my own living and spend my wages wisely. I've been before the mast for the last three years and just today returned for a visit home. Had me a little accident, nothing more. I'd rather not discuss it."

The sergeant nodded. "Fair enough, lad. *Home*, you say? *Before the mast?*" He eyed Jack more closely. "I guess that explains the sea bag the constable found in the street with you. And the constable also found this." He produced Georgey's sheathed knife and offered it back to Jack. "Very nice work indeed. You can thank me for convincing the constable not to keep it for himself."

Jack finished his water and traded the ladle for the knife, replacing it quickly inside his jacket as he felt through the rest of the empty pockets. "Thank you, sir," he answered sincerely. "Now, I don't mean to be rude, and I appreciate you giving me water and returning my knife, but if I'm not in any trouble then I'd like to leave now. May I?" Without waiting for an answer, he tried to stand but fell backwards against the wall.

"Whoa, lad." The sergeant lurched forward and caught Jack to steady him back in place. "You may certainly leave but I don't believe you're able. Better stay where you are for the time being. Where would you be going anyway?"

After several moments Jack shook his head. "I don't rightly know."

"Well then, what's the hurry?" the sergeant shrugged. "Stay put and enjoy the king's hospitality. You look quite peaked, lad. Let me get you something to eat and some medical attention. In the meantime, we can have ourselves a bit of a discussion. In fact, I have an opportunity for you."

"*Opportunity?*" Jack repeated cautiously. "What opportunity would that be?"

"Are you an Englishman, lad?" the sergeant asked.

"Of course, I am." Jack answered.

"Do you love your king and country?"

Jack hesitated. "I don't rightly know. I never quite thought about it. I suppose so."

"Of course you do, lad, of course you do. Nevertheless, you should know these are dangerous times – dangerous times indeed." The sergeant's tone stiffened as he rose and began to pace, using his hands to emphasize each point as he spoke. "England's possessions span the globe, and, in fact, the sun never sets on King George's empire, the greatest empire this world has ever known. But with that empire come threats from all quadrants by those less deserving and jealous of our hard-won fortunes. It must be us *Englishmen* that protect and defend our good king and country against the attempts and designs of our enemies, natural or otherwise, who, if they had their way, would no doubt invade old England, *our happy country*, murder our gracious king, rob us of our property, make whores of our wives and daughters, and teach us little else but the damned art of murdering one another. We must *guard* against these evil intrusions with constant vigilance."

The sergeant stopped in front of Jack and bent down, looking him sternly in the eye. "If you love your country or, at least, the liberty that your country guarantees, *now* is the time to show that affection. If you have a good heart, if you would support your king, if you treasure your God, if you hate the French, if you damn that villainous pope and all other Catholic meddlers and miscreants, then join with me, lad, to protect England's honor and virtue. Join with me, lad, and be not an inconsequential tramp cast aside by providence but instead your country's hero! What do you say to that?"

Jack gazed back at the strutting soldier in stunned silence. After a few moments he managed to murmur, "I don't rightly know."

"Well, what would stop you?" the sergeant asked incredulously, then paused to let Jack collect his thoughts.

Jack shook his head. "Sir, I'm an Englishman to be sure, but I know not what you speak of. Who are these *enemies?*"

"Lad, we are an island nation surrounded by enemies that would cast this beloved country aside without so much as a second thought simply because we are Englishmen, and they are not. Is it not enough to know that your king and country need a spirited lad like yourself? If you are so willing to fight, then fight with us! Fight for your country and serve your king. What else would you do? Is it back before the mast with you?"

"What are the terms?" Jack asked.

"Of course." the sergeant nodded. "A practical lad you are. You earn eight pence a day, minus the cost for sustenance and clothing. When you sign on you will be paid a bonus of two pounds – a handsome sum indeed, I think you'll agree."

Jack sighed and fiddled with the knife in his pocket as his other hand rubbed his throbbing face. "The truth is," he began, "I don't have a better idea, or any idea, of what I'll do from here. This morning, I woke with three year's wages in my pocket and since have been beaten like a rug and now am poorer than a ditch digger's dog. I have no family save for a den of miscreants related to me through mere coincidence. I truly don't give a damn about the king but if he can deliver me far from this hellhole and pay me wages in addition then he'll have my loyalty."

"Well, there it is, lad." The sergeant grinned as he extended his hand again to Jack. "Let's make it official."

Jack shook the sergeant's hand and nodded. "Very well then, sir, I'm your man. Do with me what you will. Just get me as far away from here as you can."

"No doubt about that one, lad." The sergeant smiled widely and clasped Jack's hand again, this time with both of his. "Aye, lad, you're going to make a fine soldier, you are. I'm never wrong on that account."

3

Democracy is two wolves and a lamb voting on what to have for lunch. Liberty is a well-armed lamb contesting the vote.

Benjamin Franklin

That Great Britain existed as it did – an unkempt, unruly, incorrigible mob of cultural misfits, forced onto Europe as if an unwanted relative at a dinner party, much less a world power – might have appeared to all but themselves a freak of nature. Long ago geologically attached to the European mainland, it seemed that even the continent itself had rejected Britain, forming it into islands and pushing them ever westward, and never an inch too far. From ancient Celtic origins, England in particular had endured Romans, Teutons, Vikings, and Normans, each invader in turn becoming themselves vanquished as their culture and influence gradually amalgamated into a relentless ethnic melting pot. The British had survived revolutions, executed monarchs, rejected popes, reconstituted governments, invented religions, and as if the very epitome of the mascot bulldog, each convulsive rebirth had threatened to leave their mother dead. After nearly two millennia of recorded turmoil, upheaval, and strife, these islands of misfits had managed not only to survive but to form a cohesive nation, if not an awe-inspiring empire. Those who knew best would argue the only possible explanation was neither inherent ability nor God-given fortune but rather pure abject obstinance.

As in the rest of the known world, most of Britain's social upheavals, at least in modern times, could be traced to religion. On the fringes of civilization since Roman times and perennially at the end of the political food chain, it came as no surprise in the 16th century when England shed its Catholic chains, long considered inconsistent with political dictates. After not being granted a divorce by Pope Clement VII from a marriage that failed to produce an heir, King Henry VIII proclaimed Rome's political influence no longer relevant to matters on the British Isles and simply replaced the pontiff with a more useful religious figurehead – himself. Not an unreasonable conclusion for any serious despot and no doubt mainland European rulers of lesser vision and closer proximity to Rome were envious.

But this new *Church of England* was not alone in its objection to the decadence and corruption of the Catholic Church. Back on the continent the base beliefs of Martin Luther grew into the Protestant Reformation, a theological schism that threatened to implode the whole of Europe. Basic tenets of this Protestantism preached simplicity and austerity, and, most importantly, held that every human being had the right to commune directly with God without the need of artificial and unnecessary intermediaries such as priests, saints, and angels, with their own agendas. Further, under Protestantism, every person's life had already been predetermined by God upon creation, making irrelevant and unnecessary the obligatory acts of faith and contrition that were considered thinly veiled schemes designed first and foremost to fill Catholic coffers. Since it was the Catholic Church that sponsored, approved and otherwise *blessed* European rulers and administrations, this radical Protestant movement challenged the very existence of any government where their theology took root.

The English version of these so-called *Protestants* also chastised the Church of England as not having gone far enough in its reforms over Catholicism, holding the government and its citizens yet hostage to self-serving, made-made political policies no longer dictated by the pope but rather now the king. They objected strenuously to England's religious business-as-usual and sought to purify their lives by a strict adherence to the word of God as was done by the early Christian believers before the Romans confiscated and bastardized the movement, bringing about unnecessary formalities and trappings that had since accumulated like mold over the previous millennium and a half. Not surprisingly, the English government considered these heretics *criminals* and persecuted the formation of such groups to the point where some illegally emigrated off the British Isles across the channel to Holland. Here, the exiles found tolerance but also a troublesome loss of their identity as Englishmen as with each passing year they and their children assimilated into the ever-present Dutch society. Again, they chose to relocate, this time across an ocean to an entirely new world where they could be left to their own devices to build a community unencumbered by Europe's misguided and unavoidable cultural baggage.

In early November 1620, the good ship *Mayflower* arrived off what is now *Cape Cod* with 102 souls, one half of whom were willing to risk everything for their religious beliefs and the other half, *strangers,* whose presence was mandated by the investors that had funded the venture. Originally bound for Virginia with a two-month journey more difficult and longer than expected and now almost out of provisions, they nevertheless turned south in an attempt to land somewhere below the Hudson River, the northern limit of their charter. Hugging the coastline, the ship became dangerously swept inland by the clutches of the strong current and shallows off Nantucket Island until a sudden providential shift of wind from the south pried them loose from the tide. With the decision now made for him, the captain, no stranger to these waters, backtracked north to safety, anchoring the *Mayflower* in the protection of the barren hooked tip of what is now *Provincetown* just inside the upper tip of the crooked arm-shaped cape. No longer mere passengers, the would-be settlers spent the next several weeks reconnoitering the inner peninsula coastline in a race against the oncoming grip of winter to find a permanent site, eventually stumbling just before Christmas upon a suitable harbor across the bay that became known as *Plymouth*. Unbeknownst to these *Pilgrims*, they had just offloaded the baggage of the tumultuous human machinations in Europe for an even more challenging burden of those in the new world.

The settlement at Plymouth was not intended as a harbinger of mass immigration but rather as simply a place where these religious malcontents could be left in peace to practice as they pleased their version of Christian faith. In addition, it would also turn a profit in terms of goods shipped back to England. In retrospect, no one of any rational sense would have repeated their act of arriving on the American coastline with little more than the clothes on their backs in the midst of thousands of indigenous heathens and so far north at the very beginning of a long, cold winter. Being neither accustomed to nor prepared for the harsh climate and lacking both adequate sustenance and the means to acquire it, half their number died before the spring. Meanwhile, the local native population watched from a distance with curiosity the seemingly futile efforts of a strange race of people they surely must have considered fools.

Europeans had been coming to the east coast of North America for more than a century prior, not to settle but rather to extract riches, mainly furs and fish. Inevitably bumping up against the indigenous population, some of the strange visitors had managed to endear themselves by trading with and befriending the natives with others, decidedly not through kidnapping and murder. But if these early white entrepreneurs brought unusual, wondrous, and useful objects they also brought germs for which the so-called *Indians* had little or no biological defense. In the area surrounding Plymouth the controlling tribe known as the *Pokanokets* had been so decimated by a sudden disease just prior to the Pilgrims' arrival that it had rendered them vulnerable to consummation by their aggressive neighboring tribes. In a grand stroke of sheer luck, the new immigrants had managed to drop themselves into the midst of the one and only native community in the vast region that had as much need of them as a game-changing political ally as they had of local sponsors, both for their mutual survival.

In the beginning the Pilgrims coexisted with the natives in a mutually beneficial relationship driven mainly by the Pokanoket *sachem*, their spiritual and tribal chief, *Massasoit*, who recognized an opportunity when he saw one. After the initial hard winter, Massasoit approached the settlers along with a dubious English-speaking interpreter named *Squanto*, who had formerly been kidnapped to England and who used his unique ability to manipulate his own influence with the Pokanokets and neighboring tribes. Massasoit agreed to provide the Pilgrims the knowledge and means to sustain themselves in return for local political top cover through their advanced weaponry and manufactured trade goods. The indigenous people soon realized that they could acquire European commodities in abundance by swapping the one resource they had plenty of – land. As the Pokanokets staved off obliteration so did the Pilgrims as both not only survived but began to thrive. Soon Massasoit was the region's leading sachem from his seat in what is now *Bristol, Rhode Island* and, as for the Pilgrims, they set an example that proved irresistible to follow by those back home with a penchant for adventure and investment or Protestant religious autonomy. Within a decade the coastline of what would become known as *New England* became dotted with settlements that began to push inland.

The Pilgrims soon realized that their chosen site of Plymouth, while rich in natural resources and well located within the protective sphere of Massasoit's control, contained too shallow a harbor for meaningful commercial trade. However, just 30 miles to the north, inside the territory of the *Massachusetts* tribe, lay a pork chop-shaped peninsula called *Shawmet* with not only depth but protection from the open seas as well as ample estuaries leading inland. This remarkable port took the name of *Boston*, a hotbed of religious dissent along the English east coast in Lincolnshire north of London, and from the beginning grew rapidly into the economic and political epicenter of the region. The steady drip of Pilgrims that arrived in Plymouth were now overtaken by a larger stream of *Puritans*, fueled by the entrepreneurial wellspring of the *Massachusetts Bay Company*. In contrast to their radical Pilgrim cousins, these more practical *Calvinists* did not necessarily advocate complete separation from the Church of England but instead a wider spectrum of reformation. Whereas the Pilgrims sought simply to be left alone to practice their rigid beliefs in peace, the Puritans instead aimed to colonize, grow, and prosper.

In the beginning the many and varied indigenous tribes took advantage of the newcomers' insatiable thirst for land, trading what they had an abundance of for wealth and items that gave them prestige, influence, and advantage over one another. Eventually it became apparent that this relationship was not in their best interest as their relative spheres of influence steadily declined in proportion to the inflowing tide of Englishmen. By 1675 the leadership of the Pokanoket had been assumed by Massasoit's eldest son, *Metacom*. In a reflection of how much the natives had allowed themselves to become assimilated to the alien settlers, Metacom had taken the English name of *Philip* or, *King Philip* as he was more commonly known, due to his boast of greatness on par with Britain's current royal monarch. Possessing neither his father's political savvy nor personal self-control, Philip, through strategic miscalculation and personal animosity toward the insatiable English land grabbers, touched off an armed conflict that quickly spread to engulf the entire region.

King Philip's War lasted nearly three years, stretching from the Hudson River east all the way into the far reaches of the region of Maine. The *Naragansetts*, the *Nipmucs*, the Massachusetts and the other tribes that chose to follow the Pokanokets and Philip's lead as well as their English adversaries exhibited a blind barbarism that differentiated not between male combatant nor women and children, bringing a level of violence, destruction, and genocide not seen since in the American experience. Whole English settlements vanished with a larger proportionate percentage of population, estimated at a full ten percent, put to death than any American conflict since. By the time King Philip was hunted down and his head mounted on a palisade for display at Plymouth, effectively ending the conflict, it had become even worse for the natives, whose scattered remains of individual and collective political influence over their land and affairs never recovered, rendering them disadvantaged against the terror-stricken biases of the settlers, the vast majority of whom no longer categorized them according to particular tribe but rather as a blurred homogenous threat simply according to their aboriginal race.

But as devastating as the conflict had been, King Philip's War served to galvanize the settlers and forever change the landscape of the still budding New England colonies. No army from Europe had come to their rescue and the intrepid colonists had defeated, with no outside assistance, a vicious foe that had sought to expunge them. The concept of militias, a longstanding tradition carried over from the origins of modern England, now became the very backbone of every hamlet, which grew as a network of self-sustaining organisms completely independent in every way. In fact, the very notion of *independence* was no lofty political concept but rather an enduring fact of life as each town became a replica of the next – its own autonomous organism with a common place to worship, a common place to socialize, and a common place to conduct military drills. The majority of the inhabitants were related to each other, interdependent within the community on farming and the various trades but above all, able to defend themselves at a moment's notice. If anyone had doubted it before, with three generations removed from the *Mayflower*, these strange English transplants had proven, if to no one else but themselves, that they were there to stay.

Around the turn of the 18th century Mother England amalgamated into *Great Britain,* assuming control of Wales as well as Scotland. The nascent American satellite footprint across the Atlantic rapidly expanded, as the intermittent drip of disenfranchised ideologues seeking religious privacy had now become a steady stream of practical-minded risk takers willing to leave their world behind across a vast ocean for the opportunity to create a quality of life they otherwise had no chance of obtaining. Fueled by charters issued by the government, the examples of Plymouth to the north and Jamestown to the south were repeated until a vast patchwork of settlements formed a colonial quilt that grew into thirteen separate provinces along the east coast of North America. Well over three thousand miles removed from the Crown, each became governed by a loose-jointed system of easy-going imperialism that incorporated a compromise between traditional central control and new world self-government; between the principle of authority and the reality of autonomy. King and Parliament managed foreign affairs, war & peace, and overseas trade, husbanding colonial raw materials into a mercantile system that conceptually provided profit for all. In almost every other respect the provinces were allowed to direct their own affairs with each colony completely self-managed by a London-appointed governor as well as provincial assemblies freely elected from within. These organic assemblies maintained the exclusive right to tax constituents and chose to do so sparingly. They appointed officials and fixed their salaries, commissioned military officers and raised troops, and controlled schools, churches, and land systems. While religious and social persecution remained rampant in Europe itself, Great Britain conversely welcomed all brands of refugees to America, where they would be naturalized as British subjects yet allowed to retain their own language, religion, and customs. After approximately a century and a half of existence, the American colonies acquired a level of independence like no other within the British Empire with these *American English* citizens enjoying more freedom and prosperity than any other governed people in the world. For the first time in human history, with the burden of government minimal, there emerged a vibrant middle class of shopkeepers, artisans, and tradesman – all individual entrepreneurs who carried on their own shoulders life's relative risks and gains – that grew into an economic and political engine that dominated the growth of every province. But like all good things this situation could not remain undisturbed and, as usual, where you find Britain's trouble you will also find the French.

France had American colonies too, mostly to the north in Canada, and also claimed the area along the Mississippi River from the Great Lakes south to the Gulf of Mexico. At the time this grand expanse was populated mostly by indigenous natives and a scattering of backwoodsmen and fur traders. As the Atlantic east coast continued to fill, the British government gradually revoked the charters that had initially established the provinces and appointed royal governors in a measure to control the rapidly growing colonial territory. But to British subjects in America real prosperity meant *land* and, like the earliest settlers, they held a ravenous appetite for it. Western borders for provinces such as Virginia had never been established – purposely, it seems – therefore, at least in Virginian eyes, their claim ran all the way to the Pacific Ocean. As much as those living in America looked to the west, London was not and never had been keen on colonial expansion past the Appalachian Mountains, as that policy was neither cost-effective nor strategically advantageous to their overarching purposes. Instead, British leadership advocated expansion north and south into Nova Scotia and Florida where that relationship would strengthen the coastal shipping monopoly and hamper their over-entrepreneurial American offspring from entering trade relationships with the French. But the provincials themselves would have none of it and, like a never turning tide, a steady stream of settlers flowed ever westward past the Appalachians, seemingly undeterred by hostile Indians, the mischievous French, and especially their own self-serving government an ocean away.

By the middle of the 18th century the situation came to blows between Europeans, provincials, and native peoples in a predictable bloody affair known as the *French and Indian War*. Called the *Seven Years War* on the European continent, the conflict was, in reality, an extension of the ongoing global power struggle between Britain and France in Europe proper that simply bled over onto the colonies like a giant family argument pushed out of the house and down the street. Unlike King Philip's War nearly a century earlier that had been handled solely by the colonists themselves and in an uncoordinated, piecemeal fashion, this conflict brought large European armies to America that sought to conduct warfare in the traditional linear manner under a central command and control. Britain used the colonial militias in a secondary role while France incorporated support from numerous indigenous tribes that saw a brighter political future aligned with the Catholic-minded French who, in addition to trying to convert them also at least somewhat valued them as human beings and were therefore more willing to act as partners rather than overlords. But through a combination of superior strategic acumen, greater military doggedness abroad and adroit political skill at home, in particular by First Minister William Pitt the elder, the *Earl of Chatham*, Britain triumphed. In 1763 the Treaty of Paris gave her all of North America east of the Mississippi, other than the city of New Orleans, as well as French islands in the West Indies and possessions in Africa. The French also turned over their claim to New Orleans and lands west of the Mississippi to Spain as compensation for that country having surrendered Florida to the British. Great Britain now emerged as the dominant power in Europe and, for that matter, the world. But ironically, this overwhelming strategic success did not bear the dividend of peace and security as intended but rather quite the opposite, as the windfalls of Canada and Florida brought new administrative problems that could not be solved within the current framework of colonial policy and management. Like a cruel joke, it was not a defeat at the hands of the hated French and divisive Spanish that portended Great Britain's internal troubles yet to come with her thirteen American colonies but, ironically, its own grand victory.

In addition to the traditional security issues in Europe, the cost of usurping the French in North America had proved horrendous, in fact, a bill that when delivered London nearly choked on. The government had always extracted revenue from the American colonies through the mercantile system of channeled commerce supported by the *Acts of Trade and Navigation*. This legislation, originally enacted in 1650, was an effort to put the idealistic theory of mercantilism into actual practice and to combat the threat of the fast-growing Dutch market. Under these provisions, trade with the colonies was to be conducted only through the British or its provincial shipping. Certain specific high-demand items, such as sugar, tobacco, and indigo, were to be carried only within the empire and trade destined for nations outside the sphere required passage first through Britain. This monopolistic law had the desired effect of funneling revenue from the colonies directly into England – but the unintended consequence of driving up prices and consequently, and some might say *predictably*, as the monetary dividend from this body of laws grew, so did the American penchant for circumvention. Smuggling of foreign goods was rampant, particularly in New England where import trade mattered most and where the irregular and endless coast-line provided a haven for illegal traffickers. First and foremost, to pay the mounting costs driven by the security requirements of an expanding empire, Britain had to maximize the output of its maritime revenue machine by plugging the leaks in the Acts of Trade and Navigation.

During the Seven Years War, flank colonies such as those in New England and South Carolina, those most directly menaced by France and Spain, had given more effort than Britain had expected. But middle colonies, especially Pennsylvania, where Quaker pacification prevailed, did far less and, in many eyes, next to nothing. It seemed only reasonable that the American colonies in total, all direct beneficiaries of victory over the French oppressors and their savage Indian mercenaries, should them-selves assist in relieving the empire's debt – to *pay their fair share*. But London had never devised a method of extracting uniform contributions from the colonies for their defense and whatever assistance appeared had always done so sporadically. Additionally, there remained the stubbornly unresolved *western question*, that of what to do with the increasing provincial horde that insisted on settling on the wrong side of the Appalachian range. A succession of ministries and Parliament had tried valiantly to responsibly meet these simultaneous problems but in typical bureaucratic fashion tackled them clumsily, piecemeal, and in untimely fashion.

On the heels of dominant military victories, the decision was made in 1762 to leave a permanent garrison of 10,000 men in America, an action sincerely intended for *frontier security*. But the relative vast distances in the colonies coupled with the reality of overland transportation expense for resupply necessitated that these troops be maintained not on the fringes of population expanse, where the threat to security existed, but instead close to major harbors such as Halifax, Boston, and New York. Those logistic subtleties were generally lost on the colonists who viewed this situation with suspicion and resentment, they themselves having inherited a heavy dose of the traditional English dread of standing armies in peacetime.

The next year, in 1763, the king issued a proclamation that *no colonial government could grant and no white man take land beyond the source of rivers that flowed into the Atlantic Ocean* – that source being the Appalachian Mountains. This policy was intended to temporarily stem the tide of settlers across that barrier. However, the colonists construed it as permanent and unfairly restrictive. From 1764 to 1767 Parliament passed a series of laws to include the *Revenue Act*, the *Stamp Act*, and the *Townshend Act*; all intended to shore up the Acts of Trade and Navigation and to both protect and extract greater revenue from Britain's monopolistic trade. These acts collectively levied heavy custom duties and user fees on goods, products, and services – stamps, paper, tea, and more – that colonists were forced to import and could not avoid purchasing in their conduct of daily life. In addition, and probably even more importantly, the Townshend Act administratively reorganized the rules that framed the separate provincial governments. Now, American-born deputies of absentee British custom officials, who had previously made their living from smuggling and bribes, were replaced by Parliament's own men – mostly Tory Scots that did not give a damn about provincial sensitivities. The Townshend Act specifically intended, for the first time, to fund salaries for colonial governors and judges to make them independent of their respective state assemblies

– in other words, to put them back in London's pocket where they belonged.

To the American colonists these collective measures seemed not only heavy-handed but, in fact, *immoral* in both concept and execution. The basic rights of all freeborn Englishmen were first and foremost life, liberty, and property, which were further interpreted to prohibit abusive taxation, particularly without consent. In general, citizens in America had always objected to certain inflexible directives from the Crown, but before, these had been mere irritants not worthy of more than the normal political dissatisfaction that any people find with their government. For roughly seven generations colonists in North America had not only been allowed, but encouraged, to manage their own affairs and had felt as secure in their status as proper British subjects as their brethren on the isles across the Atlantic. For the first time in American colonial existence, following directly on the heels of the magnificent victory against the French, there emerged a growing ground swell of dissatisfaction, organized complaints, and even violent protest against the seat of government in London, the very entity, much like a parent, entrusted to provide for and preserve their cherished freedom and way of life. But as large as these mounting problems loomed in the American Provinces, they were by no means impossible to resolve.

British politics in the late 18th century could be broadly divided into two diametrically opposed dogmatic camps composed of *Whigs* and *Tories*. The term *Whig* emanated from *Whiggamore*, a 17th century term for cattle drivers formerly used to abuse Scottish Presbyterians in their struggle against Catholics, now evolved to label middle-class liberal-minded Protestants in general. *Tory* stemmed from the Gaelic language first applied to 17th century Irish outlaws, then to supporters of Roman Catholicism and eventually Anglicanism which, in turn, buttressed English rule itself. In general, both sides agreed that government should be composed of king and Parliament; however, conservative Tories, more aligned in thought with the Church of England, believed ultimately that the divine intention of kings to rule came directly from God via birthright. Conversely, Whigs, much a product of the emerging *enlightenment* of Protestantism, believed that God concerned Himself not with kings but rather common people. The Whigs further believed that a king existed solely at the request and goodwill of those people and should therefore only continue to reign at their approval. But although God may have concerned Himself with common people, the liberal Whig execution of that interpretation decidedly *did not,* as their representation in government remained limited to roughly 400 established nobles and carefully chosen families. The vast majority of the remaining population lived largely as peasants – vestiges from the feudal system – and in no case would or could their imperial masters imagine ceding any form of government decision-making to mere *commoners.* In contrast to the lofty ideas of the ruling intelligentsia, the average citizen lived in relative squalor with no voice whatsoever in their government. For all their talk of preserving humanity, little thought or action was given to preserving humans themselves, whose individual worth was measured solely by birthright, a metric managed tightly by a ruling class of elites with little interest or incentive to increase their exclusive membership, whether Tory or Whig.

In 1763 the power of Parliament reigned virtually supreme, mainly due to the emergence of these liberal-minded Whigs, whose numbers and influence had steadily increased for the better part of the century. Having a bicameral system consisting of the *House of Lords* and the *House of Commons,* the growth of Parliament's influence and that of the ministry cabinet, which drew its strength from Parliament, had diminished the English king's traditional authority to little more than a right to accept the advice the ministry gave him. By the end of the Seven Years War, the time had long since passed when the personality and efforts of the king were of much consequence to legislation and policy. In fact, Parliament had reduced Great Britain to practically an aristocracy governed not by a powerful single monarch but rather by various leaders of the classes embodied there – in other words, the Whig aristocracy. Enter King George III who, as the British political landscape would soon lament, waged his greatest war not on external enemies but rather his own internal government.

If the British people were generally satisfied with the state of affairs immediately following defeat of their French oppressors, their new young king was definitely not. At twenty-five years of age, King George III had succeeded his grandfather, George II, only three years earlier. The third of the four *Georges* from the German *House of Hanover* that ruled Great Britain from 1714 to 1830, he was the first to be decidedly less Teutonic, having even mastered the English language. A dignified, faithful, and religious man of impeccable moral character and plain habits, he was conversely narrow-minded, prejudiced, and appallingly obstinate. Following the death of his father, Frederick, the Prince of Wales, his mother had raised him in almost complete seclusion, neglecting his worldly education and providing him little opportunity for the broadening influence that comes from contact with diversity. Along with teachings of piety, courage, courtesy, and respect for women, his mother and other tutors had also impressed on him firm views regarding the *proper* role of a king drawn from examples of certain other European rulers, that of a strong authoritarian not to be bullied by the ignoble whims of self-serving political assemblies. In this fashion, George soon developed a single-minded goal: To rescue the British Crown from the clutches of the leading Whig families, whom he saw as strangling the natural order of things – the supremacy of the British Monarchy as the wellspring of Great Britain itself – with their liberal and conciliatory views.

Temperate, conservative, and methodical, but hardly a political visionary or craftsman of enlightened foreign policy, King George aimed from the beginning to personally dominate and control Parliament, in essence to be his own first minister and cabinet. For the most part he succeeded, but only by shamelessly subverting British law through monetary bribes, granting of titles, and other means of influence peddling that reduced political leaders, hopelessly addicted to their own importance and high standard of living, to follow his lead or step aside for someone else who would. In this way, over the course of time he systematically tightened his grip on government and managed to splinter the Whig Party into relatively ineffective factions until even the *Old Whigs*, the bloc that strongly supported colonial rights by espousing the principles of England's own *Glorious Revolution* in 1688, became only a small voice in the minority. So dominant prior and wholly responsible for the success of the Seven Year's War, this idealistic and arguably naive old guard realized too late that their scheming king had literally undermined their constitution and populated Parliament and the ministry with his own bought men. In the immediate aftermath of the great struggle with France the manipulative king gave little mind to far-flung colonies such as America. His focus remained almost blindly internal toward restoring control of Britain's governmental process to what in his eyes was its rightful place – under his monarch's thumb.

Nowhere in the American colonies had the pain of England's post-1763 revenue recovering policies been more deeply felt or the dissension more loudly communicated than in New England. The physical makeup of the northern-most colonies with its rock-laden soil rendered large scale farming operations, such as those found in the southern plantations, impractical. In addition, while not illegal, the concept of slavery was not well received in the high-minded, Whig-dominated northeast and therefore removed any possibility of utilizing large quantities of that labor pool so necessary to make running large farms possible – and profitable. Moreover, New England, although relatively small in area, contained an enormous coastline equal or greater in length than that of the entire remainder of the eastern seaboard. With countless deep harbors whose rocky bottoms did not silt up, practical New Englanders relied on what made the most sense – fishing and seaborne trade. Of those who had abused the Acts of Trade and Navigation, these *Yankees* led the way and naturally, were hurt the most economically by Britain's effort to tighten its grip on commerce.

Secondly, and at least equally significant, the colonists them-selves who settled New England were much different ideologically than their brethren further south. The population roots that had taken hold drew their nourishment from the initial Pilgrims and following Puritans, the most radical of Protestants who had fled England, and by the middle of the 18ᵗʰ century had melded into the *Congregational Church*, which dominated educative, theological and political thought to the point where church and civil government of nearly each town became indistinguishable. New England became a patchwork of individual but homoge-nous theocracies knitted together by the common hardships of everyday life that all citizens of the northeast shared. Basic tenets of *Congregationalism* included democracy, simplicity, interpretive study of the word of God and, above all, the *autonomy* of the congregation. At the opposite end of the ideological spectrum from mainstream conservative Europe and even unlike their more religiously and racially mixed neighboring provinces to the south, there grew in New England a radically liberal mindset that left little room for anything short of autonomous self-rule as a general principle. This self-imposed egalitarianism had produced, unlike their parent country, a well-educated middle class of farmers, artisans, and entrepreneurs who enjoyed a standard of living that existed nowhere else on the planet. The populace was well aware of the wretched and unavoidable peasantry that existed in other British colonies such as Ireland and Scotland and even in England itself, to the point of hyper-sensitivity to any action that even hinted at threatening what they considered the successful exercise of their natural rights as freeborn Englishmen. To control their own destiny in terms of family, church, township, and province was as natural as breathing and no entity, short of the Creator Himself, had the right to change that dynamic.

At the epicenter of these staunch Congregationalists was the community of Boston with about 17,000 inhabitants, second in American colonial population only to Philadelphia. Due mainly to its fortuitous advantage of a deepwater harbor and natural port of entry as well as the industry and vision of the Puritans, the settlement had grown into the intellectual and educational center of New England, and arguably the colonies as a whole. By the end of the Seven Years War Boston had become the leading provincial commercial center in New England by developing shipbuilding, fishing, logging, and other trade industries, all a byproduct of Britain's mercantile system and all at the mercy of the Acts of Trade and Navigation. Britain's new policies in America, intended by London to protect the empire's strategic position as a world power, were viewed instead as oppressive by the colonists, who were forced to fund them. For a century and a half each of the thirteen provinces had been allowed to independently manage their own affairs with an astonishing amount of autonomy and success. Now it seemed, following their collective hard-won victory against the French, their government had inexplicably turned on them, abusing their rights as Englishmen and blatantly fleecing them with neither mercy nor regard. In New England, debates raged in town meetings and political lectures intermixed with church sermons. In Boston, the nucleus of an emerging radical liberalism underpinned by Whiggish idealism, two leaders emerged whose combination of commercial interests and democratic fundamentalism would serve as a navigational beacon for Massachusetts and ultimately the entire colonial seaboard.

Samuel Adams, trained as a lawyer like his prominent cousin, John, and a staunch believer in classic Roman virtue, was a failed businessman several times over, whose only apparent successes lay in stirring up trouble. John Hancock, conversely, was a wealthy merchant, having recently inherited in 1764 at twenty-seven years of age a veritable fortune from his uncle, Thomas – a slaver and smuggler. With Adams as the ideological brain and Hancock the chief financier, this improbable pair led the *Sons of Liberty*, an activist organization dedicated to redress perceived legislative abuses by London. Typically, middle class and educated, largely composed of shopkeepers and artisans, these Sons of Liberty were Whigs as well but with a Yankee bent of radical liberal thought found only in New England, more specifically in Massachusetts and most specifically in Boston. Related in thought but still markedly different from their British Whig cousins, who spouted principled platitudes yet in practice clung to remnants of the feudal system, these democratic extremists advocated a Puritan-born idealism based on government accountability not by the people but rather *to* the people. But for all their high-minded rhetoric, what these frugal Yankees hated far more than any intangible political lashing at some ideological whipping post, was someone's hand in their pocket – most notably their own government's.

Following Massachusetts' example, parallel groups to the Sons of Liberty soon formed in every colony professing great loyalty to their symbolic leader, King George, but using mob tactics to steer public opinion against Parliament, often in a most open and violent manner. Before long the Massachusetts government leadership that represented the interests in London, most notably Governor Thomas Hutchinson, could not claim the hearts and minds of their provincial public, particularly the population majorities that existed along the coast. The other provinces remained not far behind. Those that had settled and were born inside the colonies had forever considered themselves as *Americans* but always within the context as British citizens with no difference in status or rights between themselves and their brethren on the other side of the ocean. To do otherwise would be alien to the point of absurdity. Although Sam Adams and a minute minority, even more radical than he was, proselytized independence as inevitable, the entirety of the provinces sought only to correct the misapplication of English law by the current government in London. Because if the king, his ministry, and Parliament were allowed to even begin to treat them as anything less than freeborn Englishmen, that would open the door to the threat of reduction to an existence no better than that of the poor wretches of Ireland.

In 1768 the Massachusetts Assembly committed what could be construed as the first openly rebellious act. In February, Adams and others drafted a letter, circulated to sister provincial assemblies, proposing a formal request for redress to Parliament from the most hated Townshend Act. Although containing what they considered moderate and loyal language, the British Ministry took exception, ordering the Massachusetts Governor to dismiss the assembly, which he did, as those miscreants refused to rescind the letter. At about the same time the new London-appointed Commissioner of Customs falsely charged John Hancock with smuggling Madeira wine and had him arrested, and his sloop, *Liberty*, impounded. A Boston mob promptly rescued Hancock and his ship, wreaking so much havoc that the commissioner and his officers were forced to seek refuge on Castle William, a fortified island three miles out in the harbor. Soon, two additional regiments of British soldiers arrived from Halifax, Nova Scotia to quell the resultant riots and maintain peace. The Boston radicals from the disbanded assembly now organized an illegal convention, inviting delegates from throughout Massachusetts to address the crisis and encouraging Bostonians to openly rebel. The situation cooled only when more even-tempered representatives from the western hinterland convinced the coastal zealots of the folly of physically resisting the king's troops.

London dealt more successfully in enforcing the Townshend Act in other colonies, all of which opposed the legislation, but none of which experienced the convulsions of Massachusetts. After all, these Americans were anything but a homogenous bunch with diverse and often competing economic and political interests: Fisherman, traders and shipwrights in New England; livestock and grain farmers in New York, New Jersey, Pennsylvania and Delaware; tobacco planters in Maryland and Virginia; turpentine and tar creators in North Carolina; and rice and indigo growers of South Carolina and Georgia. Nevertheless, the relative failures of state assemblies to effectively redress grievances convinced liberal-leaning colonial leaders that the way forward was not through traditional legal channels but rather to take matters into their own hands in cooperation with merchants to enforce a boycott of British trade. Leading merchants in the north and planters in the south agreed to import no British goods, including the colonial staple – tea. This accord, however, was difficult to enforce as the colonies were not nearly so committed against the Townshend Act as they were the previous Stamp Act, which had actually been repealed in 1766 after only a year in force. Rioting and strong-arm methods by the Sons of Liberty also appalled many, pushing some of those more conservative to lean toward Mother Britain. Still others, mainly those living inland, held hostility not toward Parliament but rather the coastal cliques that always dominated their provincial governments. The collective colonies remained concerned, mainly relative to their own provincial interests, but they remained decidedly *ununified*.

In 1770, with ten years' experience as king behind him, George III managed to maneuver into place a first minister that would be responsible to *him* rather than to Parliament as the position demanded. The 2nd Earl of Guilford, commonly known by his courtesy title *Lord North*, had made his name as the leader of the House of Commons, and had also served as the First Lord of the Treasury. Unlike his Whig predecessors with strong convictions and abilities, who had been allowed to exercise their robust leadership for the perceived good of the country against a backdrop of weaker monarchs, Lord North had no such qualities and was handpicked for precisely this reason. In other words, when King George wanted Lord North's opinion, the king would give it to him.

As Lord North assumed his post it was commonly recognized that current legislation with the American colonies was problematic and in need of renovation. At this relatively early point in his reign, King George, not at all educated on and much less concerned with colonial affairs, focused solely on maintaining a proper superior-subordinate relationship, as he had been reared to do since birth. Enabled thusly by the king, Lord North brought forth a bill to repeal the Townshend Act *except* for the duty on tea, an action intended as a conciliatory gesture of good will toward the colonies but more importantly a demonstration of primacy in still maintaining a tax.

On the very day that Parliament repealed the legislation in England, March 5, 1770, there occurred in America a most violent riot. Two British soldiers in Boston had accepted work as common laborers during a local strike, thereby precipitating an agitated mob. Angry Bostonians turned their rage on a target of opportunity, a lone British guard at the Customs House, pelting him with bricks and chunks of ice, and threatening to kill him. A platoon of fellow soldiers called forth to protect the guard and calm the situation was similarly accosted and, in a panic, shot and killed four citizens. Sam Adams labeled this unfortunate incident the *Boston Massacre* and used it to great advantage as propaganda to increase resentment against the British government.

When news of Parliament's new legislation reached the colonies, the hardline Yankee radicals remained unmoved. To them, anything less than *full* repeal of the monstrous Townshend Act was unsatisfactory, and they wished to continue the total boycott of British goods until the duty on tea was also lifted. Many colonial merchants, however, no longer supported this course of action as their economic situation had by now become quite desperate. The repeal of the Townshend Act, even with keeping the tax on tea, would provide the kind of prosperity not seen in years. With an unyielding ideology and stubbornness that rivaled that of their good King George, Adams and his cohorts considered this newfound apathy dangerous, citing that duties from British tea continued to fund Crown officials, such as their own despised Governor Hutchinson, thereby eroding control by their own state assemblies and diminishing provincial liberty. But at least for the time being, frugal Yankee practicality would trump Adams' hardcore liberal radicalism.

In early June of 1772 the British customs ship *HMS Gaspee* ran aground while chasing smugglers in the Narragansett Bay in the province of Rhode Island. Overexcited locals rowed out to the stranded craft, where they beat up the crew and burnt His Majesty's Ship to the waterline. Outraged, the British government called for capture of the perpetrators for impending trial in England. No principle of British liberty was more sacred than a man's right to trial by a jury of his own community and the idea of such a hearing anywhere but in Rhode Island stirred up agitation across the colonies all the way to Georgia. Unable to find the offenders for lack of willing witnesses, London had no choice but to drop the matter. However, the *Gaspee* issue served to persuade radical-minded leaders in every province to follow the example of the Sons of Liberty in Massachusetts and form a *Committee of Correspondence* to maintain communication both internally and externally for their own collective protection.

At this juncture the radical liberal movement across the American colonies simmered, but still well below the boiling point, with a more than ample number of conservative colonials siding with their British government and many more moderates ambivalent, even in Massachusetts. Sam Adams and a tiny minority of other democratic extremists had believed from the beginning that total independence was the only viable outcome and the path to colonial salvation from the abuses of Parliament would lead inevitably to a violent showdown and that this was, in fact, *necessary*. However, even in the face of the Boston Massacre and *Gaspee* incidents, there had yet to occur an event of sufficiently grave emotional value that would drive colonial passions to a frenzy and push them past the point of no return. Sam Adams and those of his political bent saw the colonies, and Massachusetts in particular, as a keg of gunpowder needing only a proper fuse. Unwittingly, the North Ministry, in its clumsy efforts to regulate America and ever-focused inward to preserve their own self-interests within King George's new government order, provided exactly that.

In 1773, with the Townshend duty still not removed on the precious commodity of tea, an enormous amount of colonial smuggling continued, particularly with Dutch suppliers, which undercut London's effort to use the tea as economic political leverage. In May of that year Parliament passed the *Tea Act*, removing the customs tax on tea exported into England in an effort to support the financially failing British East India Company. Elimination of the government middleman, in effect, allowed the national company to be its own exporter. In the American colonies, the net effect enabled the British East India Company to actually *undersell* the smugglers but with the colonial tax still a mandate. A treasury man to a fault, fiscally minded Lord North assumed that American provincials would welcome this relief in the form of lower-priced British tea. He could not have been more wrong as it was not the price of the tea the colonials objected to but rather the idea of being forced to do something – not only being gouged but poked in the eye as well – without their consent. Colonial radicals seized the opportunity to vigorously protest what they called an *illegal monopoly* and fanned the flames of new demonstrations across the colonies, the intensity of which had not been seen before.

That December, when initial shipments of the discount tea arrived in the normal distribution centers of Charleston, Philadelphia, and New York, the ships were either not allowed to enter port or officials were *persuaded* by the usual violent mob tactics against offloading it. In Boston, three ships did arrive and were allowed to dock with the tea consigned to the Royal Governor's sons. However, before the cargo could be unloaded and as thousands of interested spectators crowded the waterfront to watch, a mob organized by the Sons of Liberty, dressed as Mohawk Indians and Negroes, forced their way aboard the vessels and unceremoniously emptied the entire shipment, a small fortune of 342 chests, into the icy waters of the harbor. When news of this *Boston Tea Party* reached London, it proved more than King George could stand as the obvious insult and wanton destruction of such a symbolic commodity eclipsed that of even a national asset, the *Gaspee*. Sam Adams and other radicals hoped Massachusetts had just elevated itself to command the British government's full attention in the most negative light possible. While not a circumstance for the king and his ministry on par with a global crisis, the situation nevertheless demanded a stern response if for no other reason than to set an example to anyone else contemplating such imprudent behavior. Not caring one whit for the sensitivities that motivated the Bostonians to take such action, King George focused solely and narrowly on the issue of *discipline*. For if his ungrateful and churlish subjects in

Massachusetts chose to stir up trouble to challenge their government's authority, they would certainly receive a full measure of what that authority could bring to bear.

With King George now firmly at the helm of both ministry and Parliament, there were scant few who would oppose him. There had been for roughly the prior decade the ever-weakening minority of the Old Whigs who had spoken out against the continued policy of extracting payment from America in the form of forced taxes, most notably the Earl of Chatham. The former First Minister and architect of victory over France that King George had ousted early in his reign who, more than anybody present in government, could speak with authority on proper American policy. But the Earl was physically ill and largely irrelevant, having been out of the political process for some time as his lofty philosophical arguments, however compelling to English sensitivities, competed with the reality of the government that the king had purchased. But in the case of the Boston Tea Party, even these Old Whigs, as did the British public in general, considered the actions in the Massachusetts province as reprehensible.

The king expected decisive action from the North Ministry, which reacted, quite predictably, with commensurate levels of severity. Over the course of the spring in 1774 Parliament devised and passed a series of edicts directed toward Massachusetts called the *Coercive Acts* to take effect as soon as possible over the summer. They were: The *Boston Port Act*, which effectively closed Boston Harbor until the city paid for the tea; the *Massachusetts Government Act*, which reorganized the province by-laws to remove political influence from the people and allow the king and Parliament to govern it directly; the *Administration of Justice Act*, which allowed royal officials to use any means necessary to enforce laws and quell riots; and an amendment to the 1765 *Quartering Act*, which allowed military commanders to house troops in buildings other than traditional barracks. To enforce these unprecedented actions, the king appointed General Thomas Gage, the current commander-in-chief of military forces in America, as the *military governor* and *Captain General* of Massachusetts. The two army regiments stationed in Boston were ordered tripled with a royal navy squadron added in support.

What the king wanted and what he succeeded in doing, at least from his perspective, was to send a clear message to the people of Massachusetts that if they would not fall in line then he would dominate them into doing so, just as he had his own government in London. This course of action was underpinned by two basic assumptions: That the situation and sentiment in Massachusetts was an isolated incident born of misguided local radicals who would never receive support from the remaining fractious and self-serving American colonies; and, most importantly – a takeaway from the Seven Years War – that the Massachusetts citizenry, like all American colonials, were merely loud-mouthed cowards with neither the capability nor the backbone to stand up to an overt show of force by the British Army, the world's finest fighting machine. The king was now finished with the weak policies of appeasement that he had previously allowed himself to be talked into as he ruefully regretted repealing the Stamp Act and all other conciliatory gestures made in the past. From here on out he would exercise his version of leadership and authority – that of a strong and supreme monarch – something that his short-sighted, weak-kneed predecessors had for too long been loath to do.

As if the Coercive Acts were not bad enough, Parliament also passed the *Quebec Act*, designed to take effect the following year, in May 1775, for the territories north in Canada that had been acquired through the victory of the Seven Years War. This legislation sought to organize the governance of a colony that was overwhelmingly populated by unworthy scoundrels – French Catholics – utilizing a structure that was anything but autonomous and decidedly despotic with control placed firmly in London. While the Quebec Act was not aimed at the American colonies, such outrageous action was viewed there with alarm, particularly in light of and in parallel with the Coercive Acts, as a harbinger of Parliament's abusive inclinations.

As news of Parliament's monstrous deeds washed over Boston from the sea, the citizenry braced themselves with each battering wave. Although such a standoff was exactly what the Sons of Liberty and their radical support base had been waiting for, it did not mitigate the realization that the Massachusetts province, and Boston in particular, were staring straight into the abyss of potential disaster, if not total, at least economically. By dictating such heavy-handed and destructive policies and underwriting their enforcement with military troops no longer tasked with frontier security but rather now holding their own people hostage, King George was literally challenging them to a fight as if they were not English citizens but rather a foreign enemy. This audacious, extraordinary, and entirely unnecessary assertion of power had a profound effect on the Massachusetts population with the conclusion drawn that their own government had gone insane and, inexplicably, no longer represented their interests as British citizens. Back in London, colonial agent Benjamin Franklin desperately sought to assure the body politic that what those in Massachusetts craved was simply redress to what they considered unfair legislature. But King George and his minions would have none of it as, thanks to the Boston Tea Party, they were now past the point of listening and craved only to demonstrate and exercise authority.

Loyalty, tradition, and pride begged Massachusetts to concede to their government however unreasonable it had become. Yet, those same cherished English values impelled them to stand firm as the Holy Grail of *liberty* lay at stake. Ironically, in London, the American colonists that Britain had formed and protected for the last eight generations had now become themselves the threat. The British government that just a decade before had so masterfully defeated its mortal papist enemies and cemented itself as the greatest empire in the world had since taken every opportunity to birth an even more insidious menace – themselves. A narrow-minded king, a weak and corrupt Parliament, and a self-centered, greedy ministry that had devolved from enlightenment to ignorance had chosen the one option – the use of its military – that was guaranteed to escalate what was, in the grand scheme of things, a relatively minor domestic dispute. King George and the government that he had confiscated righteously prepared themselves to clean up the mess an ocean away in a corner of the empire about which they collectively knew, much less cared, little or nothing about – and they were seemingly willing to do so with blood. In this way the monarch of the world's greatest power would make a classic error which many rulers had made before and many more would make again: to resolve what was, in essence, a social problem with a military solution.

Thus, beginning in the spring of 1774 and continuing through the summer a steady stream of soldiers loaded onto transport ships in England and along with assorted naval men-of-war, dutifully sailed across the Atlantic Ocean in support of their government's new hardline policy. Unbeknownst to these well-meaning representatives tasked with the business end of saving their American brethren from themselves they steered toward an ever-growing, seething cauldron of resentment and mistrust that burned even hotter than the westward sun they followed.

4

A messmate before a shipmate;
a shipmate before a stranger;
a stranger before a dog;
and a dog before a soldier.

Old naval saying

BOSTON, MASSACHUSETTS, JUNE 1774

"**M**AKE READY!" the sergeant barked curtly as he looked down the line of six men.

Jack stood stiffly in rank dressed in full kit of a leather helmet with a rounded brim turned upward, displaying the famed *Lion of England*; a black leather band neck stocking; a black waistcoat covered by a long-sleeved red coat; white breeches; gray wool stockings; and black leather shoes with black gaiters. Upon command, he and the others knelt in unison on right knee while simultaneously cocking their muskets as the butt end touched the ground, keeping a firm grip with the left hand of the middle part of the firelock, their state-of-the-art weapon spanning four-feet-nine inches and weighing twelve pounds. Keeping their heads up and torso straight while remaining motionless they looked to the right along the rank with muskets upright, the butt placed precisely four inches to the right of the inside of their left foot.

"PRESENT!"

They brought the muzzle of their firelocks down together with a swift motion as if they were one, extending their left arm to full length with the musket butt raised up high against their right shoulder. With the weapon now pointed forward, their right cheek rested close to the butt as they peered down the length of the barrel.

"FIRE!"

They methodically squeezed the trigger and braced against the explosion and recoil of the firelock that hurled a round projectile three quarters of an inch in diameter at unfathomable speed. As the smoke cleared the rank briskly rose and, with torsos erect and left foot held fast, brought their weapon back to their side and right foot back in parallel. Several paces forward where their barrels had pointed lay a dead man – one of their own – hooded and tied to a pole, now slumped to the ground with his bleeding torso riddled and mangled by His Majesty's .75 caliber solid lead ball.

Jack had only just arrived in Boston that very day in the warmth of early summer. Against a hazy blue sky, a committee of seagulls had followed the transport in, squawking loudly to welcome their entrance. Making its passage through Massachusetts Bay, the lumbering vessel had carefully picked a course through a maze of islands, shallows, and other hazards to navigation that included several warships engaged in enforcing the Boston Port Act. Since the first of the month not a grain of sugar nor drop of molasses was allowed in or out of the seaport until the city paid for every last leaf of tea they had so wantonly destroyed. For the foreseeable future the only commodity imported to Boston was the one in least demand – British soldiers.

Jack and the ship that carried his regiment had landed without fanfare at *Long Wharf*, the lengthy wooden landmark pier that extended a third of a mile into the harbor. After collecting supplies, the new arrivals strode down the brow to dry land, officially joining the growing occupation force that already inhabited the city. They marched through the port and up the main thoroughfare of *King Street*, whose narrow cobblestone ways and familiar architecture rendered the appearance of an English city. The townspeople generally ignored them as they paraded in a long red line over the crest of the heights, arriving at a large open pasture area known as the *Commons* on the back side of the city along the Charles River. Here, each was assigned space in a large nearby barn that had been commandeered and converted to a barracks.

"SHOULDER YOUR FIRELOCKS!"

Upon command Jack returned his musket to his left shoulder in unison with the others. Now at eighteen years of age and one of the youngest in the unit, he had so far taken to the rigors of soldiering quite well. Now fully grown at five feet eight inches, his lean and wiry build concealed a deceptive strength and nimbleness formed in no small part by his years at sea. Inducted to serve at the *pleasure of the king* for His Majesty's *4th Foot Royal Regiment* of Lancaster, he had begun in the autumn prior, at the training facility at Chatham Barracks in Kent, where he marched and drilled and drilled and marched, sunrise to sunset, rain or shine, every day for weeks on end, being told when to eat, when to sleep, when to relieve himself and even how. He practiced every conceivable field maneuver until he could do them in his sleep and his musket became his closest companion. Many deserted and even more bitterly complained, but never once did Jack, who learned to perform each given task to perfection as if born for them.

There were few, if any, established units prouder and more storied than the 4th Foot Regiment – *The King's Own* – as it was commonly called. Initially raised in 1680 by the Earl of Plymouth to garrison the colony in Tangiers, North Africa in 1685, it had been employed in the personal service of King James II to quell the rebellion by the Duke of Monmouth at Sedgemoor then, from 1690 to 1695 in Ireland and the Dutch Republic in fighting to establish Protestant William of Orange on the throne – two of the defining moments in modern English history. After the successful capture and defense of Gibraltar at the turn of the 18th century, King George I bestowed upon the regiment in 1715 the title of the *King's Own*. During the Scottish rebellion in 1745 they fought at both Falkirk and Culloden, one of the few units to withstand the charge of the maniacal Highlanders and credited, in large part, with defeating the Scottish Army.

With their gruesome business complete, the sergeant marched the rank back across the Commons to resume normal duties. The executed man had come from one of the already established units and had raped a young Boston woman. His actions had left the new commander-in-chief, General Thomas Gage, a stickler for the rule of law, little choice but to meter punishment – swift and harsh – in order to dissuade a riot from the Bostonians, exceptionally nervous and agitated over the Boston Port Act and other new legislation. Ironically, if nothing else, such an execution was an extension of an *olive branch* – a peace-offering of sorts. The firing squad had been chosen randomly from the new arrivals with Jack and the other selectees performing the gruesome duty without hesitation or complaint – or choice.

Whether he knew it or not at the time but would soon learn, General Gage had been given an impossible task, one that he himself had a hand in making. The fifty-five-year-old general had arrived in Boston only a month or so prior in May, replacing Governor Hutchinson, who was promptly burned in effigy by the locals to celebrate his departure for London. Gage had spent the winter in England and, as Governor Hutchinson was on his way to do, had met privately with King George as well as the ministry to render his opinion and recommendations regarding Massachusetts.

As often happens with the second son of an aristocratic family, who by mere chance of birth will inherit neither title nor estate, a younger Thomas Gage had purchased an army commission following completion of his schooling. After capable European service and several promotions, he had been deployed to the

American colonies during the Seven Years War after which, on the strength of his record, particularly in Canada, was ultimately promoted to commander-in-chief of all British forces in North America, a post he continued to maintain. Gage even had an American wife, Margaret Kemble, granddaughter of the mayor of New York, who had borne him five children. Although firmly a Whig, the steady general received the firm approval of King George during the decade after the war he and successive ministries came to rely on Gage's expert assessments in the development of American policy.

With the use of armies to quell civil disputes quite common in Britain, Gage had advocated a firm hand, and in fact, the Coercive Acts were largely a result of Gage's personal advice to the king. Like virtually every senior officer, all products of the Whig aristocracy that dominated military leadership, Gage embraced the concept of shared government but detested the idea of *democracy*, particularly as interpreted by these Massachusetts Yankees, as nothing more than self-serving, rabble hypocrisy enforced by mobs. The use of the military was quite in line with the king's thinking that such an overt show of force would cow the craven provincials back to their proper places as obedient subjects. But if Gage had any misgivings as to the *size* of that force he would be given, initially only four regiments numbering roughly 2,000 men, he apparently did not voice it.

On the days that followed over the course of the summer the 4th Foot drilled on the Commons all day every day just as they had at Chatham. The King's Own, like most British regiments, contained 477 men, divided equally into ten companies with a regimental staff for administrative management and operational leadership. In typical military fashion a regiment organized and maneuvered its companies on the battlefield so as to amass concentrated firepower, like so many self-propelled violent rectangles, set against an enemy's near mirror image. Employing tactics that had not fundamentally changed since the beginning of western civilization, eight of these companies formed in close proximity to one another in order to maneuver toward the enemy at close range so as to either break his will or smash him to pieces before he could do the same. In modern times the foot soldiers were also typically supported from a distance with cannon by separate artillery units intended to break or at least soften the adversary prior to attack.

The remaining two companies were composed of *grenadiers* and *light infantry*, the existence of each the result of new tactics evolved over the recent century. Grenadiers, normally the largest, bravest, and most experienced and dependable men in the regiment, had originally, as their name implied, been utilized as grenade throwers during sieges of walled cities. With these methods having become obsolete they now typically guarded the regiment's flank or remained in reserve to deliver a critical blow at the decisive moment to shatter an opponent's weak spot or to shore up a breach within their own. Similarly, those in the light infantry were not as large and seasoned but still brave and nimble in both mind and body. Of the two, the light infantry was a more recent development, drawing heavily on tactics learned from American Indians, typically used as harassing *skirmishers* out in front of the main body or as a fast-moving strike force able to out-maneuver and outflank the more cumbersome regular units. Innovative military tacticians had taken this concept even further and in the colonies were experimenting with the development of entire regiments composed solely of grenadiers and light infantry as experience in the Seven Years War had shown these units to be particularly well-suited to the heavily wooded and irregular terrain of North America.

Not alone on the Commons during daylight, the King's Own would be joined by a sea of red uniforms marching, turning, and wheeling about as if in a perpetual pageant. As the summer progressed the numbers grew as regiments systematically arrived from Britain. The *Royal Lincolnshires* of the 10th Foot, the *Black Knots* of 64th and the *Royal Tigers* of the 65th from Lincolnshire, North Staffordshire, and York respectively, had long preceded them all, having arrived in North America as early as 1767 during the Seven Years War. Like the King's Own, the 43rd Foot from Oxford arrived in June, and the *Shiners* of the 5th from Northumberland as well as the 38th from South Staffordshire followed in July. Later in October, the *Light Bobs* of the 52nd from Oxfordshire would appear. Except for the 64th garrisoned at Castle William out in Boston Harbor they all shared space on what had formerly been a cow pasture. The officers, of course, found billeting within the city with those good Boston citizens who had been persuaded or otherwise *volunteered* to share their homes with the British gentry.

In order to augment the land forces and police the coastline, seven British warships lay in Boston Harbor with an additional five on their way. The First Lord of the Admiralty, the 4th Earl of Sandwich, had placed in command Vice Admiral Samuel Graves, who arrived not long after Gage in late June. Neither Lord Sandwich nor Admiral Graves contained even a modicum of knowledge or interest in America and, in addition, Graves was old, nearly retired, and thoroughly incompetent. For precisely this reason the rapacious admiral had received this backwater assignment, considered relatively unimportant in the grand scheme of global maritime affairs, so that he might line his pockets prior to exit from the navy. Graves focused his attention on leveraging the Coercive Acts to extract money from the local seagoing population in the form of expensive *licenses, levies,* and other such schemes intended to block what commerce remained except through him. Other than to prepare his fleet to bombard defenseless coastal towns as his version of an example of British primacy, he did little to coordinate with General Gage who, in turn, avoided dealing with the detestable Graves whenever he could.

Although technically a peninsula Boston was in truth more of an island, nearly surrounded by water with the Massachusetts Bay and Atlantic Ocean directly to the east and a confluence of the Mystic, Charles, and Chelsea Rivers counterclockwise from north to south. To the south a narrow isthmus only 120 feet wide at high tide known as *Roxbury Neck* or simply, *the neck,* connected the city to the mainland. The only landward access in or out of the city, Puritan settlers had originally constructed an earthen wall with a wooden gate in defense against Indians, animals, and other unwanted visitors. Just outside the gate sat oft-used gallows where the Puritans – those original self-appointed beacons of tolerance – had routinely executed criminals as well as other detestables – such as Quakers – who disagreed with *their* version of righteousness. On either side of the isthmus lay tidal marshes with soft mud that rendered entrance to Boston nearly impossible except along the neck through the gate.

From the beginning, Jack had impressed the officers and senior enlisted leadership and although neither large nor experienced enough to be a grenadier he was, however, quickly assigned to the *lights,* as the light infantry were commonly known. Along with the grenadiers the lights received special attention and training and, within the King's Own, that responsibility fell to Sergeant Matthew Searles, who took charge of their every waking moment.

One of several company sergeants who had initially trained Jack in Chatham, Sergeant Searles could spot a soldier in his sleep. Older by a generation with broad shoulders, large hands, and thinning blond hair, he remained continually ramrod stiff in posture as if made of wood. Although not much taller than Jack, in a crowd he stood out as if heaven's own light shined upon him. Up close he could be utterly terrifying with an anchor face complete with a ragged scar, an old scalp wound, that ran horizontal across the length of his forehead just below the hairline. Half Scottish, he was quite familiar with the American colonies, having served there previously during the Seven Years War with the 1st Regiment of Foot. This storied *Royal Regiment* of Scottish origin had seen action during the capture of Louisburg in 1758 and the French surrender of Montreal in 1760, and, in addition, had fought the Cherokee Indians in South Carolina.

One particular skirmish in those ghastly Indian campaigns defined the good sergeant like no other, as recalled by his own captain. The captain had tussled with a trio of native warriors who, unlike their rigid foe with European protocols, had no qualms about attacking the officers who, in turn, made no attempt to conceal their status. They swarmed and knocked him off his horse, now riddled with arrows. The captain succeeded in eliminating two with his saber but was knocked down by the third who had managed a glancing blow to the captain's head. He landed sitting upright, stunned also by an arrow shot through his shoulder that pinned him against a tree. The warrior approached with his club raised high to finish him. The captain, unable to move, began to pray as he waited for the end. Suddenly the sergeant appeared from nowhere with no less than half a dozen arrows protruding in all directions from his torso and legs. Grabbing the warrior by the arm that held the weapon, the sergeant wrestled him to the ground and, finding the captain's nearby saber, hacked off the arm at the elbow, then caved in the Indian's skull with the club, his hand still gripping it.

Quiet by nature, Sergeant Searles spoke little and always in a firm but respectful manner. The consummate *master of his own person*, he hardly raised his voice except in drill. The courage, discipline and loyalty that was the hallmark of the British Army lay embodied in this thoughtful but intense man as a standard bearer for each of his men to emulate. In the sergeant's world there was no higher calling than to do one's duty no matter what the circumstances and consequences – the only thing that truly mattered in life. His men followed without question not because they feared him but because they loved him.

But respected as the sergeant and those like him might have been within their own circles, the general concept of soldiering was not considered a particularly honorable profession by most Briton's standards. Begrudgingly accepted in times of emergency as necessary evils, standing armies were considered utterly dangerous in peacetime – accidents waiting to happen, too easily manipulated by unscrupulous political leadership or even worse, too much potential to take on a political identity of their own as had happened often in the past. Those desperate miscreants willing to maim and kill simply in return for the king's shilling were considered, at best, no more than a state-sponsored mob of violent prostitutes and, at worst, outright criminal mercenaries. In a direct abomination to the very nation they served and protected, the world's finest military was ironically manned by those at the absolute bottom of a society that looked the other way when certain services were needed.

On any given day the King's Own 4th Lights formed on their section of the Commons receiving daily instruction and drill from Sergeant Searles who, when not giving commands, typically strode down the length of each rank, nodding with a slight grin as he spoke. *"Right smart, lads, right smart indeed. Masters of your persons, you are. No man can master soldiery that has not first mastered his own person. Chins up, shoulders back, stomachs in — always. Training, discipline, courage — that's what makes a proper soldier. Drinking, whoring, and brawling in this Yankee cesspool will have little ill effect on you if I have any say in it. Right smart indeed, lads, right smart indeed."*

As the summer wore on, in addition to constant drill the 4th Lights, like elements from other regiments, made regular marches out of Boston into the countryside as both a change of pace for the men and a show of presence to the citizens outside of the city. In doing so they were under strict orders not to harass the locals or harm their property. Moving out from the city gate across to the other side of the neck lay Roxbury proper, where one could turn right and cross the *Great Bridge* over the Charles River heading west or north into the Massachusetts interior or continue straight through the hamlet leading southwest or southerly along the seacoast. Once across the neck the marshes ended, opening vast and wide into a strong country with steep hills, streams, trees, embedded granite boulders and stone walls that crisscrossed the ample land like quilted patchwork.

On several occasions over the course of these country forays the lights had passed a saltwater farm, just outside of Roxbury to seaward along the marsh, tucked behind a copse of trees several hundred yards off the thoroughfare. Countless such homesteads existed in the hinterland with cleared land, large gardens, and plentiful orchards. One evening in August, Jack ventured to cross the neck on his own to visit the farm, bringing with him his mate, Percy, with an aim to trade what goods he could scrape together for some extra food. The son of a baker, Percival *Percy* Perkins could conjure from next to nothing a meal of higher standard than any of the regimental cooks could muster.

"Pleased to meet you, sir, and good day to you." Percy tipped his cap to the owner and smiled broadly as the front door cracked open to reveal a small, elderly gentleman, who stood back in the shadows holding something concealed behind his back. "Not meaning to trouble you, sir, but we would be pleased to barter with you for some supplies if you would be so obliged."

The man edged closer to the light from outside and eyed both soldiers with not a little suspicion. Percy maintained his smile as he held up a bulging knapsack. Jack merely returned the elderly man's stoic stare and raised both empty hands in a gesture that reflected he was unarmed. The man discarded whatever he had behind him, opened the portal halfway and stepped into the doorway. "Let me see what you have," he murmured to Percy in a soft but wheezy voice as he continued to eye Jack.

The old man was a quirky old sot – beady-eyed and bald – his full moon-shaped head displayed a strip of grey hair that ringed his globe like a faded crown. Small-boned, short and sinewy, his body seemed in constant motion with a series of erratic gestures never quite duplicated nor completed. He drove a hard bargain, shrewdly eyeing every move and expression of the pair of young soldiers. Jack bit his lip and stared at his boots as Percy's propensity to answer too quickly and talk too much continually eroded their bargaining position. Having arrived at the door with an ample mixture of saved wages as well as small tools and implements liberated from the army encampment, in the end they parted with it all and, in addition, an ample amount of their own supply of gunpowder. When the front door closed, Jack and Percy stood in the yard with a dozen fresh eggs, which they cradled in their helmets as if newborn babies.

"That bloody Scot," Percy scoffed as they turned up the path leading to the road. "You'd have thought he was selling the only eggs in the province. You'd have thought they were bloody filled with gold. Bloody Scots – can't really trust them, can you?"

Jack said nothing as he took a last look over his shoulder at the small farm. Reaching the main road, they turned right, following the scent of salt air that permeated the approach back to the neck. A cool breeze from the east began to blow, rustling the hardwood trees whose leaves had just begun to turn color, announcing the coming change of season. Squadrons of white seagulls patrolled the sky above the brackish tidal inlets that snaked their way through the marsh all around.

"What I can't understand," Jack mused, "is what complaint these Yankees have. A simple old Scotsman – a mere commoner like us – has land, a farm, crops, livestock – more than he needs and more than anyone back in England could rightly fathom. He's as wealthy as a lord, and he's just one of the many we've seen. It just doesn't make sense that they cry *abuse* when there's none to be seen."

The next day Jack returned to the farm alone and offered his services to the old man – *Mister Cameron* was his name – asking if he wanted assistance, not with operations of the farm itself but rather with the more labor intensive and less urgent refurbishment of the buildings and structures, which looked generally in a mild state of disrepair. Mister Cameron observed Jack with the same suspicion as before but seemingly without the hindrance of Percy, the old man agreed to take Jack on.

Jack came to the farm as often as he could, which amounted to two or three times a week, and throughout the summer helped Mister Cameron with several projects he might not otherwise have been able to accomplish. Contrary to what one would have expected, Jack had not negotiated set wages but rather was happy to accept whatever payment the old Scotsman felt obliged to give, usually a combination of food, an odd surplus tool or supply, and sometimes, hard currency. The old man never once looked him straight in the eye, constantly muttered to himself, and when he did choose to speak directly was barely understandable. Mister Cameron was a widower as evidenced by, during the few times Jack had stepped inside the actual living quarters, the lack of any female presence except a bedroom impeccably decorated for a young girl who obviously did not live there. On occasion Jack had brought Percy along for bigger projects.

One day as the summer waned in late August, Sergeant Searles called Jack out of formation at the end of daily drill. Jack stiffened as the sergeant approached with an ever-purposeful stride, stopping abruptly in front to look the young soldier directly in the eye.

"Relax, lad, I'm not going to scalp you," the sergeant said evenly.

"Yes, sergeant," Jack answered stiffly.

The sergeant inspected his subject of interest from head to toe then nodded. "You're a good lad, Halliday. You work hard. You're intelligent, fit, dependable. You train well. With more seasoning you'll make a fine soldier. I'm glad to have you in my unit but at the moment I'm a bit concerned."

Jack shook his head. "I don't understand, sergeant."

The sergeant put his hands on his hips and widened his stance. "I understand you have taken work across the neck."

Jack nodded. "Yes, sergeant. I found a bit of work with an old Scotsman on a farm just outside of Roxbury. The pay's meager, but it's pleasant to be there and more productive than drinking and whoring, which cost wages."

The sergeant grinned. "That it does, lad. But ask yourself, *why does this Scotsman not hire a Roxbury man?* Surely there are plenty that can use the work."

Jack shrugged. "I don't know. I've seen the place for some time on patrol and noticed that it looked a bit rough. Back in July I walked across the neck to the farm and offered to work for whatever terms the old man saw fit. It's not much but whatever little he gives me is more than just our wages."

The sergeant nodded. "Yes, it is, lad, but there's the problem. Whatever that old Scotsman is paying you it's less than he'd be paying a Yankee; otherwise, a Yankee would already be working there." He paused momentarily as if to let that point hang. "You're a smart lad, you are, so you must learn to use your head. Our presence in this part of the empire is not well-received by those misguided fools who believe their freedom is being threatened by His Majesty, the very entity that secures that freedom. Those damn scoundrels, the so-called *Sons of Liberty*, have a stranglehold on the entire province and particularly this city and its environs."

Jack shook his head. "I don t believe Mister Cameron bothers himself much with politics."

"Well, he's a damn fool if he doesn't," the sergeant snapped. "But that's not my concern. Lad, your Mister Cameron may be either a loyal king's man or one of those Yankee miscreants. Maybe his business sense outweighs his politics or maybe he just does not give a fishes' tit about anything except his own affairs. But the fact is he has a king's soldier taking his wages, a situation that won't be lost on those radicals so inclined to pass judgment no matter what his political leanings are. These damned Yankees yelp endlessly about their precious *liberty*. What they really mean is the *liberty* to bash anybody's brains out that does not agree with their fanatical views. Believe me – I've seen these so-called *patriots* in action before and I'm here to tell you they're not worth a thimble full of whale shit in a stand-up fight. But a drunken mob of them is surely capable of taking on one old farmer, or even a lone British soldier, for that matter."

Jack lowered his head and sighed. "What do you want me to do, sergeant?"

"Lad, it's not against any regulation for you to take extra employment and ordinarily it would be a grand idea. But it's not prudent around here in times such as these. These damned Yankees can beat the tar out of each other all they want, but we cannot afford such an incident with one of our own. There is no need to report this up to the officers and neither will I force you to quit. But as your sergeant and someone who knows a little something about these people, it's my duty to encourage you in the strongest terms to sever this relationship both for the sake of yourself and for this Mister Cameron. For your want of extra wages and that old man's want of cheap labor, it's not going to end well."

"I understand, sergeant," Jack answered dutifully.

Sergeant Searles fixed Jack with a determined gaze. "Good lad, then," he said with a quick grin. He clapped Jack on the shoulder and strode back across the Commons, disappearing into the ever-present sea of marching red.

Jack walked to Roxbury that very afternoon, passing the neck at low tide where the cool late summer air blew the pungent smell of the mud flats across the long marsh grass. He spotted Mister Cameron puttering about the yard gathering materials for that day's project – new shingles for an outer section of the barn. Having already gone to the trouble of traveling, Jack worked until sundown and when the old Scotsman shuffled over to hand him several eggs, a fistful of nails and a few weathered coins, Jack merely nodded and watched in silence as Mister Cameron ambled back into his doorway and disappeared. Stuffing the nails and coins into his pockets and cradling the eggs in his uniform helmet, Jack simply turned and started back up the path toward Boston.

5

*America is a mere bully, from one end to the other, and the
Bostonians by far the greatest bullies.*

General Thomas Gage

BOSTON, MASSACHUSETTS, NOVEMBER 1774

"Bloody hell, mate, you'd think I was sitting here with
a damn corpse." Percy nudged Jack, who sat next to
him on a bench at a table. "Have you nothing to show
for yourself except silence and a frown?"

Hunched over with his hands cupped around a flask, Jack
stared down into a pint of ale. "Sorry, Perce," he answered with
a forced a smile, "could be the weather."

"Right you are, mate. So much for this Yankee climate.
Even on a good day it's either too cold or too hot for a proper
Englishman's liking. I can't imagine what value the Crown sets
on this God-forsaken place.

The pair scanned the bustling main room of the *Kicking Mule,*
packed to the rafters with jostling grenadiers and light infantry
from the 4th Regiment, all in uniform. Outside, the weather had
turned quite snotty with howling wind and a sky that had earlier

disgorged all manner of precipitation so vile that it could have stopped an army – and it had. A *nor'easter*, the locals called it, and for three full days every living creature in Boston took refuge in whatever manner they could. The storm blew from the open ocean across the exposed bay such that it seemed the city itself would be swept away. Now, on the tail end of that tempest the wind backed to the northwest as the precipitation disappeared and the temperature plummeted from merely raw to outright frigid. Anything and anyone unfortunate enough to be left outside would now transform from thoroughly soaked to frozen stiff.

Boston had been so squeezed by the Coercive Acts that the economic situation grew grimmer by the day. But of all the things hard to come by, finding a drink was the least of those and, in fact, a pool of local establishments seemed a growth industry, particularly around the waterfront district, fueled mainly by the British Army. Every regiment had adopted their own watering holes with each claiming several, annexed as necessary by individual companies with the King's Own assuming residence in the Mule shortly after their arrival earlier that summer. As was becoming more the norm, the 4th Grenadiers and Light Infantry went their own way, taking what they considered the best for themselves. The Mule's owner, a short and burly fellow, claimed an affinity for King George – at least to British ears – a stance, no doubt, most closely linked to lining his own pockets. Like many Boston merchants that struggled to survive, political orientations took second place to feeding their families as they held their nose to cater to the British. As long as the soldiers chose to spend their meager earnings on drink and gambling, Yankee entrepreneurs would transfer British monetary resources in whatever manner they could.

But the Coercive Acts had done much more than cause just economic turmoil in Boston and the Massachusetts province – it had sent a shock wave throughout the entire 13 colonies as had never been seen before. After all, if King George and Parliament could take such action against one province, they could do so to any of them. In an unprecedented act of unity and upon recommendation of Sam Adams and the Massachusetts provincial leadership, all the colonies except for Georgia agreed to send representatives to Philadelphia in September for the purpose of deciding how to jointly address what they considered the illegal and immoral edict. If Lord North and his ministry had calculated that their hard-nosed legislation would serve to isolate Massachusetts from the remainder of their self-serving and ever-squabbling brethren American provinces they were soon to find out they had instead pushed them together for what came to be known as the *Continental Congress*. Efforts by Loyalists to prevent this illegal, and frankly, *revolutionary* committee proved fruitless and, in some case, even dangerous as the Sons of Liberty and similar mobs along the Atlantic seaboard wasted no small effort in exerting their special brand of brutal influence.

By the end of the summer the full influx of red-clad soldiers that so proudly and overtly paraded about the greater Boston countryside left no doubt to the citizenry that King George and Parliament did not consider them full-fledged British subjects, but rather something much less. After a century and a half of relative success at managing their own affairs, under no circumstances would they allow themselves to be transformed into a backwards social prison state such as Ireland. Driven by the constant overt show of force, the realization that their own government was fully prepared to do them harm prompted a frantic race toward self-defense as each township began to arm itself in earnest.

As a practical matter, General Gage understood that the Sons of Liberty might stir the radical pot all they wished but their actual ability to create a security threat was directly related to their capability to acquire arms. Neither Gage nor any other professional British officer believed that this motley crew of yokels known as *militias* could actually mount a credible challenge, but they could certainly become a nuisance if properly motivated, organized, and supplied. Therefore, the prudent course of action was to simply disarm them. Without the necessary weapons, ammunition, and training, these militias would be no more than toothless tigers that would render meaningless the ever-increasing violent rhetoric from the misguided zealots.

Of all the commodities necessary for the provincials to make military threats, gunpowder was by far the most critical. The Yankees possessed no indigenous ability to manufacture gunpowder and what amount they managed to import, steal, or otherwise acquire they had squirreled away in magazines all over New England. Having enjoyed no success in bribing Sam Adams and other radical leadership inside the Sons of Liberty, General Gage nevertheless had managed to corrupt others further down in the hierarchy to include prominent Boston Doctor Benjamin Church, who had needed money to fund his mistress. Along with considerable support from a cadre of hardcore Tory Loyalists, Gage managed to develop a reliable intelligence network and over the course of the summer he learned the locations of the major Yankee storehouses and set to work to eliminate them.

Just six miles to the northwest of Boston across the Back Bay lay the largest single store of gunpowder in New England, kept in a stone tower on a remote hill in the hamlet of Somerville. In late August General Gage had learned from his spies that certain towns had begun preparing themselves for trouble by removing their allotment of powder from the stronghold with more planning to follow suit. Before sunrise on the first day of September several companies of handpicked regulars from the 4th Foot and others, led by the King's Own commander, Lieutenant Colonel Maddison, moved by boat across the harbor and up the Mystic River on the back side of the Charlestown peninsula. As the unsuspecting populace slept, the soldiers landed without incident and at first light secured the fortification without resistance, having kindly requested the keys from the local Tory sheriff. They confiscated the powder in its entirety, some two hundred fifty half-casks as well as two brass field pieces from neighboring Cambridge, transporting them all back to Boston before the noon hour.

Gage had planned the operation perfectly except for the aftermath reaction. Over the following days word of this heinous *robbery* became fully known along with wild rumors of British atrocities. Hordes of men from all over New England swarmed into the area, most of them armed and *all* of them angry as hornets with the accepted estimate counted at about 30,000 – more than ten times the British number. They congregated mostly in and around Cambridge across the Charles River from Boston indulging in the grand Yankee tradition of a full-out riot, beating up every local Tory within reach and dispossessing some of the more affluent of their homes and belongings. As those on the peninsula watched from the opposite bank the enraged mobs cut a swath of destruction as they punched, hacked, and burned their way toward Boston, stopping short of the city itself.

The *Powder Alarm*, as it came to be known, had a profound effect on the British, one that was interpreted differently by those on the scene and those across the ocean. The size of the mob and the speed of its formation shocked General Gage into the realization that he did not possess adequate forces to militarily dominate the Massachusetts province apart from only Boston proper. He consequently spent the ensuing days fortifying the gate at the neck with brick, stone, and timber, placing heavy cannon and a large ditch across the path. He further restricted entrance or exit only to those with strict permission. For all practical purposes, Boston now became a fortress island with a steady stream of panicked Tories seeking refuge from increasing persecution. Many on the opposite end of the political spectrum also took the reverse action, departing Boston if they could relocate to the safety of like-minded relatives outside the city. Over the autumn, the general began a campaign of missives to the king and ministry requesting reinforcements of 20,000 additional troops – an unrealistic number in the eyes of London that would have threatened to cripple the security effort for the remainder of the empire.

King George, conversely, considered the Powder Alarm as validation of Massachusetts provincial weakness as the leaderless mobs had merely blustered into the atmosphere with neither the capability nor stomach to mount a credible, organized, and unified threat. He wondered why a sharp action by his military commander against such poltroons would not settle the matter and crush the craven Yankees' spirit for good. That Gage would use the occurrence as justification for additional forces proved perplexing, as the same general had personally assured him earlier in the spring that all would be handled expediently with the ample resources already provided.

For their part Sam Adams and the Sons of Liberty, appalled that such action as confiscation of the Somerville powder should have been taken against placid, law-abiding citizens such as themselves, vowed to never let it happen again – and they did not. Soon after they had so effectively organized a resistance movement and alternate government complete with its *Committee of Correspondence* that all of Massachusetts became virtually independent of General Gage's authority except for inside the confines of Boston. They tightened their surveillance of daily redcoat activities and using their committee network managed to keep the hinterland well-informed and alerted to any British movements inside or outside the city. As autumn wore on, the British now retired into an unsure posture of inaction and indecision, their leader thus earning the moniker of old *Granny Gage.*

Jack finally raised his head as he turned to Percy. "Where the hell are those two scoundrels, your so-called *mates?*"

"Went to have a piss, didn't they?" Percy answered with a smirk.

"Well, they must be pissing all the way across the neck," Jack scoffed. "I wouldn't be surprised if they ran out and left us to pay."

"Nonsense," Percy answered, feigning surprised at such a notion. "Why would they do such a thing?"

"Because they're damn Irishmen," Jack stated flatly. "Both are well known cads that would cheat their own mother out of her last pence if presented the opportunity. We ought to be suspicious that they've suddenly taken such a shine to the likes of you and me and want to chum with us in public. I don't trust either one of them and neither should you. In fact...."

"There, laddies." A voice appeared from behind. "Bet you thought we'd run out, eh? Here's a fresh pint to whet your whistle. Come now, Halliday – drink up, laddy. If Perkins here had not vouched for you himself, we'd think you were raised in a goddamn nunnery, for Christ's sake."

Jack coolly eyed the two returnees as he drained his current tin and replaced it with the new one. He wiped his mouth with a sleeve and scowled at the Irishmen, both of whom grinned like Cheshire cats as they resumed their seats across the table. Grenadiers both, they seemed pressed from the same mold – farm boys over six feet tall with powerful shoulders, large necks, and long arms. Of the two, Patrick Flaherty to the left was the talker with a mop of dark hair and hands that practically engulfed his flask. To his side, Robert Ahearn had thicker facial features with a veiny, large bulbous nose that was now turning slowly but surely the color of his red hair.

"So, laddies," Flaherty continued, "what kind of mischief can we make tonight?"

Percy glanced back over his shoulder toward the front window. "It's not quite night yet."

"Close enough, laddy," Flaherty answered, "so we must make ourselves a plan. Otherwise, the laddies in here will drink what's left of their earnings before they've a chance to give it to us."

The Boston regiments had not been paid for well over a month but thankfully beating the storm into port a ship had arrived with chests of coins that the quartermasters gleefully doled out as if they themselves were responsible. Now, with each soldier having a relative fortune in his pocket, the city taverns were bursting at the seams with those not on duty compelled to ride out the storm in the warmest, driest place they could find which, not surprisingly, happened to offer plenty of drink and gambling.

Flaherty turned to Ahearn and gently elbowed him in the shoulder. "What say you, Robert?"

"I would say a game of dice is in order," Ahearn answered immediately, his grin remaining in place as if permanently affixed.

"A game of dice! Of course!" Flaherty offered this revelation a tad bit too practiced. "What do you say, Perce? We've made our reconnaissance and the laddies 'round back are well in their cups. There's a king's ransom for the taking. We could make it ours."

"I don't know how to play dice," Percy offered somewhat hesitantly.

Flaherty shot back an incredulous glance that could have been genuine. "Don't know how to play dice? Well, even better – we can teach you. But what soldier doesn't play dice? What have you been learning in the lights?"

"Many of the other lads play dice and cards," Percy stated. "I never have."

"Well then," Flaherty quickly regained his equilibrium. "What the hell do you do when you're not drilling?"

"I cook," Percy answered, a bit sheepishly. "I'm a baker's son."

"You cook? What the Christ for? Do we not already feed you?" Flaherty gave a belly laugh as he glanced at Ahearn, still fixed with the same silly smile. "You're a baker, are you?"

"Yes, I am," Percy answered, now trying to feign some pride. "My father has a bakery in Lancaster, and I grew up cooking there. It relaxes me now over here."

Flaherty shook his head and looked again at Ahearn. "Did you hear that, Robert? A *baker's son* he is." Ahearn's grin transformed into a scowl as Flaherty turned back to Percy. "Your father has a bakery in the city? What in God's name are you doing here, laddy? Why are you not back there making a decent living? Someday you could have that bakery for yourself."

"I don't want my father's bakery nor any other," Percy answered indignantly. "I don't want my father's life, stuck in that same bloody place day after day – a bloody slave he is. I want to see a little bit of the world."

Flaherty and Ahearn laughed in unison. "A *slave* you say?" Flaherty offered as he slapped his palm hard on the table. "Well, you're going to see the world alright, laddy. Let me know how you like the look of it past the point of a bayonet. And if you haven't figured it out yet, you soon will as there is no greater *slave* in this world than the bloody likes of us."

Flaherty shook his head as Ahearn folded his arms and continued to chuckle. Flaherty's tone now turned from amusement to annoyance as he looked to the ceiling, speaking to no one in particular. "A damn baker's son and he joins the bloody army. Wants to suffer for the king as a distraction, does he? If my bloody father had been a baker I would sure as hell not be sitting here. Lord in heaven, it's all gone pear-shaped." Flaherty leaned back in his chair and gazed in the distance, silent for at least the moment.

Ahearn pushed further forward and peered now at Jack. "And what about our stoic friend here? Can we get a game of dice from you, Halliday? Or do we also have to teach you as well?"

"I don't play dice," Jack answered flatly.

"Don't tell us you're a bloody baker as well," Ahearn continued, his irritating grin now returned.

"No – I don't play dice," Jack stated, "in fact, I don't gamble at all."

"Don't gamble?" Ahearn nudged Flaherty, who continued to stare in the other direction. "Did you hear that, Patrick? We have ourselves a couple of schoolgirls here. Do you mind telling us why, Halliday? If you don't know how, that is one thing; but if you don't *like* it, that is quite another. You can't *trust* a soldier that doesn't gamble – certainly not in our regiment."

"I bloody well don't give a goddamn who you don't trust," Jack snapped, raising his voice. "I work hard for my wages and prefer not to donate them to a couple of highwaymen like yourselves!"

"I'm going to forget that insult," Ahearn answered, his grin waning again, "only because you're new. But let me give you a piece of advice. We all work hard for our wages but taking the king's shilling isn't enough. You get by in this business on your wits and there's nothing wrong with making something extra. Those that can, do it, and those that can't will donate to others until they can. How else could we afford a drink in this God-forsaken hole?"

"I don't need to risk losing the wages I've earned for the sake of a drink," Jack lectured. "There's honest employment for those who will look."

Ahearn leaned forward. "And where, exactly, is *that*?"

"Across the neck." Jack answered, probably a bit more smugly than he should have. "I found employment with an old farmer."

"I see," Ahearn scoffed, "an old Yankee farmer with a redcoat hireling. *That* must be the pride of the village," Ahearn chuckled. "What are the terms? You plow his field, and he gives *you* a front row seat to his lynching?"

Jack did not answer, instead taking a long swallow of ale.

"Wait right there." Flaherty came back to life, pointing a finger at Jack. "You're the bloke that worked for an old Scotsman outside of Roxbury, aren't you?"

Jack remained silent, glowering behind his pint.

"We heard all about that, didn't we, Robert?" Flaherty continued, his smile returning. "Some dumb bastard in our own lights they said it was. Burned his farm to the ground, didn't they, those bloody Sons of Liberty? Tarred and feathered that old codger and dragged him off behind a horse. Don't suppose he survived that one, now did he? There's some good ol' Yankee civic spirit for you, eh, Halliday?"

Flaherty and Ahearn erupted in laughter and banged their flasks together before taking a long swallow each. Jack pounded his flask on the table and bolted upright. "Enough!" he shouted and pointed at Flaherty. "Mister Cameron was a good man – a sight better than the likes of you! He didn't deserve what he got, and I won't stand for your insults of him!"

Flaherty rose more slowly, looming like a giant from across the table. His smile vanished as he looked down at Jack's shaking finger. "Don't threaten me, laddy," he growled. "For I eat the likes of you for breakfast. Sit back down before I box your ears. And any *insult* wasn't meant for your dear Mister Cameron. Only a damn fool would've taken such work in this cursed place. The Sons of Liberty may have crucified that old Scotsman, but you handed him over like Judas. I imagine you got your sack of coins – and you want to question *my* character?"

Jack suddenly launched himself over the table sending all four flasks spilling to the floor. Using his knees as leverage he drove into Flaherty's chest and clamped his hands firmly around the Irishman's rather large throat. Ahearn and Percy were on the pair immediately with Percy grabbing Jack from behind by the waist and Ahearn reaching in to separate Jack's arms by the wrists. Like a top-heavy, four-headed, drunken beast, the cluster wavered and stumbled, finally toppling in a heap onto the ale-soaked floor. Flaherty rose first, rubbing his throat amid the cheers and shouts of the surrounding patrons.

"Goddamn you, Halliday," he wheezed. "You've a lot to learn, laddy. You're nothing but a damn street urchin – raw and undisciplined. I can tell by the way you move."

Jack rose as well with Percy still holding him from behind and Ahearn blocking his path to Flaherty. "I can move well enough to throttle the likes of you," he sneered.

"What's going on here?" The owner, short with a solid frame, arrived holding a wooden club and flanked by his two nephews, equally stout and slightly taller. Ignoring Percy and Jack the trio fixed their attention solely on Flaherty and Ahearn.

"No worries, sir," Flaherty answered, still rubbing his throat, "a little misunderstanding among mates is all. We'll clean up the mess."

The owner stared hard at Flaherty then motioned his nephews to leave. "You know the rules in here, corporal," he addressed Flaherty sternly, "there's no fighting allowed. I know your colonel personally and I'll not hesitate to bring this to his attention." He pointed a stubby finger straight at Flaherty. "You know what happens then, don't you, corporal?"

Flaherty stiffened. "Yes, sir. Our apologies. Come now, lad-dies," he turned to the others, "let's pick up the floor."

"I'll have none of it," Jack stated defiantly as he wriggled away from Percy. He then turned and marched toward the doorway.

"JACK!" cried Percy as he started after him.

Ahearn grabbed Percy by the collar from behind. "Let him go," Ahearn directed. "Better for all of us if he does."

Jack pushed through the door at almost a trot, slamming it behind him as he burst outside into a wall of cold air. The vile precipitation of the nor'easter had vanished, leaving in its wake a bitter cold wind that blew swirling through the now dark streets. He cinched his coat tight around his neck and, with hands in his pockets, leaned into the biting wind as he started up the hill back to the encampment at the Commons. He walked quickly, head down and staring at the ground, continually cinching himself down into his coat as if to disappear.

"Evenin', gov'ner."

Startled, Jack pulled up short and looked up. Before him stood a man that had suddenly appeared in the street, about the same height but thicker with a flat nose and missing front teeth.

"Soldier, are you?" the man continued with in a voice that seemed to whistle. "And where might you be going on a fine evenin' such as this?"

With hands stuffed deep in the pockets of a thick overcoat the man smiled in an easy manner, bundled in a long scarf and wool cap. Jack attempted to sidestep away to the right, but the man matched him, still remaining in front. Jack stopped again and peered past the man to either side of the street seeing only two rows of dimly lit wooden buildings that disappeared over the crest of the hill.

"Just out for a walk is all, sir," he finally answered.

The man nodded and widened his smile. "Just a walk, is it? A bit chilly for a stroll, wouldn't you say? A man out here at this time of night in this sort of weather usually has a purpose. Could I interest you in a bit of warm female company?"

"No thank you, sir," Jack replied. "Just want to get back to the Commons, if you don't mind." Jack shifted this time to the left and again the man stepped in his path.

"Come now, gov'ner," the man pleaded with hands removed from his coat, "just inside the doorway is a pretty lady who would love to meet a soldier such as yourself. For a small donation you could spend some time, get yourself out of the cold for a while."

"No thank you, sir," Jack repeated. He now stepped forward into the man, knocking him slightly backwards.

The man grabbed Jack by the arm. "See here, gov'ner! That was bloody unnecessary! I offer you a little local hospitality. Come 'round back and spend some of those wages you just received. It'll be good for everyone."

Jack did not answer but rather wrenched his arm away. Positioned now on the other side of the man he turned to hurry up the street in his original direction but suddenly stopped again, his path now blocked by several men all holding what appeared to be ax handles. He turned back toward the man, who resumed his smile. There were more men with clubs that appeared in this direction as well. The man approached again slowly as he balled his hands into fists.

"Now, gov'ner," the man said evenly as his eyes narrowed, "no doubt you're the reasonable sort. Let's make this easy for the lot of us. If you don't want to come 'round back, then just empty your pockets of those wages right here and you'll be on your way back to the Commons in a shake. Should be a quicker trip as you'll be a tad lighter." The surrounding men chuckled as the man's smile hardened to a scowl as icy as the ground. "Otherwise, we'll beat you all the way back to Mother England, you bloody lobsterback."

Jack had made the mistake of wandering alone after dark and this on a night when all of Boston knew every soldier had just been paid back wages. With much of the city out of work the majority of the inhabitants, the roughest sort even in the best of times, had been reduced to something less than human with gangs of ruffians roaming the streets like packs of wild dogs. Every soldier knew that, wages or not, a mob such as this meant to thrash a vulnerable symbol of their misery simply because they could. The ruffian's smile returned as he studied Jack intently.

"All right," Jack answered shakily as he clenched his fists inside his jacket, "I'll give you my wages." He reached slowly into his coat, grasping not his purse but instead Georgey's knife. But as he started forward the man suddenly swung around toward a commotion behind. Flaherty stepped out of the darkness striking the ruffian hard in the side of the head with his fist the sound of which resembled a melon being dashed on the ground. The man collapsed motionless into a heap.

Flaherty grabbed Jack by the collar, drawing him in. "Stay close, laddy," he ordered, "and do like I tell you."

Ahearn also emerged from behind Jack, brandishing an ax handle obviously taken from one of the ruffians. The two grenadiers worked as a team to engage three men that attempted to oppose them. Ahearn held his club by each end, blocking blows and herding the attackers toward Flaherty, who efficiently cracked their heads with his fists. The remainder of the scoundrels fled down the hill into the dark.

"PERKINS!" Flaherty shouted.

"COMING!" Percy answered.

"For Christ's sake, MOVE!" Flaherty barked. "Gather the remaining clubs and give one to each of us!"

"RIGHT!" Percy replied as he scurried around the circumference returning with three ax handles.

Ahearn bent over the ringleader, sprawled face down motionless on the cobblestone street. "This one had a busy evening, Patrick!" Ahearn offered as he rifled through the man's pockets. "Seems we made a profit after all." He emerged with a sack full of coins and placed them in his own coat. As the man groaned Ahearn struck him hard in the ribs, causing him to writhe in pain on the street like a fish. Ahearn beat him repeatedly then started toward another nearby that was attempting to crawl away.

"Forget the rest, Robert," Flaherty ordered. "That one was in charge and the others won't have much. PERKINS! HALLIDAY! Form up in a line behind me. Robert, take up the rear! Move! There'll be a mob here soon – you can count on that."

The quartet quickly started up the road with Flaherty in the lead and Ahearn trailing last, looking side to side as they trotted.

"Corporal Flaherty," Jack attempted from behind.

"Silence, Halliday," he ordered. "We need speed not conversation."

"But," Jack continued.

Flaherty turned toward Jack and pointed a finger in his chest. "Whatever you have to say, private, is unnecessary. Whatever else you may be, whatever else you may think, you're still one of us. And if you want to survive, we stick together. I hope you just learned that."

As the group hurried in silence up the hill through the darkness, Jack cinched up his coat, lowered his head, and once again leaned into the bitter wind.

6

They came three thousand miles and died
To keep the past upon its throne.
Unheard beyond the ocean tide,
Their English mother makes her moan.

Epitaph on the Concord Bridge

BOSTON, MASSACHUSETTS, APRIL 18, 1775

Jack woke suddenly, startled by a hand on his shoulder.
"Come, lads – up now," Sergeant Searles whispered as he
shook each soldier gently but firmly. "We have work to do.
Bring your haversack with a day's ration but leave your knapsack.
Make sure you have a full cartridge box with thirty-six rounds
and enough powder. Now come, lads."

Jack rose slowly from the straw atop wooden boards on the
ground that served as his bed and donned his boots and coat.
Although dark inside the barracks, he saw nearby Percy, Michael
Higgins, and George Bridges. In fact, the entire company seemed
to be moving.

"What's this all about?" Jack asked no one in particular. "What time is it?"

"Half past nine or thereabouts," Higgins answered. "Better hurry, Jack – we're marching."

"At night? Where to?" Jack wondered out loud as he yawned, reaching inside his coat to scratch his belly.

"Nobody knows," George answered, his ever-present smile evident even in the dark. "Quite strange it is. Seems Granny failed to consult us once again."

The 4th Lights had marched many a time since arriving less than a year ago but always in the daytime and never after dark. The four soldiers dressed quickly, then joined the rest of the unit as they moved silently, under strict orders not to wake anyone else. By just past ten o'clock they were formed with about 800 men in the most remote end of the Commons at the water's edge of Back Bay, brushing the remaining cobwebs from their heads as they stood silently in the cool, crisp air. A full moon rose in the clear southeastern sky, illuminating the water like a lantern as Massachusetts warmed from a reportedly mild winter to an early spring. The pungent smell of the exposed mudflats permeated the air as brackish water reversed course and now ran inland back up the Charles River for what would be an unusually high spring tide – a *young flood*, as the locals called it.

The officers and sergeants organized their men as it quickly became obvious that, besides the odd hour, something even more unusual was afoot. These missions had always been drawn from single regiments however, in contrast to that practice, there formed no troops from the *hat* companies – as the regular companies were referred to – but rather solely grenadiers and light infantry from each Boston regiment, as well as a company of marines. Further, each of those companies had without explanation been taken off regular duties three days prior with no drilling, marching, or standing guard but rather only eating and sleeping until further notice – something the soldiers had noted with curiosity but not complaint.

Being the most senior of the regimental commanders, Lieutenant Colonel Smith from the 10th Foot had been placed in charge of the operation. He arrived last, amidst disarray and confusion, there having previously been no central leadership across the differing regimental units to assume overall control. A methodical and plodding officer with an indolent but stalwart reputation, he wobbled in red-faced and out of breath looking disheveled, evoking a predictable exchange of bemused glances by the men. In fact, all the men had been dragged out of bed at this odd hour only to be mingled with elements from other regiments whom they tended not to like, much less trust, with no idea where they were going or what they were doing and, even worse, to be led not by their own officers but rather a bulbous blunderer. Confronted now with embarrassment, the colonel acted in what the men had come to know as typical officer fashion – that is, yelling and cursing at anyone close to him simply for the sake of doing so.

"'When in trouble or in doubt, run in circles, scream and shout,'" George quietly quipped, drawing chuckles from the men around him and a hard stare from Sergeant Searles.

The Continental Congress that met in Philadelphia the previous September had done so in a sincere effort to speak with one common American colonial voice to rationally explain their legitimate grievances as Englishmen to appeal for redress and depart from the current path toward a military clash. The radical delegates from Massachusetts, such as Sam Adams and his cousin John, did not push their *independence* agenda as it was enough of a victory for them merely to have such a unified gathering in light of their province's dire situation. Neither did the sensitive and polarizing topic of *slavery* emerge as it was well-understood that delegates from those southern provinces that depended economically on that institution and who resented any such hidden agenda from the north would have packed up and departed on the first mention of it. Ultimately, the Congress produced a set of *resolves* based on those formerly written back in Boston by Doctor Joseph Warren, an esteemed leading citizen and Sam

Adam's brilliant protégé. Arriving in London by mid-December, this written offering pledged unwavering allegiance to the mother country and that it would act as a body solely in self-defense. It argued that the Coercive Acts were illegal under the British construct and quite beneath the wisdom of a great nation to attempt to enslave its people. Finally, the resolves made clear that the colonies were prepared, if necessary, to resist as a whole to include a total boycott of British-made goods.

Now was the time for London to take advantage of the chance to negotiate with those more moderate than the Massachusetts hotheads, as the Congress contained a majority that leaned heavily toward loyalty to the Crown. But King George would have none of it as he viewed the Congress as another example of feckless American weakness that operated solely from a disadvantaged position. He rejected the resolves outright if for no other reason than their very existence. His narrow view for a remedy, naturally shared by the ministry, of a triumphant military confrontation to put the colonials back in their place, had become a course of action practically etched in stone. Although they could not outright say so, this was exactly what Sam Adams and his still relatively small minority of Boston radicals were counting on, so as to remove the argument from moderate and Loyalist leadership in the other provinces that King George would compromise, thereby leaving no alternative but to declare independence – a consequence they considered inevitable. That the military governor, General Gage, had persisted in painting an apocalyptic picture in Massachusetts and requesting additional troops proved a growing irritant to the king and ministry, and over the winter in London a movement began to replace the inexplicably lackluster and timid general with someone having more nerve to use the ample resources provided against such undisciplined amateurs. As far as the king was concerned, neither the Powder Alarm nor the formation of the Continental Congress gave cause to rethink his stance on America but rather his choice of commander-in-chief, who he squarely blamed for the inability to fix the ever-deteriorating situation.

On the heels of the first Continental Congress the Massachusetts Provincial Congress met for the first time in mid-October 1774, presided over by John Hancock and with representation of all 240 townships except for Marshfield. Here they established the *Committee of Safety*, an executive arm tasked with building and strengthening a viable military capability. To that end they created the *Minute Men*, a rapid response force of 50 men from each militia company expected to equip and hold themselves ready at the shortest notice from the Committee of Safety. As the colonials could no longer purchase arms, munitions, and gun powder from Great Britain, a mad scramble ensued to obtain these items wherever they might be found, not just limited to Massachusetts. Not long afterward, in the autumn the Crown-appointed governor of New Hampshire sent word to General Gage that he feared the store of armaments at Fort William and Mary, located in Portsmouth at the mouth of the Piscataqua River and guarded only by five men, was endangered by the increasing active local militia. Gage quickly made plans to send a contingent of regulars by sea to bolster the small detachment and cover the land approaches to the fort with cannon from the warship. When the Sons of Liberty in Boston got wind of that intent, they dispatched their most trusted courier, Paul Revere, to travel the 60 miles and warn the Portsmouth militia commander, who quickly organized and executed an attack on the fort. No one was hurt but the militia absconded with more than 100 barrels of gunpowder, 16 cannon, shot, and 60 muskets. Similarly, Rhode Island militia also raided Fort George in Newport's harbor taking 44 cannon, including large 24-pounders.

Outraged at this Yankee insolence spreading now into the rest of New England, King George vowed to crush the resistance at its source. He held a series of cabinet meetings in mid-January designed to formulate the proper response resulting in actions that, for all intents and purposes, declared war on Massachusetts. At the end of January, the American Secretary, Lord Dartmouth, penned orders to General Gage, which were not sent until March and which the commander-in-chief did not receive until mid-April.

These instructions commanded Gage to arrest the radical leadership and to take offensive action at the time and place of the general's choosing. The directives also reported the intention to further dispatch three additional general officers to *assist* him.

General Gage now sat between a rock and a hard place. Over the winter he had, above all, feared this very development and since the Powder Alarm in September had done his best to shape the king and ministry's thinking for them to understand that a much larger force than originally envisioned would be necessary to subdue Massachusetts. Unfortunately, those attempts at education had accomplished just the opposite and served to convince the king and rest of the puppet ministry that Gage was not up to the task and was instead himself the problem. Having pleaded for reinforcements, Gage had received not 20,000 men as requested but rather a contingent of 500 marines and three additional warships yielding a total of eleven regiments, consisting of approximately 3,500 men. With such a paltry force relative to the task there existed no action he could take that would produce the crushing blow the king demanded and worse, would surely push the Yankees further into a state of rebellion. Also, not lost on Gage was the reality that one of the three soon-to-arrive generals was intentionally sent as his replacement should he fail. Setting his professional military judgment aside and risky as it was, he resigned himself to do the king's bidding, not for the good of England but rather, like the scores of other leading men that danced to George III's tune, as a measure to preserve both his position and reputation.

Over the winter Gage's intelligence network had gathered solid evidence regarding hidden arsenals spread throughout the hinterland, the largest of which lay in Concord, roughly 20 miles distant, where leadership of the Sons of Liberty also often gathered. The capture of such a cache, while not of strategic significance, was within his force's capability and, although it would surely enrage the Yankees, more importantly it would also mollify London – at least for the time being. The key to success was to act quickly, much like the operation in Somerville, before the militias could organize and respond, and to count on the Yankee propensity for cowardice in the face of professionals. Except for the exclusive use of an elite and nimble composite force consisting of only grenadier and light infantry companies, the plan was straightforward. The expedition would move by water across the Charles River to a sparsely inhabited area, then hurry inland on foot to reach the objective by dawn to locate and capture or destroy the illegal munitions by midmorning, leaving time to rush back to Boston by early afternoon. Gage's second in command, Brigadier General Lord Hugh Percy of the 5th Foot, would wait behind in Boston with a heavier reserve force of 800 men that included artillery, if needed.

The King's Own were among the first loaded into the transports as Jack slogged through the mud and backwash with the others to take a place in a triplet of longboats lashed together and staged at the water's edge. Packed together like salt cod, with no room to sit, these overloaded craft lay so low to the water that it seemed they should sink. Towed by rowboats manned by sailors, the flotilla inched across Back Bay toward the opposite shore well over a mile distant, the only sounds the creaking gunwales and gentle splashing of muffled oars. Nearly an hour later the first wave arrived off the Cambridge marshes at Lechmere Point near a lone homestead called *Phips Farm,* owned by a staunch Loyalist. They disembarked as the boats ran aground, allowing the troops to wade ashore in frigid water up to their knees only to find precious little solid ground in a swamp rapidly filling with the incoming tide. Shivering in the cold moonlight as the wind whipped off the water across the exposed marsh, they waited for what seemed like an eternity as the transports made a second trip and returned with the remainder of their numbers, along with horses for the officers. Lieutenant Colonel Smith then formed the unit in a long column with elements of his own 10th at the head and the King's Own second with the rest behind in order of regimental seniority. Somewhat after two o'clock in the morning they began to march, already more than two hours behind schedule.

Led by a local Tory guide, the gaggle tromped back and forth across Phips Farm, practically an island now with the high tide nearly fully in, holding their muskets and ammunition high while traversing flooded footpaths and inlets in waist-deep water so cold that their testicles cinched up tighter than a Dutchman on market day. Finally emerging from the quagmire onto a muddy but firm road they paused to let the sergeants check their gear as more rations were distributed, these provided by the navy – an unidentifiable lump so infested with maggots that most men immediately donated it to the darkness. From here they started forward at a decent pace, moving in silence as best they could to make up the time lost in the crossing.

With the annoyance of the landing now behind them, the men began to settle into the familiar rhythm of a march although their legs still shook from the frigid water and soaking wet pants. Eight hundred bayonets glinted together in the moonlight as the men's breath mingled in the still, crisp night. Formed in a narrow column Percy marched to Jack's left with Michael and George directly in front as they shouldered their muskets and hurried in silence through the deserted countryside. They soon passed through Cambridge, observing more activity than expected on the north side of town as these exasperating Yankees seemed not to care to sleep even though the hour was nearly three o'clock. Exiting the village they heard church bells begin, first in Cambridge behind and then in the distance, as well as sporadic shooting – *signal muskets,* someone whispered. Along the road the vanguard in the lead happened upon several unsuspecting countrymen whose horses, wagons, and goods were confiscated as they were ordered to join the march as a precaution so as to not alert their neighbors. Several miles on, they reached the village of Menotomy with much the same scene as Cambridge; there they paused.

Here, Lieutenant Colonel Smith received reports from British officer scouts that had captured Yankee alarm riders, to include Paul Revere, that the countryside had been alerted and that a potential force of 500 militia planned to oppose them just ahead in Lexington. Unbeknownst to Smith and for that matter, Gage, the Sons of Liberty had known of the expedition well ahead of time and the Committee of Correspondence had already initiated their well-tested alarm system as soon as the troops began to form at the Commons. Paul Revere had rowed across the harbor to the Charlestown peninsula and William Dawes had traveled by horse unstopped through the gate and over the neck, crossing the Charles River via the Great Bridge into Cambridge, both men working westward door-to-door to spread the alert as well as enlisting others to assist. In fact, Revere had already reached Concord well before Smith's force departed Phips Farm and, in addition, had warned Sam Adams and John Hancock in Lexington, where those leaders currently hid.

Lieutenant Colonel Smith, increasingly anxious to all who viewed him, ordered his second in command, Major Pitcairn from the 2nd Marines, to take the first six companies of light infantry and forge out ahead of the main body. Pitcairn was the polar opposite of the colonel in every way – an energetic and capable officer but an impetuous hothead who shared the popular view that the only proper handling of these insubordinate colonies was to burn them to the ground and start anew. Led by the good major on horseback and another industrious marine, Lieutenant Adair as well as a Tory guide, Jack and his group of lights hurried out of Menotomy at an even more rapid clip than before, marching in steady silence along the narrow, wooded road somewhat illuminated through the trees by the moon. Smith took this opportunity to send a rider back to Boston as a precaution to alert Lord Percy that reinforcements would be needed. Not long afterward the column of light infantry halted again, this time not in a town but rather in the thick of the woods. Word quickly filtered back that intelligence patrols posted along the route the day prior had captured more local inhabitants that seemed to know too much about their mission and that there could be as many as 1,000 men ahead. The redcoats knew all too well the Yankee penchant for bald-faced lying but, nonetheless, the tension in the column grew like steadily tightening piano wire. Sergeant Searles suddenly appeared alongside with instructions.

"Soldiers, load your firelocks," he commanded, his voice not much above a whisper. "Do it quickly."

"Sergeant, what is happening?" Percy asked as the man the soldiers trusted most came within earshot.

"Just a precaution," the sergeant answered calmly as he continued down the column. "We have reports of activity ahead. Just a precaution. Load your firelocks and waste no time."

Each soldier dutifully lowered their musket and reached into their cartridge box, producing a .75 caliber solid lead ball threaded together onto the end of rolled cartridge paper filled with black powder. With their teeth they tore a small hole in the end opposite the ball and poured a small amount of powder into the priming pan near the stock end then shutting the pan. They next loaded the cartridge, ball on top, into the muzzle hole of the barrel, pushing it all the way down with a long steel rammer. Replacing the rammer into its slot on the wooden barrel stock, they returned the musket to their shoulder having completed the entire process in the dark in less than 30 seconds.

"Just a precaution?" Percy muttered as he finished loading and reshouldered his musket with an accentuated thud. "I'll be damned to believe that."

"What attitude is this?" George whispered loud enough for those around him to hear. "Granny has invited you out in the countryside for a nice evening stroll for which you should be thankful."

"Bollocks, George," Percy retorted a bit sharply. "When has Granny bade us stroll at night and when have we loaded ball before? I don't like the look of it."

"He's right about that," Michael added. "What do you think, Jack?"

Jack remained silent for a few moments as they peered into the surrounding woods, the growing moonlight illuminating the outline of numerous trees interspersed with stone walls. "I don't know," he finally said. "Just do what the sergeant says and hope for the best."

"I don't like the bloody look of it," Percy whispered again as the column started forward, now more anxious than before. They passed from the woods into rolling hills with vast fields on either side of the road as the four o'clock hour brought the hints of dawn in addition to the still high moon. In the distance emerged increasing musket fire as well as glimpses of shadowy figures drifting across the fields in parallel to the column. With each step those sounds of once faraway shots grew closer as did the tolling of church bells, no longer distant, in every direction.

Just before daybreak, with the emerging predawn light at their backs and having now marched ten miles they rounded a gentle turn and entered Lexington, a hamlet of roughly 900 inhabitants and 120 buildings. Toward the still dark west they approached a triangular-shaped common area, a pasture that delineated the center of town, and bore right at the apex along the road on the edge.

"COLUMN RIGHT! FORM PLATOONS! WHEEL LEFT!"

Although most soldiers could not see him, Lieutenant Adair suddenly shouted orders nearby. At a trot the line circled to the right of a large meeting house as someone nearby wondered aloud why they were suddenly conducting field exercises. Only the first two companies, the 10th, and the 4th, actually marched onto the common green with the remaining four companies behind having turned left along the road on the opposite side. Near the center of the green and with their backs to the meeting house the two lead companies automatically formed a line of battle three deep.

"POISE FIRELOCKS!"

Placed in the front row, Jack and the others around him swiftly lifted the musket off their shoulder, holding it upright with both hands in such a way as to prepare for any one of several potential follow-on orders. The collective slap of so many pieces raised in unison broke the stillness of the morning followed by a clamorous battle cry. "HUZZAH! HUZZAH! HUZZAH!"

With the view before them now unobstructed, the soldiers noticed with disbelief a startling sight. Not even fifty yards away along the far end of the green appeared through the dim light approximately six dozen or so colonial militia formed in a loose line two-deep. The term *formed* must be used generously, as in stark contrast to the British neat lines they seemed no more than a band of farmers on pause from a hunt with rag-tag appearance in both dress and posture, each of them dangling a personal firearm with the casualness of an afternoon hunter. Around the edges of the green, scores of wide-eyed onlookers scurried about. For several silent moments the opposite forces stared at one another, both seemingly mesmerized by the other's presence. Mouths became dry and stomachs tightened as the red-clad soldiers grasped that this was no drill. Anxiety gripped the King's Own as they waited for the next move. "Bloody hell," Percy whispered.

Having ridden around from the opposite side of the meeting house Major Pitcairn now appeared from the left to plant himself between the two deployed companies on one end of the green and the militia on the other. In crisp scarlet uniform atop his white horse and sporting two pearl-handled pistols in his belt, he moved slowly from left to right with sword raised as he shouted at the colonials.

"LAY DOWN YOUR ARMS! LAY DOWN YOUR ARMS AND DISPERSE!"

The militia did not move but instead simply stared back in silence, most with mouths open like codfish.

"DAMN YOU, REBELS!" the major screamed even louder. "YOU DAMN VILLAINS! DISPERSE! LAY DOWN YOUR ARMS AND DISPERSE!"

One of their number, indistinguishable from the rest but apparently their commander, turned to the group and spoke briefly. The gaggle now broke ranks, each man slowly shouldering his weapon and shuffling toward the back of the green with no more order or urgency than as if having been dismissed from church. Suddenly, with neither provocation nor warning, a shot rang out. Jack and those around him searched in vain for the source. Seconds later, with no command given, the platoon to Jack's left let loose a full volley at the straggling provincials, striking several who fell to the ground. To the amazement of the redcoats a dozen or so of the startled farmers answered, raising their weapons where they stood to return fire in sporadic fashion. Again, without command a second platoon volleyed in return and then, like a dam bursting, the good order of the British line broke with the majority rushing forward through the drifting smoke yelling wildly with bayonets lowered.

Percy started to break as well but Jack, who had stood fast, managed to grab him by the arm. "No, Percy!" he insisted firmly as they both watched Michael and George rush forward into the fray.

"Bollocks, Jack!" Percy swore, exasperated. "What the bloody hell is happening?"

"I don't know," Jack answered. "But don't move until we're told."

"SOLDIERS, HOLD YOUR FIRE!" Major Pitcairn turned toward what remained of his lines and screamed. "KEEP YOUR RANKS AND HOLD YOUR FIRE! GODDAMN IT! I SAID KEEP YOUR RANKS AND HOLD YOUR FIRE!" The major's horse wheeled in circles as he repeated his orders. Moments before the epitome of authority, now he seemed little more than an amusing turnstile as he vainly attempted to slap with the flat of his sword any soldier within reach who rushed past him.

One of the closest militia that had fallen now rose to his knees and attempted to reload his weapon. He promptly received two bayonets run through him by the oncoming soldiers and he collapsed again, now motionless. Those colonials that remained on the green, whether wounded, brave, or just plain daft, suffered the same fate. The rest scattered about in all directions, disappearing behind buildings and into the woods. Like a bizarre cross between a riot and a game of *hide and seek,* dozens of redcoats chased the farmers about the village in a running gun-battle, with the British officers chasing both, concerned chiefly with preventing destruction of provincial property. Lieutenant Colonel Smith arrived not long thereafter with the remainder of the force and, with the look of something close to hysteria, hastily found a drummer and ordered him to beat a recall. Slowly but steadily, and under harsh criticism of the officers, the unruly participants in the fox hunt returned to their companies and the column reformed on the green, sweaty, out of breath, and giddy like schoolboys.

The men stood in place for what seemed an inordinate amount of time, long enough for the smoke and smell of gunpowder to dissipate, as the colonel held a council with the soldiers close enough to hear the heated exchange. Several junior officers pleaded with Smith to abandon the mission and return to Boston immediately as the purpose for which they had come was now compromised. The colonel listened as if a statue and replied dispassionately that he had been issued specific orders and thought it proper to obey them. He then dismissed the subordinates as if naughty schoolboys, some of whom skulked back like beaten dogs to their waiting men. The fife and drummers struck up a tune as the colonel bade the column to give three cheers and empty their muskets with a victory salute as they marched past the green in high spirits, leaving strewn about the town eight dead and nine wounded provincials. On the British side only one man from the 10th had been hit in the leg as well as the major's horse shot twice. The biggest casualty, it seemed, was the notion that the militia would not dare to oppose the professionals.

To the dismay of many who had no choice but to follow in the footsteps of their comrades, instead of turning in the direction of Boston and the newly risen sun, they instead departed Lexington to the west to march further inland. With the day barely begun they soon entered the next village of Lincoln where the scene could not have been more different than the other hamlets recently traversed earlier in the dark. Instead of bells ringing, dogs barking, and townspeople scurrying, not a soul stirred. The town had been abandoned, obviously in anticipation of the British arrival. As the low sunlight reflected off the long line of bayonets pointed skyward the eerie stillness contrasted with the shrill music of fifes and the drumbeats mixing with so many boots tromping in unison. The column exited the ghost town with their newfound exuberance giving way again to tension along the long line of red uniforms. Several minutes later and well past the outskirts they were curiously met by an organized unit of about 150 militia that advanced to within a few hundred yards, then promptly reversed course to march back down the road. Like a grand parade the British followed this escort all the way to the next town of Concord with both units striding into town with their own versions of marching tunes. The British halted near the center of town as the militia continued and exited at the north end.

With scores of armed provincials spotted lining a nearby ridge to the east, Lieutenant Colonel Smith promptly ordered the light infantry up to the heights to clear the yokels off, keeping the grenadiers on the road. The lights ascended in single file, scampering up the crest that overlooked the road and village only to find upon arrival that the colonials had scurried to a second ridge further to the north. Well out of range but well within earshot, the Yankees casually loitered there as they screamed insults using one hand to brandish their muskets and the other to gesture obscenely. The lights promptly descended the hill back into Concord proper with several of their number stopping to fell with amusement the colonial liberty pole that stood at a nearby cemetery on the heights. As the lights rejoined the main body, now halted on the town common, the colonel and major climbed back up the hill to the cemetery where they surveyed the countryside with spy glasses. Facing east into the rising sun the men below squinted as they watched both officers point in several directions with the agitated colonel jabbing his fat finger in the air and waving his arms about like a round marionette. As the new morning sun warmed their still damp uniforms some of the men correctly ascertained that this village must be the objective. A quick survey of the hamlet revealed a typical white Congregational church dominating the center flanked on either side by large, neatly kept wooden buildings, one of them a tavern. A small river ran like a spine just west of town in a south to north direction, acting as a border and servicing at least one mill.

The two senior officers soon descended back to the common and began to organize the men in earnest with the time now just after seven o'clock and the mission more than three hours behind schedule. All ten companies of grenadiers, led by Major Pitcairn, were instructed to conduct a house-to-house search for military stores. As the grenadiers rummaged about, the light infantry would secure the perimeter, or more specifically, the critical choke points leading into the village. Four companies of lights would cross the bridge north of town and continue two miles west to search a farm owned by Colonel James Barrett, commander of the local militia and a prominent Concord citizen. Loyalist scouts reported that a good portion of the militia, including those that had escorted them into town, had passed over that bridge and were forming on a small ridge several hundred yards farther to the north called *Punkatasset Hill*. To ensure the expedition's safe return back across the north bridge, three additional companies of light infantry would remain there to protect the crossing. The remaining company was detached to secure another bridge south of town, where minimal threat was perceived.

The 4th Lights marched out of the village with the six other companies about a half mile north where four continued over the river to Barrett's farm, leaving the remaining three to guard the bridge under the command of Captain Walter Laurie from the 43rd Foot. Laurie promptly ordered the 4th and 10th across to the west bank, keeping his own Oxfordshires on the east side. Jack moved with his unit over the narrow wooden structure, taking up a position in formation just on the other side.

"At ease, lads. Break ranks but remain close." Sergeant Searles walked down the line, speaking calmly but firmly. "Break ranks but remain close. We may need to reform quickly. Get some water and something to eat. Hold onto your firelocks and keep a keen eye."

Jack and his mates took a much-needed drink from their canteens and walked to the riverbank near the bridge. More of a brook than a proper river, the stream nevertheless swelled well over its normal depth due to winter runoff and its waters hastened past as if on some hurried errand. Their eyes followed the oncoming water upstream as far as they could back toward the town where they could hear the commotion even at that distance. Back in the town proper Lieutenant Colonel Smith and his staff established a temporary headquarters at the tavern where the officers could procure refreshments. The grenadiers systematically moved from house to house, conducting inspections under strict orders not to molest the citizens. Major Pitcairn meanwhile rushed about like a whirling dervish hell-bent on enforcing the king's law and threatening to personally throttle any Yankee transgressor.

"Can you imagine the scene, lads?" George offered. "Our grenadiers exercising their best example of civic restraint? The likes of Flaherty and Ahearn on their best behavior? Slick smiles, hat in hand, stooped slightly at the front door feigning politeness all the while licking their lips? *'Good morning, ma'am. Mind if we come in and have a look 'round? Rob you blind? Destroy the damn place? Do you have any cannon about? Women to rape?'* Yes, I'm sure such a visit is just what these Yankees need to endear their loyalty to the Crown."

"Not good." grumbled Michael as he nibbled some dried beef. In contrast to the short, stocky and swarthy George Bridges he was slim and almost sickly looking, prematurely gray and beginning to bald. Serious as a preacher, he continued in his ever-dour tone. "Not bloody good. We're exposed here. No cover. No room to maneuver. No tactical advantage. Not bloody good at all."

"Are you worried about that band that met us on the road?" Jack answered. "More musicians than militia. Surely, they're hiding by now."

"They're on that hill up there." Percy pointed behind to the north. "Less than a quarter mile away by the looks of it."

"And what good are we doing over here?" Michael continued. "We're hemmed in with our backs to the river. We should have stayed on the other side of the bridge where we can defend ourselves better if we have to. This is a bloody choke point."

"You already have us in another scuffle, do you, Higgy?" George chuckled. "Didn't you get enough already this morning?"

"That was a carnival back there," Michael answered. "Took them by surprise we did. Roughed them up pretty bad and they're bloody well not going to let that go."

"Just a bunch of farmers," Jack stated.

Michael looked over his shoulder and lowered his voice. "The officers might say that, but I think they'll have a thing or two to learn before this day is over. They may be farmers, but now they're *angry* farmers. And we have yet a good twenty miles to march back through *their* countryside. We should've gone back after the scrap at Lexington. In fact, we shouldn't be out here to begin with. Did you hear the bells and firing all night? I'm telling you those devils are running to find every musket they can. They may not fight us here, but they're going to fight us somewhere along the way. Every minute we stay here looking for who knows what, their numbers grow. It won't take long before there are more of them than us – many more. We should've gone back after Lexington. Not bloody good at all."

Jack nodded but never got the chance to answer as smoke suddenly appeared in the distance above the center of Concord.

"Bloody hell!" Percy remarked. "Surely those damn grenadiers aren't burning the town!"

What started as thin wisps of grey suddenly erupted into a billowing black cloud that could only have been generated by a building. A murmur moved like a wave through the idle companies on either side of the bridge as red flames now began to lick above the treetops only several hundred yards distant. Behind them a long line of armed men marched hurriedly down the path that led from Punkatasset Hill to a clearing a hundred or so yards to the west of the bridge assembling themselves into a steadily growing formation.

"KING'S OWN! BACK ACROSS THE BRIDGE! MOVE!" Sergeant Searles strode by, grabbing each soldier to give him a nudge. "QUICKLY NOW! NO TIME TO FORM! JUST MOVE!"

Jack and the others made for the bridge as both companies hustled in a gaggle, crowding and jostling their way onto the narrow platform only wide enough for three or four abreast as they hurried over the river. On the other side, officers and sergeants hastily untangled their respective units and formed them in the road close to the bridge. Back across the west bank the militia had swelled to about four times the British number and began to approach the river. Captain Laurie hurriedly organized his Oxfordshires into a defensive position on the bridge itself with men in front kneeling and others standing behind. He sent several soldiers back across to pull up the planking but quickly abandoned that effort as the colonials were advancing too quickly. The farmers moved in surprisingly good order with some fanning out along the river's west bank.

"They mean to come across that bridge," Michael stated. "We're burning their town, and they'll not give a damn who we are. They're coming to fight."

To the south, black smoke from Concord continued to pour into the sky. A militia officer at the head of the column frantically waved his arms and shouted something to Captain Laurie, pointing for the 43rd to clear away. Although they had not received orders to do so several soldiers on the bridge fired random shots that landed harmlessly in the river except for one that grazed a militiaman. As Laurie scampered about in a futile attempt to regain control the 43rd followed with a full volley from about 75 yards, the sudden crash of the muskets in unison startling the companies behind. Most of the balls sailed high but two of the closest militia along the river fell, one of them shot clean through the head.

The colonial officer, now quite animated, pointed toward the rising smoke of the British muskets and cried, "FIRE, FELLOW SOLDIERS! FOR GOD'S SAKE, FIRE!"

Although not all the militia were able to do so at least a couple hundred of them let loose a barrage concentrated at the soldiers on the bridge. The Oxfordshires shattered like bowling pins as men crashed backwards onto each other. Their entire unit seemed to dissolve as the militia poured on more fire and advanced onto the bridge itself.

"STAND YOUR GROUND! POISE FIRELOCKS!" Sergeant Searles shouted from the left. "I SAID STAND YOUR GROUND, GODDAMN IT!"

The 43rd now turned and began a hurried departure from the bridge leaving at least six men down and two writhing on the ground near the bank. The Oxfordshires who could moved in rapid motion as they streamed past the 4th in the opposite direction, some bloody and hobbling badly. Their officers were nowhere to be seen with the leading edge of the militia now half-way across the bridge. Jack looked at the exasperated sergeant and then to Percy, Michael and George, whose faces had all gone ashen white. Before the sergeant could speak again the entire British unit turned to follow, scampering in a hobbling sea of red uniforms back toward Concord with a horde of angry Yankees close behind.

7

The die is now cast. The Colonies must either submit or triumph.

King George III

CONCORD, MASSACHUSETTS, APRIL 19, 1775

The light infantry ran as fast as their feet would take them and did not look back until they reached the center of Concord, where they stopped – leaning on their muskets, out of breath, shaking from fatigue, hunger, and fear. All around them confusion reigned as officers shouted and soldiers ran about like children chasing butterflies. As the sun now approached its zenith, they were drier and warm for the first time that day, the flight from the bridge having been at least good for something. Lieutenant Colonel Smith and Major Pitcairn again ascended to the cemetery above the common, talking and pointing most seriously as they looked through their spy glasses to the east. The militia had chased the three companies nearly all the way back into town until met on the outskirts by a reinforcement of grenadiers led by the colonel himself. The village, as it turned out, had not been torched but rather only a couple buildings mistakenly set on fire by overzealous grenadiers who, after realizing the consequences of their inattention, had worked in earnest together with the townspeople to extinguish the blaze. Once content that their homes and businesses were not in danger the militia simply melted back into the woods to reclaim their position on the heights to the north.

The quest for military stores abruptly ceased and the expedition now searched for horses, carriages and bedding, all commandeered to carry the numerous wounded that had been placed in the local boarding house, now a makeshift hospital. The four companies that had pushed west to Barrett's farm had returned from their mission, having found nothing except the usual Yankee contempt. Unbeknownst to them, the townsfolk had learned of their mission and just ahead of their arrival had barely managed to move most of the armaments to Barrett's farm where they buried much of it in the surrounding fields. Upon their re-crossing of the north bridge these companies had met no resistance however, to their great alarm, they discovered the east bank littered with dead comrades – one of them apparently scalped. In all, the expedition had turned up precious little except for a few cannon and a handful of musket balls – hardly enough to mount a parade, much less a rebellion.

At about noon, the hour at which General Gage had intended the expedition to already have returned to Boston, Lieutenant Colonel Smith descended from the cemetery and, after pacing back and forth like a pigeon at a picnic, gave the order to march. The column reformed and started out of the village along the same road from which it had entered, this time without music, as sullen as a funeral procession, carrying the wounded officers as best they could in various chaises and carts. Injured men from the lesser ranks walked, if they could, and the more severely hurt were simply left behind.

Along with the 43rd the 4th had been mauled so badly they were forced to fall in with other units. Again, Jack and his comrades were dispatched in one of several platoons of light infantry to cover the main body's flank to the north, parallel to the road. They re-ascended the heights that revealed ample rolling fields stretching east, those once empty pastures now crawling like armies of ants with scores of militia in motion in the distance. The countryside presented an irregular landscape of sloping grass divided by stone fences and interspersed with tracts of woods filled with granite faces and large boulders – not at all the kind of easy, open terrain generally found in Europe that lent itself to the British traditional set-piece way of fighting. Shortly the wooded heights descended, giving way to open grassland where the light infantry rejoined the main body as it crossed a narrow bridge over a brook near a curved intersection on the road. Jack and the others intently eyed the hordes of armed men that shadowed the column but remained a couple hundred yards distant from the choke point. Concealed behind a nearby homestead's buildings and stone walls they shouted obscenities and fired over the heads of the column. Suddenly, as the grenadiers at the end of the column passed over the bridge, several of the last turned and shot at a small number of militia that had dared to approach within range.

For those that had clung to the hope that, given even the recent bloodshed at Lexington Green and the Concord bridge, the growing numbers of armed provincials would be content to remain concealed in relative safety, this cavalier action from the trailing grenadiers removed any doubt as to where the line of restraint would be drawn. Like a dam bursting, hundreds of militia now swarmed the bridge from both sides with whole companies firing in large volleys at the long line of redcoats. Jack flinched at each shock of the sound and heat from scores of muskets as he craned his neck back to spot at least half a dozen grenadiers sprawled behind in the road. The column did not stop but continued forward as on both sides of the road hundreds of armed farmers paralleled them well out of range, racing ahead through the fields toward the woods in the distance. The soldiers were ordered to quicken their step now hurrying at a trot and leaving dead and dying comrades in their wake.

"BUCK UP NOW, LADS!" Sergeant Searles shouted as he passed beside Jack and the others. "STAY TOGETHER

AND KEEP YOUR EYES FORWARD! COURAGE AND DISCIPLINE! DON'T STOP FOR ANY REASON! WE'LL FLANK THEM AHEAD!"

In another half a mile they approached a rise where a barrage of unseen muskets let loose from behind a stone fence that lined the road. Michael Higgins took a ball through the neck, his blood spraying both Jack and Percy just behind. Dropping his musket and clutching his throat he crashed backwards into Jack, who managed to catch him while still maintaining his firelock.

"Bloody hell!" Percy exclaimed as he and George each took hold of Michael and helped Jack pull him out of the column to keep him from being trampled. As their profusely bleeding friend writhed in agony the trio rushed him toward the rear of their unit where they might place him on one of the various wheeled contraptions. They arrived at a flat cart being pulled by an old horse that contained three wounded officers and just enough space for another body. As they attempted to lift Michael onto the cart the nearest officer kicked him off with his remaining good leg.

"MORONS!" the ensign screamed. "He's dead!"

Jack looked down at his friend, who had gone limp, blood still streaming from his neck. Michael breathed but in shallow gasps as the holes in his neck gurgled, with Percy and George trying their best to stem the bleeding with rags they obtained from their haversacks.

"Sir," Jack answered as they continued to walk beside the cart holding Michael, "he's not dead. We...."

"MORONS!" the ensign repeated. "He bloody well will be. Look at him, for Christ's sake. We need firepower here, not bloody nurse maids. Just drop him on the ground and return to your place. Who is your sergeant, goddamn it?"

Just then Sergeant Searles appeared. "I'm their sergeant, sir," he answered crisply as he quickly studied Higgins' wound.

"Good," the ensign snapped. "Take your men forward where they belong and leave the dead one behind."

"Yes, sir." The sergeant answered dutifully then turned his attention to Jack and the rest. "Lads, just leave him be – he's gone."

"But sergeant," Jack hesitated as both Percy and George looked on, frozen as statues, "he's…."

"He's *gone*." Sergeant Searles repeated emphatically as he placed a hand on Jack's shoulder. "Leave him, lad and get back forward – now!"

Jack looked down for the last time at Michael, his eyes staring skyward, and face gone even paler with a torn-away throat. With eyes welling in tears the trio gently laid their limp friend on his back in the nearby grass. "Good-bye, Michael," they each whispered in his ear.

"Come, lads." The sergeant prodded as the trio turned and followed him at a trot.

"Shoddy discipline I should have to say, sergeant," Jack heard the officer shout from behind. "I'll have a word with your superiors!"

"Yes, sir," Sergeant Searles turned to answer, "I will inform them myself." He then addressed the three in a low and even voice that did not hide his temper. "Move forward back into the column. Stay together. Don't stop. We've much work to do, lads. Do as I tell you and focus ahead or you'll not see the sun set."

Under constant fire from behind they quickly returned to their places, stepping over several dead or dying men in their path as the column continued past a tavern down the sloping road crossing back into Lincoln township. The twisted route before them rose and fell amid orchards and cultivated fields with small streams in the low parts and tracts of woods filled with hardwood trees still barren from winter. Men with muskets poured into the next tree patch across a brook only a few hundred yards ahead with seemingly no end to their growing mass, as by now there was no doubt the provincial numbers seriously outweighed the British forces. Like Jack, the surrounding men paled as they searched ahead nervously and quickened their pace.

"PERKINS, BRIDGES, HALLIDAY – FALL OUT!" The sergeant's voice boomed with a focusing effect. "FORM UP WITH ME HERE AND FOLLOW CLOSELY! NOW MOVE!"

Jack soon found himself trailing George and Percy in one of numerous flanking parties, groups of ten to twenty light infantry detailed to parallel the column off the road. By now the militia tactic was obvious – to ambush the column from the cover of trees, boulders, and stone fences, and then flee. However cowardly as it was viewed by professional soldiers, it was certainly effective in reducing their numbers. The light infantry, specifically designed for this very task, would attempt to flank these assassins from behind and flush them out before they could inflict their violence on those in the road. The platoon quickly happened on a handful of them as the main body approached the woods near a turn in the highway. The farmers laid every which way behind trees and rocks and were so focused on the column that they did not detect the soldiers in their rear. These Yankees fired into the road individually with no one in charge to coordinate their efforts, each one furiously reloading as if possessed by the Devil himself. Sergeant Searles charged the platoon forward with bayonets, huzzaing like wild men, scattering the ambushers in a frenzy, like hens from a fox. This scene was repeated multiple times as the flankers hurried to keep pace with the main column as it passed through Lincoln, the Yankees nonetheless able to litter the road with red-clad bodies. The main column on the road pressed on, now moving quickly at a trot as the flanking parties paralleled on either side as best they could. Trudging through the swampy, thicketed lowlands and irregular wooded rises – tough work for even the fittest – before long they grew dog tired, gasping for breath and sweating like Dublin whores. Wracked with thirst and their canteens long since emptied, any would have traded even their musket for a drink of cool water. Each time they reached a rise it seemed there stood before them another – and another.

As Jack's platoon reached the summit of one particular hill, they heard the drumbeats signaling a recall and not a moment too soon, as they had become too weary to follow the column that now stood halted in the road. Amid constant musket fire they returned to the main body, approaching as the officers attempted to reform what had turned from a disciplined unit into a rag-tag mob of walking wounded. Major Pitcairn, now dismounted, waved his one good arm as he nursed the other, his fine white horse having been taken out from under him. The colonel was wounded as well – shot through the leg but still on his mount. In fact, there seemed not one officer who had not taken a ball as the Yankees hiding in the woods had aimed at them in particular.

But the efforts of the officers proved to no avail. With hundreds of Yankee muskets popping around them from every direction and men dropping where they stood as if trees felled from an invisible ax, Jack found himself along with those that could, hurrying forward down the road on the backside of a hill, each man for himself, with George and Percy no longer in sight. No more than a horde now, they hurried headlong through the gauntlet of fire up the longest of rises toward Lexington, having little choice but to flee or die as brazen attackers now emerged from the woods by the dozens, approaching the road now in plain sight to take point-blank aim. Out of ammunition, many soldiers threw down their pieces and surrendered. Others simply sat on the side of the road with their heads in their hands to await whatever fate was coming. Jack raced with those that still could, desperately following the sea of red backs that ran for their lives up the road. Musket fire poured so thick from each side that their eyes burned, and their lungs choked from the great cloud of smoke that enveloped them. Suddenly their own officers appeared before them with bayonets presented, threatening quite convincingly to run them through if they did not assume some semblance of order. Falling into line with eyes pointed down toward their feet they moved like zombies, following the next man as if already dead.

At this point of near mutiny, futility, and despair, where the collapse of the entire expedition lay just a few more Yankee musket shots away, there suddenly occurred a sound so unforeseen that at first it went unnoticed – cannon! British cannon.

Little by little they dared lift their heads to fix the location of the distant booming. Around the next corner with a view into the center of Lexington there stood before them Lord Percy with his glorious reinforcements, having just arrived from Boston. The message that Smith had managed to send back to Boston via fast Loyalist horseman had not managed to reach Lord Percy until later than intended however, he nevertheless had arrived just in time. These saviors formed in a line of battle just east of Lexington Common and from their center rained down artillery fire with two six-pounders into the woods surrounding the road. Jack cheered with the others as one ball struck the meeting house, exiting the backside in a shower of splinters. Most of the nearby Yankees well within range turned tail and ran with some not so lucky spread across the ground like fertilizer. Gathering what strength remained in them, Smith's men staggered into Lexington, collapsing on the very green which they had occupied earlier that morning. Receiving fresh water and a nibble of jerked beef they soon fell asleep – but not for long.

"Wake up, lads. We've work to do."

The 4th Lights woke to a familiar voice and hand on their shoulder although not so gentle as earlier that morning as Sergeant Searles worked to reconstitute what was left of the Kings' Own. "Come now, lad," he ordered curtly as he pulled Jack to his feet and pushed him forward. "Form up with the others over there. Now move!"

Jack staggered to the other side of the green to join his company now reduced to about half its strength, the remainder dead or too wounded to be effective. Spotting Percy and George the trio simply greeted each other with a nod, too physically and emotionally drained to muster anything more.

Lord Percy now assumed command of the entire force and set about in earnest to reorganize them. They had yet a good sixteen miles to return to Boston but this time not having the luxury of naval transport but rather the necessity to march the long way across the Great Bridge in Cambridge and through Roxbury to the neck. Instead of a long strung-out column Lord Percy, with now a much larger force that needed to defend itself, formed three interlocking rectangles. Assuming that the pressure would come mainly from the sides and especially the rear, he placed the smallest rectangle first, about fifty men whose task it was to clear the road. Behind, the second rectangle formed what was left of the Concord expedition including the wounded, and in the rear he placed the strongest third of the new men supported by the two six-pounders. To the sides the all-important flankers would again be utilized but this time in larger numbers that would be able to keep pace with this tactical formation not intended for speed. In reserve would be Major Pitcairn's marines, who could move to whatever quadrant needed their help. Lord Percy understood that the Yankee farmers had his total force vastly outnumbered but that they did not possess a central organizational capability with which to coordinate and direct the individual militia companies into anything more than flies buzzing around at their own will. In sharp contrast to Smith's failed attempt to outrun the swarming mob the supremely competent Lord Percy would accept the fact that he could not and instead would methodically engage them to fight his way out in deliberate and orderly British fashion.

As was the norm that day, the organization for departure took longer than anticipated with the force not moving out until well after three o'clock. A stark change of attitude now emerged within the ranks, the former panic and desperation having been replaced by anger and want of revenge. With the destruction of colonial property no longer a concern Lord Percy, as a tactical measure, ordered several buildings burned as the militia had used them for cover. As the British started forward again the rising smoke of Lexington billowed thick in their rear, removing any doubt that Percy had thrown in his lot for a fight to the death.

On the right of the road to the south, four or five regular hat companies from the newly arrived King's Own were detailed to secure a rocky, wooded ridge that ran upwards of one hundred feet and, to the left where lay open fields and pastures, an even larger force from the 47th deployed to guard an intrusion from the north. Placed in the more protected second rectangle, Percy,

George, and Jack moved forward like cattle in a herd under the heavy crackle of musket fire from behind, the militia having wasted no time in resuming their mischief. The six-pounders boomed with regularity, a constant reminder that the action in back was hot. They had walked maybe a mile when Jack again felt a hand on his shoulder.

"Well, Patrick – look here! Is it not our favorite privates, Perkins, and Halliday? And what's this – smiling George Bridges as well."

Jack turned to see the large forms of Flaherty with Ahearn close behind, both grinning ear to ear with their smarmy smiles.

"Seems you lot beat the reaper at his game today, did you not, laddies?" Flaherty continued. "He's a fickle ol' bastard, isn't he? One moment you're enjoying a delightful stroll in King George's fair countryside and the next your head has gone clean off! It's all just a game of dice, isn't it?"

Percy and George remained silent, but Jack managed to blurt out a reply. "It would appear so, corporal."

"Oh, come now, Halliday. Why so formal on such a festive occasion? We're mates after all, are we not? And you Perkins – how's your father's bakery looking to you today, laddy? I'd wager that you'd donate a testicle to be there right now instead of having some damn Yankee ventilate you like a fife, eh?" Flaherty nudged Ahearn as they both laughed heartily. "Patrick and I've been thinking," he continued. "We've a plan to make a profit and could use some dependable laddies like yourselves. What say you?"

Jack shook his head. "What profit do you see here with a thousand-fold scoundrels that want to put us in the ground?"

"Oh, I know what you're thinking, Halliday," Flaherty began as if selling his coat, "that this has all gone pear-shaped. But believe me when I tell you that providence has shined on us today. These are the moments that don't come along often enough for the likes of us poor soldiers. But when the opportunity arises you must seize it. Stick with Patrick and me and we'll triple your wages for the year. We'll just need the word and a few staunch men. And that word is coming now."

"CORPORAL FLAHERTY!" A familiar voice of authority cut through the air.

"Yes, sergeant!" Flaherty stiffened as Sergeant Searles approached from the front.

"You and Ahearn pick out a dozen men. Make them a mix of lights and grenadiers. I have a job for you up ahead." The sergeant pointed to the top of the formation not far in the distance as he continued to head that way. "Now move and meet me there!"

"Yes, sergeant!" Flaherty answered curtly then grinned at Ahearn. "There we are, Patrick – *Ask and you shall receive.* Our prayers have been answered."

Flaherty turned back toward the trio of privates. "HALLIDAY! PERKINS! BRIDGES!" he barked as he started off. "Follow Corporal Ahearn! Patrick, take these three forward. I'll gather more and meet you directly."

Ahearn merely nodded and looked in the direction of the three subordinates: Jack motionless as a statue, George with his fixed smile, and Percy with the expression of a stunned mullet.

"What's the problem?" Ahearn snarled in a low raspy voice. "You heard Corporal Flaherty. We have a job to do – one that'll line your pockets."

"I don't like the sound of it," Jack offered. "I don't need to go."

Ahearn's smile disappeared as he stepped forward and bent slightly, placing his nose about an inch from Jack's, his breath freshly laced with rum. "Maybe you misunderstood the sergeant, private – we're not *asking* you. Now move!"

"Yes, corporal," Jack answered with more than a little indignation. He motioned to the others as all three followed Ahearn toward the head of the formation.

The landscape from Lexington back to Menotomy changed significantly just as it had in reverse order earlier that morning. Now instead of mostly rural farmland that existed past Lexington to Concord the road became more thickly settled with houses, barns and all manner of utility buildings such that the village of Menotomy proper seemed indistinguishable from its outskirts. This preponderance of shelters now became a hazard to the

British as the Yankees ahead used them most effectively as cover for their lethal attacks. In fact, forward units had reported that freshly arrived militia companies were at that moment setting ambushes in their path, having been engaged by flankers and only partially dispersed. Packs of these snipers, many cut off from their main units, were holed up in several abandoned homes close enough to the road to remain a threat. Buildings nearest to the road were put to the torch as time and ability allowed still others that needed to be cleared. What leadership remained from the battered units of the morning began to organize their men for that work. As Jack's trio approached the head of the formation, they met Sergeant Searles giving final instructions to Flaherty as one of their officers, Lieutenant Barker, looked on.

"Corporal, take your men forward to that house yonder," the sergeant ordered crisply as he pointed diagonally to his right. "Clear it thoroughly and rejoin us as quick as you can. There's a swarm of these devils yet up ahead."

"Right, sergeant," Flaherty answered as he let slip a wry grin toward Ahearn. "The English start these fights, don't they, Robert? But us Irish always finish 'em."

The sergeant's face grew grim as he squared his shoulders and leaned into the larger grenadier. "I need your energy, not your rhetoric, corporal! Just do your bloody job! I want that house cleared, NOW! Save that sharp tongue of yours for the Yankees!"

"Yes, sergeant," Flaherty replied with his grin still intact. He turned to his newly formed squad and shouted. "MOVE, LADDIES! FOLLOW ME!"

There were twenty in all – twelve grenadiers and eight lights that trotted loosely behind Flaherty, who headed straight for the objective about an eighth of a mile distant and a good stone's throw off the south side of the road. They crossed a field and gardens, stopping about a hundred yards away from a brown wooden one-story structure built in the typical style with a steep pitched roof, large center chimney and smallish square windows covered by what the locals called *Indian shutters*, which allowed the windows to be closed with muskets protruding out from slits.

Flaherty called the lights to the front for instructions. "I'll circle 'round to the other side with the grenadiers. You men wait here. Upon my signal, parade in line to fifty yards directly in front of the house then present and fire a volley at the building. Halliday – you're in charge. Move quickly and don't hesitate. Is that clear?"

"Yes, corporal," Jack answered, still glaring.

"Good. Watch for me over there." Flaherty pointed to the far side of the front yard. "After your volley we'll start from behind that small barn and enter the front door. Once we're in the building set up a perimeter lookout and wait for another signal. Got it?"

"Yes, corporal," Jack replied again.

"You'd better," Ahearn whispered in Jack's ear. He eyed Jack coolly as he and Flaherty started off with the rest of the grenadiers, their large backs lumbering toward the side of the house.

Jack turned to the remaining men, who looked at him wide-eyed in silence. He motioned them to get behind him in a line. As they waited for their cue, they took the opportunity to scrutinize the objective. The front door of which Flaherty spoke was situated central to the house, painted a deep red and slightly elevated from the ground with three simple granite slabs below acting as stairs. In front of the bottom slab squatted what looked to be an elderly man, propped with a musket behind a crude barricade of stacked logs, shingles and other wood scraps. Each window on either side of the door to include from above revealed muskets poking through the Indian shutters.

After several long moments Flaherty appeared exactly where he said, about a hundred yards away, well in Jack's view but hidden from those in the house. Flaherty raised his arm for a moment as he met Jack's gaze then brought his hand down and pointed forward. Jack bade his men rise and marched them in quickstep to the agreed upon position where they presented their pieces and fired in unison, the shots bouncing harmlessly off the wooden siding. No sooner had they finished when their fire was returned by those inside with several shots landing in the dirt by their feet as others whistled past their heads, the sound like a hand slapping hard on water.

"Bloody decoys, we are!" Percy exclaimed.

"GODDAMN YOU LOBSTERBACKS!" the man behind the barricade screamed at the lights as he furiously reloaded. "THIS IS MY GODDAMN HOUSE AND YOU'LL BLOODY WELL NOT TAKE IT! I'M AN ENGLISHMAN, GODDAMN IT! YOU'VE NOT THE RIGHT!"

Flaherty and his grenadiers had been on the move since the volley exchange traversing the hundred yards to the doorstep with amazing speed. The owner never got a second shot as, upon reaching the barricade, Flaherty bayoneted the old man in the chest with no more effort or care than if he had pitch-forked a pile of hay. The man fell to the ground writhing and screaming as Flaherty kicked him flat on his back, placed a boot on his neck and ran him through the torso again. The rest of the grenadiers followed with the first half-dozen wielding a large pine log scavenged from the property and, rushing the house with a loud *HUZZAH! HUZZAH! HUZZAH!* they knocked in the front door with one blow. With Flaherty in the lead and before the Yankees inside had time to reload, the dozen grenadiers stormed through the entry followed by the rapid flash and muffled popping of musket fire that beckoned no mercy.

Seconds later Flaherty emerged from the doorway through a cloud of burnt gunpowder. "HALLIDAY!" he shouted, "SECURE THE PERIMETER! THEN REPORT IN HERE!"

The lights outside quickly finished reloading then surrounded the house, stationing their numbers in a circle and within view of each other. Once satisfied of no further immediate threat, Jack bade the men remain and he then entered the house. Before him in the main living area lay strewn about a half-dozen plainly dressed men, contorted into various positions as if randomly dropped. All dead, each had been alternately shot, then bayoneted and finally their heads bashed in with the butt end of a musket. The floor washed in a growing pool of blood as the room buzzed in a flurry of activity with the grenadiers stuffing private possessions in their haversacks like hyenas stripping a carcass.

"Halliday!" Flaherty called from across the room, "There you are, laddy. Take what you can. We have but a minute."

Flaherty stood at the far end of a long dining table across which lay the body of a teenage boy, his brains dumped out like so much egg salad. The grenadier picked up a spoon from the table and, after wiping the brain matter off with the boy's shirt, tossed the utensil in Jack's direction, the silver glinting curiously in the dull light as it travelled end over end as if in slow motion. Jack caught the thin object without taking his eye off Flaherty, who winked with a smile from ear to ear. Jack stared at the spoon then placed it gingerly inside his coat pocket near Georgey's knife then turned to walk slowly back out the front door.

"JACK!" Percy cried outside as he approached in earnest, moving quickly with long strides. "Jack! Come quick! We have a prisoner."

Jack followed to the side of the house where stood two more light infantry clutching by the arms what appeared to be a provincial militia, well in his fifties and dressed poorly in the typical farmer fashion. He wore a glazed look of shock as he held a bloody hand onto what remained of his left ear that hung down between his fingers.

"He just staggered over here out of the woods," Percy offered without prompting. "Didn't seem to know or care that he walked right into us. He doesn't have a weapon and won't say a damn thing. What should we do?"

Jack looked again at the farmer, who simply stared straight ahead blankly.

"Bring him to the front yard," Jack answered. "We'll take him back to the ranks and give him to the officers."

Just then the grenadiers began to exit the house, laboring as they carried their haversacks stuffed full. Flaherty spotted Jack and signaled him to reform. Percy went to collect the other men around the house as Jack pushed the farmer on toward the grenadiers, nudging him in the back with the butt end of his musket. The man remained silent as he wobbled forward as if in a trance.

"What have we here, Halliday?" Flaherty asked as Jack reached the front of the house, all grenadiers having now exited and congregated in the yard as they made final adjustments to carrying their newfound possessions. "Found a new mate, have you?"

The rest of the grenadiers chuckled as they eyed the man warily.

"A prisoner," Jack reported. "Found him wandering 'round back. He's not armed but he's wounded in the ear."

"Yes, indeed he is, laddy," Flaherty answered coyly as he studied the man. "ROBERT!" he called out across the group. "Come take care of this prisoner!"

Ahearn emerged from the rear and circled around. Approaching from behind to within a couple yards of Jack he lowered his musket and rammed his bayonet square in the man's back. The man screamed and lurched forward landing face first at Flaherty's feet. As he writhed on the ground Ahearn placed a foot on the man's back between the shoulder blades and drove his bayonet into the soft area at the base of the skull where the neck meets. He rapidly twisted the musket several times until the body went limp, withdrawing the bloody blade with a sucking sound. Flaherty nudged the man's head with the toe of his boot, lifting the bloody face then letting it drop. "We don't take prisoners," he stated flatly to no one in particular as he wiped his boot off across the man's coat, "least not the likes of these. Our business here is finished. LET'S MOVE!"

As Lord Percy's force churned its way through the center of Menotomy the relatively good order that had existed began to degenerate into something more resembling an organized mob. The surrounding woods teemed with militia as they continued to pour in like a rising tide with leaderless groups using whatever makeshift cover they could find to stage an ambush. Packs of soldiers broke away on their own accord to alternately fight hand-to-hand in yards and ransack those buildings closest to the road. Those assailants hiding in houses galled the redcoats exceedingly but paid for it with their lives and property as they were put to death without exception and the dwelling torched. What officers that remained tried to stop it but realized the futility as the red swarm flooded through the town in a rolling riot. Amid the constant popping of muskets in every direction and the booming of the six pounders behind, they exited Menotomy leaving in their wake the charred wreckage of the hamlet along with several dozen dead comrades.

To this point Lord Percy had fared relatively well. He had rescued Lieutenant Colonel Smith's expedition from certain destruction and had managed to fight his way back to within eight miles of Boston, more or less intact, with unrelenting use of flankers to the sides and cannon covering the rear. But for all his success in the now waning hours of the late afternoon the most difficult test lay before him. Unbeknownst to Lord Percy and the rest of his men they were surrounded by nearly 5,000 militia from at least 30 towns who had answered the call that had started the night before. The alarm system devised by the Sons of Liberty had worked as intended, honed to perfection by the constant practice marches of the British out of Boston. In two days, there would be on hand more than 16,000 militia from all reaches of New England. The effectiveness of Lord Percy's combined force of 1,500 had been reduced by almost twenty percent by those killed, wounded, captured, or deserted. The Yankees now held a numerical advantage of four to one that grew with every passing moment.

Unlike Smith, Lord Percy's much heavier laden force had departed Boston by land over the neck then had turned right at Roxbury to cross the Charles River into Cambridge via the Great Bridge. Yankees had pulled up the planks from the bridge but had deposited them close enough nearby such that Lord Percy's men were able to make repairs enough to get the troops and cannon over. Having at the time no concept of the forces that would oppose him, Lord Percy chose not to wait for the bridge to be adequately repaired to bring across the larger provision wagons filled with ammunition and food. This supply train left behind and supported only by a minimal protection force did not manage to cross later as they were promptly captured.

The water route that Smith had used earlier to get his men across the Charles River was not an option for the return, as no boats waited. To reach the safety of Boston, Lord Percy would need to retrace his steps through Cambridge and re-cross the Great Bridge, where a great mass of militia now flooded to oppose him. The fighting here would eclipse that of Menotomy with the bridge no doubt torn apart again to prevent his traverse. If not able to cross the river, if he even made it that far, Lord Percy would be pinned against the north bank by overwhelming numbers of rabble and forced to surrender or be decimated. The other option was to not cross the Charles River at all but instead dash east from Cambridge to the Charlestown peninsula that lay just over the harbor from Boston between the Charles and Mystic Rivers. Much like Boston this peninsula's land entrance consisted of a narrow, marshy neck about a hundred yards wide that could be defended once across and also covered from either side by British warships. Having lost the supply wagons and with his ammunition running out, Lord Percy had little choice but to turn his forces left at Cambridge and hasten them approximately three miles to Charlestown. Not anticipating this and having no central command authority with which to coordinate a blocking movement, the bands of militia scrambled like packs of dogs to give chase as Lord Percy's cannon covered the British escape with their last remaining rounds.

Approaching Charlestown Neck, Jack and his comrades straggled forward in the fading light like zombies as hordes of women and children scattered in their path in a panic headed in the opposite direction. Once on the other side they climbed the backside of the peninsula up the heights to Bunker Hill and then down again toward Charlestown village situated on the shoreline. Lights began to gleam as darkness descended on the city of Boston only a quarter of a mile south across the mouth of the Charles River. Jack and the others found a place to sit in the tall grass to wait for the transports that would eventually come to ferry them back. No one said a word as they listened to the symphony of cannon from the warships on either side of the peninsula that raked militia positions inland as they tried to approach the neck. Major Pitcairn and his marines were the final force to cross, fighting doggedly even in the dark to protect the rear until the last of their number reached safety.

Jack looked out across the harbor as he sat next to Percy and George, the latter with his ever-fixed grin to accompany a now wide-eyed stare in the distance. Percy placed his face in his hands and shook his head. "Michael? Where's Michael?" he sobbed. "Bloody hell, those Yankee bastards had better give him a proper burial."

Jack placed his hand on Percy's shoulder. "We might just get him back to bury him ourselves."

Percy trembled as he continued to cry. "What do we do now, Jack?"

"I believe we do nothing, Perce," Jack answered softly. "We do nothing and wait for tomorrow." Jack's head then sank down onto his arms folded across his knees as he placed a hand inside his coat and felt the silver spoon tucked in the pocket next to Georgey's knife. Within moments he fell fast asleep.

8

A dear bought victory; another such would have ruined us.

General Henry Clinton

BOSTON, MASSACHUSETTS, JUNE 17, 1775

"Jack! Did you hear that?" Percy stooped over Jack as he lay on his straw mattress, gently nudging him in the back. "Jack – wake up!"

"What is it, Perce?" Jack rolled over and sat up, rubbing his eyes in the dim pre-dawn light. "What is it?"

"Cannon, Jack! *Our* cannon!"

Jack dressed quickly and followed Percy outside of the barn toward the direction where the unmistakable booming seemed to emanate.

"There it is again!" Reaching a place with a view of the entrance to the Charles River Percy pointed across the harbor toward the Charlestown peninsula where several hundred yards off the coast a lone British warship fired a salvo. "The *Lively*, I believe," Percy offered. "Twenty guns – nine pounders. But why?"

In a moment they understood as both now stood with mouths agape. Across the quarter mile stretch of water, past the town of Charlestown itself and above on the heights, the very place where two months prior they had found life-saving refuge from the march from Concord, a horde of Yankees feverishly worked to build a makeshift defensive structure from dirt and wood. The entire high ground teemed with activity as hundreds of men dug, chopped, sawed, and hammered while others delivered material and supplies, all seemingly impervious to the warship's efforts to stop them.

"Bloody hell," Percy exclaimed as more of the unit arrived on scene to include Sergeant Searles.

"Have a good look, lads" the sergeant chuckled, "you'll be making their acquaintance later today – you can count on that."

"Surely they do not mean to come over, do they?" Percy asked.

"Perkins, you are as daft as a mackerel," the sergeant stated flatly as he pointed. "They're not coming over here – we're going over there. Look over yonder toward the top of their works. If we don't get up there and push them off, those rascals will mount cannon that can reach us here. They're daring us to engage them, and we'll certainly oblige."

"Any orders, sergeant?" Someone chimed in from behind as now the veteran had the full attention of the rapidly gathering crowd.

"None yet, lads, but you can be sure orders are coming. Go back and ready your kit. Make sure your firelocks are clean and in top working order. No drilling today on the Common. Instead, we drill across the river. And this time we'll show these scoundrels a proper stand-up fight."

General Gage's failed attempt to capture military stores at Concord had proved a disaster, the product of a bad idea poorly executed. The British had lost approximately a fifth of the force that had marched – killed, maimed, or deserted. However, the biggest casualty of all was the notion that cowardly Yankee rabble would not or could not stand up on their own and fight. If not for the leadership and tactical ability of Lord Percy, the entire British force would have been decimated or captured if for no other reason than the sheer overwhelming numbers of militia.

Now, two months later, more than 20,000 armed and angry volunteers from all corners of New England and beyond manned positions on the outskirts of Boston, that peninsula protected only by the surrounding water and a heavily fortified gate at the neck. Gone now was any vestige of civility toward local Loyalists, whose homes were confiscated or destroyed, families scattered and many simply murdered. Those who could sought shelter in Boston, where General Gage allowed them to enter but conversely did not allow exit for those who sided with the so-called *Patriots* for fear of losing a suddenly newfound precious commodity – *hostages*.

Although the aftermath was clear, accounts differed as to who started the fighting at Lexington, with British officers at the scene insisting it had been the Yankees. For their part the Sons of Liberty had immediately launched an investigation that involved testimonies from hundreds of eyewitnesses to include captured British soldiers. This ensuing version was rushed to England by Doctor Warren, who chartered for that purpose the fastest ship available that easily slipped the naval coastal blockade and provided an exceptionally comprehensive rebel account to both the British government and London newspapers. King George and his ministry marinated in the Yankee version of the truth, which laid blame squarely on the British, as they waited uncomfortably for General Gage's official report. That did arrive more than a week later however, the brevity of data and obvious lack of details proved more informative than any facts contained. Once again flying into a rage, similar to that at the news of the Tea Party, and rather than reconsider his analysis and approach, the king could only bring himself to affirm his belief that the Massachusetts province had not been dealt with forcefully enough. Like a person with a splinter in his finger who only drives it deeper in by trying clumsily to remove it, he vowed to ratchet up the military pressure and remove anyone under his thumb who could not or would not serve that purpose. By the end of the summer both Gage and Graves would be recalled to England and, along with the American Secretary Lord Dartmouth, they would be replaced for the want of suitable aggression.

Back in Boston, on the heels of the historic debacle on the road to Concord, Gage now had to contend with the reality that his sphere of influence consisted solely of the ground under his feet on the relatively small peninsula of the city itself. Against his better judgment, Gage had risked his reputation, the political situation, and the lives of his men in order to please his king and remain in favor. Now he would be beaten with his own stick, as he had stirred up a vast enemy army of his own English brethren with their intentions unknown. Instead of serving to quell a riotous province, as was his mission, he and his forces now had to work for their very survival. The Yankees took what feed and livestock they could from the islands in the bay and what they could not take they destroyed in plain sight as neither Gage nor Graves possessed the ability to stop them. Food was rationed, as resupplies reached the city by sea in a trickle.

By the end of May a few British vessels bringing relief straggled into Boston, one of those a frigate carrying the three new senior officers foretold of in March – Major Generals William Howe, Henry Clinton, and John Burgoyne, all of whom bore decent reputations as experienced fighting men. Along with them came an additional directive, written well prior to the march on Concord, placing Massachusetts under martial law, thus removing any semblance or pretense of civilian government. The influx of the three new generals, all of whom held the party-line belief that Americans were inept cowards, prompted Gage to take what aggressive action he could, and he subsequently planned a breakout across the harbor to occupy the Charlestown peninsula on June 18th. As usual, the Sons of Liberty quickly learned of the plan and on the evening of the 16th assumed positions on the peninsula heights to begin building fortifications to block such a landing.

As morning broke on the 17th to reveal the Yankee menace in plain view across the harbor, Gage and his new senior staff hastily devised a response while the navy began a steady cannonade on the yet unfinished construction and also on the Charlestown Neck to dissuade the arrival of reinforcements. The straightforward plan involved the transport of a landing force across the Charles River to clear away the threat and secure the peninsula. Gage's new immediate subordinate, General *Billy* Howe, would command the assault with more than two thousand men composed of ten companies of light infantry, ten companies of grenadiers, four whole regiments and part of a fifth to include artillery. Next in line, General Clinton, would remain in Boston with a seven-hundred-man reserve force, if necessary, of two regiments and two battalions of marines. The operation commenced in the early afternoon directly after lunch as those making the crossing marched through the city down to the waterfront where the first wave boarded more than two dozen barges. Looking much like giant red caterpillars, the watercraft methodically snaked in two long lines across the harbor to the Charlestown Peninsula, their mounted bayonets gleaming in the sun. The day had started cool but now began to warm nicely as civilians within sight of the harbor gathered on their rooftops to watch an early summer spectacle.

As the sailors rowed the first wave toward the landing zone, Jack and his comrades stood basking in the warmth, all the while entertained by the symphony of cannon that boomed about the harbor.

"Should be making better use of our shipping," Percy remarked as they passed a large warship that discharged its guns in a thunderous clap, blanketing them in a cloud of smoke. "A wasteful effort I should say. Can't elevate their cannon high enough to be effective and the land battery behind on the North End is too far away. The most our shipping can do from here is destroy Charlestown proper with incendiary shot as that's bound to be thick with snipers. We'd be better served to have our shipping come up high on either side of the peninsula to cover the neck with cannon while we land there and choke off the peninsula without a musket being fired. The Yankees would be forced to either surrender or starve. Making a landing at the bottom and coming up the hill is far more work and risk."

Jack shook his head and chuckled. "You might be right, Perce. Maybe one of these days Granny will ask for your counsel."

"And what about this haversack?" Percy quipped as he patted the shoulder-mounted bag now resting on his stomach. "Granny gave us enough provisions for three days. Bloody hell, I seem to be carrying a small child. What say you, George?"

George merely shrugged but did not answer, preferring to stare straight ahead toward Charlestown with his ever-present grin.

"I can't imagine we'll be there three days," Jack answered instead. "These Yankees on the hill can't hide behind trees and stone fences this time. I expect they'll run as soon as we march on them."

"They have something up their sleeve, they do," Percy replied. "Why would they choose to fight us in the very manner which we excel and they don't? Surely, they don't think they can prevail."

The approaching Charlestown peninsula was pear-shaped, oriented from southeast to northwest with the neck at the stem about a mile from the bottom where the landing force approached. No more than half a mile wide at the base, to the left lay the village of Charlestown at the southwest corner. Directly ahead on the eastern-most corner was the chosen landing zone, Moulton's Point, which delineated the mouth of the Mystic River that ran alongside the northern edge of the peninsula to the neck. Following the peninsula from the base up toward the neck, treeless pastureland rose roughly seventy-five feet over a third of a mile to *Breed's Hill* with steep slopes on its western and eastern sides. Continuing up another quarter mile sat *Bunker Hill*, the highest point at well over a hundred feet, and behind that a slope of about another third of a mile that ran back down to the marshy neck. The Yankees had chosen to place their main fortifications on the lower Breed's Hill closer in cannon range to Boston. Here they constructed a square earthen *redoubt* about six feet high for more than 100 feet on each side with a V-shaped *redan* projecting toward Charlestown and a narrow gorge in the rear for entry and exit. Extending a few hundred yards from the base of the redoubt northeast toward the Mystic River was an earthen breastwork constructed similar to that of the redoubt walls. Behind and beyond the breastwork were also built three arrow-shaped piles of wood called *fleches* pointing toward the Mystic River to guard an approach from there.

At about one o'clock, the flotilla landed at Moulton's Point with half the number necessary for the operation. The Yankees could have opposed them here, in their most vulnerable circumstance, but were dissuaded by two British frigates just offshore that swept the approaches inland with grape shot. As the navy continued to pound the peninsula the barges departed and returned by mid-afternoon with the second wave and General Howe. Immediately upon his arrival the good general split the force roughly in half placing the hat and marine units supported by several flank companies under the command of Brigadier General Sir Robert Pigot, sending him left in the direction of Charlestown in parallel with the base of the redoubt. Protected by the 35th's grenadiers the artillery pushed four six-pound cannon to the top of relatively low Moulton's Hill in order to fire on the redoubt at closer range. Howe led the remainder, all grenadiers and light infantry, along the coast up the Mystic River, his tactic to outflank the redoubt to the right along the more vulnerable northern quadrant while Pigot kept what looked to be the bulk of the militia busy between the redoubt and Charlestown.

The pleasant earlier weather now turned hot and sticky on the back end of the afternoon, as Jack and the others plodded their way fully loaded like pack mules. What had looked from the harbor as easily navigable terrain now proved a quagmire of marshland, fences, brick kilns, and clay pits, all masked by tall grass. To make matters worse they quickly discovered that the six-pound cannon they labored to pull had been mistakenly supplied with twelve-pound ball rendering those contraptions as well as the ammunition a useless hindrance. They tediously trudged forward with the redoubt, breastwork, and fleches well to their left until a point where they detected a rail fence ahead, which looked to be reinforced and fortified as a continuation of the breastwork. To outflank the fence, Howe split them yet again, keeping the grenadiers for himself and sending the light infantry farther right toward the river down a ten-foot embankment to the water's edge. Once on the beach the King's Own formed just behind the lead company, the 23rd Royal Welsh Fusiliers, with the entire force of well over three hundred led by a Fusiliers' officer. They marched more easily now along a thin strip of hard sand in a column four abreast, their muskets held near the waist with bayonets fixed and projecting forward as they braced themselves to break any resistance by sheer force of mass and intimidation. A few hundred yards farther lay a newly built stone wall about waist-high, a makeshift extension of the rail fence above, behind which contained militia in numbers roughly equal to theirs. At one hundred yards the Yankees presented their firelocks as the British kept their pace, waiting for the order to charge.

Jack turned to Percy and George, both of whom stared ahead white and grim. Like most of the surrounding comrades it was their first such engagement. "Don't worry, lads," Jack whispered, "they'll run."

"Bollocks, Jack," Percy answered flatly. "They haven't run yet."

Jack peered forward about a dozen yards to the front of the column as they closed to sixty-five yards from the wall, then sixty, then fifty-five. A silence hung over the beach like a curtain waiting to drop with only the sounds of their boots scuffing through the sand. The column tensed like a coiled spring in anticipation of the impending order, preparing to answer in a great *Huzzah!* to commence an assault once inside fifty yards.

Of all the horrors of 18th century battle there was nothing so terrible as staring into the face of a bayonet charge made by determined men. Even with the recent developments of modern warfare that rendered the ability to engage the enemy from an ever-increasing distance, the most effective method of carrying a fight was still close-in, a reality that had not changed since the invention of warfare itself. Properly employed by trained pro-fessionals, a wall of massed seventeen-inch metal spikes could break a defense before even reaching its objective. Only the most disciplined and stoutest of hearts could stand before it to await the conclusion and most never did. Much is written of the prowess of the British Army in protecting the empire, but it was the bayonet upon which England owed its greatest debt.

Unbeknownst to the approaching British the men on the other side of the wall happened to be of the stoutest sort – the 1st New Hampshire Regiment commanded by Colonel John Stark, a first-generation English immigrant and hardened veteran of the French and Indian War. Having recognized the vulnerability on their left flank along the river the militia on-scene commander, Colonel William Prescott, had dispatched Stark, who plugged the gap with a hastily constructed stone wall and now prepared his force to defend it. The light infantry approached the wall with the militia deployed behind in three distinct rows, not at all a group of ragtag motley farmers. As the Fusiliers' officer raised his hand to signal the bayonet charge there erupted from the first row of militia a clap of thunder and disgorgement of fire and smoke that struck the head of the British column as if a sheet of lightning. The forward element of the 23rd disintegrated like dandelions blown by a stiff wind with arms and other parts flying from bodies as if a giant scythe tossed what was left of them backwards in bloody chunks. The second row of militia promptly fired next with similar effect as suddenly Jack found himself pushed into the adjacent water at the bottom of a bloody pile of mangled bodies and pieces of such. He wriggled about coughing and choking in the mud under the great mass, aware of the catastrophe above him only through the screaming and repeated blasts of the Yankee muskets that raked their position without quarter.

"GET UP, HALLIDAY!"

Jack felt a firm hand grab his collar and pull him free, covered in a mixture of brackish water, muck, and blood.

"HALLIDAY!" Sergeant Searles shook Jack, yelling in his face. "HALLIDAY! DO YOU HEAR ME, LAD?"

Jack murmured something close enough to an affirmative as the sergeant shoved him in the opposite direction. Jack took a step on wobbly legs as if it were his first, falling over a body in his path, kicking it unintentionally in the stomach. Percy coughed and gagged as he lay half-floating, half-rolling in the shallow water and mud of the shoreline. The sergeant grabbed them each with one hand pulling both to their feet. "CLEAR OUT OF HERE, THE BOTH OF YOU," he screamed. "FIND YOUR WEAPON AND REFORM DOWN THE BEACH! THIS IS A KILL ZONE – THEY HAVE IT SIGHTED! NOW MOVE!"

Jack grabbed the closest musket and held it by the top of the barrel, using it to lean on as he stumbled forward amidst the scores of bleeding stragglers, leaving behind dead, or dying comrades heaped on the now blood-red sand. He staggered back from whence he came with what was left of the column well out of range of the militia, who did not pursue but rather remained fixed behind the stone wall, cheering wildly over the wailing cries of his wounded comrades still piled on the beach.

"Bloody sons-of-bitches," Jack muttered to nobody.

"Right you are, Jack," Percy answered from the right as George now managed to join them, bleeding from both ears and covered head to toe in seaweed and muck.

"PERKINS! HALLIDAY! BRIDGES! THIS WAY!" Sergeant Searles now called from near the embankment. "FORM UP IN THE FIELD ABOVE! THAT'S IT – UP YOU GO!"

With the load of extra gear still on their backs they scaled back up the sandy rise with a push from the good sergeant, not nearly as easy as the trip down. Percy and George had to pull Jack up the last few feet as his right knee suddenly failed, having been well twisted under the great heap on the beach. Hobbling forward to the growing congregation of light infantry in the pasture they fell in with the remnants of the company, all taking seats in the tall grass. The sergeant soon arrived and inspected each of them, further culling the most seriously injured.

"Are you hurt, Halliday?" the sergeant asked Jack, who shook like a fluttering leaf in a strong wind.

"He is, sergeant," Percy answered instead.

"Hell, if I am!" Jack countered sharply as, with the aid of his musket and under great duress, he managed to rise, keeping most of his weight on his left leg.

"Good lad," the sergeant stated without hesitation. "Get a drink of water and check your gear. Clean your piece and give it a dry load. We move up the hill in five minutes."

Percy, George, and Jack looked at each other with heavy eyes and shook their heads as the sergeant strode away. Nearby rested what was left of the grenadiers, who had been similarly beaten back from their assault on the rail fence above the beach. For several moments none spoke, taking what precious rest they could. Having just deposited a third of their column dead on the beach and leaving behind in the grass others among them too wounded to continue, the light infantry formed what was left into three columns composed of not even half their original number. The task now was to approach the same rail fence as the grenadiers had just attempted, this time, as a decoy intended to keep the force along the fence occupied while the grenadiers to the left would close on the fleches in a play to get behind the breastwork that jutted toward them. General Pigot's forces would also assault the redoubt further left from the other side of the peninsula with the ultimate goal of enveloping the main body of the militia and squeeze them like a vice to drive them back up the hill from their entrenched positions.

Jack limped along as best he could, wincing with every step over the uneven sloping ground deceptively obscured by the tall grass. Approaching the rail fence rising three hundred yards in the distance the rebels began firing artillery down from upper Bunker Hill finding targets on the light infantry's lines as well as the grenadiers to the left. Farther left, Charlestown proper lay fully ablaze from the incendiary rounds shot by the navy to level the town and drive out snipers that harassed Pigot's forces as they skirted the inferno toward the opposite side of the redoubt. With the light infantry columns still 100 yards from the fence, Howe and the grenadiers closed on the fleches, hotly peppered by musket fire from three sides. Several small fences laid in the path, low enough to be hidden by the tall grass but high enough to slow their approach as Jack and the others labored over these impediments, still burdened by their excess gear.

From the left the grenadiers give a great *HUZZAH!* followed by the repeated intense blasts of several hundred rebel muskets. Once inside fifty yards from the objective the entrenched defenders opened on the light infantry as well, sweeping the first few men from the top of the fence as they attempted to scale it. In the face of increasing heavy fire the officers urged them forward as the sergeants tried to maintain organization to allow for rapid navigation of the fence. But like the grenadiers before they bunched up in disarray at the bottom as those in the process of climbing were launched backwards, riddled with lead shot. Once again Jack found himself at the bottom of a great pile of bleeding men screaming for their lives with their last breaths as he wriggled free from the writhing melee shouting in pain as his ever-worsening twisted knee contorted itself to allow his egress. Covered in new blood he found his musket and managed to stand. Those who could were already engaged in a quick retreat in the opposite direction and he did not need further encouragement to join them. Some ran, most stumbled, and a few even crawled back down the slope to the starting point, where once again the lights formed in the tall grass even more bewildered than before.

Not far away stood General Howe, where a scattering of officers attempted to piece together what remained of the grenadiers, who had fared even worse than the lights and were nearly decimated at the fleches and breastwork. All twelve of Howe's personal staff were gone, either killed or mortally wounded, as the ashen-faced general stared grimly up the hill in anger and disbelief. On the other side of the field, General Pigot had failed as well, his units beaten back by the same savage musket fire as they attempted to storm the redoubt. Several of the remaining officers begged to give up this folly and return to the beach but Howe simply motioned them away before returning his attention up the hill. Each of the newly arrived generals had earlier presented their recommendation to Gage but it had been Howe that convinced the commander that the slovenly band of poltroons on the peninsula possessed neither the will nor capacity to withstand a coordinated land attack by a professional force. But withstand it they did and, in fact, gave back even better.

In truth the British had, in blatant disrespect of the Yankee capability, broken with the tactical convention normally afforded to such an offensive operation in that they divided their forces in the beginning at the beach and then again after that. A good portion of those forces had made their initial attack in unprotected lines versus massed columns, and they had not waited for proper artillery support. All this with several dozen pounds of excess weight on each soldier's back against an enemy assumed too inept and cowardly for concern. They had barely put a dent in these farmers' makeshift fortress and had far from persuaded them to flee. In response those supposed cravenly yokels had littered the pasture with the so-called professionals. For these miscalculations the British had in the course of an hour paid dearly but now, it seemed, embarrassed by the stubborn Yankee rabble and fueled by equally stubborn pride, Howe resolved that his force would return to Boston victorious or not return at all.

A low cloud of smoke hung suspended in the hazy, hot, and humid air as the late afternoon sun descended toward the curtain of towering flames that engulfed Charlestown proper, producing a glimpse of Hell itself. The once pleasant summer day had turned decidedly oppressive as the soldiers rested in the tall grass and drained the last of their canteens in a small measure of relief and to wash the acrid taste of burnt gunpowder from their mouths. An eerie silence blanketed the peninsula as the waiting Yankees dug in up on the hill stared down intently.

"George!" Percy cried somewhat sharply, "George! Where are you going?"

George took another step down the hill then stopped and turned back toward Percy and Jack, his ever-present smile suddenly replaced with a blank stare.

"George," Percy repeated, "where are you going? What are you doing?"

George hesitated then stated flatly, "I'm leaving."

Percy looked at Jack, who leaned on his musket and maneuvered on his good knee to step closer. "What do you mean *leaving*?" Percy continued, "Where would you be leaving *to*?"

George gave a casual glance around "Going down the hill back to the beach, I reckon."

"*Down* the hill? You can't go *down* the hill."

"Well, I'm sure as bloody hell not going *up* that goddamn hill. That bloody Billy Howe would butcher us all and I'm not having it."

"But, George, if you go back down to the beach you'll be rounded up as a deserter and shot."

"I don't bloody well care, Perce. I don't give a bloody damn about this bloody hill. I'm not going back up there for Billy, or Granny, or England. I'm done."

"Jack, do something – please!" Percy turned to his other friend. "He's going down the hill. You know what *that* means."

Jack stared silently at George for several long moments as he tried unsuccessfully to speak. "George…" he finally managed in a low tone as other soldiers began to look on. George…I don't give a damn about that hill either…or Billy…or Granny…or England…or the damn Yankees for that matter. And I doubt any of the rest of us do either. The only thing I give a damn about right now is getting through this day in one piece and the only way I see to do that is to stay together." Jack shifted on the musket as he turned to point behind. "Percy's right. You go back down to the beach, and you'll be rounded up for a deserter – that's for certain. Every one of us wants to go back down to the beach but we're not. We all want to get off this damn hill, but we can't do it by ourselves. You don't need to go up that hill for Billy or anybody but yourself and the rest of us. Don't go down, George. Stay here with us – it's our best chance together."

"No," George simply answered as he turned abruptly and strode away. Jack, Percy, and a dozen others watched as he slowly descended.

"Bloody hell, Jack," Percy whispered as they watched their friend disappear into the tall grass below. "We're not going to see him again. First, Michael. Now, George. Gone."

Jack shook his head. "I don't know, Perce. Life hasn't been kind to me. Seems all I ever get is a dog end. I never complained, and I'm not complaining now. But I won't turn my back on those that won't turn their back on me. Our chances on this hill don't look good but staying together is the best chance we have. And if I die – so be it."

Percy looked at Jack as he swallowed hard and tried in vain to answer.

"PERKINS! HALLIDAY! BRIDGES! FORM UP OVER YONDER!" The familiar voice of Sergeant Searles broke the silence. After half an hour's respite he appeared from the direction of the officers, his face stern and emotionless as he approached in his ever-straightforward gait. "Form up," he commanded flatly. "We're moving again, lads. Strip off your kit and leave it here. Where's Bridges?"

Neither Jack nor Percy answered, both looking down with sullen expressions.

"Gone is he? And what about you two – do you want to go as well?"

Jack looked up as he leaned on his musket and looked square into the sergeant's piercing eyes. "And where would we go?"

The sergeant nodded. "Good lads then. For today your courage will define the rest of your lives. Every one of us is afraid of going back up that hill but we must do it, nevertheless. Courage is not the absence of fear but rather the mastery of it. Courage is a choice. Those who choose the easy path to allow themselves to be ruled by fear will forever be a vassal to their own doubts. But those who choose the harder path will master their fear. This is why Britain rules the world. We're all going to die someday but that occurrence is fixed and there's nothing any of us can do to change it. But if today is that day then let's die in *that* direction," he raised his voice as he pointed up the hill, "like proper soldiers, not common cowards. You two forget about Bridges now and do your jobs. Is that clear?"

"Yes, sergeant," both Jack and Percy answered in unison.

"When you get up yonder," the sergeant continued to point, "you put a bayonet into anything that moves that doesn't have a red uniform. Killing is good, lads. You kill as many of those devils as you can, and you don't stop killing until I personally tell you. Is that clear?"

"Yes, sergeant."

"Do your duty and put your faith in providence. Understand?"

"Yes, sergeant."

"God may love a bastard, but he reveres a soldier. Now move!"

The arrival of four hundred reinforcements from the 2nd Marines and 63rd Regiment as well as the correct size ball for the six-pound cannon removed any doubt of British intentions. The men gladly unlimbered the excess equipment from their backs, heaving the heavy knapsack and rolled blanket on the ground with a satisfying thud. Jack and Percy fell in with a composite unit of what remained of the light infantry to the far right of the remnants of the grenadiers. Moving up the hill the lights and grenadiers marched in well-ordered columns as Jack grimaced with the first step forward and, in fact, with every step as his knee had stiffened considerably. To the far left as before the main force under Pigot also marched as the two converged on the Yankee position like a giant red pincer. This time there would be no feints, no decoys, no attempt at complicated flanking maneuvers as Howe had decided they would charge the redoubt and breastwork with the full weight of their forces in a straight-on headlong bull rush like the wounded and desperate animals they had become. Given their dwindled numbers and the time of day it had not been stated but nevertheless well-understood by all that this would be the last attempt, come what may.

As in the prior attack, the Yankee artillery started from three hundred yards with the sniping crossfire somewhat closer in.

British artillery opened up as well, creating havoc now along the enemy lines where none had previously existed. As before, the militia waited until the redcoats were well within fifty yards of them before they gave the first musket volley, the grim result of which buckled the columns. But this time, unlike before, instead of a second volley of consequence there followed only the scattered popping of a few guns. For all their magnificent effort the disorganized militia command structure had failed to provide enough ammunition and the naval cannon had adequately prevented resupply across the neck as the Yankees now exhausted their last available rounds. As the redcoats approached, the defenders disgorged one last volley then showed their backs, quitting their defensive positions as fast as they could.

The grenadiers to the left reached the breastwork first while the column of lights edged around it to the right toward the fleches and rail fence. All the while the six-pounders cleared swaths of militia from their entrenchments as the cannons enfiladed the breastwork with brutal effect throwing up giant sprays of dirt and gore. Within moments the grenadiers were up and over the earthen wall and with a great *HUZZAH!* they scampered behind with their bayonets lowered as Pigot's men also poured into the main redoubt from the left. The lights were not far behind as they skirted between the fleches and rail fence, encircling the breastwork to pinch off any escape. Many militia had already begun to flee while others remained in place seemingly stunned by the rapid British advance. Not possessing bayonets, the desperate defenders now wielded their muskets like clubs while others feverishly tried to reload with whatever ammo they had managed to retain. Jack's column dissolved into the confusion as pent up frustration turned to unbridled anger. Somebody pushed past, knocking him firmly from behind and still favoring his knee, he lost his footing and toppled into a somewhat concealed ditch behind one of the fleches, rolling down a slight incline and landing on his back.

Jack sat up quickly to find a militiaman before him several yards away on his knees and stuffing a handful of nails into a rusted firelock. Older than Jack but not by much, the Yankee wore a floppy wide-brimmed hat above a large forehead, prominent nose and square-cut jaw. The whole of him looked to be a farmer as if he had on that very day left his crops to fight. Too slow, hurt, or just plain stupid to have already quit, the man fixed Jack with a wild-eyed gaze that no portrait artist could have duplicated. Startled but still maintaining hold of his musket with both hands Jack scooted back toward the incline in instinctive fright as he pawed the ground with his good leg in an unsuccessful effort to rise and flee. The unlikely pair stared at each other for several frozen heartbeats before the man dropped his firelock and withdrew a hatchet shoved in his belt. Still off balance on his backside Jack swung his musket with the bayonet forward in an effort to protect himself. The man lunged toward Jack and with the hatchet slapped the musket out of Jack's hands, momentum carrying the man forward as the hatchet whirled past Jack's face into the ground near his ear. Jack grabbed the man's extended arm with his left hand and reaching with his right inside his coat for Georgey's knife he stuck the blade as best he could into the man's ribcage. The man cringed and screamed, convulsing like a fresh caught fish as Jack withdrew the knife and caught him again, this time square in the sternum, just as Georgey had taught him. The man went limp falling forward onto Jack, who quickly pushed him to the side as he withdrew the knife, wiping it on the man's ragged pants before replacing it in the sheath.

Jack remained on his back for a long moment, heart pounding and breathing heavily as he stared up into the acrid smoke that continued to hang low in the sky. With a shaking hand he located his musket and slowly managed to rise to his knees, leaning on his firelock and sweating profusely. With more than a little effort he climbed out of the ditch and limped out from behind the fleche back up the incline toward the ongoing melee, whose roar hit him like a giant ocean wave as he approached the clamor.

A chaotic mixture of fleeing militia gushed from the redoubt's only exit in the rear like a wine sac being squeezed as scores of redcoats scaled up and over the earthworks into the trenches on the defensive side. Those Yankees that chose to stay fought with axes, shovels, picks, or just their bare fists. Many grabbed their now empty muskets by the barrel and swung frantically at the heads and shoulders of the rapidly growing red mass that continued to pour over the walls. The rabid grenadiers mercilessly lanced each and every one of them including those who suddenly chose to beg for mercy as dozens of bayonets thrust again and again into the shrieking bodies that piled inside the redoubt. Outside the redoubt the escaping militia on the fly were chased like turkeys up the hill as the British poured lead balls and steel shafts as best they could into the mass of fleeing backs.

Jack turned right and followed the rolling chaos up the hill as he saw officers and sergeants working to organize men back into their respective units. Several militia companies on the flanks, including the 1st New Hampshire that had engaged the lights earlier on the beach, managed to retreat in good order as they gave cover to their more panicked comrades. These disciplined units traded volleys with what scattered British platoons had managed to form as they backed their way off the peninsula allowing most of the militia to run for their lives down the backside of the hill and across the neck. Jack found the King's Own at the crest of the heights where above the din he followed the voice of Sergeant Searles, who cursed the reformed column for their lack of discipline.

General Clinton had arrived as well, having just marched up from the beach with more fresh forces sent over from Boston. Clinton continued down to the neck, where he set up a defense, he and Howe having decided not to pursue the militia further. As the generals had intended from the beginning the British now owned the peninsula but at a cost they never imagined as the fields behind them lay littered with dead and wounded like pebbles on a beach. For those who survived, there would be no rest as they were formed into scavenging parties to salvage the living and pick up the dead, the latter of whom were thrown onto flat, horse-drawn carts in heaping piles.

Twisted knee and all, Jack did not shirk the task as he and his unit worked a section between the breastwork and the redoubt. Here the grenadiers lay where they had fallen, grotesquely stacked like cordwood as Jack and Percy heaved one after the other onto the lorries. They suddenly paused when two of those hoisted were Flaherty and Ahearn, each mangled almost beyond recognition by so many musket balls that they nearly fell to pieces when lifted. Jack gagged as he turned away toward Charlestown, the once pristine village now a ghastly shell of blackened rubble smoldering in the waning daylight, no less violently consumed than the British themselves. Across the harbor an eerie silence carried the noise of Boston all the way up the hill. He exhaled deeply and coughed, the violence of which disturbed his knee.

"My God, Jack – what have we done?" Percy offered nearby. "All this for a bloody patch of grass? Another scrap like this and there'll be none of us left."

"We're still alive," Jack answered in a low murmur. "That's the important thing."

"PERKINS! HALLIDAY!" Sergeant Searles called out from several paces away as he approached. "Quit your lollygagging! It's getting dark, and we've work to do."

"Yes, sergeant," the pair answered in unison as they turned to hoist another dead grenadier.

9

War is a mere continuation of policy with other means.

On War, Karl von Clausewitz

YORK ISLAND (MANHATTAN), NEW YORK, FEBRUARY 1777

"Damn that bloody Scarecrow," Percy exclaimed as he shook his head in mock disbelief. "How could any person possibly have that much to say? Are you still watching this, Jack?"

"I already gave up," Jack answered in a bored tone as he looked in the opposite direction. "I can't bear to look anymore."

"If I talked that much," Percy continued, "my lips would fall off."

Jack turned to join Percy as they peered into the large window across a small, snow-dusted lawn only a short distance from where the two soldiers stood with a horse and wagon. Inside the window of the well-appointed main building of a sprawling farm, a well-dressed aristocratic group sat before a long table filled with more food and drink than they could possibly consume. Seated at the far end of the table a tall, thin man with a long but exceedingly handsome face and dark, wavy hair who wore a red officer's jacket motioned his boney hands and arms furiously in the air as his jaw moved up and down in frantic synchronization.

"What in God's name could he possibly be telling them, Jack?"

"Bloody hell if I know," Jack answered in disgust. "But all night he's had a full plate in front of him with more food than I've seen in a year. I could eat that whole turkey myself, and he hasn't touched a morsel. Little wonder he is but a stick."

Percy chuckled as their old mare snorted as if on cue, pawing the ground with her hoof. "By now he may have given them the entire history of England. Told them how he's personally won every war we ever had and even some we haven't. Damn that bloody Scarecrow, Jack."

That *bloody Scarecrow* would be one Captain Reginald Henry Garthwaite, commander of the Light Infantry Company of the King's Own 4th Foot Regiment. Recently arrived at the unit just before Christmas, Captain Garthwaite had made an immediate impact on his new subordinates in indelible fashion. The product of a wealthy family whose lineage could have easily defined the very meaning of English aristocracy, his older brother, Edward, stood first in line to inherit the vast, long-held estate dating back to before King James I. His father, Ronald, a man of impeccable character and an esteemed Whig, held peerage with the likes of the Howes. But if an apple usually falls not far from the tree, in the case of Reginald it seemed as if a cosmic giant had descended to Earth and kicked that object into the next universe, leaving Ronald little choice but to exercise that old English tradition of remitting the second son or the family fool, in this case one and the same, into the care of the military in hopes of divine transformation or at least an honorable death so as to not tarnish the surname.

Midnight had long since passed to the wee hours of the morning when the candles in the window finally extinguished and shortly thereafter the front door opened.

"Percy!" Jack called in a whisper as loud as he dared. "Percy, get up!"

Jack had huddled next to the standing mare, leaning on the friendly beast to keep warm as he positioned himself out of the wind but still able to see the front of the house. Percy had since taken a prone position in the rear cargo box area of the wagon, snoring so loudly as to ensure both Jack and the horse would remain awake. Jack quickly moved to the back and reached inside to vigorously shake his friend. "Percy, get up! He's coming out!"

Percy stirred, then bolted upright. "What? Bloody Scarecrow! Where?"

"Be quiet!" Jack admonished, covering Percy's mouth. "He's at the doorstep. Get out of there now!"

Jack half dragged Percy from the wagon as the pair hurried to appear as if they had never moved from their original stations. Satisfied they were properly in position with muskets at the ready, they stared ahead and waited. Before them, on the top step of the low granite stairway that led to the front door, stood their commanding officer frozen in place as if a frightened cat trapped on a tree branch. Although there existed a metal rail on one side to guide him down the mere three steps to the bottom the bewildered captain could seemingly not fathom how next to proceed. After a brief silence he began to mutter to himself and turn slowly in circles, traversing across the several feet of the top granite slab like a child's wobbly spinning top. With his back to the two soldiers his face bounced off the wooden siding of the front of the house, lurching him backwards into a teetering perch on the edge of the precipice. At six-foot four inches and thin as a waif, his coat suddenly caught a gust of wind toppling him further backward with his arms outstretched like a broken main mast of a ship at full sail. His feet found nothing except air as he fell like a giant puppet whose master had suddenly let go of the strings, dropping him into the yard in a colossal, mixed-up heap of boney limbs. Jack and Percy immediately set their muskets aside and rushed forward across the lawn, reaching the captain in scant seconds as he rolled and flailed about in the thin layer of snow. Both soldiers grabbed him beneath the shoulders as they attempted to pull him to his feet.

"GODDAMN YOU, PRIVATE!" the captain screamed. "GET YOUR BLOODY HANDS OFF ME! I SAID GET YOUR DAMN BLOODY HANDS OFF ME!"

Jack and Percy looked at each other and promptly released the captain, causing him to fall face-first into the combination of snow and muck now created around their feet on the lawn. The captain managed to rise to his knees as he commenced to crawl forward on his forearms and continued to bellow.

"GODDAMN YOU, PRIVATE! YOU SHALL NOT TOUCH A GARTHWAITE! BLOODY PEASANT! I WILL HAVE YOU FLOGGED!"

The captain lifted himself enough to swing his fist at no one, only to lose his balance and flop back down into the snow.

"GODDAMN IT, SERGEANT! I WANT THIS MAN COURTS-MARTIALLED! DO YOU HEAR ME? HE WILL NOT LAY A HAND ON ME! BLOODY PEASANTS, ALL OF YOU!"

The captain struggled to his hands and knees again as he continued to swing at thin air with the only positive result being that he managed to slowly lurch himself forward toward the wagon. By now the recently extinguished candles inside the house became lit again. The front door cracked open slightly to reveal at least two faces that peered outside from the thin opening. The captain continued his methodical crawl, alternately screaming, swinging, and falling, with the two soldiers remaining just out of reach flanking him to either side and behind. Finally reaching the wagon, he tried to stand but could not. Jack and Percy both grabbed him from behind, quickly and firmly, and with one great shove lifted his long, thin frame into the cargo box, which elicited a fresh round of threats and profanity with renewed vigor as the captain lay sprawled across the flat, wooden boards. As the captain tried in vain to kick them, Jack and Percy quickly latched the rear gate shut then hurriedly assumed their positions in the front as they started the horse out of the driveway, soon out of earshot from the murmurs that came from the doorway.

Once they were on the road, a light snow began to fall again, complementing the cessation of noise from behind except when the captain managed to lift his head over the side of the cargo box to vomit. After several miles heading south on the road that ran along the Hudson River, now just before daybreak, they reached the outskirts of the village proper toward the lower tip of the island, where the King's Own had been assigned quarters at an old warehouse facility formerly used to store feed. Sergeant Searles met them soon after they cleared the security checkpoint and stopped at the small house that served as Captain Garthwaite's quarters. Percy halted the wagon at the head of the walkway as the sergeant stood ramrod straight in the early light in front of the building, remaining silent as he peered into the cargo box without expression. He motioned for the two soldiers to dismount and help; all three took hold of their vomit-soaked, unconscious commander by his legs and shoulders to carry him inside the building. The captain woke briefly to wriggle as he cursed loudly. "SERGEANT! I WANT THESE MEN COURTS-MARTIALLED AND LASHED AT DAWN! DO YOU HEAR ME? I WANT THESE BLOODY PEASANTS LASHED!"

Sergeant Searles muttered what passed as an acknowledgement as the trio hurried inside the house, stripping the captain of his stench-ridden coat, and placing his incapacitated carcass onto his bed. The sergeant rounded up another soldier currently on guard duty and placed him outside the captain's door with instructions to leave it open to listen and check that the sleeping officer did not choke on his own vomit. He then brought Jack and Percy back outside where the horse and wagon had already been disposed of and bade them recount the recent events. The sergeant listened with pursed lips and an ever-tightening jaw as the pair narrated the evening in detail, then stared hard at each of them with a frightening stone-cold gaze.

"You will say nothing of this to anyone," the sergeant whispered sternly, "ever again in your life. If I hear talk of this going 'round the camp, I'll know exactly where it came from. Rest assured the captain will remember none of this but if I hear of it from another soldier's lips, I *will* have you both flogged. Do you understand?"

"But, sergeant," Percy protested, "such talk is already going around the camp for this isn't the first time nor even the second."

"But we won't say anything of tonight, sergeant," Jack added. "You can count on that."

Sergeant Searles tensed again as he shot them one last stern gaze. "Well done, lads. Now, get out of here."

* * *

What had started in Boston on a hot, muggy day nearly two years prior as a relatively small battle for a scraggly hill across the harbor on the Charlestown peninsula had ended as a pivotal strategic point of no return for all involved. For better or worse the *Battle of Bunker Hill,* as it subsequently became known, elevated the colonial crisis to another level that galvanized both British and American resolve in an unalterable direction that dictated every decision that followed. Although technically a *victory* as defined by military convention – having captured the ground – the hor- rible cost struck England as if a massive defeat. Well over half of the 2,000 participating redcoats had resulted in casualties, severely crippling General Gage's ability to do anything more than maintain his precarious grip on Boston proper, much less mount another offensive effort outside the city. Moreover, a previously supposed cowardly and inept band of farmers had proven them- selves ready, willing, and able to stand up to the world's finest army in a traditional set battle for which the British excelled, with the vast majority of the rascals escaping as if naughty hooligans running from a mischievous deed. No longer could King George, his ministry, and Parliament, explain the situation as merely a case of civil unrest needing simple increases in oversight and discipline, but rather now was regarded as rather an unbridled violent rebellion requiring a substantial military response.

For their part, the collective provincial militia had lost about a quarter of the British numbers as well as the Charlestown peninsula itself, including the charred remains of its formerly pristine lower village. One of the fallen was the beloved Doctor Joseph Warren, leading Boston citizen eclipsed only in patriotic standing by Samuel Adams and John Hancock. In contrast to the British *"victory"* the militia *defeat* would boost morale and validate their effort as they set about to construct defensive works on the land surrounding Boston to press their advantage in the form of a siege. From the Massachusetts perspective they had driven home the point that they were willing and capable of fighting for their rights as freeborn Englishmen even against their own tyrannical government and they fully expected this action would go far toward convincing King George to restore or otherwise grant them autonomous governance. In this line of thinking they could not have been more misinformed, misgiven, and generally erroneous than even the king himself.

But while Bunker Hill would change much strategically, geographically it changed virtually nothing. Gage and his forces remained bottled up in their micro kingdom of Boston to which they could now add the remnants of the Charlestown isthmus across the harbor, which they fortified with vigor. With logistic support from the hinterland completely cut off the British relied solely on their shipping, which landed all too infrequently, rendering never more than a three-week supply of barely edible food. Not a tree remained in the city as the army burned nearly all the wood they could find, including even piers and houses belonging to Loyalists. The army drilled on the Common as usual, always with a wary eye across the river, as their numbers increasingly dwindled from disease that took hold from the unsanitary environment with as many as dozens a day dying from smallpox. All the while a steady caravan of civilians streamed in from across the neck, each with a story more horrible than the previous, having been driven from their homes by lifelong neighbors now turned into an angry mob of looters and murderers stripping them of every worldly possession and dignity for nothing more than the continued support of their king and government. With resources already strained to the limit, General Gage nevertheless graciously welcomed every one of them. This military and humanitarian stalemate hardened itself in place throughout the summer like a newly made clay pot drying in the sun surrounded by an angry horde that waited to smash it to pieces the moment the chance appeared.

Earlier in May 1775, the colonials had called their second Continental Congress which, like the first, convened in Philadelphia with representation by twelve provinces, lacking again only Georgia. Prompted by the actions on the road to Concord the month before in April, it seemed the delegates were of unanimous mind that preparation for armed resistance was the obvious prudent and unavoidable course of action. However, they sharply disagreed on the aim of such initiative, with the conservative majority from the southern and middle colonies favoring a political settlement on American terms, meaning continued loyalty to the king but complete autonomy from Parliament. The small but determined minority from New England, chiefly radically liberal Massachusetts, continued to argue unsuccessfully for complete independence. New York, Pennsylvania, and South Carolina, in particular, maintained deeply rooted economic ties with Britain that they were loath to disturb, much less discard.

Enter George Washington. The son of a respected Virginia planter, his father had died when he was but ten years old, leaving him and his half-brother, Lawrence – older by fourteen years – to care for the modest estate of 4,000 acres. Self-educated, Washington apprenticed as a teen in land surveying, served as an officer in the Virginia militia, and married into money at age 26. Endlessly ambitious, at times impetuous and courageous to a fault, it could be argued that five years earlier in 1754 he had personally planted the seeds of the coming Franco-British conflict by badly botching his leadership of an expedition to oust the French from the *Ohio Country* in western Pennsylvania. He later served with distinction during the French and Indian War as part of the Virginia militia under General Edward Braddock during an Indian massacre of British forces at Monongahela, Pennsylvania. Having subsequently been refused a commission in the British Army, a slight he never forgot, he nonetheless grew into a provincial leadership role and served as a Virginia delegate to the Continental Congress, along with Thomas Jefferson and Patrick Henry. A masterful horseman, avid hunter, and devout member of the Anglican Church, he was every bit the Virginia colonial version of an English country gentlemen that sought to surround himself with the finer things in life. Fully aware of the stakes at the Second Continental Congress, he purposely attended in his militia uniform and on June 17th, ironically the very day of the clash at Charlestown, was unanimously elected as the commander-in-chief of the newly authorized *Continental Army,* currently comprised of the various militias ensconced outside Boston.

With a seeming split personality this Congress authorized raising such an army from all the colonial provinces while simultaneously drafting a petition to King George pledging their loyalty and explaining their actions as British citizens. The *Olive Branch Petition,* as it became known, was an attempt to avoid further military escalation and bloodshed as the conservative majority of Congress maintained the belief that their king would consider the prior actions at Concord and then Charlestown in a positive light as validation of their right to autonomy. Penned initially by Thomas Jefferson, whose draft was considered too inflammatory, the final version was written by John Dickinson – a staunch believer in British reconciliation – and adopted by Congress in early July just as newly-commissioned General Washington arrived on the outskirts of Boston to assume command of the military effort. As the radical liberal minority fumed in frustration at their naïve moderate colleagues, they understood the greater necessity of maintaining a unified approach and had acquiesced to supporting the petition as had the moderates to authorizing an army.

Following close on the heels of the news of the British disaster at Charlestown, the Olive Branch Petition was delivered in late August to Lord Dartmouth and King George, the latter of whom refused to even read it. The king had, in fact, already decided his position a week prior, issuing a *Proclamation of Rebellion,* which stated that elements of the colonies were in an *open and avowed rebellion*. He further added to this stance in late October, giving a speech in Parliament explaining that the rebellion was driven by a *desperate conspiracy* of insincere leaders who sought independence, not reconciliation, which would necessitate increased military efforts to include *offers of foreign assistance* to prosecute a military solution. The Congress issued a response to London in early December reiterating their continued loyalty to the king and maintaining their desire to avoid the calamities of a civil war but also insisting on their right to autonomy as British subjects to include armed resistance as necessary. This exchange served to highlight the continued folly of the colonial southern and mid-coast moderate majority who, much like their obstinate king, were ill-equipped to view reality through anything other than their own foggy lens.

Washington began his summer mission in Boston having told his wife, Martha, to expect him home by autumn. In fact, no one on the colonial side, particularly those in Massachusetts, anticipated that the standoff would last very long. The new commander-in-chief took control of a rag-tag patchwork of mainly Massachusetts as well as other New England militias that had no command structure, no common understanding of coordination, no common uniforms, no common weaponry, no common tactics, no common training, little tenting, few cannon, and scant gunpowder. The only fabric that knitted these units together was their distaste for the mistreatment they had suffered under King George, his ministry, Parliament, and their ardent desire to resist being further abused. The first task for Washington was to count his forces, which took eight days and revealed approximately 17,000 men, of which 3,000 were unfit or absent. This compared with roughly 7,000 redcoats, about half the provincial numbers, bottled up in Boston and Charlestown. Publicly, Washington praised the New England men for their willing service but privately he detested them for their lack of professionalism, slovenly manners, and practice of electing their officers, largely unqualified with an annoying and self-defeating penchant to placate their men, not lead them.

Washington soon called a council with his senior staff to determine the feasibility of an attack on Boston. Included in this body were subordinate local military officers from Massachusetts who had acquiesced to Washington's leadership as well as his second-in-command, Major General Charles Lee, a former lieutenant colonel in the British Army generally regarded as having the finest military mind in the provinces. There were some in Congress who had preferred Lee to head the fledgling military effort, as he possessed the extensive large operational experience that Washington did not. But with unity of purpose the prime colonial objective, the political practicality of maintaining a centrally located Virginian in charge along with Washington's own impeccable reputation had rendered such a compromise palatable to all – or at least palatable enough. As was his aggressive nature, Washington wanted to attack the British quickly in order to finish what had been started. Having no navy with which to threaten the harbor with cannon and otherwise land troops from the sea, such an attack would have involved an amphibious operation from their land positions using makeshift barges to cross the tidal marshes of the Back Bay directly into the teeth of the most fortified enemy positions and would depend on a small window of opportunity only at or near high tide. This idea was unanimously voted down as excessively ambitious and logistically complicated with a strong chance of the invading force becoming bogged down in the mud and helplessly slaughtered by British artillery, a risk they could ill afford to take. Distasteful as it was to sit on his hands, Washington nonetheless accepted this verdict. With the British in Boston too weak to break out and the continental forces lacking the proper assets to break in, the situation settled into a protracted and monotonous stalemate as militia units from provinces below New England began to arrive. Washington did not make it home to Virginia in the fall.

For the remainder of 1775, the British government, for their part, did not remain idle as it wrestled with a new paradigm it had never imagined possible. King George moved to make examples of weaklings as he sacked all who he blamed as too conciliatory and ineffective. General Gage, just as he had imagined, was recalled to London in favor of his second-in-command, General Howe, who assumed duties as Commander-in-Chief of North America. Gage, the undisputed expert in American affairs, had undoubtedly sealed his fate when he initially accepted the job under the auspices of having sufficient forces to do the king's bidding. Once in place he could neither protest for additional troops nor effectively employ the number he had. In the end he had followed the path of least resistance by doing what he was told although he knew it to be folly, a decision that ultimately cost him his job and reputation.

General William Howe's older brother, Admiral Richard Howe, replaced the inept and corrupt Admiral Graves as head of the navy in North America, a signal that King George now intended to install the strongest team possible. The Howes were peers of the king and had played with him as children and, although ardent Whigs, were considered two of the finest military officers England possessed. Their oldest brother, Brigadier General George Augustus Viscount Howe, beloved by all in the American colonies, had died a hero at the Battle of Ticonderoga during the French and Indian War. First Minister Lord North also replaced the American Secretary, Lord Dartmouth, with Lord George Germaine, a conservative hardliner much approved by the king. In keeping with the general political trend, North effectively doubled down on blindly following the king's lead rather than taking an opportunity to pause for objective strategic reflection.

The grand victory of the Seven Year's War less than a generation earlier could be directly attributed to then First Minister William Pitt, an incredibly capable leader with a firm understanding of the relationship between the government, the military, and the people. Respected, influential, and enlightened, the free-thinking Pitt was a leading Whig more interested in what he considered best for his country rather than his own personal gain – just the sort of man King George loathed. The king and Pitt had clashed almost immediately upon the young king's assumption of the throne such that the new monarch took immediate steps to marginalize him. Eventually installing the uninspiring and easily manipulated Lord North as First Minister, it was easy for the king to further populate his ministry with those who would keep their proper place and not oppose him. In Lord Germaine, the king received not just a vassal but a soulmate, as the new American Secretary chomped at the bit to ram fire and brimstone policies through Parliament with nary a thought of anything less than a good lashing for the American colonies.

On the heels of the king's October rebuke in Parliament that body, even more hawkish than ever, issued in December the *Prohibitory Act* that disallowed trade with America and authorized the British Navy to seize provincial shipping abroad – effectively declaring *war* now on the whole of the colonies and not just Massachusetts. With the context of the colonial struggle now transformed from a geographically limited civil uprising to a vastly broader operational undertaking, the strategic value of Boston also changed to an expendable asset of limited military worth. Accordingly, General Howe began to make plans for an eventual evacuation.

While the moral victory at Charlestown emboldened Congress into believing they were worthy to oppose Great Britain on a more strategic level, a practical problem to such ambitions was Canada, where Britain kept significant forces. What Congress had to fear, and rightly so, was a movement from the British along the St. Lawrence Seaway down through Lake Champlain into New York to capture and control the Hudson River in concert with a sea-borne invasion of New York Harbor itself. Possession of America's largest logistical center would set the table for British reach of the entire Atlantic seaboard to facilitate blockades and isolation, most importantly of New England. Increasingly anxious over the stagnant situation in Boston and given the threat in Canada, General Washington undertook what assertive action he could and, in the autumn of 1775, sent two land forces north – one up the Hudson through Lake Champlain and the other through the Massachusetts district of Maine wilderness under Colonel Benedict Arnold. Their plan was to attack the city of Quebec from two sides and capture the fortress commanded by General Guy Carleton before it could be further reinforced, thus neutralizing the British threat in the north. For a variety of reasons, not the least of which was poor planning, this endeavor failed miserably as the colonial forces found themselves out-led by Carleton, out-fought by the British professionals, and out-lasted by the Canadian winter. What was left of the invaders drifted back south over the winter like scattered ashes in the north wind. For his troubles Benedict Arnold received a severe leg wound that would hobble him for the rest of his life.

The failed campaign in Canada proved not only a blow to the fledgling Continental Army but also to the moderate majority in Congress that continued to promote the likelihood of British capitulation for American autonomy. A decisive victory at Quebec might very well have cemented the colonial political momentum for those moderates as well as provided impetus for intervention by France, who watched with interest from the shadows like a hungry wolf, salivating at the prospect of a hatchling America no longer under the protective wing of Mother England. As far as the French were concerned, the contest for expansion into North America was not over and they still had a score to settle with the British. But they were not ready to reenter that arena unless and until convinced that the colonies could sustain themselves politically and militarily to a point at which few yet believed possible.

Until 1776, the ideological argument for the soul of America was confined largely to those representatives to Congress and the educated elite from their respective provincial assemblies. Suddenly, out of nowhere, emerged a man that with pen and ink succeeded to galvanize the will of the common people more than any appointed official or military victory could have. Thomas Paine was a transplanted Englishman who had been an utter failure at everything he had ever tried, lacking somehow the responsibility and discipline for respectable employment. Along the spectrum of political leanings, he edged so far to the end of democratic idealism that any further movement may have caused him to disappear from the universe altogether. He authored a pamphlet called *Common Sense* that urged the colonies to declare complete independence, arguing that the key to America's shackles and chains lay not with a far-removed villainous king and his minions but rather with the very idea of the monarchy itself – an unnatural and abhorrent abomination of nature. Striking a deep chord in thoroughly Protestant America, he compared the concept of a monarchy to that of the papacy, which every God-fearing colonial fundamentally believed was directly responsible for the wars, government abuses and all other political pestilence that existed in Europe, if not the entire world. As this suddenly obvious truth spread across the colonies like an out-of-control fire, it burned away at the platform upon which stood the colonial moderates' argument of conciliatory resolution with their king.

But if Congress and the Continental Army had bungled away opportunities for a decisive resolution, so had the British. In the winter months of 1776, Howe sent his subordinate, General Clinton, recently arrived with him less than a year prior, down the Atlantic coast from Boston with a small armada of five newly arrived Irish regiments totaling 1,500 soldiers. Bolstered by a belief that hordes of Loyalist support awaited such an initiative, the aim was to secure the southern colonies with a relatively easy and low-risk effort. With an eye toward the fortified city of Charleston, South Carolina – then known as *Charles Towne* – Clinton attempted an assault on the outer defenses at Sullivan's Island, where he was promptly beaten back due to poor intelligence and stiff resistance by rebel militia that just weeks earlier had snuffed out the local Loyalist military capability.

Earlier, in May 1775, on the heels of Lexington-Concord and prior to the failed expedition to Canada, Colonel Benedict Arnold with a small force of New England militia to include Ethan Allen and his *Green Mountain Boys* from the district of Vermont managed to capture Fort Ticonderoga on Lake Champlain in the upper New York province. Originally built by the French, the fort stood lightly guarded by the British, who surrendered without a fight. The fort contained roughly 60 tons of heavy cannon and artillery, which later that winter an industrious supply train led by former Boston bookseller Colonel Henry Know dragged nearly 300 miles through the snow to Cambridge. In early March 1776, Washington's army entrenched themselves and the guns overnight atop Dorchester Heights, which overlooked Boston to the southwest much like the Charlestown Peninsula to the north. Like a recurring nightmare from the previous June, the British awoke to again find Yankee scoundrels looking down on them but this time with firepower capable of reaching into the city and harbor as well as approaching sea lanes. That General Howe had not chosen to seize that ground first, proved a point of contention among the professional officer class with many believing their leadership was interested no longer in fighting but only on planning an evacuation. Choosing not to assault the heights as he had at Bunker Hill, Howe struck a deal with Washington that would allow British forces to quit Boston without razing it if the rebels would allow them to depart unmolested. In mid-March Howe loaded every last man, woman, and child, including more than 1,000 civilian Loyalists and whatever equipment they could carry, onto warships and transports and sailed out of the harbor like a great invasion in reverse, bound for Halifax, Nova Scotia. Having occupied the city of Boston for well over than a decade, the British forces would never return.

Although the Canadian debacle in 1775 was a serious blow to the American effort to gain political leverage, the British setbacks at Charleston to the south and Boston to the north in the late winter of 1776 emboldened the Yankees once again. Early that summer, the thirteen colonies called yet another Continental Congress in Philadelphia, this time to decide on an actual *declaration of independence*, a determination previously eschewed by all provincial representatives except the radical minority bloc from Massachusetts and, to a lesser extent, greater New England. The shrewd Boston politicians, led chiefly by cousins Samuel and John Adams, had waited patiently for such an opportunity – never pushing their opinion too hard, always conciliatory, willing to listen and, most importantly, supremely confident in the knowledge that they were ideologically correct and that in time the whole of Congress would ultimately come their way. Now, the whole of the delegation had arrived at a difficult impasse in large part of their own making. Without control of Canada, they could not hope to force King George and Parliament to capitulate on their terms of autonomy. Without independence they could not impress France – a suitor born in Hell if there ever was one – to openly render ample quantities of political and military assistance, lacking which their collective survival would be doubtful. Driven by *Common Sense* and the liberal movement's newfound popular fervor as well as the lure of France's potential deep pockets, the dominant position of the conservative majority rapidly eroded. Backed into a corner by the very providence they prayed to, what remained of the moderate coalition swallowed their better judgment and threw in their lot with the democratic radicals by declaring *independence* in a unanimous vote. As viewed by the gob-smacked British, such an irrational action by their offspring seemed, among other things, *amusing, as* they could find no logical explanation for a people willing to cast away the protection of the world's mightiest empire in the name of *abuse* in favor of courting a Catholic nation of pope-mongers who had perfected that concept.

As the Continental Congress passed the point of no return by declaring independence, so too did the British take a fateful leap of faith by no longer considering the colonials across the Atlantic as merely misguided brethren but rather proper foreign *enemies* and thus began to execute their new American strategy accordingly. Simultaneously, as if in a strangely choreographed play, just as Congress finished, signed, and distributed its *Declaration of Independence* in Philadelphia and beyond in early July 1776, the initial wave of a massive British armada arrived by sea in New York Harbor and began to entrench itself on Staten Island. Over the summer the influx did not cease as the mouth of the Hudson resembled a forest of masts, and by the middle of August the king's troops numbered 32,000, including 8,000 mercenary *Hessians*.

The inclusion of the latter Germanic *barbarians* deeply troubled the colonials regardless of their loyalty as it was criminal enough for King George to make war using his own professional soldiers, but wholly unthinkable that he would leverage his still-obvious ties with the region of Hesse-Cassel to hire savage thugs known explicitly for their cruelty and inhumanity.

Once Howe had evacuated Boston in March, General Washington quickly shifted his operations to New York as that strategic seaport represented the next logical location for a British reappearance, this time in greater force. But here Washington had a massive problem with the situation quite different from that of Boston. Initially staging his forces around the village at the lower end of York Island he needed to defend an area surrounded by water without the benefit of any armed vessels against a foe with the most powerful navy in the world. The new colonial commander-in-chief also begged Congress to raise a professional army, as he deeply mistrusted militias as nothing better than *destructive, expensive, and disorderly mobs*. Washington's gentile Virginia upbringing and his experience in the French and Indian War informed him beyond a doubt, much as they had the British, that reliance on militias, particularly those from New England, where an idealistic and independent bent made obedience to orders optional, would render military operations impossible on the scale now required. Congress countered, based on the recent successes in Massachusetts and South Carolina, that militias had proven to be as viable as they were cost effective. In addition, the members of Congress harbored a deep-seated distrust of standing armies, even an American one, and therefore disregarded Washington's professional assessment by flatly refusing his request.

From the beginning Washington struggled to place his forces in such a way as to maximize their effectiveness. To begin with, although he knew where Howe had staged – just several miles south on Staten Island – he could not be sure where the inevitable attack would come as the British possession of a navy provided so many options. Militias from both north and south streamed in and out of their own accord, continually rendering an inexact number with which to work, estimated at no more than 20,000 troops, a force substantially smaller than that of Howe. In the end, in opposition to standard military convention, Washington divided his forces roughly in half, leaving one group to fortify the main population center of lower York Island and placing the other across the East River to entrench itself at Brooklyn to defend against what he and his staff considered the most probable British landing.

Upon arriving on scene earlier that summer in grand fashion, General Howe did what he would soon become famous for in the American theater – *nothing*. Having clear numerical superiority with uncontested control of the waterways, he enjoyed the distinct advantage of choosing the time and place of the inevitable engagement. Inexplicably he seemed reluctant to commit his forces, thus allowing Washington additional time to organize and prepare a defensive posture. Some later supposed Howe's lethargy a product of his family's staunch Whig principles with a trickle-down effect of granting leniency to his American brethren, whom he certainly did not respect but may have pitied. This was, in fact, a sentiment not uncommon among the senior British military gentry.

Finally in late August, Howe put roughly half his troops ashore below Brooklyn as expected at *Gravesend Bay* on Long Island with Washington's forces entrenched just to the north along the steeply wooded *Heights of Gowan*. After another delay of nearly a week Howe put those forces in motion using artillery to decoy an attack along the coast and fast-moving light infantry to exploit a carelessly unguarded gap at *Jamaica Pass* to the east. With Washington's main defenses now outflanked and panicked, the British poured in behind and with professional precision decimated the colonial militias, a good number of whom discarded their arms and ran, pushing the chaotic and tattered provincial horde west into Brooklyn village by day's end, trapped with their backs to the East River. Here Howe inexplicably paused again, allowing Washington to escape in two days' time by rushing what remained of his broken force back across the river to York Island under cover of a sudden and fortuitous storm, thus saving the entire American cause from obliteration.

With General Howe just across the East River in Brooklyn and his brother, the admiral, in complete control of the entire harbor and adjacent waterways, Washington had no choice but to abandon his position on lower York Island or be crushed in a vice. Having made this decision, Washington fully intended to burn the lower village to the ground in a standard military measure to deny the enemy its comforts. Although a squeamish Congress forbade such action, rebel sympathizers, mostly from Connecticut, took on the project themselves, destroying about a third of the town before being caught and hanged by the mainly Loyalist populace. With shooting flames in their wake and militia deserting in droves, the remnants of the rebel army scurried north as quickly as they could up the western side of the island along the Hudson River. As was now his established pattern, once across the island, Howe less than vigorously drove his troops in pursuit, allowing the bulk of the rebels to extricate themselves again. For the next two months the British chased Washington and his army in a cat-and-mouse game through the Westchester area on the mainland north of York Island before finally cornering them in mid-November back on the island at *Fort Washington* located on the northwestern heights along the Hudson. Thinking they possessed the advantage of making a fortified defensive stand the Continentals were instead embarrassingly routed with a loss of not only 3,000 men but also a vast majority of stores and ammunition. General Washington again managed a narrow escape, this time across the river into New Jersey with not so much of an army as a dwindling force of shell-shocked and disorganized stragglers. Leaving his subordinates Generals William Heath and Charles Lee to the north with several thousand men, Washington scurried south through New Jersey with about 3,000 troops, his main objective to simply survive by avoiding a major confrontation with the British.

Pursued by General Cornwallis and 4,000 redcoats that almost managed to catch him, Washington escaped across the Delaware

River near Trenton in the nick of time, taking all available boats with him. Here the British turned back, content now in early December to organize themselves for the winter, mainly in New York Harbor, while leaving the Hessians to hold down the east side of the Delaware River. In an act of true desperation with his army about to evaporate due to expiring militia enlistments, Washington returned across the icy tributary during a storm in the early hours of Christmas morning in a surprise attack on the Hessians at their outpost at Trenton – still drunk from festivities the night before. General Cornwallis raced from New York to engage him as the forces skirmished at Princeton before the Americans once again managed to escape intact back across the Delaware. As the new year began, both sides retreated for good to their respective winter quarters, the British in New York Harbor, and the Americans about 30 miles to the northwest in the scraggy foothills of Morristown, New Jersey. From this position Washington could both monitor Howe and move farther away if necessary.

It could not be said that the year 1776 ended, just six months after boldly declaring independence, as Congress had intended or desired. The path to American independence directly depended on a viable military capability with which to pressure or otherwise influence the British government. With the war effort having gone nearly as poorly as possible, in the eyes of many, Washington had proven himself a questionable commander-in-chief with his personal leadership and commitment undisputed but his operational acumen severely in doubt. Whispers began to circulate calling for replacement by others thought more capable and seasoned, chiefly his subordinates, Major Generals Lee and Horatio Gates, the latter also a former British Army Officer. Both quietly worked behind the scenes to encourage such dialogue. The militia had proven themselves worthy to stand up to the British Army in limited, tactical engagements but totally incapable of dealing with the type of large-scale pitched battles in which the professionals excelled. The small victory at Trenton and credible action at Princeton came not a moment too soon, inconsequential on anything greater than the tactical level yet enough to spur morale and provide an emotional boost as the tourniquet Washington needed to keep his army from bleeding to death, at least for the winter – in that respect it had been strategic. Against every instinct he possessed, Washington was not in position to engage the British on their terms in open traditional warfare and, at least for the foreseeable future, his task was not to win giant battles as much as it was simply not to lose them, or more accurately stated, to be judicious to even attempt them. All hope for independence lay solely on Washington's ability to keep his army intact and as the new year turned to 1777, it was barely that.

Fortunately for Congress, the fumbling of their Continental Army had been counter-balanced by the lassitude of General Howe, who had fought as if with one hand tied behind his back; content to severely wound his ragtag colonial opposition but stopping short of knocking it out. In direct conflict to the will of hardline Lord Germaine, the Howe brothers seemingly preferred to conduct operations against their American brethren in a way that left room for unwanted political compromise instead of a fight to their complete demise. As 1777 began, with the British Army nestled comfortably in New York Harbor and the tattered refuse of the stubborn Americans just out of reach to the north in Morristown, both sides rested for what they expected to be a decisive campaign when the weather warmed again.

* * *

YORK ISLAND, NEW YORK, APRIL 1777

"Halliday! Wake up, lad!"

Jack felt an all-too-familiar hand on the shoulder jostle him awake as he lay on a makeshift bed of boards, blanket, and straw. He sat up as Sergeant Searles looked him in the eye before quickly moving to the next sleeping soldier.

"Get up, lad – we've work to do. Take your kit and musket, and form with the company outside."

"What is it this time, sergeant?" Percy murmured.

"What does it matter, private!" the sergeant snapped with an edge uncharacteristic even for this early hour. "Just move!"

Jack dressed quickly in the dimly lit warehouse, then formed with the remainder of the company outside. He watched and waited in silence as the quartermasters issued rations and ammunition, enough for one day. Still well before sunrise on a crisp spring morning, the 4th Lights formed in a double column and started a brisk march out of York village, headed north along the west highway that paralleled the Hudson River. Percy and Jack exchanged curious glances, as it had not been long since they had traveled this exact route with their slovenly commander who now rode ahead of the column on a handsome, recently purchased white stallion.

They marched for more than two hours without pausing until reaching the general vicinity of the captain's recent dinner engagement. Here they left the main road and turned inland down a long driveway that ended at a wealthy estate even larger and more handsome than the previous grounds Jack and Percy had seen with fields for crops and buildings so numerous that it resembled a village in and of itself. The column halted briefly before being reformed in a small field surrounded by majestic maple trees in front of the main three-story house with six chimneys; the house was immaculately painted rusty yellow with black trim and shutters. The soldiers looked anxiously in the distance in the ever-increasing predawn light for some semblance of an enemy. Finding none, their attention soon turned toward Captain Garthwaite, who approached the main entrance on his horse, wearing a hat fashioned out of raccoon fur, a style common to certain Indian tribes and now curiously popular among aristocratic circles. From the front door emerged three young women dressed as if attending an important social engagement and behind them two older couples attired in similar fashion. The handsome captain dismounted and falling to one knee, removed his furry headpiece and bowed deeply for several seconds. As the girls giggled and the couples clapped, the captain sprang to his feet and jumped back on his horse, wheeling in circles with his sword drawn. Waving the saber high above his head he galloped back toward the soldiers, whooping a war cry of some indistinguishable variety.

As sunlight began to peek above the trees Sergeant Searles stood nearby with his fists clenched and jaw tightened, his normally rigid posture even more so stiff that he seemed as tight as an archer's drawn bow, ready to release an arrow. As the captain arrived the sergeant barked the all too familiar orders that set the company in motion on a series of parade drills that crisscrossed the field in precision battleground movements. This carried on for well more than an hour as the 4th Lights fought a mock engagement against an invisible foe with the spectators watching from the side on what looked to be a recently built set of small viewing stands. As the soldiers traversed the makeshift parade grounds, they could see at one end of the field a line of a dozen or so *Yankee militia* dummies mounted on wooden crosses and stuffed with hay. Their dress was a mixture of old coats and blankets with a semblance of muskets crudely carved from branches placed leaning at their sides. Their heads had been sewn on with angry faces painted and adorned with an array of floppy farmer's hats. The exercise culminated with the *honor* of a bayonet charge awarded to Jack's squad to run through the dastardly villains after which the captain, with the loudest of *huzzahs,* ran down the entire line on his stallion and lopped off their heads with his sword. The captain continued his gait to face the viewing stands where he again wheeled the horse in circles now up on its hind legs and, with saber still drawn flashing high in the air, gave one last war cry. He then galloped back toward the men at which time the company reformed back into a column, promptly marching off the field and back down the drive leading toward the main road.

Jack looked at Percy who returned his glance with a bemused expression as the captain pranced by on his horse toward the front, still adorned in his raccoon cap.

"Well done, sergeant!" the captain called over to Sergeant Searles, who strode down the column on the opposite side. "Give the men an extra ten minutes of sleep tomorrow!"

"Yes, sir," the sergeant growled in reply, his jaw tightening like a vice. "Private Perkins!" he continued as the captain moved from ear shot. "Do you have a complaint you want to share with us?"

Jack kept his eyes fixed on the man's back in front of him as the steam from the sergeant's breath wafted past.

"No, sergeant!" Percy barked.

"Too bad," the sergeant answered with his nose practically pressing into Percy's face, "because I'm looking for someone that does."

10

I will let loose the dogs of Hell
Ten thousand Indians, who shall yell
And foam and tear, and grin and roar,
And drench their moccasins in gore...
I swear by George and St Paul,
I will exterminate you all.

Excerpt of Proclamation by
General John Burgoyne
Ticonderoga, New York, July 4, 1777

As the armies of Generals Howe and Washington settled into their respective winter quarters, intrigue and dysfunction brewed in London – as if there were not already a plethora. Having served under General Howe in Boston and subsequently in Canada, Major General John Burgoyne had returned to London for the winter of 1777. A woman-chasing gambler and established playwright, the royal court favorite, *Gentlemen Johnny,* approached Lord Germain, Lord North, and eventually King George with his new script for success in America. The idea involved placing a force in Canada above Lake Champlain that would forge south to secure the Hudson River Valley to sever New England, the *head of the snake,* from the remaining lower colonies – a concept eerily similar to what had prompted the Continentals to move on Quebec. To the dismay but not surprise of the liberal Whigs, who considered the flamboyant Burgoyne *more sail than ballast,* the conservative hardliners, ever seeking to curry favor with the king, swallowed the idea whole. Thus, in early March 1777, Burgoyne departed England in transports stuffed with a force of 7,000 troops split roughly between British professionals and German mercenaries for an exceptionally ambitious and risky mission along a vast expanse of American wilderness. Never explicitly stated by Burgoyne but rather tacitly assumed, was the support of and coordination with Howe's forces located relatively close in New York Harbor at the bottom of the Hudson.

But as Gentlemen Johnny sailed west across the Atlantic General Howe formulated his own plan for his soon-to-be-renewed American campaign. In the traditional European understanding of the conventional rules of war, the capture of an enemy's capital city spelled doom for that foe. However, a far cry from an actual country but rather merely a gaggle of thirteen separate provinces that had somehow managed to follow each other in the same direction, America had no such formal seat of central government. Lacking such a prize to seize, Philadelphia was nonetheless the largest and most influential colonial population center and also where the diabolical Continental Congress sat and therefore, by default, became Howe's obvious target. With full knowledge of Burgoyne's campaign already in motion, Lord Germain approved Howe's plan to take Philadelphia, undoubtedly with the under-standing that to do so the general and his army would have to depart New York Harbor to march *away* from the Hudson River some 100 miles through treacherous New Jersey. Saddled with a prior military reputation for cowardice and intimidated by ideologically opposed and politically connected senior Whigs, particularly those of impeccable military standing such as the Howes, Germain merely *mentioned* Burgoyne's plan in corre-spondence with General Howe but never specifically *directed* him to support it. Thus, lacking clarity and direction from their

American Secretary both subordinate generals developed and executed their campaigns in isolation from each other.

Burgoyne reached Quebec via the St. Lawrence Seaway in early May with a smaller secondary force under Lieutenant Colonel Barry St. Leger landing further southwest in Lake Ontario at Oswego, New York intending to push east along the Mohawk River to where it joined the Hudson in Albany. Gentleman Johnny's command performance commenced at the top of Lake Champlain in mid-June with an army of just over 8,300, bolstered by ample artillery, contingents of Loyalist militia and about 500 Indians. The latter mix of local tribes salivated at the chance to ally themselves with the British in return for the opportunity to exact their vicious brand of retribution on the scourge of colonial frontier expansion. In addition to the already established usage of barbarous Hessians, the willingness of the British to enlist utter *savages* was not lost on colonial inhabitants of upper New York and western New England, who flocked in droves to join the fast-swelling militias intending to repulse the invaders. In addition, Burgoyne himself stoked the fire even hotter by issuing an arrogant and ill-conceived proclamation that threatened Indian retaliation on those who chose to resist him. Whereas abstract political arguments of British tyranny by leaders in faraway places along the coast may have fallen on deaf ears of those further inland, the terror of savage Indians certainly did not, as for nearly two centuries there had existed no greater menace to their individual, family, and community security. If any provincials in Burgoyne's path still needed motivation to resist his aggression, Gentlemen Johnny had unwittingly supplied a large helping.

After navigating southward over Lake Champlain Burgoyne's heavily burdened force began to chop its way through the dense forest of upper New York. Meanwhile, General Howe loaded the bulk of his troops in lower New York onto navy transports and sailed south, leaving his second-in-command, General Clinton, with a smaller fraction to hold the environs of the harbor. Choosing the longer but least opposed route by sea to Philadelphia, Howe did not bother to report this change of plan to Germain before departure, having recently conceived of it due to a lack of requested reinforcements with which he felt necessary to travel over land through volatile New Jersey.

Burgoyne initially found success in upper New York, as his army recaptured Fort Ticonderoga and sent the American garrison led by the bellicose and incompetent commander, Major General Philip Schuyler, fleeing into the wilderness. Burgoyne reached the Hudson River in late July with the idea to drive further south to Albany, approximately 100 miles below his logistic center now established at Crown Point near Ticonderoga. But the more progress his army made, the longer and thinner his logistic line stretched until ultimately, the dense woods, incessant partisan ambushes and the capriciousness of his Indian allies began to take their toll. In truth, sensitive to the western aversion to Indian atrocities and in complete contrast to what he had promised both sides, Burgoyne had purposely held his indigenous forces in check even as local colonial leadership fabricated propaganda to the contrary. Prevented from conducting warfare and butchering as they saw fit, the native warriors began to skulk away in disappointment and disgust. By mid-August, with supplies and food rations dwindling, Burgoyne dispatched a force of 600 Hessians on a foraging mission near Bennington in New York's Vermont district. This scavenging party, along with a second Hessian unit sent to reinforce it, were both shot to pieces by 2,000 New England militia led by General John Stark and his New Hampshire volunteers – the same unit that had held the makeshift wall on the beach at Charlestown two years earlier. Burgoyne soon also learned that St. Leger would not be joining him, having quit his expedition from Oswego. Battered, disheartened, and over-extended, but still unwilling to turn back, Burgoyne continued to drive for Albany in a production that was at this point not going according to script.

Meanwhile to the south, General Howe landed in Maryland in late August at the top of Chesapeake Bay and proceeded north overland toward Philadelphia. Not having previously known his enemy's intentions, Washington hurried his rag-tag army of approximately 11,000 south from New Jersey to oppose the British advance, much *encouraged* by a panicked Congress. Over numerous engagements, Washington proved no match for Howe as even though the continentals fought with honor and tenacity, they were constantly out positioned by the more professional British for whom *operational maneuver* of large forces was second nature. Purposely avoiding direct pitched battles Washington did not intend to sacrifice his army, and along with it the entire cause, for the sake of one city – although he nearly did so unwittingly on several occasions – but always somehow managed to avoid that decisive crushing blow that would have done him in. Howe and his army took possession of Philadelphia in late September, marching into the open arms of many Loyalists and right on the heels of a desperate Congress that had fled only scant hours before. Badly bruised but still not beaten, Washington had little choice but to situate himself somewhere out of easy reach of the British but close enough to watch them, choosing the protective hills of Valley Forge about eighteen miles to the northwest.

On September 18th, as Howe was positioning himself to capture the de facto colonial capital, Burgoyne was intercepted by a larger force of 12,000 Continentals at Bemis Heights near Saratoga led by Major General Horatio Gates, who had replaced Schuyler. Gates' subordinate, Benedict Arnold, had been promoted to Brigadier General for his actions in Quebec. Much detested by Gates, Arnold's brilliant tactical leadership produced a rout of the British and again at the second battle on October 7th with the American force now swelled to 20,000. But Arnold was once again severely wounded in the same leg as before and, in addition, an infuriated Gates dismissed him from command for insubordination. Acting on increasingly desperate pleas of help from Burgoyne, General Clinton feigned an attempt at reinforcement by sending a force of 7,000 men north from lower New York but ultimately recalled them as he realized the impending debacle on which he did not want his fingerprints. Trapped, decimated, and no longer having the resources to defend himself in hostile territory, the curtain came down on Gentleman Johnny's drama, as he surrendered to the Americans on October 17th.

As Burgoyne's campaign ground to a halt in upper New York and with Howe comfortably ensconced in Philadelphia, Benjamin Franklin continued his diplomatic mission in Paris to lobby the French government to join the war on the American side. Arriving late in 1776, Franklin had been so well-received as to enjoy national celebrity status with full access to government officials. *Le sage de Boston* proved intriguing; besides satisfying the aristocracy's eccentric curiosity with Franklin's purposeful plainness, the French had a bone to pick with the British, a bone so large that it threatened to choke them.

Since their resounding defeat in the Seven Years War the French government had spent the last decade and a half retooling and rebuilding its military, particularly the navy, in preparation for what they viewed as the inevitable chance to reengage their rivals – the only real question being *when*. King Louis XVI and his Foreign Minister, Charles Gravier comte de Vergennes, had listened to the odd but persuasive American but, so far, saw fit to only give him lip service and to his colonial brethren a few crumbs of token covert logistic support, as France could not take the risk to enter such a conflict with a junior partner not capable of winning more than minor skirmishes.

But after the news of Burgoyne's defeat at Saratoga reached Paris in December 1777, Vergennes spent the dawn of 1778 recalculating the American situation. Due to a combined assessment of France's increased military strength, an observed pattern of British bungling, and a reasonable belief that Spain would assist; he drew a new conclusion that now considered the embattled American Colonies a risk worth taking. Sensing a Franco-American partnership in the making, London now offered a deal to Congress similar to what the colonies had originally proposed in 1775, with full autonomy except for continued loyalty to the king. This overture proved too little too late as Congress would now settle for nothing less than complete independence even if they had to sell their souls to the sordid French. In early February a commission led by Franklin received the signature of King Louis XVI for separate treaties of *friendship and commerce*, and *alliance*, both of which Congress ratified in May. With France having not only recognized America as an independent entity but, even worse, entered into a partnership, the British had no choice but to declare war on their sworn enemies. The conflict was no longer a domestic issue.

For Great Britain, the entry of France into the fray was nothing less than a disaster for which they had only themselves to blame. A good and decent man in almost every respect but blindly obstinate to a fault, King George, in his noble quest to rescue England by restoring the monarchy to its primacy, had unwittingly handicapped his government by populating it with those whose chief ability was doing what they were told. Long gone were the spirited debates and healthy exchange of opposing ideas that had formerly existed under William Pitt's tenure as First Minister. When the king wanted his ministry's opinion, he would provide it to them and the monarch now reaped the harvest of that planting. The king, his ministry, and the majority of Parliament had never understood why America had chosen a path of armed rebellion. How could a tiny minority of misguided hotheads lead a more rationale majority by the nose into war against its parent, the greatest society in the history of the world? Where were the multitudes of Loyalists that should be flocking to the aid of the king's troops? What had started three years ago as an isolated, minor civil insurrection with the assumption of a quick conclusion, had now grown in size and scope to what could never have been imagined, much less predicted, and with no end in sight. Nevertheless, the good king and his minions could not be bothered to rethink their hardened analysis that the Americans were no more than disobedient provincial ingrates for whom the proper course of action mandated a heavy-handed policy of military retribution – the very fuel that stoked the fire.

If the good king and his followers had bothered to learn, they would have understood that what the Americans wanted was what they had always enjoyed from the beginning of their colonization – what they had already been provided by their government that now wanted to take it away – the rights and ability to govern themselves at the local levels as free Englishmen. But the abusive overreach from London, the incessant taxes, the introduction of standing troops, and the constant erosion of self-government had revealed a tyrannical parent that threatened to cast an egalitarian middle-class into the same subjugated abyss that defined the population of other British colonies such as Ireland and even in England itself. To quell the American riot, King George had advocated liberal use of the proverbial *stick* without an accompanying *carrot* and, in doing so, had pushed away droves that might otherwise have rallied to his side or at least remained neutral, the very multitudes that the Crown assumed to be waiting in the wings to assist. The leading Whigs in England, effectively neutered as a political bloc but not completely silenced, had continued to beat this drum even as their mantra fell on deaf ears. Well-meaning to a fault but stubborn as the day is long, King George could not begin to comprehend or even bring himself to consider that he and his bought and paid for hawks might themselves be the problem.

No longer able to afford to focus solely on their disobedient colonists, the British had no choice but to turn their attention and priorities to their mortal enemies, the French. What had started as a pinprick on Lexington Green three years before had now festered into a raging global infection that threatened amputation of the appendage if not demise of the entire body. France possessed a navy that could move men and supplies just as well as Great Britain and threaten British dominance along the eastern seaboard as well as their even more critical economic interests – the colonial *Holy of Holies* – the sugar production in the Caribbean. Even worse was the possible invasion of the England itself as too many naval assets were in service elsewhere. No more just a simple family scuffle, the struggle for the American colonies had metastasized into another world war which Britain neither needed nor wanted and was not prepared to undertake.

In light of the new French reality, the British occupation of Philadelphia suddenly became a liability as it stretched the military arm too far from its main body in New York Harbor. With both Congress and Washington's so-called *army*, dilapidated as it was, still in existence the conquest of the pseudo capital had produced nothing more than to serve as lavish winter quarters sponsored by local Loyalist gentry for General Howe and his officers. The unsupported General Burgoyne and his forces had been left to die on the vine in the New York wilderness, which had created an opening into which the French had readily stepped. The massive British effort in 1777 had not produced a victorious ending as expected but instead dug an even deeper hole. In keeping with his narrow-minded nature that rejected any possibility of objective self-evaluation the King George again needed scapegoats – and quickly.

In May 1778 King George, much as he had with General Gage, recalled General Howe to London and replaced him as commander-in chief with his immediate subordinate, General Sir Henry Clinton. With arrival of French forces imminent, Clinton's first order of business was to evacuate Philadelphia and consolidate his military in the strategically logistic stronghold of New York Harbor. Terrified, and rightfully so, that the jackals of the independence movement would emerge from the hinterland for their blood, the Philadelphia Loyalists begged Sir Henry to save them. Clinton obliged in part for humanitarian reasons as well as the strategic necessity to preserve the good will, whether actual or potential, of other Loyalists throughout the colonies. In mid-June, he loaded 3,000 civilians and their belongings onto his transports and sailed them out of the Delaware Bay, narrowly missing an arriving French fleet that would have destroyed or at least trapped them. Shortly thereafter, he started his army north by land to New York – treacherous New Jersey be damned. The campaign of 1778 had begun, no longer an effort to quell an internal uprising but now a full-fledged war with France allied with the very colony Britain had rescued from that enemy less than a generation prior.

* * *

MONMOUTH, NEW JERSEY, JUNE 28, 1778

Jack wiped his dripping face with his sleeve as he struggled to place one foot in front of the other in the long column of soldiers that moved excruciatingly forward. Still well before midday, the temperature and humidity seemed even heavier than the thick wool uniforms they wore. As the word came back to pause for rest, each man found what meager piece of shade he could and waited for the water cart to pass, canteens having run dry.

"Damn this cursed place," Percy growled as they both sat next to a bush. "Unbearable it is. Cold as the Arctic in the winter and hot as Africa in the summer. I say we just let the Yankees have it."

As the water finally arrived, Jack and Percy filled their canteens then drained them immediately in time to fill them again. Several of their number filed past them, carrying yet another victim of heat stroke by his arms and legs to be placed up ahead on the endless line of baggage carts.

Percy shot Jack a quick grin and nudged him in the ribs with an elbow. "Another lucky sot that will not have to walk to New York."

"My eyes are sweating, Perce," Jack answered as he rubbed them. "It stings to even blink."

Having departed ten days earlier, Clinton's army had now tramped to the vicinity of Monmouth Court House in northeastern New Jersey on its way northward to an embarkation point at Sandy Hook at the entrance to the Hudson River. Surrounded by tall pine barrens and navigating on roads covered with sandy dirt, the column stretched for more than two miles with a hefty baggage train of 1,500 wagons sandwiched between a contingent of 4,000 German mercenaries at the head and 6,000 British behind with a rear guard composed of grenadiers and light infantry, including the King's Own.

"Jack!" Percy suddenly exclaimed. "Did you hear that?"

Jack was already in motion struggling to stand from his stiffened position and suddenly hampered by his knee. Both he and Percy peered into the woods to the column's right as an unmistakable popping sound, faint but clear, emanated from the east.

"Muskets," Jack murmured as others around him scrambled to their feet, weapons in hand.

"HALLIDAY! PERKINS!" Sergeant Searles barked as he appeared, as usual, from nowhere, marching through the sea of red that waited for orders. "Form down yonder by that stump! I want squads to the left and right! We'll flank these partisans on either side of the column then rejoin up ahead! You know what to do!"

The arrival of the *partisans* was no surprise as the New Jersey province was famously infested with them. In fact, they had become business as usual as any British military movement more than a marching band was sooner or later met with these would-be assassins hidden in the woods. Never continental soldiers, sometimes organized militia, but more often than not simply loose bands of opportunistic democratic sympathizers with more ambition than brains and no sense of respect for proper military convention – at least the British version. By now the redcoats had finely honed their tactics to neutralize this threat by deploying light infantry as fast-moving flanking units that skirted around behind these villains as they faced forward to aim at the approaching main column.

Sergeant Searles rapidly formed several squads of six men, each led by a corporal, to fan out into the woods from various starting points on either side of the column. As the units departed, Captain Garthwaite approached on horseback from ahead to receive an explanation from the sergeant, his familiar long and crooked silhouette revealing his usual slumped and disheveled appearance. The good captain had enjoyed a jolly good frolic in Philadelphia as the Loyalist gentry had seemingly opened their doors en masse to such a dashing aristocrat. He had kept an around-the-clock social calendar, imbibing alcohol and bedding women at a frightening rate and, in fact, had managed to drag one of the choicest strumpets with him now securely ensconced somewhere inside the baggage train. Of all those reticent to leave the friendly confines of an adoring city with a seemingly limitless store of admiration to travel 100 miles overland through hostile territory crawling with murderous Yankees, Captain Garthwaite had no equal.

Jack and Percy exited the road and stepped into the woods as the fourth and fifth men respectively in their squad led by Corporal Kelly, a solid soldier that typically said little. They moved due east in a single file in a trot between the sparse thin trees across the sandy forest floor covered with pine needles. Trudging across several shallow ravines they reached the top of one, slightly winded and sweating profusely. The corporal raised his hand for the squad to halt.

"Are we well, lads?" Kelly asked as he turned to face his small column of men, each of whom nodded in the affirmative. Although musket fire could still be distinctly heard in the distance, they had yet to make contact with any partisans. "Take a drink, lads, and we'll...."

BOOM!

In an instant the entire squad launched violently backward as all six men crashed back down the ravine. With the man in front riding him like a sled Jack slid through the sand to the bottom as the entire column piled onto him like an accordion that had been squeezed and released. Jack and Percy squirmed out from under the now motionless mass as they stayed low on the ground.

"Bloody hell!" Percy cried as he knelt to brush himself off and check for injuries. "What the bloody hell was that? Are you all right, Jack?"

"I think so, Perce." Jack's right leg buckled as he tried to stand. "Damn it!"

Percy grabbed Jack by the shoulder to steady him. "What is it?"

"My knee," Jack answered angrily. "Again. Goddamn it!"

"Can you walk?"

"I bloody well have to as we're sure as hell not staying here."

Jack winced and limped as he and Percy inspected the remnants of the squad that lay in a mangled, blood-soaked pile before them. Percy rapped his knuckles on the round metal object embedded in the third man's breastplate, small enough to fit in his palm. "Three-pounder," he stated flatly. "Martin's dead."

"As are Brian and Thomas," Jack added as he surveyed the other two that had been in front, each with a fist-sized hole shot clean through their chests. "Bloody hell."

"What do we do now, Jack?" Percy asked as they watched the sixth man pick himself up and depart down the ravine in rapid fashion with nary a look back to either of them.

"Jeffrey!" Percy called after him.

"Never mind, Perce. We will stick together, us two. We need to find our way back to the column and get some help to retrieve our mates."

Locating their muskets they crawled back up the ravine on their knees and elbows, peering carefully over the edge when they reached it.

BOOM!

Another cannon shot whistled through the trees above their heads as they buried their faces in the sand.

"Bloody hell, Jack," Percy repeated. "Since when do bloody partisans have cannon?"

They peered again over the top of the ridge removing their headgear carefully to minimize their profile. About 300 yards distant stood an artillery crew busily cleaning a small cannon mounted on large wheels. Finishing their task the crew quickly readied the gun for transport as a man dressed in a faded blue uniform pointed in their general direction. From behind the field piece emerged more blue-clad men carrying muskets and heading toward the ravine.

Jack ducked his head back down. "Bloody hell, Perce," he stammered. "Damned if those are partisans! Those are bloody Continentals! We need to find the sergeant – now!"

Percy did not need more prompting as they both slid back down the ravine and ran hurriedly in the direction of their previously departed comrade, Jack wincing with every step. Using the ravine as cover, they continued for several minutes until reasonably certain of not being trailed.

"Where are we, Jack?" Percy queried as he stooped, trying to catch his breath. "Which way back to the column?"

"I think ... this way." Jack pointed, equally as winded. "Let's give it a go up here."

They climbed up the gully on their elbows and knees, peering once again from the top of the ridge. Finding nothing amiss in the sparse forest before them they scampered completely out of the crevice and pushed forward. Now out of the insulation of the ravine they could hear the once sporadic musket fire in the distance that had increased to exchanges of unit volleys and cannon – sure signs of a formal engagement.

"This way," Jack whispered as he motioned with his hand. "Toward the noise."

If Howe's conquering army had enjoyed a lavish winter with ample hospitality, Washington's forces certainly had not. At the complete other end of the spectrum the American paupers endured a tough winter in makeshift encampments complete with a stark scarcity of resources due to an almost non-existent logistic support system that had been managed – or mismanaged – by an exiled and dysfunctional Congress. But although Washington's army had barely survived their meager existence over the winter one might have said they also prospered. The defeat of Burgoyne had not only ushered in the French but also had attracted a plethora of European military officers eager to make a name for themselves. In late February there arrived Frederick William Augustus Henry Ferdinand, more commonly known as *Baron von Steuben*, a soldier of fortune of dubious background that claimed a Prussian aristocratic heritage as well as service under Frederick the Great. Although he spoke little English except for profanity, Washington had taken a liking to the rough-cut Baron and allowed him to train his motley troops in close-order drill – and train them von Steuben did.

With France now in the picture Washington had waited eagerly from his perch at Valley Forge to learn the next British move. Once the overland march back to New York became apparent the ever-offensive minded Washington could not pass on the opportunity to attack with his newly upgraded troops. Led by volunteer French nobleman Marquis de Lafayette and second in command General Charles Lee, a rebel force roughly equal to Clinton's snuck up behind the column, the British all-important rearguard, commanded by Clinton's second, Lord Charles Cornwallis. Still not possessing the capacity to oppose the British in a direct pitched battle Washington nevertheless aimed to take a chunk out of them however he could.

BOOM! BOOM! BOOM!

To Jack's left the American cannon thundered again, still out of sight but close enough for his ear drums to buckle under the discharge compression. He and Percy hit the ground on their stomachs as these salvos were answered in the distance ahead.

"That's too close," Jack stated. "We need to skirt around to the right."

The pair rose and resumed a careful trot, their heads swiveling side to side as they frantically searched the woods for the slightest hint of movement. The fighting to their left continued to intensify as cannon volleys traded back and forth in a steady barrage. They soon reached the edge of a small, square field, a couple hundred yards across, stopping just inside the tree line as they scanned out across the open knee-high grass.

"Bloody hell, Jack!" Percy exclaimed in a whisper. "What have we here?"

Jack did not answer as they both focused hard toward the center of the field where sat a crooked figure atop a white horse. It looked to be a lone British officer, stooped in the saddle, wavering back and forth as if a tree blowing in the wind.

"Bloody hell – it can't be!" Percy grabbed Jack by the elbow and shook his head. "Is it?"

Jack peered hard across the field as he nodded. "It is."

"Bloody Scarecrow! What the Christ is he doing?" Percy asked. "Just out there all by himself. Is he hurt?"

"Can't tell. But he'll get his fool head blown off if he stays there."

They scanned the field again but could see no one else.

"We can't leave him out there," Jack continued as he turned to Percy. "We need to get him."

"What?" Percy returned Jack's serious expression with a look of utter astonishment. "You're not serious?"

"We cannot just leave him there, Perce," Jack repeated emphatically as he started out into the field.

"Bloody hell," Percy muttered in reply as he reluctantly followed.

They traversed the hundred or so yards quicky, approaching the unmistakable profile of their captain from his right and slightly behind, stopping just a pace or so from his knee. The captain did not acknowledge them but remained stooped and swaying with his eyes closed as he snored loudly.

"Bloody hell, Jack – he's asleep!" Percy exclaimed with chuckle.

"CAPTAIN GARTHWAITE!" Jack called up to his commanding officer. "Sir, it's Privates Halliday and Perkins from the King's Own! We need to…"

BOOM!

A cannon ball suddenly screamed through the field bouncing not fifty feet from where they stood, plowing a path through the grass before bouncing into the woods where it crashed into a tree that toppled with a loud crack.

The captain suddenly jolted awake. "What's this? Ragamuffins!" he blurted with drowsy irritation. "Where's the sergeant?"

"We don't know, sir," answered Jack in his most formal tone. "Sergeant Searles sent us on patrol and…."

"Don't sass me, private! Goddamn you – I said where's the bloody sergeant?"

Neither Jack nor Percy answered as they stared at the captain like deaf mutes, watching as his shaky hand removed a pewter flask from inside his jacket. Looking straight ahead he took a long pull then wiped his mouth with his sleeve. Replacing the flask inside his jacket he now brandished his sword, waving it high above his head. The *hanger* was a short, thick weapon commonly worn by many officers and much utilized by mounted cavalry to be swung down to break the shoulder blades of foot soldiers to render them unable to further wield a musket.

"Bloody ragamuffins!" the captain repeated as he coughed hoarsely. "The sergeant sent *you*, did he? He didn't inform me. I'll have him lashed! Where in bloody hell *is* he? Where are the bloody Yankees?"

"Sir," Jack protested, "the Yankees are thick behind us and on their way. We must leave here. We...."

"PEASANTS! BLOODY PEASANTS!" the captain ranted as he continued to stare into the distance and slash the air with the hanger. "Do you take me for a fool? Bring me the bloody sergeant or I'll have you lashed! I'll have you all lashed – LASHED I SAID! Goddamn it!"

"Jack, he's gone mad," Percy whispered. "He's going to get us killed or captured. We must get out of here!"

"No, Perce," Jack whispered in return. "He's just drunk. We can't leave him out here – even like this. Especially like this."

BOOM!

Another cannon ball screamed through the field nearby and into the woods, this time throwing up dirt that found the eyes of the horse, which jerked its head as it threatened to rear up.

"Whoa!" Percy cried as he instinctively reached for the reigns.

"Bloody peasant! You'll not touch my horse!" the captain yelled as he suddenly brought the blade down hard and high on Percy's shoulder, the sharpened edge biting diagonally into Percy's neck three quarters of the way through to nearly sever it. Percy teetered on one foot before toppling to the ground under the horse, the light of life in his eyes extinguished like a snuffed-out candle.

"BLOODY PEASANTS!" the captain continued to rage as he raised the sword again above his head, fixing his gaze on Jack.

Jack did not hesitate as he dropped his musket and withdrew Georgey's knife, ever present inside his uniform. Captain Garthwaite swung the hanger down again at Jack, who ducked in toward the horse and grabbed the captain's arm, using the momentum to pull him down from the animal. As the captain slid from the saddle Jack drove the knife hard into the center of

196

his chest below the sternum. They both fell together to the ground with the captain landing on his back screaming and Jack on top pinning him with the knife held firmly in place.

"HALLIDAY!"

Jack turned to see Sergeant Searles approaching from about fifty paces, hurrying forward in long even strides. Withdrawing the knife from the captain's now motionless body, Jack stood and faced the sergeant.

"Halliday!" the sergeant barked as he reached him. "Where's your squad? What's Captain Garthwaite's horse doing here? Where's the captain?"

Jack did not answer but instead merely stared at the sergeant in stunned silence. He watched the sergeant's eyes grow wide as the senior soldier surveyed the scene on the ground behind Jack – Captain Garthwaite on the ground, the bloody knife in Jack's hand, the bloody sword in the captain's hand, and Percy under the horse nearly decapitated.

"What in the bloody Christ is this, lad?" the sergeant asked as tears welled up in his eyes. "Bloody fool. This can't be." He quickly checked the surroundings then fixed his gaze on Jack. "Run, lad," he ordered swallowing a large gulp of air. "Run before somebody sees this. Run and don't stop. RUN!"

Jack swallowed hard and nodded. He bolted for the woods in the direction from where he and Percy had come. Wincing with each step, he did not look back.

11

Those who would give up essential Liberty, to purchase a little temporary Safety, deserve neither Liberty nor Safety.

Benjamin Franklin

MONMOUTH, NEW JERSEY, JUNE 28, 1778

Jack ran. Neither the heat nor his knee nor the raging battle seemed to slow him. He plowed through the woods in a straight-line mad dash that would remove him from the area as soon as possible. Around him in the distance muskets popped as figures appeared, then disappeared, with cannon balls whistling through the air and knocking down trees as they bounced, plowing up swaths of the forest. Having left his own musket in the field far behind he moved unencumbered, except for his knee, like a passing ghost. As the sounds of fighting began to fade, he stopped long enough to discard his heavy red coat, his head gear and other military vestiges as buried his face in the water of a shallow brook. He adjusted his course easterly and continued at a hurried pace but not so frantic. Soon he came to a narrow road, of which he took advantage, walking for hours in long quick strides as he peered ahead and around for any signs of human activity. As the light dimmed in the evening he stopped, taking up a position below a broad fur tree well off the path. Sleeping fitfully, he rose at first light and continued east.

Well after midday he arrived at a marshy expanse of inland water, turning south along a sandy road that led toward a cluster of ships. Tied alongside a rickety wooden pier that jutted out into a small inlet sat three freight haulers, each well under a hundred feet. Hesitating at the brow leading up to the first, a well-worn two-masted schooner, he swallowed hard and stepped aboard.

"You there!" called a voice that came from inside the open main hatch on the deck out of which emerged a short, thick man with a swarthy complexion and cropped, sparse gray hair. "Can I help you, lad?"

"Yes ... yes, sir," Jack stammered, "Sorry to startle you, sir. I mean no harm."

"You look more startled than me, lad," the man chuckled with his hands on his hips as he started hard at Jack. "What's your business here?"

Jack stared down at his feet and pawed at the deck. "I ... I...." he fumbled before finally looking up and locking eyes with the man. "Sir, I would be looking for passage."

"Passage?" the man mouthed the word as if it were foreign. "Passage to where?"

"I don't rightly know, actually. Anywhere, I suppose."

"Don't rightly know? A bit odd isn't it? Folks that want passage usually know where they want passage to. But this is a working ship, lad. I don't take passengers."

"I can work, sir. I have three years before the mast and know what I'm about."

The man eyed Jack even more carefully, studying the ill-fitting shirt and pants that Jack had managed to abscond from the drying laundry of a farmstead recently passed. "You don't look much like a sailor, lad. Do you have a name?"

"I am Peter ... Peter Smith."

"Well, Mister Smith," the man continued, now a bit more relaxed, "I'm headed south, back from a trip to New York Harbor.

I pulled in here to make some repairs. It's just me and my two grandsons and I could actually use a little help from somebody capable. I'll tell you what, lad. We've a couple days' work to fix our steering gear. I'll try you out and if you prove useful you can stay aboard. I can feed you, but I can't give you wages."

Jack nodded and breathed a small sigh of relief. "Fair enough, sir. I can't ask for more than that."

The man extended his hand and shook Jack's firmly. "Name's Martin Chase. This here's the *Harriet* out of Portsmouth, Virginia at the bottom of Chesapeake Bay, where we're headed. She's not much to look at, but she's sturdy and can move with a load on, just like my wife, for which she's named." He called down into the hold and shortly two younger boys soon emerged on deck, both in their teens and resembling him with short, thick features. "This here's Jacob." He pointed to the oldest with reddish-blond hair then to the younger with darker brown. "And this here's Isaac." Both boys merely nodded as they stood their ground and stared at Jack in silence.

"Lads," Mister Chase offered as he pointed to Jack, "Mister Peter Smith will be with us for a couple days. Make him feel welcome. Lord knows we can use an extra pair of hands at the moment." He turned to Jack and raised his palms. "Enough socializing now – let's get back to work."

Mister Chase led Jack down below to the after part of the vessel where the four of them labored to repair the complicated mechanism consisting of a series of ropes and pulleys that transmitted inputs from the wheeled helm on deck above to the rudder mounted on the stern and extending below the waterline for directional control of the vessel. Jack worked diligently as Mister Chase soon gave him the main task of splicing and fitting the all-important hemp cords, some of which had failed and come apart.

"That's a handsome knife, lad," Mister Chase commented as he stood over Jack's shoulder. "May I see it?"

Jack hesitated a moment before stopping his work and handing the knife up to the older man.

"Very nice indeed," Mister Chase continued as he alternately gripped and released the handle. "Good balance. Fine workmanship? Where'd you get it?"

"A gift from a friend."

"Well, he's quite a craftsman he is, your friend. Are you willing to trade it?"

"No, sir, I can't," Jack answered with certainty. "I don't have much in this world and that knife is quite dear to me."

"Yes, I see," answered Mister Chase as he cheerfully returned the knife to Jack. "A valuable piece like that would fetch you a handsome return. If I had a cargo full of those I could do quite well."

They worked all day until the heat gave way to evening thunderstorms. As the sky grew dark and violent, Jack sat with the others sheltered below deck sharing a dinner of smoked fish and cheese. They retired soon after, each atop a blanket that covered the ballast of bricks that lined the bottom of the cargo hold. Jack woke in the morning to the sound of shouting topside. Emerging from the main hatchway he saw Mister Chase and the older grandson standing nearly nose to nose on the foredeck, each with a wide stance and hands on hips.

"Well, you're as dumb as the mackerel we ate last night, lad!" Mister Chase bellowed as he leaned even closer toward Jacob's face. "Do you think if your father were still here you'd be having a different conversation?"

"I doubt my father would turn his back on his country," Jacob answered as he folded his arms across his chest.

"You can't even remember your father. But I do. He was once a fool like you, but I can assure you, as a grown man, he wouldn't see it any different than me."

"I don't believe you."

"You never do." The elder man answered flatly as he turned and began to walk astern. "But I'm growing tired of this." He spotted Jack near the hatchway. "Come now, Mister Smith – you're awake. With your help we've repaired the steering gear sooner than anticipated. The wind's shifting and the tide's slack. Let's take the opportunity to quit this place and put to sea. The Lord has a way of providing, doesn't He?"

Jack nodded and fell in with Mister Chase and his grandsons to prepare the ship to get underway. The stifling heat and humidity of the past few days had finally been broken by a front that, in addition to the storms the night before, had ushered in cooler, drier air that blew conveniently from the northwest. With Martin Chase at the helm, they let go the lines from the pier and raised the schooner's fore and aft-rigged sails, allowing the freshening breeze and beginning ebb current to carry them into the muddy green tidal river. They soon exited the small inlet, brushing through some moderate surf into the open ocean where the water turned blue, and the wind strengthened even more. With land growing smaller in the *Harriett's* wake, Jack stared back past the marsh in the direction of Monmouth to the west.

"Were you expecting someone to see you off back there, lad?" Mister Chase chuckled from his station at the helm near the stern. "A farewell committee?"

"No, sir," Jack answered as he quickly turned away.

"Come, Mister Smith, and take the wheel. She seems to be steering fine. Keep the wind on the port quarter and an easterly course like so. When we get more water under us, we'll turn south."

Jack did as Mister Chase bade as the four settled into the standard shipboard routine with each taking the helm for a four-hour watch and in between sleeping or conducting repairs and maintenance as necessary. In about three days they arrived at the wide mouth of the Chesapeake Bay just before sunrise with a following wind that had veered to the north. Turning west they entered the bay and steered for Portsmouth, Virginia still a good twenty miles distant as all four hands now came on deck. During the course of the short voyage Jacob had managed to avoid his grandfather but now the previous argument suddenly erupted once again in earnest. With the younger Isaac at the helm and a glimpse of the orange-yellow sun peeking over the horizon astern, Jack moved as far aft as he could to remain clear of the renewed confrontation again taking place on the foredeck just inside the jib sail.

"How many times do we have to have this conversation, lad?" Mister Chase exclaimed as he threw up his hands before replacing them on his hips.

"I didn't bring it up this time, Grandfather," Jacob answered as he pointed a finger, nearly poking it into the older man's chest. "*You* did!"

"You'd best watch that finger, lad, before I snap it off and feed it to you!"

"I'm not afraid of you, old man," Jacob continued along with the finger. "I'm not afraid of anyone or anything."

"Yes, and there's the problem," Mister Chase answered as he leaned in closer. "You're too goddamn stupid to be afraid."

"I'm not *stupid*, Grandfather. And this is the problem with *you* – you just won't listen because you think you know everything and everyone else is just *too goddamn stupid*."

"I know you don't care anymore what this old man has to say. But think about your grandmother. What would it do to her to see you march off to fight? She's already lost the only son she had and now she must risk also her grandson? What would that do to her, lad?"

"Grandmother is a patriot, she is. She would be proud of me – something you can't bring yourself to be."

"Your grandmother and I are already proud of you, you damn fool. You don't need to march off and join some damn army to prove anything to us."

"It's not about you or Grandmother or anyone else for that matter – it's about *me*. I want to be part of it. I want to make something of myself. I want more than … than…."

"Than *this*." Mister Chase finished the sentence. "Is *this* not good enough for you, lad?"

Isaac at the helm suddenly gave a nervous look over in Jack's direction.

"This boat has damn well provided for us since before you or even your father was born. *My* father had a boat and his father before him. Between them they earned enough to provide a better one for me and I'm damn proud to have it!" Mister Chase's voice now rose to a bellow as he stepped forward, his chest pressing into that of his grandson. "I raised you, lad as my own son and you can be a damn fool if you want, but you won't insult our family livelihood and this boat – one day it'll be yours!"

About the same height as Jacob although a tad bit heavier, Mister Chase began to push his grandson across the deck toward the gunwale. Isaac turned to Jack with a look of panic as he cried, "Mister Smith! Take the helm please!"

But Jack was already on his way forward and arrived at the pair as they wrestled around the deck up near the bow with hands clasped hands around each other's throat. Mister Chase had the advantage as he pinned Jacob on his back against the gunwale with his shoulders edging out over the water below. Jack reached in between to separate the two without success as each seemed oblivious to his presence.

"My name … is not … Peter Smith," Jack blurted in between breaths as he wrestled along with the pair. "My name … is Jack … Halliday… and I … am … a king's soldier."

Mister Chase and Jacob suddenly ceased the struggle as they turned to Jack, each with a shocked expression.

"I'm a king's soldier," Jack repeated more easily as he let go of both their shirts and staggered back. "Or at least I was. King's Own Fourth Foot Light Infantry out of Lancaster. If you'll permit me, I can tell you a thing or two about that business."

Both grandfather and grandson said nothing but merely stared at Jack with their mouths open.

Jack pointed at Jacob. "I had such a conversation once with my so-called father, except *he* was the one that wanted *me* to leave. I wanted nothing more than for him to want me to stay. But I ran off and joined the army not long ago when I was just about your age. I had no idea what or why they might be fighting, and I didn't really care. I was sent here to America, where I soon found myself on a hill across the river from Boston. The Yankees had taken the high ground there where they could mount cannon and threaten the city, so we meant to dislodge them. Until then they had fought like cowards, ambushing us from behind trees and stone walls and then running away. But on that day, they decided to fight us proper and for a while they gave us as good as they got. It took us three attempts to break their defenses and they managed to kill or maim about half our number. In the end their shot ran out and we overran them to claim the hill and push them off.

"Along the way I happened upon a Yankee about the same age as me. He meant to split my head down the middle with an ax, so I took my knife and thrust it into his heart." Jack removed Georgey's knife from its sheath as Jacob gasped and staggered back a step. "This knife." He raised his voice as he held the weapon aloft. "That Yankee's gone from this world but not from me. He comes to visit me often and though I knew him only a moment, I remember every line on his face, the color of his eyes, the part of his hair. In fact, most of the people I knew best are dead. My mate, Percy, is dead – just days ago. His neck was severed by our own drunken captain. I killed that man also before he could murder me as well. I'm here now before you and your grandfather, begging for passage, because if I'm found I'll be shot as a deserter. Five years a loyal soldier and now hoping that you'll carry me away is all I have to show for it.

"If you think that you're going to *make something* of yourself in the army you better think again. I still don't quite understand what the fight is about with you Yankees and I can't say I really care. But for the likes of those that would be a soldier on either side, the common compensation is death or worse. If you're exceedingly fortunate, you'll wind up right back here where you started in one piece and of sound mind. I would give anything to have your grandfather, your grandmother, and your brother, who don't want you to go anywhere but instead wish for you more than anything the means for which to make a decent living. If I were you, I'd think a little harder about what I just told you before you run off to fight. Otherwise, you may find yourself trading an opportunity that few have for the wrong end of a blade such as this."

Jack replaced his knife in the sheath as the pair simply stared at him in silence. He returned to his position near the stern and for the next few hours there were few words spoken, with each man mainly keeping to himself. They skirted the southern banks of the Chesapeake reaching the Elizabeth River further to the west in the afternoon where they found a berth in Portsmouth Harbor, tying up to a pier among a maze of other vessels. With the *Harriet* now secured, Jack watched as Jacob strode down the brow and disappeared into the port environment.

Mister Chase approached shortly and clasped his hand on Jack's shoulder. "He's going home for a few days to think about things. And what about you – *Halliday* is it? What are your plans now?"

"I don't have any plans, sir," Jack answered. "I'm a deserter as I told you. The day before I met you, I was marching from Philadelphia on the way to New York with my unit under General Clinton. It was a hard way of life but at least I knew I'd be fed and have a place to sleep. Now I find myself in a strange land where I know not what the next day will bring. I need to find a way to sustain myself."

Mister Chase shook his head. "I wish I could help you, lad, but it's all I can do at the moment to provide for myself and the family. Why not stay on board a few more days? Tomorrow, Isaac and I will head up the bay to Annapolis. I think I know someone there that could use a lad such as yourself."

"That's generous, to be sure, sir – more generous than I've a right to expect. I'll accept your offer. But I must ask you further not to mention my situation to anyone."

"That's not any on my business, lad. But you have my word."

Jack nodded as Mister Chase slapped him on the back then strode down the brow with Isaac, following in the direction of the older grandson.

The next morning the *Harriet* got back underway and headed north up the Chesapeake Bay. The journey took the better part of three days, as Mister Chase preferred to anchor at night rather than risk collision in the more confined waters. They arrived at a small but busy harbor just before sunset, having to anchor before being placed at a berth the next morning. About midday, with the ship secure and Isaac left on board, Jack followed Mister Chase down the brow and into the bustling port. They continued out of the waterfront and through the small, well-kept city, passing numerous shops and enterprises that lined the main street leading from the harbor. Dozens of people circulated in the business district, many of whom seemed to know or at least recognize Mister Chase as they acknowledged him with a wave or at least a nod as he and Jack passed. If the ongoing war had devastated the likes of Philadelphia, New York, and Boston to the north it showed little negative effect on this thriving mid-Atlantic trading post.

Soon the downtown gave way to an open, rural setting with homes and farms that became increasingly dispersed as the pair continued inland. After more than a mile or so they stopped before a handsome brick home with a large field behind where several cattle grazed. They entered the yard via a circular half-moon driveway and approached the large front door well protected beneath a portico designed to accept large or multiple carriages. Mister Chase knocked on the door using a heavy hinged device attached for that purpose and waited patiently. The door was soon opened by a short, stout, middle-aged Negro woman attired in impeccably neat fashion with a black dress and white lace. She said nothing but merely smiled warmly at Mister Chase and motioned them both to enter. Jack followed into a large foyer that transitioned to a hallway leading toward the rear of the house. On either side of the foyer, wide openings revealed large, well-appointed rooms decorated with handsome portraits and furniture upholstered with fine, richly colored fabric. The woman quickly departed as other well-dressed Negro servants moved about the hallway and adjoining rooms conducting various housekeeping tasks. Mister Chase stood calmly with his hands clasped by his waist as Jack's eyes followed back and forth along the symmetrical lines of the perfectly fitted rooms.

From the hallway soon appeared a man in a tailored white shirt, about the same height as Mister Chase but of slighter build with pale skin, coal-black hair pulled back in a ponytail, and dark brown eyes. He strode to the foyer quickly and reached to clasp the hand of Mister Chase. "Martin," he said with a thin smile, "it's good to see you, man. To what do I owe the pleasure of a visit to the house? You normally send a runner when you land. How did the last trip go?"

"Well enough, I suppose, all things considered," answered Mister Chase. "I offloaded the entire shipment at the usual place in Brooklyn. There's not enough being manufactured up north these days for me to load so we left empty. On the way back south I developed a problem with my steering gear and had to put into Jersey near Avon for repairs – which leads me to the reason that I came here personally."

Jack continued to peer around the inside of the house as if in a trance. Mister Chase grabbed him by the arm and pulled him forward. "Arthur, I want to introduce you to Jack Halliday. I took him aboard while in Jersey and he's proven a great use to me in a short time. He's a sturdy lad and quite dependable. I wish I could employ him permanent, but I don't have the means at present. The next best thing I can do is to offer him to someone who does. I know you've been considering some extra help. He has my personal recommendation."

Having totally ignored Jack's presence until now the other man turned and eyed him intently as if he were the only thing that existed. He offered his hand to Jack, who accepted it nervously. "I am Arthur Coleman," the man stated confidently. "Arthur *Xavier* Coleman. I'm the landowner here. I manufacture shoes and other footwear on the premises. My business has been growing and Martin is correct that I've been considering taking on more help. Where are you from, lad?"

Jack hesitated slightly. "I'm from Liverpool … originally."

"I'm a Welshman, myself, but with family roots back in England. I came here as an indentured servant when I was much younger than you. If you're willing to work, you can make something of yourself." Arthur Coleman continued to study Jack, slowly circling around, and inspecting him head to toe. "There's

certainly plenty of work around here. You have good bearing and
seem strong enough. Martin and I have known each other for some
time, and we've done a good bit of business. I respect his opinion."

Mister Coleman stopped in front of Jack and looked him in
the eye. "Tell you what, lad – I'll take you on for sustenance for
a month. If things work out, I'll keep you on and we'll talk then
about wages. When can you start?"

"He can start immediately," Mister Chase answered.

Mister Coleman remained silent as he waited for Jack's reply.

Jack nodded as his eyes never wavered from the gaze of Mister
Coleman. "Yes, sir, I can start now."

"Well then," Mister Chase stated cheerfully as he clapped
Jack on the shoulder, "that settles it. I'll leave you in the care of
the Coleman family." Mister Chase took Jack's hand and shook
it warmly. "Good luck to you, lad."

"Thank you, sir," Jack replied. "I'm not sure if I can repay you."

Mister Chase chuckled. "Repay *me*? Oh no, lad – I consider
us even on that account. But if you can do for Arthur as you've
done for me, that'll be all the thanks I need."

Jack nodded as he let go of Mister Chase, who turned back
to Mister Coleman.

"Arthur, since I'm here, we can discuss our business now, if
you'd like. Do you have another cargo ready for me?"

"You're back a little earlier than I expected. But give me a
day or two and I can gather one together and deliver it down."

Mister Coleman raised his hand and seemingly out of nowhere
appeared a thin, elderly Negro man who approached the trio
from the hallway in slow, short steps.

"Isum," Mister Coleman ordered in an even tone, "take our
new man, Master Jack, down to the barn and organize his own
quarters."

"Yes, sir," Isum answered as he nodded, then motioned toward
the hallway to Jack.

Mister Chase gave Jack a final nod as he walked into a side
room with Mister Coleman. As the pair disappeared around the
corner Jack turned to follow Isum toward the back of the house.

12

Do not waste good iron for nails or good men for soldiers.

Chinese proverb

ANNAPOLIS, MARYLAND, SPRING 1779

Jack sat at a wide wooden work bench that butted up against the wall and ran down its length, which stretched nearly to the far end of the barn. Spread out on the work bench along the wall were every type of tool imaginable – awls for punching holes in leather, hot burnishes that rubbed soles and heels to a shine, sole knives for shaping, stretching pliers to fit the uppers, marking wheels to denote the lacing holes, size sticks for measuring, saws, mallets, and a seeming unending inventory of other implements necessary for the making of footwear. The bench itself was organized into stations where specific tasks were performed, then passed down the line. Across the barn there was a small foundry and metal-smith shop to fashion buckles and other necessary items. Outside not far away stood a separate smaller building that housed a tannery.

Less than a mile southwest of the Severn River along Weems Creek, Arthur Coleman's property comprised about 25 acres that contained several buildings, including the handsome main house nearest to the road. Across a stout wooden bridge that spanned the shallow waterway nearly 100 yards wide, the land opened to more than 200 acres of rolling pasture dotted with cattle. With shoe making the main industry, the Coleman operation also included other lesser but compatible enterprises such as dairy and meat production as well as custom manufacture and repair of metal parts. While the military struggle to the north had ravaged and destroyed the lives and fortunes of many, the capital of Maryland and mid-Atlantic coast trading center of Annapolis had remained largely unaffected, with Arthur Coleman along with many other such merchants managing to profit in no small measure. Aligned with a network of business partners such as Martin Chase, he had expanded his reach out of the Chesapeake Bay north up the Atlantic coast where the British invasion and occupation of New York and Philadelphia had created a nearly insatiable appetite for his goods, especially military footwear. Mid-Atlantic traders had plied for years the population centers of New York, Newport, and Boston where the abundance of manufactured goods were easily offloaded in the Chesapeake Bay. The war and lead up to it had diminished or even put a stop to much of the manufacture and export from the north; however, utilizing his network of capable shippers, Arthur was able to quickly take advantage of the sudden need to import shoes and boots. Unlike his Yankee brethren that traded in potentially worthless Continental paper dollars, the British paid in hard metal specie, the most respected currency in the world.

Arthur Coleman had come to America from Wales when barely six years old, along with his brother, Benjamin – twelve years his elder – shortly after his parents and two sisters had died in a fire of suspicious origin on their family farm in Brecon. They were both taken as indentured servants by a wealthy Annapolis landowner and physician, Doctor William Davies, a widower with no children. Unlike the other colonies, Maryland had been originally conceived and settled as a haven for Catholics and was generally allowed to exist as proof of religious tolerance in the

New World. Doctor Davies, a Welshman and staunch Catholic whose family had immigrated to escape persecution in the homeland, was happy to take the two boys through an arrangement brokered by existing relatives that had been close to the Coleman family. Brother Benjamin died of smallpox soon after arriving but surviving young Arthur remained with Doctor Davies for nearly two decades, staying on well past his indentured commitment, growing close to the elderly man as if a son. When Doctor Davies passed away, having no surviving relations, he willed all his wealth and possessions to the only family remaining in his life – Arthur. Nearing his late twenties Arthur suddenly found himself propelled into a station in life that he never could have realized back in Wales. Doctor Davies, himself a learned man and community leader, had ensured Arthur was well-educated and had even tried to steer him toward the professional study of science and medicine. But Arthur, an average student at best who had applied himself with determination if for no other reason than loyalty to and appreciation of Doctor Davies, was not cut from that academic cloth. From the beginning Arthur had proven industrious and most comfortable working with his hands, spending much of his youth in the company of Doctor Davies' dozen or so slaves, who taught the boy how to repair and build all manner of things. With new wealth at his disposal and a foundation of influential contacts gained through a life with Doctor Davies, Arthur gravitated to the area for which he was most naturally suited – business.

Perceiving a market and growing an available labor pool of talented artisan slaves, Arthur began to produce leather goods in earnest that quickly gained a reputation for high quality. He began an export trade that steadily spread by water throughout the Chesapeake Bay and north over land to Philadelphia. Before long Arthur's standing in the Annapolis community as a merchant had surpassed even that of Doctor Davies. As ambitious in love as he was in business, Arthur pursued and married Margaret Wilson, a local beauty nearly a decade his younger and daughter of Doctor Samuel Wilson, a longtime friend of Doctor Davies and patriarch of one of the most respected families in Annapolis. Margaret soon gave birth to a girl, Priscilla but died doing so, leaving Arthur to raise the child alone. Deeply affected by the unfortunate turn of events Arthur threw himself into caring for his daughter as well as building his business, both of which blossomed extraordinarily.

As Jack stared down the long work bench, a Negro man approached from the side carrying an arm full of cow hides.

"What do you want me to do with these, Master Jack?"

Jack shifted on his stool and hesitated before pointing to an empty space nearby on the bench. "Put them there, Custis. We'll deal with them tomorrow. I think we've done enough for today."

"Yes, sir, Master Jack," Custis answered in a sincerely dutiful tone as he worked his way to the indicated area.

Custis never moved fast but rather quite effectively, as wasting effort was not his nature. He stood an inch or so taller than Jack but was thinner in a frail sort of way. About a decade older, he looked even more advanced with a full head of premature gray hair and deep lines that framed a long face dominated by sad, droopy eyes. Unlike the other Negroes on the premises, Custis did not speak to Jack for the first several months after his arrival preferring to remain out of the curious young white man's sight like a shy cat. But ever so slowly Custis had come out of hiding to approach the farm's strange addition in ever increasing and painful gestures of communication that resembled a tree attempting to grow where it normally should not as it struggled to find purchase for its roots and sunlight for its leaves. Custis knew leather craft like no one else and organized the other Negro workers, now numbering 20, into maximum efficiency to produce high-quality footwear. Custis did not speak much but when he did it was generally to give direction that rarely received question and he eventually showed Jack every intricacy of the operation from growing the cattle to tanning the hides to shaping the metal work to constructing every conceivable shoe.

"Custis, what do you think of these?" Jack pointed to a large wooden box of newly finished shoes nearby on the floor.

Custis quickly examined several without expression. "Uppers are a little off and these soles are uneven."

Jack took the shoes and inspected them as well. "I don't see it," he muttered as he shook his head. "Rejects?"

"No, they'll do. But they'll not fetch top price from those that know the craft. Those were made by Augustus."

Jack looked at Custis with surprise. "How do you know Augustus made those?"

Custis reached back into the box, feeling around without looking, then randomly pulled out a shoe. "Bethesda," he stated as he dropped the shoe back in and pulled out two more. "Chloe … and … William."

Jack shook his head. Which of those are mine?"

"Yours are in a special box, Master Jack – for donation to blind folks." Custis answered with a grin as he reached for a second crate. "What should we do with this one here?"

"Custis," Jack answered with mild annoyance, "why do you insist on asking me things that you already know the answer to? You know exactly what we're going to do with that batch."

Custis did not answer but continued to grin.

Jack continued. "How long have you lived here and worked for Mister Coleman?"

"All my life, Master Jack," Custis exclaimed proudly. "I'd say some thirty odd years or so, but I'm not exactly sure."

"All your life," Jack repeated, "and you've made shoes all that time?"

Custis nodded. "Been making shoes ever since I can remember."

"Did your parents teach you? Did your father make shoes too?"

"Can't rightly say. I can't remember ever seeing my father. I believe Doctor Davies sold both my father and my mother a long time ago. Isum and Maddie in the main house pretty much raised me. And Samuel taught me to make shoes. Samuel used to be in charge around here – everybody listened to him. But he died some years back. Nowadays no one really wants to be in charge – most of all, me. That's why we're glad to have you, Master Jack."

Jack ignored the last comment and continued with his current line of questioning. "And you've never been anywhere else?"

Custis shrugged. "Sometimes Mister Coleman takes me with him into town to deliver goods to the docks. But I can't say that I like going."

"Why's that?"

"Just don't like going, Master Jack. Nothing there to interest me. I'd prefer to just stay here."

Jack gazed at Custis in amazement. "Is there some other place you'd like to go, maybe just out of curiosity?"

Custis shrugged again then shook his head. "Nope," he answered flatly, "got all I need right here. Every time I go into town, I see unhappy people and hear bad news. I'd just as soon stay here. Got all I need right here."

"I see," Jack said. "And you're happy here?"

"Happier than most. Happier than you, Master Jack."

Jack's eyes widened. "How do you know *that?*"

"Well, let me ask you. You've been around the world, have you?"

"Not quite – been around part of it."

"Well, did that make you happy?"

Jack hesitated as he lowered his head. "I suppose it didn't."

"See there, Master Jack, I'm right. I'm *always* right."

Jack pondered this a few moments before he spoke again. "If you're always right, then why do you need to ask me what to do when you've been here all your life and know this operation better than I ever will?"

Custis chuckled. "Master Jack, I have to tell you – for someone who has been a good way around the world like you say, you don't know so much. The answer is simple – because you're a white man. You've been brought in here to run this place otherwise you wouldn't be here."

Jack stared back in amazement. "Mister Coleman has said no such thing to me. I'm only here by pure chance, and I only remain because he needs extra help."

Custis shook his head. "If Mister Coleman only wanted an extra pair of hands he would just go out and buy himself another Negro. But white men don't buy and sell other white men – they hire them. White men *buy* Negroes like me and *hire* white men like you. That's the way things are. I'm not privy to what Mister Coleman told you, but I have no doubt that you've been brought on here to be something more than just one of us, otherwise Mister Coleman would've got himself another one of us."

Jack raised his head and looked straight into the back man's curious brown eyes. "How do you know that, Custis?"

Custis reached down into the wooden crate and felt along the bottom. Without looking he withdrew a shoe and presented it to Jack. "The same way I know that you made this."

* * *

"Nice to have you here, Jack." Arthur Coleman spoke in his soft low tone as he smiled. "Do you mind if I use your given name, lad?"

"No, sir," Jack answered a little nervously.

"How long have you been here now? Eight months, is it?"

"Nine," Priscilla answered quickly as she glanced furtively in Jack's direction with a shy grin.

"Yes, sir," Jack offered tentatively, "and thank you for inviting me to dine with you."

Arthur Coleman, his daughter, Priscilla, and Jack sat at a medium-sized round table placed in the center of a room located in the back of the house just off the kitchen. In contrast to the more ornate formal dining area this room was considerably smaller, almost square and decorated quite plainly. In fact, nothing at all adorned the walls except behind Arthur where hung a brass Catholic crucifix, and above that a picture of Priscilla's mother, who bore an uncanny resemblance to her daughter.

Isum smiled as he placed a small silver spoon in front of Jack, who merely returned the gesture with an awkward nod. Jack normally took his meals in the main barn where he worked and slept with either Isum or Mattie bringing him whatever was left over from the Coleman's kitchen. On occasions, when invited, he would join with the slaves, who normally ate as a group and cooked their own food. In any case, the staff ensured that Jack did not go hungry, and he never complained even though much of the food was thoroughly foreign to him.

Mattie followed close behind her husband with the first course, a nut-based soup served in a delicate white china bowl painted with a detailed city scene. Thanks to the talents of Isum and Mattie, the Colemans ate well with a mixed cuisine drawing both from the bounty of the Chesapeake region as well as a mishmash of West African dishes. On this day, in addition to the soup, the menu offered pan-fried crab cakes, beans with bacon and for the main course a large leg of chicken grilled and served atop a bed of rice with red gravy. As the last bowl of soup was placed before Arthur Coleman, he bowed his head and spoke. "Let us pray." He then crossed himself in the Catholic manner touching his right hand first to his forehead then alternately to his breast and finally to his left and right shoulders. "In the name of the Father, the Son, and the Holy Ghost. Bless us o' Lord in these Thy gifts that we are about to receive from Thy bounty through Christ our Lord. And thank you, Lord for the company of our guest, Master Jack, who we have become quite fond of over the last nine months. May he continue to prosper here with our family. In the name of the Father, the Son, and the Holy Ghost. Amen."

Jack tried clumsily to imitate the hand motions of Priscilla and her father as the young girl stifled a giggle. Arthur Coleman raised his head with a satisfied smile and reached for his spoon. "Let us begin," he said calmly as he took the first sip of soup. Jack and Priscilla quickly followed.

"Are you religious at all, Jack?" Arthur Coleman asked after his first swallow.

"No, sir," Jack answered as he shook his head, "not really."

"Did your family not bring you up in a faith?" Arthur continued as he ladled another sip.

"No, sir," Jack answered as he gazed downward toward his bowl. "It seems we had no need of it."

"Well, to me," Arthur offered, "the ritual we have before our meals in this room is sacred. You seem curiously to me; a lad much like me in many ways – a stranger in a strange land, taken away from your home maybe not on your own terms. Am I right?"

Jack said nothing as he put down his utensil and gazed at Arthur Coleman without expression.

Arthur also put down his spoon as he continued. "I came to this land when I was a mere child. I have few recollections of my parents but the strongest one I have by far is saying a blessing before the meal. Whatever happens outside of this house, if nothing else, I can always remember who I am and where I came from when we pray before eating. My family were Catholics and devotedly so. For that reason alone, they were persecuted, and my brother and I forced to flee across an ocean. Even here in this land, Catholics may not be welcome, so we keep it just to ourselves and especially in this room where we take our meals when not entertaining. It's a dangerous world we live in, lad, but also one filled with opportunity. Every man needs to maintain a sense of who he is if he is to succeed in it. My faith has provided me that sense when all else might fail."

Jack merely nodded in response as both he and Arthur raised their spoons to resume. They ate in silence for a short while before Arthur spoke again with a glance toward Isum, who stood dutifully behind Arthur and to the right. "My extended family seem to have taken an unusual liking to you, Jack. They may be my property, legally speaking, but they are to me so much more than that. In many ways they are my eyes and ears to the world, and I have found them to be expert observers of human nature. They are rarely wrong on the issue of character, and I trust their opinions explicitly. I will not do business with those they disapprove of. I don't have to ask their opinions but merely just watch their reactions. So, tell me lad, what's your secret?"

Jack did not answer at first but just stared into his now empty bowl, swallowing the last of what he had in his mouth. "I have no secret, sir," he answered quietly as he wiped his lips with his napkin.

Arthur chuckled as he passed his bowl to Isum. "Well, you must, lad, even if it's a secret to you."

Jack looked briefly at Isum, who gathered also his and Priscilla's bowl before disappearing from the room with a wide grin.

"It's good to have family, lad," Arthur continued, "no matter where you are. Can you tell us a little about yours? You must miss them all the way over here." Both he and Priscilla looked patiently at their guest as Jack lowered his head as if to pray and stared down at the table.

"I don't really have a family, sir." Jack stated flatly. "They're gone."

Arthur nodded with a concerned expression. "I'm sorry, lad. We did not mean to trouble you."

"Not gone like *that*," Jack continued as he raised his head. "I never really had a family in the sense like this one – but rather people that happened to be around as I grew up. They're not gone from this world, but I don't expect that I'll see them again and, in fact, I'd prefer it that way."

"Well," Arthur offered as he and Priscilla exchanged a quizzical glance, "now that you're here with us you can be part of *this* family. You've proven yourself more than willing to pitch in and contribute and we'll take care of you."

"Yes, sir," Jack answered promptly and nodded as Isum returned with three plates of food that he placed in front of those seated.

Arthur tasted the first bite then nodded approvingly. "Now, Jack," he continued after swallowing, "I don't mean to pry about your circumstances, but I'm curious. As a man recently arrived from England – at least more recently than me – what are your views on the current troubles here in America?"

Jack chewed and swallowed as Arthur put down his fork, awaiting an answer. Priscilla paused as well and looked up from her plate. "Well," Jack began, "I'm really not much for politics."

Arthur furled his brow and exchanged a glance with his daughter as he slowly shook his head. "Not much for politics?

Surely you must have an opinion as a man most recently on both sides of the ocean, no?"

Jack shook his head and looked Arthur straight in the eye. "No, sir, I don't. I know there is trouble here and many people have lost their loyalty to the Crown, but I really can't say that I understand why."

"Don't understand why? Really? The people have not lost their loyalty to the Crown but quite the reverse – the Crown has lost its loyalty to the people." Arthur paused and stared at Jack. "When I came to this land many years ago, a man was free to be as successful as his imagination and industry would take him. There was plenty of opportunity for all – you just had to go out and find it. Provinces like Maryland were left alone to govern themselves and conduct trade as we saw fit. Now the king and his ministers want to take that away and impose an abusive form of control on what goes on here, to include extorting illegal taxes and immoral regulations. Am I to understand that this is all news to you, lad?"

"No, sir," Jack shook his head, "I've heard that perspective before. But being as you say, recently arrived, the one thing I've noticed is that the citizens here seem to have more than plenty – more than can be imagined by anyone that lives in England."

"That is precisely the point, lad," Arthur stated as he leveled his finger in Jack's direction, "and we mean to keep it that way. What happens in England is fine for England and it's not going to change. But we won't accept that manner of abuse over here. The reason that we have what we have is because we govern ourselves with minimal control. We'll govern ourselves as Englishmen despite these tyrants that have seized their grip on these provinces and mean to enslave now us through coercion and force."

"Father," Priscilla interjected as she gently touched Arthur's arm, "must you get worked up like this for Jack's first dinner?"

Arthur picked his fork back up and began to eat in silence as Priscilla and Jack did the same. After several minutes Arthur started again. "You know, Jack – and I say this with all sincerity – it's not so important *what* your opinion is as it is to have one.

It reflects thought and engagement. Any man that does not or will not pay attention to that which goes on around him willingly condemns himself to be ruled by the efforts of others, more often than not, less noble than himself. There are too many people in this world who are perfectly happy to be blindly pushed along, provided they get their daily bread. I have learned over my lifetime that the only way to prevent being manipulated by the results of the political process is to insert oneself into it. Have you heard of the *Sons of Liberty*, lad?"

Jack put down his fork and nodded. "Yes, sir. They're quite well known."

"Good! Very influential in these parts and especially here in Annapolis. I have a surprise for you if you are up for it," Arthur offered with a slight grin.

Jack looked at Priscilla, who rolled her eyes. He then turned back to Arthur. "I don't understand, sir."

"No need to understand at the moment, lad," Arthur chuckled. "You just come with me tomorrow morning and you'll understand all that you need. Ah – here is Isum with the next course."

* * *

Jack stared at the gently rolling Maryland countryside as it eased by in the opposite order from his initial ride to the Coleman farm with Martin Chase the previous summer. Now with winter long waning, the surroundings glistened with remnant moisture as hardwood trees strained to renew their leaves. The one-horse wagon creaked over the soft, muddy road as Arthur Coleman guided them ever closer to Annapolis with Jack to his side in the front and Custis on a board behind facing backwards. Not long after the edge of the town proper and well before the port district they stopped in front of a plainly built boarding house and tavern commonly known as *Rupi's* after its proprietor, Rupert Stone, whose family lineage laid claim to the founding of the original settlement seven generations prior. Disembarking the wagon, Arthur handed the reins to Custis as he and Jack walked up the granite slab steps onto the porch. Jack followed Arthur as they pushed through the wooden front door into a foyer that resembled a former living space, then continued deeper through several rooms and eventually to the back that opened into what looked like a cross between a barn and a large meeting hall. Spread across the dusty floor were a dozen or so large tables where scores of men sat talking as they drank from large flasks.

Jack turned to see a tall, thin man with wide shoulders, graying hair, and a large, hooked nose, approach in a long gait. He placed his long hand on Arthur's shoulder and smiled. "Mornin', Colonel."

Arthur nodded and replied, "Morning, Rupi. What's the count so far?"

"Still a bit early, sir, but I think most of them are here. Fancy a drink?"

"No thank you – not yet. Jack?"

Jack mumbled an almost unintelligible "No thank you" as he locked eyes with Rupi, who still grinned widely.

"Who have we here, Colonel – a new recruit?"

"We'll see, Rupi. Let me introduce you to Master Jack Halliday. He works for me at the farm."

Rupi removed his hand from Arthur's shoulder and extended it to Jack. "Pleased to meet you, lad. I don't believe I've seen you before."

"No, you have not," Arthur answered before Jack could. "Let's get started, shall we? The others can fall in as they arrive. Where's the captain?"

Arthur quickly scanned the room until he caught the eye of a man at the far end by himself at a table. The man tipped his flask high to finish the drink, wiped his mouth on his sleeve, then rose stiffly from the table as if he had been glued there. A portly man, Captain James Cady wobbled over toward Arthur, who did not wait for him to reach.

"Captain," Arthur called in his best version of a booming voice, "have the sergeant form up the men. I'll be out in a moment."

"Yes, sir, colonel," the captain answered. He then wheeled around, nearly falling over, as he headed for a large door in the

222

rear. The rest of the crowd begrudgingly followed suit as they drained their flasks and slowly rose to exit, some grumbling as they staggered to locate their weapons.

As the room cleared, Jack followed Arthur and Rupi out the back door, which led to an open rectangular field several hundred yards long and a couple hundred yards wide across which, on the far side, ran a line of hardwood trees that hid a creek below, the typical landscape of the area. Men of various ages ranging from late teens to elderly stood in a loose block formation, each dressed in their own version of a uniform and holding their personal hunting firelock casually on their shoulder or loosely by their side. Some wore wide-brimmed hats, others a triangular-shaped cap – a tricorne, others a scarf wrapped onto their head and still others no head-covering at all. There were green coats, blue coats, gray coats, brown coats and seemingly every variation of those colors with no two looking exactly alike. The men talked among each other and joked as they threw friendly insults at the captain's equally rotund twin brother, Sergeant John Cady, as he paced across the ranks before them like a waddling duck. Arthur and the captain casually conversed nearby about daily business as if oblivious to their surroundings. For a full ten minutes men continued to stream into the formation with each arrival receiving a cheer as they hurried from the back of the building to the field, their pace growing quicker in measure with their tardiness.

Finally, the sergeant called the mob to order. "A-TEN-HUTT!"

The gaggle loosely came to attention as the sergeant repeated the command, each man with his own interpretation of the order in terms of action and posture.

"LEFT – FACE!" the sergeant barked, more or less, as each man shuffled in a ninety-degree turn.

"SHOULDER – ARMS!" The men now placed their musket leaning on their shoulder of choice with the butt end cradled in the corresponding hand.

"FORWARD – MARCH!" The mob now stepped forward in motion with the sergeant paralleling on the right side. Arthur and the captain ended their conversation as the latter followed the group, trailing loosely behind.

Jack watched from a distance as the formation crisscrossed the field in a series of directional maneuvers as Arthur joined him. "They're a fine group, they are," Arthur commented as he moved a bit closer to Jack, "our Annapolis Militia. I'm quite proud of them."

Jack said nothing as the formation continued for about 30 minutes, then returned to its original location. The sergeant dismissed the men as they broke ranks and hurried back into the tavern, laughing and joking amid good-natured jostling as if schoolboys. Jack followed Arthur inside behind the gaggle and took a seat at what acted as the head table near the entrance along with Rupi, the captain, the sergeant, and a few of the older men. The room vibrated with loud conversation as the female staff hurried from table to table providing large flasks of foaming liquor, making sure to serve Rupi's table first. Placing himself next to Jack in the middle of the bench Arthur stood and hoisted his mug above his head as he spoke to the entire room.

"One cheer for our militia!" Arthur brought the flask down to his mouth for a long drink as the crowd responded with a shout. "Two cheers for the Sons of Liberty!" The men yelled even louder as he repeated the procedure. "And the last cheer for Mother England!" Arthur tipped the flask skyward, emptying its contents, then slammed it on the table amid a most raucous roar after which every man drained their drink as well.

"Now, lads, I have an announcement to make," Arthur continued as he wiped his mouth with his sleeve, the room becoming quiet. "You all know what has happened and continues to happen in these colonies as our abusive government foregoes the principles of our English heritage and tramples our livelihoods with an invading army. Thank God that pestilence remains well north of us and has not come to our land. But I have been informed by agents of our Congress that the Continental Army, led by General Washington, continues in great need of men and a quota will be levied on the Maryland Province, as it will be in others, to bolster the ranks that bravely continue to battle the great scourge of King George, his ministry, and our Parliament. It would be an honor to serve such a cause and for any man that would take up arms to defend our home. Maryland would be indebted to him for eternity. I expect to have more details in due time and will promulgate those when they become known to me. For today, let's enjoy each other's company and rejoice that we remain the Annapolis Militia in the service of our city, our province, and our English principles of liberty for all!"

"HERE, HERE!" the men cheered as Arthur returned to his place at the table and signaled for another round of drinks.

"Well, lads," Arthur asked with a slight grin to those seated before him, "what do you think of that bit of news?"

"Bound to happen," replied Captain Cady. "Expected it, didn't we?"

"The French are about now," added his brother, the sergeant, "with men and ships to help us."

"Come now," answered a man at the end of the table, "when have the French ever proved dependable?"

"Who needs the French," asked another, "when there are men such as us? The French are no better than the wretched Hessians as they fight not for their own country."

"HERE, HERE!" answered the table as each man took a long pull at his newly filled drink.

"The First Maryland under Colonel Smallwood gave those lobsterbacks a good showing in Brooklyn," offered the captain. "Decimated they were but still stood their ground. If only the rest had fought as well, we'd have chased them from New York."

"HERE, HERE!" answered the table again.

"We had them in Boston long before," added Sergeant Cady. "Our cousin was there and said the redcoats were penned in the city like so many hogs, too afraid to come out and fight. Raped women and girls, they did, and burned people's houses to the ground just for their own amusement. More criminals than soldiers, they are."

"HERE, HERE!"

"I heard that on the road to Concord," the captain continued, "they ran like school children discarding their weapons and begging for mercy as the militias marched to oppose them. They scattered in disarray, and many were captured hiding in basements. Some took advantage of the men gone to fight and ransacked homes. The world's greatest army is no more than a pack of common thieves!"

"HERE, HERE!"

Jack did not raise his flask but instead slammed it hard on the table. He had not been drinking along with the rest but rather sitting in silence with an increasingly tight jaw. The sharp sound startled the group around the table, who now lowered their drinks and fixed their eyes upon him.

"What's this, sir?" Captain Cady asked. "Is there a problem?"

Jack did not answer, his jaw cinching even further and his knuckles beginning to show white as he increased his grip on the handle of his flask.

The captain turned to Arthur. "Colonel, your man seems in distress. Have we somehow managed to offend him? Is he not of like mind with the rest of us?"

Arthur maintained a bewildered expression but said nothing as Captain Cady, his face gone red, returned his attention to Jack. "Out with it, lad, lest your silence speak for you – and ill of you at that!"

Jack slowly raised his eyes to meet the captain across the table and stared hard for several moments, the anticipation hanging like a storm cloud. "You men know not of what you speak," he finally uttered in a low even tone. Several at the table leaned closer in earnest.

"Know not of what we speak?" the captain asked with an incredulous smirk as he looked around the table.

"You know not of what you speak," Jack repeated, now louder, "and those that listen know even less to believe it."

Captain Cady stood and slapped his palm hard on the table. "Colonel Coleman, who is this stranger brought into our midst that upon his first words would address us as if we were buffoons?

We offer him hospitality and he repays us with insults! Who is this ingrate and by what authority does he talk to us so?"

Arthur remained silent as he slowly turned his dumbfounded stare toward Jack. The entire room now fell silent and turned their attention to the main table.

Jack slowly rose and stood erect to face the captain across the table as he scanned the scores of angry eyes set upon him. "My apologies to Colonel Coleman," he began with a measured tone, "who has been nothing but gracious to me. I wish no ill will to come upon him for my sake because he knows not what I am about to tell you. It was not my intention to start trouble here, but I cannot remain silent and listen to your rhetoric any longer."

"Well then, lad, perhaps you have some rhetoric of your own that you would enlighten us with." Captain Cady motioned his arm around the room with a large grin as the onlookers chuckled all except for Arthur Coleman, who continued to stare at Jack as if at a ghost. "State your case, lad," the captain continued, "and it had better be good. I've a mind to run you out of here on a rail and I'm willing to bet that I'll find plenty of help."

Jack placed both hands on the table and leaned forward closer to the captain. "Running unarmed citizens out on a rail is something you lot do quite well. On the other hand, actual *fighting* is not."

A tense murmur now swept through the room as each man's eyes now aimed at Jack like daggers.

"I was on the road to Concord, "Jack continued in a measured tone, "when the so-called *militia* hid behind trees and stone fences conducting themselves more like assassins than proper soldiers. On the Concord Bridge after the engagement there was a wounded man hacked to death, his head stove in with an ax by one of the citizens as he waited on the ground for help. I was on the hill at Charlestown where the Yankees built a defense and at first gave us a straight-up fight but in the end, against a disciplined force, ran like scalded dogs off the peninsula. I spent that evening picking up what was left of my brave comrades who died like Romans.

I was interned in Boston when those from the countryside who were loyal to the king sought refuge, driven from their homes by their own neighbors for the crime of remaining loyal to the Crown. I was in New York when we landed at Brooklyn and swept away the various ragtag mobs that attempted to oppose us, then chased General Washington up York Island where he managed to escape across the Hudson River with no small measure of luck. We further engaged his army in New Jersey and Pennsylvania in battles so numerous that I can scarce recall the details except that each time those scoundrels were defeated they managed to accomplish the one thing at which they excelled – running with their hides still intact.

"No, my good fellows, thank you for having me here and I mean you no insult. I am Private Jack Halliday of the King's Own Fourth Regiment Light Infantry and upon risk to my person as well as the reputation of my sponsor, your Colonel Coleman, I cannot abide to accept such rhetoric for what I know firsthand to be utterly incorrect."

Silence hung for several suspended moments like a giant curtain as Jack remained standing, staring out across the room at the angry eyes that remained fixed upon him. Sergeant Cady now rose and pointed his stubby finger at Jack.

"You, sir, purport yourself to be a king's soldier? You're obviously not one now. What foul wind brings you to our gathering?"

"Not quite a year ago we quit the city of Philadelphia and marched through New Jersey to reposition ourselves in New York. We were engaged from the rear of our column by General Washington's forces at Monmouth. It was there my service ended. I will not speak of that."

"A deserter then," continued the sergeant as he looked around the room. "But no matter – that's no concern of ours. But you speak as if someone that has *right* on his side and lecture us as if children. Do you also share the king's hatred of the cause we support, that is, our natural rights as Englishmen to govern ourselves and to not be abused by the very Crown to which we hold dear? What say you on that account? Think very clearly on your answer as although we may not measure up to your lofty standards as soldiers, make no mistake that every man here will fight to the death to defend their right to liberty!"

Jack paused before he answered. "Yes, I have heard this complaint many times and I must admit I don't understand it. You enjoy already as citizens of the Crown in these colonies more wealth and prosperity than any commoner in England could rightly conceive, much less expect. I can't help but think that you bite the very hand that feeds you. But *liberty* you say? I can't help you on that account as I have never known such a thing."

The sergeant returned Jack's gaze as if dumbstruck. "A man that doesn't know *liberty* doesn't know *life*. For what cause then did you enlist in the king's army and take up arms at severe risk to yourself?"

"For no cause at all except to sustain myself with employment and improve upon my circumstances."

"To *improve upon your circumstances*, you say?" the sergeant scoffed. "What previous circumstances did you have for which being a dog in King George's army was an improvement?"

Jack stiffened amid the many chuckles but did not answer.

"On this side of the Atlantic," the sergeant continued, "we fight for our rights as Englishmen and that cause is worth dying for!"

"HERE, HERE!" shouted the crowd.

Jack slowly shook his head. "That's certainly a worthy notion, and you may fight for such a thing once a week in the field behind this tavern and you may toast to precious *liberty* a thousand times here in this hall. But no man who expects to survive the reality of the battlefield, much less carry the day, fights for such lofty ideals once he stares for the first time into the face of death."

"What then, sir, does one fight for if not what he believes in?" Sergeant Cady asked with a bewildered expression.

"I'll give you my best answer so that you and the others may judge me accordingly as to whether I'm a knave in your midst who should be treated like so many other so-called *Loyalists*. I have seen a chunk of the world but know little of it and even less of politics. I've neither love nor ill-will for King George and understand next to nothing about the forces that brought me to this land. But you speak to me of *liberty*, and I wish you luck to have it. As for me, I have but one expertise that has, for better or worse, sustained me until recently when I came into the employment of Colonel Coleman. I can tell you without a shred of doubt that if you wish to take up arms against the likes of the king's army all the lofty ideals in the world will not amount to a thimble full of whale shit and, in fact, they'll flee like children from you the first time your hair is creased with a musket ball or worse, you stare at the business end of a wall of oncoming bayonets wielded by professionals who mean to use them. No – if you want to fight and live to fight yet again, you must learn to fight for one thing and one thing only – you must fight for the man next to you and for nothing else. If you can't do that then you'll die and with you your precious cause. For your *liberty* is nothing without the courage to risk or even lose your life for and with those who would do the same for you."

With that, Jack finished his drink in a large gulp, stepped away from the table and strode from the room amid complete silence. No one followed.

* * *

"Priscilla, wake up." Jack gently shook the bare shoulder next to him. "Wake up."

Priscilla turned her head full of dark, tangled hair and rolled onto her back, opening her eyes. She turned to Jack and smiled.

"You have to go back," Jack whispered. "It's starting to get light."

Through the windowpane on the rough-hewn walls of the simple room the faint outline of trees began to appear. Priscilla giggled. "Why are you whispering? There's no one else here. Don't you understand that I can pretty much do as I please?"

Jack shook his head. "I see very well that you do as you please, but I think there's a limit to what your father will accept."

"My father loves you, Jack."

230

Jack smiled. "So, you keep saying. But I doubt he'd love me very much longer if he knew you were here. Please, Priscilla, get dressed and go back to the house."

Jack watched Priscilla as she returned the smile and rose from the straw matting reaching for her nightgown draped on a nearby wooden chair as shrouds of dim outer light faintly highlighted her young shapely form.

"Are you really a soldier, Jack?

Jack hesitated. "Why do you ask me such a thing?"

"Because the entire town is talking about it. They say you're a British soldier. Is it true?"

Jack sighed as he sat up. Yes, I was a British soldier."

"But why, Jack? Why would you do such a thing?"

"This is a conversation for another time. Now please, go back to the house before it gets too light."

Priscilla jumped back onto the matting and rolled into Jack's arms. "My love – every morning it's the same worry. And every morning I return to my room as if I had never left. Custis watches and will warn me if someone is coming. But why, Jack? Why would you come across the ocean to bring us harm?"

"I didn't mean to come across the ocean to bring anyone harm. It's just that ... that ... that I never really thought about it. It's not so much that I wanted to come here, or anywhere, but I needed to get away from there."

"Where is *there*, Jack?"

"You know I'm from Liverpool."

"Yes, and you left your family to come here to fight?"

Jack stiffened. "I told you several times that I don't have a family."

"But I don't believe you. Your mouth says one thing, but your eyes say something else. There is much hurt in your eyes, Jack."

Jack did not answer as he looked away.

"I would give anything to have a mother," Priscilla continued as she repositioned herself to meet Jack's gaze. "Mine left me so long ago." She reached up to grab Jack's jaw to fix his eyes toward hers. "Look at me, Jack. We're your family, now."

Jack sprang out of the matting, dropping Priscilla on the blanket. He donned a pair of britches laying close by on the floor. "Priscilla," he stated emphatically, "it's getting light. If you don't go, I'll carry you back myself."

Priscilla smiled as she rose and put her arms around Jack's neck. She gave him a long kiss then pulled away giggling as she cinched her nightgown and walked out the back. Jack moved to the window where he could see her in the half-light disappear into the small patch of trees that separated the working buildings from the main house.

Close to turning summer, it had been more than a month since Arthur Coleman first brought Jack to the Sons of Liberty. Following that testy introduction the militia leadership had unanimously voted to invite Jack to join their ranks. In a typical show of Yankee pragmatism even the Cady brothers had argued, in fact, most stringently, that Jack's knowledge outweighed whatever differences existed and petitioned Colonel Coleman to bring the former professional soldier in. Jack had reluctantly agreed and over the course of the month acted mainly in the capacity of an *advisor*, focusing on the areas of close-order drill and formation movement. In an amazingly short time, the Annapolis Militia no longer looked like a band of farmers but rather had begun to resemble a disciplined military unit that moved together with precision and purpose or, more accurately, like *masters of their persons*. The citizens of Annapolis and their militia did not seem to care that the quiet young man employed by their most prominent citizen had been one of King George's soldiers, as he was now *their* soldier.

As Jack turned away from the window, he spotted Custis emerging from the trees along the same path as Priscilla had used, moving quickly toward the barn in uncharacteristic long, hurried strides. Moments later a gentle but firm knock on the door announced Custis' arrival as he entered before Jack could open it. Custis stopped just past the doorway, staring wide-eyed at Jack as his lips moved without a sound.

"What is it, Custis?" Jack asked, his brow furled. "You look like you just saw a ghost."

"Master ... Master Jack," Custis managed to stammer, "Mister ... Mister Co ... Co ... Coleman wants to see you right away. Wants to see the both of us."

Jack turned to look back out of the window at the path leading into the woods. "Is something wrong?" he managed.

"Yes, sir, Master Jack. Very wrong. It can't get any more wrong. You best get ready to pack your things."

Jack glanced around the room, which contained all he had in the world. He swallowed hard, then hung his head and sighed. "I knew it. All right, Custis. Let's go see Mister Coleman."

Jack followed Custis back out of the door as they walked quickly in silence, navigating the short route to the main house. They entered the back without knocking and made their way inside to the parlor, where Mister Coleman typically preferred to conduct business, the same room where Martin Chase had presented Jack the year prior.

Isum intercepted the pair with his typical stoic expression, escorting them to the parlor entrance. "Master Jack and Custis, sir," Isum announced clearly, then departed quickly with a nod.

At the far end of the well-appointed rectangular room sat Arthur Coleman intently writing with a quill behind a large handsome wooden desk. Both Jack and Custis stood silently at the entrance until Mister Coleman motioned them in without looking up as he continued to write. They approached the desk and waited for a long moment before Arthur Coleman placed the quill down and looked up at them with a tired expression. "Well," he offered as he looked at Jack directly, "it's finally come to this."

Custis began to shake as Jack set his jaw and shifted his gaze to the ground. "I ... I ... I am very sorry, sir," Jack managed to stammer. "I ... I ... I ...."

"What's done is done," Arthur Coleman continued, "and we must now take appropriate action."

Jack hesitated, then slowly looked up, trying in vain to speak as his eyes began to moisten.

"This is not unexpected, and in fact, we've been waiting for this development. We've received an edict and there's nothing to do but comply."

Jack stared at Arthur Coleman with a confused expression as he wiped his eyes with a sleeve.

"The Continental Congress," Arthur Coleman began earnestly, "have levied a quota of men from Maryland for the Continental Army under General Washington. Also, for Virginia, Pennsylvania, and others, as well. As a colonel in our militia, I've been selected in accordance with the lottery. As an improvement on that circumstance, I've arranged to provide substitution of more than equitable compensation. You and Custis will serve in my place in addition to a generous donation to Congress – funding desperately needed for the cause and a contribution more valuable than any other I could make with my own person."

Jack gazed ahead, dumbfounded, as he wiped the remaining moisture from his cheeks.

"I'm sure this is as much a shock to you as it was to me. But you would do me and this family – *your* family – a great honor if you would accept this responsibility. As I have no male children, upon your return I'll make you my sole heir." Arthur Coleman rose and, placing both hands on the desk, leaned forward on his arms. "Most importantly, Jack," he continued, "I'll give you permission to marry my daughter. I see the way that you two look at each other. Don't think you have me fooled on that account." Arthur Coleman winked and managed a fleeting grin as he extended his right hand across the desk. "What do you say, Jack? Will you honor our family by accepting this commission?"

Jack remained motionless with eyes bulging wide and mouth agape. Ever so slowly he reached his hand forward which Arthur Coleman clasped in both of his and shook vigorously as he smiled widely.

"Good lad!" he exalted as he released Jack's sweaty palm. "It's settled, then. I'll inform the proper authorities and make the necessary arrangements. Congratulations! It's a proud day in the Coleman household!"

Jack nodded and continued to stare ahead as Arthur Coleman departed the parlor, which returned to its early morning silence broken only by the hard swallow of Custis.

13

Then said Jesus unto the twelve, Will ye also go away? Then Simon Peter answered him, Lord, to whom shall we go?

Gospel of John 6:67-68 KJV

MORRISTOWN, NEW JERSEY, LATE JANUARY 1780

Jack hid his hands inside icy sleeves as he held the wagon reins while the mare to the front snorted glistening clouds of mist that hung in the damp, frozen air. He cinched up his coat and shook his head as rime fell like dust from his wide-brimmed hat. The barren woods around him blended indiscernibly with the ever-building fog. Here the impending storm was deceptive as the leading edge brought a relatively warm precipitation mix soon to be followed by a steep drop in temperature that would freeze everything in its path. With Annapolis nearly 200 miles behind, the trek northward had proved difficult with roads hampered by increasing accumulations of snow now piled well above the wagon on either side. Somehow, a path had managed to be trampled through by traffic that left on the ground a hardened, uneven white layer now just soft enough to hinder progress. Seated to the left beside him, Custis merely stared down and shivered, having uttered nary a word since departure more than a week before. Now approaching the Continental Army encampment at Morristown, they sought to beat nightfall and the worsening weather.

Moving slowly but steadily, Jack and Custis exited the woods for a field, across which they traversed several hundred yards, pelted harder by the frozen heavens no longer impeded by the looming barren trees. Approaching the resumption of forest ahead, a cave-like opening gradually appeared that revealed an uphill path. Just before the mare reached the entrance a man suddenly appeared, having hidden himself in a cutout made in the tall snow along the path. He grabbed the horse's reins.

"Whoa, there," he commanded as the horse and wagon halted. "Good girl."

The man stood out ahead of the horse with arms folded across a long coat. He was tall with broad shoulders and a wide floppy-brimmed hat worn low enough to obscure his face. After several moments of study, he approached the wagon on Jack's side. "Where might you be going on a day such as this?" he asked in a low growl.

Jack shifted in his seat as he stared at the man. "We're bound for the Continental Army encampment at Morristown ahead. May I ask who you might be that you see fit to impede us?"

The man briefly removed his hat to shake off the ice revealing an ugly scar that ran from the top center of his forehead down across his nose and over his right cheek and ended at his ear that looked as if the bottom half had been chewed off. He replaced the hat over his brown eyes and hair as he answered. "I'm the outer guard – Morristown militia."

A second smaller figure now appeared, remaining shadowed just inside the entrance to the path, his arms also folded across a long coat. The man at the wagon continued. "What business have you with the Continental Army?"

"We've come from Annapolis to augment the Maryland forces," Jack answered carefully.

"And what's in the wagon?"

Jack hesitated. "A hundred pairs of boots that our sponsor has donated. I have a letter of introduction that explains this."

"A letter, you say? May I see it?"

"No, sir," Jack answered flatly, "you may not. My instructions are to show it only to General Washington or his staff."

The man grunted in a half-laugh as he stepped to move along the length of the wagon, circling slowly around the back and stopping on the other side next to Custis, who continued to shiver and stare at his feet. "Is this your nigger?" the man inquired to Jack across the bench.

"This man is the property of our sponsor, Mister...."

"YES, I AM!" Custis raised his head and answered in an uncharacteristic loud voice. He frantically looked at Jack, then returned his gaze to his feet.

The man stepped back a pace or two to reveal a musket barrel protruding from the bottom of his coat as he continued to keep his arms crossed. "A hundred pairs of boots, a sturdy wagon, a tired horse, and a shivering nigger, but no proof of what you claim. It seems you're far from home and at a disadvantage. As a security precaution I'll take the wagon, to include the nigger, and deliver these myself to General Washington. You may pass the short distance on foot to whatever business you have."

Custis looked again at Jack with a frightened expression.

Jack leaned on Custis to the left, stretching closer to the man. "How is it, sir, that you comprise the *outer guard?* Let me see the proof of *that* if you want to negotiate with me for passage. If not, these are the words of a highwayman with no authority whatsoever."

"Rest assured that I have such authority," the man growled again, "and moreover, a dozen more men up ahead in the woods that I can call down in an instant."

Jack peered ahead into the tunnel that rose through the trees into darkness, then turned his gaze back to the man. "If you have more men up ahead, call them down and you may take the wagon. Otherwise, I believe it's just the two of you and the two of us."

The man cast a glance toward his second, still somewhat obscured inside the edge of the woods. He loosened the top half of his coat and slid the musket up so that butt end protruded up near his collar. "It would seem that you prefer to make this difficult," the man stated. "My men and I are well-armed. Are you?"

"I am," Jack answered. "But if your man behind you is armed, why doesn't he show himself so that I may know for sure?"

"What weapons do you have?"

Jack slowly undid the middle button to his coat and placed his right hand inside. "I have two pistols inside my coat – one for you and one for your second."

"Now you ask me to believe *you*?"

"You may believe whatever you choose."

The man fell silent and stared at Jack. He looked to his half-hidden assistant and back again, pawing the icy ground with his foot.

"If all you have is that musket," Jack resumed, "it's of little consequence. I can see by the stock it is of an origin common to the British Army. The outer guard would have a weapon furnished by the Continental Army, probably acquired from France, wouldn't they? But no matter. Given the current weather and the angle you now hold it inside your coat, which is too open to protect it, the firing mechanism is surely wet and most likely won't operate to make a spark. At best it is but a club."

The man's eyes narrowed as he clinched his coat tighter.

Jack continued. "Since the light's running short and we've no interest in a quarrel, I'm willing to bargain with you, but not according to your outlandish terms. I'll give you each a pair of boots. They're of the finest quality. For that you'll allow us to pass unmolested."

The silence hung heavy in the frozen air as a mist began to form along the grass in the field. The man shook his head. "Very well. I'll take six pairs each – and I'll choose which ones."

"Three," Jack snapped. "That is final. And you may choose them."

"I require to see your pistols," the man added.

"If you require to see my pistols it will be the last thing you ever see. Rest assured that I won't hesitate to put a ball between your shoulder blades. You pose a large target and from this distance I shall not miss."

The man stared hard at Jack again and nodded. "Very well. Three pair each."

"Stay where you are." Crossing over the shivering Custis, Jack descended from the wagon, keeping his hand inside his coat and his eyes on the man. He walked to the back of the wagon and lifted a large blanket that lay over numerous burlap sacks filled with boots. He motioned to the man and tossed him an empty sack. "Please be quick – the weather's worsening. Your assistant stays where he is."

Jack remained several paces behind as he watched the man carefully pick through the boots with one hand, still cradling his musket with the other. When the man finished, he turned and hoisted his now burdened sack over his shoulder.

"One last thing," Jack instructed. "Follow this path to the other side of the field. Your man as well. When we can't see you anymore, we'll leave."

The man sneered as he hesitated then motioned for his assistant to join him – a young teenage boy – as the pair slowly started in the opposite direction. Jack watched until they disappeared into the whitish grey that obscured the trees on the other end of the field. He climbed back onto the wagon, took the reins, and started up the hill into the misty forest.

* * *

With the British reconsolidated in New York Harbor for the season, Washington likewise took refuge at Morristown, just as he had the first winter three years earlier. Roughly 30 miles northwest of New York Harbor, the location allowed him to monitor actions of the British while maintaining a line of communication north to New England and south to Philadelphia, where Congress had returned following evacuation by the British. Rugged terrain interspersed with broad swamps guarded the approaches to

Morristown with the Watchung Mountains behind providing for ample visual surveillance and signaling. His army, numbering somewhere over 10,000, had straggled in throughout December, destitute and in dire need of food, clothing, supplies, and pay, with nearly 6,000 enlistments set to expire by the end of the month. Out of necessity and after several failed efforts from Congress, Washington had appointed his most trusted subordinate, Brigadier General Nathaniel Greene of Rhode Island, to take charge of the Continental Army logistic effort as *Quartermaster General*. A man of action, like Washington, Greene had chafed at the assignment, wanting instead to command on the battlefield. Also, a man of ample competence, his much-needed leadership and management delivered an impact as the movement of resources rapidly improved, although not nearly to the level ultimately needed. As newly recruited men flowed into camp the winter harshness and threat of disease caused nearly as many to depart.

From the beginning of his tenure as commander-in-chief, Washington had advocated for a permanent army as he considered the reliance merely on militias as woefully inadequate to contest the British. However, on the heels of the Declaration of Independence, Congress held the opposite point of view, influenced and justified by militia successes at Lexington/Concord and then again at the Charlestown peninsula. Besides requiring a level of funding that the fledgling colonial assembly was unprepared to bear, a large standing army represented a visible pillar of the very tyranny they sought to dislodge. Moreover, command of such power could become a dangerous political weapon in the hands of he who controlled it no matter how impeccable his character. History was rife with examples of such. In fact, Oliver Cromwell's role in Britain's civil war and his refusal to relinquish power, a mere century ago, lay still fresh in the minds of all Englishmen. But after the disastrous display by the American forces at the Battle of Long Island and throughout the remainder of 1776, it could no longer be argued that the militias alone were up to the task of standing toe-to-toe with the British in the kind of major engagement necessary to defeat them. If the triumph of the

American cause depended mainly on the sustained existence of a viable army, the militias, by their local and limited nature, proved operationally and strategically insufficient just as Washington had originally maintained. Forced to risk another Cromwell – or even Caesar – as a matter of survival, Congress acquiesced to the commander-in-chief they trusted and authorized the raising of a *Continental Army*.

The Christmas Day victory at Trenton in 1776 had buoyed the sunken spirits of the army as well as much of the American populace. However, the subsequent and inevitable exodus of troops due to the expiration of short enlistments had been staggering. Congress re-thought its manpower authorization and began to devise schemes to bolster the army through longer enlistments and increased pay as best they could. Still under the illusion, at the time, that the conflict would not last long, the period of commitment typically called for *three years or the duration of the war* with the monetary burden born by the individual provinces that were levied manning quotas. With the conflict now entering its sixth year, reliance on the militias had steadily waned, gradually replaced by continental units generally organized according to geographical origin. This produced a more standardized and dependable fighting force but, much like their British counterparts, tended to attract those on the lowest end of the socio-economic spectrum motivated not as much by ideological passion but rather a guaranteed sustainment they could not otherwise secure.

That the Continental Army had survived so far, and with it the American cause, was nothing short of a miracle as well as a testament to Washington's personal leadership ability. Continually bested by his professional British counterparts in the art of large operational movement, Washington's ability to inspire, organize, recognize aptitude, and empower subordinates had mitigated his shortcomings in the optimum positioning of his forces. The ability to maintain Congressional support to his advantage in the face of an unrelenting tirade of naysayers that wanted him replaced may have been the greatest talent of all. His natural proclivity to constantly attack had been tempered by a realization that of prime importance for his army was not so much to *win* but rather to *exist*. As long as the colonies had the means to resist militarily, they could maintain the hope of independence. This strategy had resulted in an inconclusive stalemate prolonged enough for the British to blunder into giving France an opening. As Washington's forces hunkered down in Morristown, they needed the winter to bolster themselves for the next fighting season in what had proven to be a war that continued longer than anyone had imagined.

* * *

"Custis, can you read it again?"

Custis rolled his eyes as he nodded. Like several other Negroes at the Coleman farm, he had been taught to read at an early age. "How many times have we done this, Master Jack? No doubt you have it memorized."

"I do have it memorized. But I just want to hear the words, as I like the way they sound from you."

Seated across from Jack at a modest wooden table in the common area of an inn that served as transient quarters for the army, Custis withdrew a scrolled paper from a handsome leather satchel. With meticulous dexterity he untied a thick string of the same material that secured it, carefully pulling the paper straight with one hand on the top and the other on the bottom.

"Dear General Washington," he began, "please accept my sincere greetings and salutations. This letter serves as notice of my intentions to continue to support our noble cause and to present to you my employee, John Halliday and my servant, Custis Coleman, who have been nominated by me, with full confidence, to act in my stead in order to fulfill the manning quota levied on the province of Maryland by Congress for the purpose of augmenting the Continental Army, whose actions and reputation under your leadership during our honorable struggle have been nothing less than spectacular. If it would please you, Sir, it is my intention that you commission John Halliday as a lieutenant, with

243

commensurate duties and responsibilities, as you will find him skilled in the art of military drill and wholly steadfast of heart and mind. As for Custis, please assign him as your good judgment dictates as you will find him well-suited for general duties, particularly those that require a high degree of technical skill and acumen. In closing, I wish you and the Continental Army continued success and all the blessings that Providence is capable of providing in your gallant endeavor to deliver us from eternal tyranny. Written this 26th day of December 1779 and signed by my hand, your humble servant, Colonel Arthur Xavier Coleman, Commander of Militia, Annapolis, Maryland."

Custis slowly rolled the paper back up, carefully tying it again, then handed it over to Jack. "It's yours now, *lieutenant*."

"Lieutenant," Jack repeated softly as he accepted the scroll. "I'm not a *lieutenant* yet."

"You soon will be," Custis stated as he rose. "Shall we go?"

Jack looked across the room to the main doorway, whose narrow windows across the top revealed thin rays of early morning light. He did not get up.

"Is there something wrong, Master Jack?"

Jack shook his head and placed it in his hands.

Custis sat back down and fixed his eyes on Jack, stuck in his seat and staring in the distance. "I don't understand. What's the problem?"

Jack looked up but continued to stare ahead in silence. Finally, he swallowed hard and answered. "Custis, I can't be an officer."

Custis looked quizzically at Jack. "What do you mean? You have a letter from Mister Coleman that states his intentions. Surely, they'll make you an officer."

"That paper may say as much but you don't understand." Jack balled both his fists and set them firmly on the table. "Military officers are educated. They come from important families. They have pedigrees. Military officers are not of the lower sort." Jack hung his head again. "Like me."

"The *lower sort*? You have a letter from Mister Arthur Xavier Coleman, Colonel of the Annapolis Militia, one of the most prominent men in the Maryland province that requests you receive a commission. How can you be the *lower sort*?"

Jack pounded his fists on the table. "A letter that I can't even read!"

Custis nodded and looked the other way as they sat in silence for a while until he returned his gaze to Jack, whose eyes now watered. "Master Jack, I don't believe that they will expect you to read as much as they will expect you to lead. Men will see that you have courage and ability. They'll follow you and not care a whit from where you came. I'm right about this."

Jack said nothing as he wiped his eyes.

"The reality is," Custis continued, "we have an obligation to Mister Coleman. We can't return home until we fulfil that obligation and, to do that, you must be commissioned in his place, and I must be enlisted along with you."

Jack nodded as he looked at Custis. "You're right. I'm low born, to be sure. But I have freely accepted such an assignment from Mister Coleman, who's placed his trust in me. But you, Custis, have no such bargain."

"What do you mean?" Custis scoffed. "Mister Coleman has certainly obligated me to accompany you. It says so in the letter."

"But you were given no choice. You weren't asked. And will you not return in the same state as you departed – as Mister Coleman's property? Why not leave here while you can and head farther north, where many Negroes live as freedmen? It's quite common in Boston and York Island and also Philadelphia. It would be easy for me to say that you simply disappeared. Nobody would know the better."

Custis smiled and shook his head. "You must understand, Mister Jack, that a trust has also been placed in *me*. I've served Mister Coleman all my life and I must say that I'm not the worse for it. I may be his *property* but that's not an issue I care to dispute. I may not have been asked by Mister Coleman to accompany you but make no mistake that he sent me because he knew that I would not, as you say, *simply disappear*."

"But given the opportunity, would you not want to make a new life as a freedman? This is the opportunity – one you may not ever get again."

"Opportunity as a *freedman*? What's that really – a *freedman*? Free to do what? Free to go where? At the farm I have family and security. At the farm I'm respected. My life has meaning and I lack for naught. But out here – a so-called *freedman*? Do you mean *free* to be a Negro without means in a world without pity that must start again at the very bottom? Whose worth is less than our wagon full of boots? Where could I possibly go where I wouldn't have but a mere sliver of what I already possess with the Coleman family? No – *freedman* is a concept that's no more than a ghost."

"Mister Coleman gave me some means to be used as necessary for our journey. I'd gladly give it to you."

"Whatever you have, it's not enough to guarantee that I wouldn't eventually end up in the employment of someone not half the man of Mister Coleman – or worse. If you wish, we can agree that from this moment on that I'm such a *freedman*, but as such I choose to return to the farm in Annapolis to resume, as you say, the status of Mister Coleman's *property*. The reality is, there's no such thing as *freedom* for me, but instead, just a choice of masters. And I don't choose as a master the cruelty and uncertainty of a world that doesn't value me to begin with. I choose instead my home on the farm where freedom is irrelevant, and I need it not."

"I see, Custis," Jack nodded, "I hadn't considered it in such that way. And in that way, I envy you more than you can imagine. In my life I've had neither home nor family, at least not one that is worth returning to. I haven't for one moment felt the security you speak of, where I wasn't merely helpless, being swept by the river current fighting to stay afloat and unable to find a purchase on land. But Mister Coleman has offered me that security with the hand of his daughter, who I dearly love. I cannot and will not fail them or I'll die in the attempt. For the first time I have a path."

Jack rose and extended his hand across the table. "It's settled then, Custis. We must fulfil our obligation to Mister Coleman and return home – for you to resume your life and for me to begin a new one."

Custis accepted Jack's hand and pulled himself up. "Agreed, Master Jack. This is best for the both of us."

"No need to discuss this again, Custis. Our way is clear. Let's take the first step."

Custis nodded as Jack clapped him on the back. The pair strode out the door into the frigid morning air where the mixed precipitation of the day before had given way to a bitter cold. They clinched their coats tight against the brisk northwest wind that whistled through the now icy streets of Morristown. Retrieving their horse and wagon from the adjacent barn, they quickly traversed the small village of four or five dozen houses, arriving at a large, white, handsome wooden home.

The *Ford Mansion* served as headquarters for General Washington and his immediate staff. Built in 1774 by Colonel Jacob Ford, Jr., prominent citizen and Eastern Battalion Commander of the Morris County Militia, the property sat on 200 acres of land deeded to Ford by his father. One of the most prominent families in the New Jersey province, the Fords owned interests in nearby iron mines, iron forges, a gristmill, a hemp-mill, and a gunpowder mill, all of which now served the colonial cause. Colonel Ford had died of pneumonia three years prior in January 1777 shortly after his participation in the second Battle of Trenton subsequent to Washington's daring crossing of the Delaware River. Following in the same year, his widow, Theodosia Ford, like many residents, had rented the house to colonial troops, many of whom developed smallpox that ravaged the town. Washington had since implemented a policy of inoculation that largely eradicated the problem. Nonetheless, even if the village did not welcome the idea of his army's return, such was the reputation of and respect for Washington that Theodosia gladly made her home available to the general, his wife and his staff, as she crammed herself and four children into the two remaining rooms.

"I'll wait here," Custis offered, "as I usually do."

"You can't wait here," Jack answered. "Your name is in the letter, too. They'll need to see you. Besides, who else can read if necessary?"

Flanking the central main entrance of the house stood two tall, well-built soldiers of General Washington's Guard armed with muskets and dressed in heavy grey-blue coats and leather helmets with a white plume. They eyed the new arrivals intently as one of them approached the wagon, signaling the pair with a wave not to dismount.

"Can I help you, sir?" The soldier addressed Jack as he maintained both hands firmly on his weapon, conspicuously at the ready before him. "Please identify yourself and the nature of your business. Keep your hands where I can see them." The second soldier remained at the door but also removed the firelock from his shoulder.

Jack cleared his throat and sat up straight. "I am Jack Halliday, and this is Custis Coleman. We are arrived from Annapolis as part of the Maryland quota for the Continental Army. I have a letter for General Washington."

"May I see it?"

Custis slowly produced the letter from his satchel, untied it, and handed it to Jack, who passed it down to the soldier. The man scanned it quickly and nodded then rolled the paper back up and returned it to Jack.

"Very well. I'll take you to the staff officer. We'll see to your horse and wagon."

Jack and Custis descended from the transport, each with a knapsack that contained their belongings. The soldier motioned to the second at the door to come take the reins.

"The horse, the wagon, and its contents are a gift to the general from our sponsor, Colonel Coleman." Jack informed both soldiers. "We need them no more. In the back are nearly a hundred pair of quality boots."

"Very well." The first soldier nodded. He then brought Jack and Custis to the door as the second led away the horse and wagon.

They entered a small foyer with a handsome wooden floor, partially covered with a matted rug, upon which the soldier tamped off the snow from his boots. Jack and Custis did likewise before following down a hallway toward the back of the house, stopping outside of a room with a closed door.

"Wait here, please." The soldier instructed. He knocked twice and entered, assuming a rigid posture as he made his report just inside the entry. "Captain, I have two men here newly arrived from Maryland for the army. They bring a horse and wagon with a hundred pairs of boots. They have a letter for the General." The soldier handed the letter forward, then resumed his place as the trio waited with Jack and Custis just outside the doorway. "Yes, sir," the soldier soon answered whoever was inside then turned to Jack and Custis with a nod. "You may enter. Leave your knapsacks here."

As the soldier quickly departed, Jack and Custis stepped into the room, rectangular with a welcoming fireplace across from the doorway. Sparsely furnished with little decoration, at one end sat a large wooden desk behind which a burly man was seated, dressed in a grey-blue jacket hanging on wide shoulders. He resembled a small bear with a large round head and ears, a thick head of black hair and full beard that hung beneath his bulbous nose. He put down his spectacles and stared at the pair before him with dark brown eyes.

Captain Matthew Isaac Littlefield hailed from the more isolated region of the Massachusetts province, about 90 miles west of Boston in the village of Springfield along the Connecticut River. Roughly five generations prior at the onset of King Philip's War, the meager Puritan foothold in the hinterland frontier had nearly been eradicated by the Nipmuc tribe, who burnt Springfield and surrounding towns to the ground. Like many other New England settlements, that horrific experience had galvanized the survivors in such a way that left little doubt that the only path to continued existence lay in a strict reliance on God and each other. Such was the heritage of Captain Littlefield, the son of a minister who, like his father and ancestors before, had held a musket and marched with the town militia since childhood.

Armed elements from western Massachusetts had arrived on the coast not long after the British incursion into Concord and helped form the defense of the Charlestown peninsula. Their growing numbers welcomed the arrival of General Washington and his organization of the subsequent Boston siege, even if they were not a little put off by having a Virginian in charge. Matthew Littlefield, then a private, proved skilled in helping gather, sort, and ration the myriad of goods that streamed in haphazardly from the far reaches of New England and beyond, first for his own unit then eventually on Washington's staff. If nothing else, the general had a knack for spotting talent and, having great need for such men, had plucked Littlefield from his unit, increasing his responsibility and arranging for an officer's commission inside the newly forming Continental Army.

Captain Littlefield replaced his spectacles as he clutched the letter in his hands, meaty but peculiarly small for his otherwise thick frame. He read the correspondence thoroughly and looked up at Jack. He read it a second time, looked up at Custis, then returned his gaze to Jack. "You would be John Halliday?" he asked in a low, soft voice, not much more than a whisper.

"Yes, sir," answered Jack, crisply, standing straight as an arrow with shoulders squared.

"And you are an *employee?*"

"Yes, sir."

"Do you mean an *indentured servant?*"

"No, sir. I owe Mister Coleman no term of service and we have no contract."

"And how long has that been?"

"Going on two years now, sir."

"I see," the captain replied as he turned his gaze to Custis. "And you must be Custis Coleman then?"

"Yes, sir," Custis answered quite uneasily.

"And you are a *servant?*"

"I'm the property of Mister Coleman. He's my master."

"A *slave*, then."

"Yes, sir."

The captain removed his spectacles again and placed them on the desk as he leaned back and rubbed his eyes. He pushed forward again, resting on his elbows as he stared intently at the pair. "Please help me to understand. An employee, a slave, a horse, and a wagon full of boots? It would seem that your *Colonel* Coleman releases himself from obligation with great advantage. No doubt he's also lined the pockets of some in Congress. Are you sure that you trust him?"

"Sir, our Mister Cole …." Jack began to answer as the captain raised his hand to stop him.

"That's not necessary," the captain shook his head as he pointed to Custis. "I want to hear it from him."

Custis bowed his head and rubbed his hands, then looked up and nervously spoke. "Our Mister Coleman is a good man. He's much more than the commander of the Annapolis Militia. He is one of the most prominent and respected citizens in the Maryland province."

"Please tell me more."

Custis cleared his throat. "Mister Coleman is a landowner of an estate upon which there is a farm with crops and cattle. The farm produces much, most notably leather, which is fashioned into items that are traded far and away to increase the wealth of the farm and to provide for the many under his care. The many boots we brought are of the finest quality and will be well-received by those that wear them."

The captain nodded. "And how many other *servants* such as you does your Mister Coleman possess?"

"Twenty at last count."

"Twenty human beings imprisoned by a detestable institution at odds with humanity, all working to increase the wealth of an owner who claims the military rank of a *colonel* but shirks his duty when called himself to be a servant and instead purchases a replacement with the currency of those that cannot similarly

refuse. To whom much is given, much is asked. We all may prosper according to our circumstances but our conduct in doing so
will ultimately be judged by God. Jesus said, '*It is harder for a
rich man to enter the kingdom of Heaven then for a camel to pass
through the eye of a needle.*' A *rich man*, not in terms of physical
wealth but rather one that would consider himself immune from
spiritual debt. Since your master chose to send you here in *his*
place to fulfil *his* obligation then, while you remain you will
carry the status as a freedman. When your military obligation is
fulfilled, I have no responsibility to return you to him. Do you
understand?"

"Yes, sir," Custis answered as he returned his eyes to the floor.

The captain returned his gaze to Jack. "And you, Halliday –
you state that you're not indentured?"

"No, sir. I have no binding obligation. Mister Coleman pro-
vides me lodging and sustenance."

"And also wages?"

"No, sir, I receive no wages. But I'm compensated well enough
and lack for nothing."

The captain nodded. "Really. And you're here from Maryland?"

"Yes, sir."

"Yet, you don't have the tongue of a Marylander."

Jack shifted nervously. "I'm from Liverpool, in England."

"Yes, of course. And where and when did you arrive?"

"Sir, more than five years ago in the port of Boston, in the
summer of '74."

The captain stared at Jack for several moments then leaned
forward on the desk. "'74? A curious year indeed to immigrate to
Boston. You have the manners and bearing of a soldier – are you?"

"Yes, sir," Jack answered as he stared straight ahead. "I was."

"Tell me."

Jack swallowed hard as he re-squared his shoulders and
straightened himself. "I was a private in the *King's Own* Fourth
Foot Royal Regiment of Lancaster, Light Infantry Company."

The captain raised an eyebrow. "A *private* in the Fourth
Lights?"

"Yes, sir"

"Hell, if you don't say." The captain now leaned back in his chair and studied Jack harder. "Then you were on the road to Concord and at Charlestown and then at Brooklyn?"

"Yes, sir."

"And you campaigned with Billy Howe through New Jersey and Pennsylvania and the occupation of Philadelphia?"

"Yes, sir."

"Ha!" The captain slapped his hand on the desk as he pushed forward onto his elbows and smiled. "My eyes be damned." The smile slowly faded as he leaned back again. "Tell me then, private – why was it so necessary to burn Charlestown to the ground?"

Jack cleared his throat. "Sir, it's my recollection that the action was taken to remove sanctuary for the many snipers that harassed our left flank adjacent to the village."

The captain waved his finger. "The bombardment didn't end until long after our marksmen, who were protecting our right flank, departed. The continued cannonading prevented the inhabitants from salvaging the remaining structures and therefore they had no choice but to abandon the village and all their possessions to the ravaging flames. It burned completely and well past the point where the marksmen were a factor. But you were on the right flank, yes?"

"Yes, sir. We marched with the Twenty-Third Fusiliers on the extreme right flank, at a beach along the northern side of the peninsula. We aimed to skirt the defenses below the fortifications on the hill."

"And what of it?"

"We were met by Yankees at a stone wall they had thrown up across the beach to the waterline."

"That would have been Colonel John Stark and his First New Hampshire boys. He's *General* Stark now."

"Mauled us bad, they did," Jack continued. "Pushed us into the river and turned it red. My memory is the taste of blood and saltwater."

"I imagine that's a taste you'll never forget." The captain folded his arms. "Continue please, private."

"Many died there at the waterline, but our sergeant led us off the beach and reformed our remainder in a field back in the direction from whence we'd come. We stayed close to the hill out of musket range and also small cannon. At that point I realized I had injured my knee but could still walk. We soon pressed forward again through the tall grass, above and parallel to the beach with the grenadiers to our left closer to the hill. But we were stopped again at a rail fence that stretched for some distance toward the hill. The fence was high and the Yankee fire thick, and we were compelled again to retreat."

"Many of your number fell at the fence," the captain nodded as he spoke thoughtfully, "some draped over it like drying laundry. The grenadiers that attacked the breastwork to our left below the fort also suffered greatly as our defense there was strong. But the worst we saved for those to our right who attempted to approach from the direction of the burning village. They took the heaviest loss as we decimated them almost to a man."

"You were there," Jack stated with an expression of mild surprise.

"I was," the captain answered. "I was but a private myself at the time with our Springfield Militia. We had arrived at Cambridge more than a month prior having answered the call for the aggression at Concord. Some of our officers and older men had fought the Indians and seen action in the war with France but for most of us it was the first time in battle. Our company manned a section of the rampart that faced the harbor, and we could see the whole of the peninsula below us. I can finish the story, if you would allow me. It's a scene that is forever etched in my memory. But I must be blunt."

"Please, sir."

"We watched as you struggled at the fence, stacked up like cords of wood, astonished that you hadn't bothered to remove your kit as that only served to hinder your movement. The only explanation, one would conclude, was a complete disregard for

our ability to repel you, a decision for which you paid dearly as
the clumsiness of your progress made you easy targets. The grenadiers closer in were brave but their numbers were not enough as
you had divided your force in half to attack the hill from both
sides without either having the numbers necessary to overcome
our defenses on either. Again, the only possible explanation was
a lack of tactical proficiency, for which you're not known, or a
lack of respect for our ability, for which you're very well known.

"You retreated a second time to the bottom of the hill from
whence you came. It was now long into the afternoon and the heat
was stifling. You didn't know that your second rush had forced
us to expend much of what remained of our ammunition. There
was plenty of ball and powder on the other side of the neck, yet
it had not managed to reach us. We scraped together what best
we could, enough for another good volley or maybe two. Many
of our number wanted to quit the hill then but the officers bade
us to remain. The good Doctor Warren himself had taken up a
musket and assumed a place on the rampart not far from me.
As long as he remained, no other man would leave. And so, we
waited as we knew there would be yet another rush.

"Finally, you started up the hill again with bayonets and your
kit now removed. This time you had support of cannon, which
played on our defenses with effect. There were noticeably fewer
of you but no longer divided as before. As you closed the main
works, we gave you a volley and then another as best we could
– but this time not able to repel you. Your grenadiers were the
first to breach the rampart to our left as they leapt across with
a terrible *Huzzah!* We tried to oppose them with whatever we
could place in our hands but were no match for so many bayonets. They spared no one, not the wounded or even those that
surrendered or otherwise begged for quarter. Outmatched now
with so much red now pouring in, we had no choice but to flee
lest we all be put to death. The last thing I remember was seeing
was one of your officers shoot Doctor Warren between the eyes
with a pistol. We ran up the hill and back down the other side
to the neck and across, every man for himself, and didn't stop

until reaching Cambridge." The captain shook his head. "Yes, I remember like it was yesterday."

The captain fell silent as he looked away, seemingly mesmerized by his own thoughts. Custis stirred and glanced at Jack, who continued to stare straight ahead with his jaw set firm. The captain finally spoke again. "Yet, you survived, private. And for your part, how did you fare?"

Jack spoke carefully. "None of our number wished to return to the hill as we considered ourselves more than fortunate to yet be alive. But we were ordered to advance yet a third time and so we did, this time in a proper column. We approached the rail fence as we had prior but now our cannon managed to clear the area and we were not so much opposed. No longer having need to scale the fence we instead skirted it to the vicinity of the fleches where we crossed behind the breastwork and started up the hill. There was a volley and then another, and then – nothing. We now rushed forward toward the fort. Here my knee faltered, and I fell into a ditch behind one of the fleches. In the ditch was a Yankee with the look of battle shock. He may have been hurt. We fought as he aimed to cleave my head in two with an ax and I had to kill him. I then managed to crawl out and continue upwards, my company already well ahead. When I reached the fort, I saw chaos with the backs of many militia moving hastily to the top of the hill and over. We chased them for a bit, as disorganized as they were, but were soon ordered to reform. With what remained of the day and well into the night we spent retrieving those fallen in the fields below."

"Fools and drunkards in charge of our supply," the captain shouted, leaning forward and pounding his fist on the desk. "For the want of mere ball, you never would've pushed us off that hill. You never would've claimed that victory."

Jack shook his head. "Sir, believe me when I tell you that whatever *victory* we may have claimed came at a cost too dear."

"And so," the captain's voice returned low as he leaned back again in his chair and stared at Jack, "it would seem our destinies have crossed yet again. Two soldiers on the same hill but on opposing sides. We could have made our acquaintance under much different circumstances you and me, but providence, it would seem, had other ideas." He reached forward to retrieve the letter, holding it in front of him. "Let's return now to the business at hand. Your *Colonel* Colemen recommends that you are to be made an officer – a lieutenant. That's a weighty proposition for a mere private. I know well myself. So, tell me, how do I know that you'll execute those duties honorably, with loyalty to our cause and not still cling to those of King George?"

Silence hung over the room for a long moment until Jack began to speak, slowly in an even tone. "Sir, I care naught for King George nor my homeland in England, which I don't wish to ever see again. As for your *cause*, I truly don't understand it but that matters not. I stand before you today solely at the behest of Colonel Coleman, who has given me an opportunity, the likes of which I've no right to expect, but from whose hand I'm compelled to accept as no one has ever treated me so well. I'm betrothed to his daughter and, upon my return, I'll take my place in his family."

The captain raised an eyebrow. "Betrothed to his daughter you say? Interesting, indeed. And you'd risk your life for this family?"

Jack nodded. "I would, sir. I'd risk my life and ten more if I had them. At Charlestown I understood that in order to live I must go up that hill. It's no different here. If I want a life in the Coleman family, then I must climb this hill, too. I'm no stranger to battle and hardship, and will not falter on that account, sir."

"I don't care for your Colonel Coleman," the captain declared as he shook the letter, "who by his very hand reveals that he's not fit to assume the role and responsibilities of a military officer, a distinction he no doubt enjoys to his own advantage but the duty of which he doesn't execute. Nonetheless, the issue at hand isn't him but you, as *you* stand before me, not he. There was a day not long ago that I'd discard such a letter without hesitation as an insult to the notion of our noble cause and as further proof that our brethren to the south are not committed as necessary to reject the yoke of this tyranny but rather prefer to dither in wait to ascertain the direction of the winds rather than assert themselves in causing them. But you, lad, I see, aren't made for such things. You don't understand our cause, as you say, and yet you'll fight. There are many who understand our cause very well, and yet they refuse to defend it.

"If you were on that hill at Charlestown, on that wretched day, that's all I need to take the measure of you and I care not that you were, at that time, in the service of the tyrant we now oppose. I see before me two men who've placed their fate in the hands of providence to do their duty even as their sponsor shirks his own. I'll therefore honor this request, however outrageous it may be, and enroll you both into the Continental Army under General Washington. It would seem the way of the world that those who bear the burden of military service are always those least able to avoid it. Do either of you have any reservations before we proceed?"

"No, sir," Jack answered straightaway with vigor.

"No, sir," Custis echoed somewhat more reservedly as he bowed his head toward the floor.

"Very well," the captain stated as he returned the letter before him on the desk. "John Halliday, you'll receive a commission as a second lieutenant and Custis Coleman, you'll be enlisted as a private. You'll join the Maryland unit and Colonel Smallwood will administer your oaths. But I'll further assign you under me, at least for now, as I believe you'll be of best use in that capacity as any man with service in the British Army can no doubt help with our training effort. Private Coleman will drill with the Marylanders, but I'll also assign him duties commensurate with his abilities."

The captain retrieved a quill pen and blank piece of paper and hurriedly scribbled a note, handing it to Jack. "Make your way to Jockey Hollow and give this to the quartermaster. He'll issue you the necessary supplies."

"Yes, sir," Jack replied as he accepted the note.

"But one last thing," the captain mentioned as he smiled and clasped his hands together with his elbows again on the desk. "Are you both men of God?"

Jack hesitated as he folded the paper and placed it in his coat.

"Yes, I am," Custis answered fervently.

"And you, Halliday?"

"Not particularly, sir," Jack responded.

"Not particularly?" the captain repeated. "Do you at least believe in our Lord?"

"Yes, he does," Custis offered.

The captain waved his hand at Custis then pointed to Jack. "I want to hear it from him."

Jack shuffled slightly as he stared straight ahead. "Sir, I don't think much about it. I would say that I've no opinion on the matter."

The captain leaned back and chuckled. "Surely you don't think you are here of your own accord and that I'm here of mine? And that we both yet live because of our own good works? But no matter. The men under my command, and particularly the officers, attend Sunday service. It's the essence of what binds us together. I'll expect to see you there. In time you may see fit to acquire an opinion."

"Yes, sir," Jack answered flatly.

"Very well then. You're dismissed. Welcome to the Continental Army, Second Lieutenant Halliday and Private Coleman."

14

At Uncle Joe's I liv'd at ease;
Had cider and good bread and cheese;
But while I stayed at Uncle Sam's;
I'd naught to eat but faith and clams.

The Adventures of a Revolutionary Soldier,
Joseph Plumb Martin

MORRISTOWN, NEW JERSEY, EARLY FEBRUARY 1780

"COME, BROTHERS AND GATHER! LET US GATHER AND PRAY!"
Dressed in a long brown coat with a black scarf around his neck, a woolen cap and mitts, a tall, gaunt man shouted from atop a large stump. Around him many lesser stumps poked out from the frozen white ground before him where the snow had been removed down to not quite half a foot. Jack and Custis ambled along with a multitude of others into the crude clearing at the far end of the army encampment that occupied an area known as *Jockey Hollow.*

"COME, BROTHERS AND GATHER!" the man repeated with outstretched hands as puffs of steam emanated from his mouth. "LET US GATHER FOR THE LORD ON THIS JOYOUS MORNING! LET US GATHER TOGETHER IN PRAISE ON HIS DAY!"

Located about four miles southwest of Morristown, roughly 900 acres of sloped land had been cleared of hardwood trees now converted to a *log-house city*, sectioned in accordance with each Continental Army regiment. Brigadier General Greene himself had surveyed it, at Washington's behest, deeming the uneven terrain not as agreeable as he would have preferred however suitable enough for the purpose. From the central parade ground at the bottom, rows of some 1,200 log huts ran up the hillside, constructed with the felled trees, mortared with chunks of clay and with hand-split shingles for the roof. They stood sixteen feet long, fourteen feet wide and six and a half feet tall with no windows, a fireplace at one end and a dozen wooden bunks with loose hay for bedding stacked three high along the inside. The structures nearest the parade grounds housed the common soldiers with the junior company officers, only four to a cabin, above and with the most senior field grade officers furthest up the hill. General officers, like Washington, were billeted in Morristown village itself according to the goodwill of the residents. Inhabitants at Jokey Hollow included units from New Hampshire, Massachusetts, Rhode Island, Connecticut, New York, New Jersey, Pennsylvania, Delaware, Maryland, Canada, and a smattering of other foreigners. The Virginia and North Carolina regiments had been detached prior to bolster the growing British threat in the southern provinces.

"COME, BROTHERS AND GATHER!" The man lowered both his hands and voice as he smiled widely. Jack and Custis jostled with an assortment of others to find a place to stand nearby. "Let us pray."

The man stood on the highest stump that marked the center of the straight side of a half-moon-shaped area that had been cleared as best it could. Seven blizzards in December alone had hammered the area already filled with November snow as the poorly clad troops had raced to erect their dwellings. Five more storms followed in January and now February had brought such cold that whatever could not move to keep warm had frozen solid. With the season only half over, none from the northern provinces could recall, even from family history, a winter so severe. The soldiers gathered looked more like scarecrows, many with mere strips for clothing and some using rags to wrap their feet. When Jack had arrived at the quartermaster to receive his *issue of necessary supplies,* he was awarded only a tattered blanket and a sneer, the latter being parted with more readily.

"Come, brothers, let us pray," the man on the stump repeated as the crowd bowed their heads. "Lord, we are gathered in Your presence once again seeking strength and wisdom. Hungry we may be. Shivering we may be. Naked we may be. Yet we stand united in this great cause that You have laid before us. Though we may falter we shall not fail for Your grace and mercy descends upon us like the many snowfalls You send.

"Tell me, brothers," the man raised his arms and his voice, "why are we here? Why are we here in this lonely, forsaken glen, with not enough to clothe us, not enough to feed us and damn near no wages as promised? Why are we not with our families in the warmth of our own homes tending to our own affairs of prosperity as free Englishmen? I believe you know the answer – because we are no longer free Englishmen! Our forefathers came to this land several generations ago to make a new life in a new world where they could prosper, each according to his own industry, where courage and ingenuity were the coin of the realm. That promise has been taken from us by an abusive king and his ministry that would strip us of a rightful inheritance over which only God has the authority to either grant or deny. For this reason, we must be reborn as a people, reborn as free Englishmen. I tell you that we must be reborn to enter a new worldly construct just as we must be reborn spiritually to enter the kingdom of God! Each and every one of you is an instrument of that glorious rebirth and your labors shall be rewarded here on this earth as they shall be in heaven. For the Lord sent his only son not as a peacemaker but rather to divide – to force our choice of whose purpose we shall serve. Listen now to a reading from the Gospel of John, chapter three, verses one through eight."

The man reached into his coat producing a pair of spectacles, which he placed on his nose, and a small book that he opened and held before him with both hands. Shivering, he read. "*There was a man of the Pharisees, named Nicodemus, a ruler of the Jews: The same came to Jesus by night, and said unto him, Rabbi, we know that thou art a teacher come from God: for no man can do these miracles that thou doest, except God be with him. Jesus answered and said unto him, Verily, verily, I say unto thee, Except a man be born again, he cannot see the kingdom of God. Nicodemus saith unto him, How can a man be born when he is old? can he enter the second time into his mother's womb, and be born? Jesus answered, Verily, verily, I say unto thee, Except a man be born of water and of the Spirit, he cannot enter into the kingdom of God. That which is born of the flesh is flesh; and that which is born of the Spirit is spirit. Marvel not that I said unto thee, Ye must be born again. The wind bloweth where it listeth, and thou hearest the sound thereof, but canst not tell whence it cometh, and whither it goeth: so is every one that is born of the Spirit.*"

He closed the book and removed his spectacles, placing both back in his coat. "Let us reflect on Bother Nicodemus. '*There was a man of the Pharisees, named Nicodemus, a ruler of the Jews: The same came to Jesus by night.*' You may recall that in those times the Pharisees and Sadducees were religious sects who sought to lead the Jews in religious interpretation of how one should comport oneself according to the laws that Moses gave. They differed in that interpretation, but such a fine point is not relevant for our discussion here. What is relevant is that Nicodemus was also a ranking member of the *Sanhedrin*, the great Jewish court in the capital of Jerusalem. A consummate holy man of his day, a rabbi, with enormous, and I would dare say, *unquestionable* moral and legal authority. The Romans, to make their occupation work, depended on the Sanhedrin to control the Jewish masses and in return maintained for them a place of high standing and preferential treatment in their gilded cage society. Yet here he was – sneaking in the dark like a thief to speak with Jesus. Such a man of high standing could not risk his reputation by making this kind of visit in the light of the day in full sight of his esteemed peers as Jesus, this charismatic but politically dangerous stranger from the hinterlands of Galilee chose to surround himself with the very unwashed rabble, whose behavior the more pious Pharisees constantly and publicly admonished for the sole purpose of manipulating them. For Jesus had most openly and unabashedly taken issue with the Pharisees, the Sadducees, and the Sanhedrin itself for corrupting God's law to serve mainly themselves and, in doing so, He had most severely threatened the Jewish leadership's credibility, relevance, and most importantly, their authority. SOUND FAMILIAR?"

The man waited as the crowd murmured in agreement. "Yes, one of King George's men ol' Nicodemus was, was he not? Yes, a regular *Parliamentarian!*" he chuckled as the crowd began to curse. "But for all his so-called wisdom the most learned Nicodemus did not understand this concept to be *reborn*. He did not understand because the imperative of maintaining his vaulted position had limited his thinking to only that which served such purpose. He did not understand because the voluntary construct of his existence did not allow him to understand. Bound and shackled by his own self-worth was Nicodemus, and yet here was this mere peasant from Galilee, this unwashed pilgrim, this lowly provincial who should otherwise be bowing to the authority of the Sanhedrin and liking it, this Jesus, instructing him otherwise. Here was this Jesus handing him the key to enlightenment. But would he take it?"

The man paused for a moment as he surveyed the crowd that stood silent before him. He raised his arms as he raised his voice. "So, I ask you, brothers, will *YOU* take the key? Do *YOU* understand? Do *WE* understand? Do we understand that to be redeemed we must be reborn? That to enter the Kingdom of God we must cast away our old selves that within which we exist in ignorance of our own egos? That we must instead make a voluntary decision to walk the path as an obedient servant to

God, and only God, so that we may flourish as a means to help our neighbors and, in doing so, all of mankind? That, likewise, we as free Englishmen on this continent and here in this lonely outpost in order to prosper as a people must collectively do the same?" He lowered his arms and leaned forward, speaking almost in a whisper to the intently silent crowd. "My brothers, I say to you truly – we are all *Nicodemus.*"

He paused, then stood back erect and produced from his pocket a small object that he held high above his head for all to see. "Consider the lowly acorn, my brothers, one of nature's most humble creations, I think you would agree. It is constructed with a hard shell and a cap on top. A large tree produces thousands that fall on the ground and scatter. It is a worthy creation in and of itself and if left in this unaltered state it remains but an acorn. One might say there is nothing ill-conceived about an acorn and that to remain an acorn, as created by its maker, would be a worthy course of events – nothing wrong with that, right? But let us pause to think deeper. Did God really create the acorn for it to remain only as such? Did He? For if you crush the acorn and break it open, essentially destroying the carcass of its former existence, you allow light and water to enter. If planted in the right ground under the right conditions, that broken acorn now receives nourishment it could not have otherwise and over time flourishes into something that was impossible to formerly conceive. And hence, that same mere acorn no longer resembles its former state but is *reborn* to become a mighty oak tree whose worth is multiplied a thousand-fold. And without the existence of these mighty oaks there would eventually cease to be acorns altogether, would there not?

"So, I ask you, brothers, what then is the acorn's true purpose? For not all acorns grow to an oak, as most remain intact on the ground where they fall to spend their existence merely as acorns, do they not? For to grow to an oak the acorn must be transported to a suitable place, then cracked open and destroyed – forever altered. Does not every acorn possess this potential? Yes, but few ever realize it. Why?

He produced the book again. "Let us consult once more with John fifteen, verse sixteen. *"Ye have not chosen me, but I have chosen you, and ordained you, that ye should go and bring forth fruit, and that your fruit should remain: that whatsoever ye shall ask of the Father in my name, he may give it you."* Beautiful passage, is it not? Jesus spoke these words only hours before his death to the Apostles who, like yourselves, may not have understood the gravity of their situation. Brothers, I tell you, and doubt me not on this, that *YOU* have already been chosen, that *WE* have already been chosen to do the Lord's work. It is not *you* that chooses God for such a purpose as this but rather that it is *God* that chooses *YOU!*

"For Jesus also said – Matthew ten, verses thirty-four through thirty-six -- *'Think not that I am come to send peace on earth: I came not to send peace, but a sword. For I am come to set a man at variance against his father, and the daughter against her mother, and the daughter-in-law against her mother-in-law. And a man's foes shall be they of his own household.'* My brothers, for are we not on this very day in such a struggle? Make no mistake – Jesus did not come to unite the world but rather to divide it – to force a choice, each according to our own free will. Every one of us here today, right now, has been called to the side of the righteous – and we have answered in kind. Though hungry we may be, shivering we may be, naked we may be, God has chosen us to be reborn in this great endeavor. And we have heeded that calling. Like that lowly acorn we, sinners that we all are, will ourselves serve as the nourishment for this noble cause to which we humbly oblige so that this new nation will not remain a simple acorn under tyranny but rather will one day become that mighty oak tree. That we will become a nation under God as God has intended that such a nation of free men should be."

The man bent so as to place the acorn by his feet and deliberately ground it into the stump with his boot. With that he stepped down from the stump and disappeared into the crowd as they began to disperse as they had formed, in a slow, cold silence. Walking back toward the cabins with the others across the hard-packed, snow-covered parade grounds, Custis turned to Jack. "Did you understand all that, Lieutenant Jack?"

Jack shook his head, staring at the ground as he walked. "No," he answered. "He talked in circles, didn't he?"

Custis chuckled as he shook his head. "No, not at all."

"Then tell me, what was all that about an *acorn*?"

Custis stopped in front of Jack and faced him. "Don't you see, lieutenant? *You* are that acorn."

* * *

A sudden knock broke the morning silence inside the cabin as all four inhabitants turned their heads toward the sound. Captain Wojciech Wadwicz, the most senior of them, moved toward the nearby door, having just poured his second cup of tea. His younger twin brothers, Lieutenants Pawel and Piotr rose from their seats, along with Jack. The door opened to reveal a stern-faced Captain Littlefield, who addressed his Polish counterpart. "Good morning, sir. May I come in, please?"

Captain Wadwicz nodded in silence, then stepped aside as Captain Littlefield entered, stomping his feet and brushing his coat of a hint of snow fallen from trees. "Looks like another storm brewing. I need to speak with Lieutenant Halliday, if I may."

Captain Wadwicz looked to Jack then pointed to his teacup as he nodded to Captain Littlefield.

Captain Littlefield hesitated with his brow furrowed then chuckled. "Oh, a cup of tea. Yes, that would be lovely."

Captain Wadwicz nodded, motioning Captain Littlefield toward a chair at a crude table near the fireplace at the end of the cabin which, unlike the enlisted men's structures, had such an amenity at each end. Jack had been assigned to billet with the Polish officers who, like him, had been separated for special duty to assist with training. Artillerymen by trade, their military leadership experience in a standing army was invaluable in the continuation of the professionalization effort that General Washington had initiated through Baron von Steuben at Valley Forge two years earlier. Several years older than Jack, the Poles had arrived toward the end of the summer by way of Paris, having received commissions upon recommendation by Colonel Tadeusz Kosciusko, the Polish engineer of exceptional standing. His talent had helped defeat Burgoyne at Saratoga as well as lead construction efforts for numerous other Continental Army fortification projects. Like Kosciusko, the Wadwicz brothers had departed their homeland due to the civil unrest in the Polish-Lithuanian Commonwealth, fueled by their puppet king's apparent acceptance of Russian domination. From an aristocratic family of substantial lineage, they spoke French and, of course, Polish, but only a smattering of English gleaned over their short time of service. Possessing ample resources, they had managed to acquire a sufficient quantity of tea, the existence of which was kept confidential inside the cabin.

Jack approached from the end of the room and stood rigid before the table. "Lieutenant Halliday reporting, sir."

"Very good to see you, lad. Sit down, please." Captain Littlefield motioned to Jack as he pushed out an adjoining chair with his foot. He leaned over the tea to savor the rising steam. "This won't take long, unfortunately."

Jack sat as Captain Wadwicz also placed a cup of tea before him. "Dziekuje," he addressed the Polish captain and nodded.

Captain Wadwicz nodded in return then moved to join his brothers on the far side of the room near the second fireplace.

"You speak Polish, lad?" Captain Littlefield asked in surprise, his furry brow knotted.

Jack grinned. "I know only *thank you*. But it's a word I use a lot as the brothers have been most kind to me."

"Yes, we're grateful to have them here." Captain Littlefield shifted in his seat and took a sip of his tea. "But as much as I'd like to linger, I must get to the point. I've several more stops such as this and time is short."

"What can I do for you, captain?"

"You've been here but a short time but as you are no doubt keenly aware, we're dreadfully short of supplies. The quotas for rations placed on the surrounding counties aren't enough to

sustain us and their arrival is spotty at best. What meager provisions from other provinces that General Greene has been able
to arrange through Congress have been held up due to the snow
or been turned back altogether. To say we're in dire straits would
be an understatement. I dare say the entire camp would desert if
they could survive leaving.

"The boots you brought were a godsend and Private Coleman
has been most instrumental in fitting them to the neediest of us.
I've assigned him to assist the quartermaster and he's proved his
worth in no time. But now I've an important chore for you as
I've been given the task of organizing local forage patrols. You
and other such officers will lead groups of a dozen men to nearby
farms that I'll direct you. There you'll negotiate with the owner
for hay, grain, livestock, and any other means of sustenance he's
willing to part with. Under no circumstances will you or any of
your men molest the owner, his family, or his property – on this
point General Washington's desires are firm and those found
culpable of even the slightest offense to the local population
will be held accountable in the strictest manner. You'll depart
immediately to this dwelling on the main road leading south
from the village."

The captain withdrew a map from his jacket, unfolded it and
placed it on the table. He pointed a stubby finger to a section
near the center. "You'll proceed to this location with all possible
haste in order to return before nightfall. Any questions?"

Jack silently studied the map for a moment then suddenly
looked up. "Sir, with what instrument do I negotiate?"

The captain shook his head. "I've naught to give you but
a letter of guarantee from General Washington that the owner
will be reimbursed in full at such time when the funds can be
procured. You're to take an accurate account of all that you're
given and affix your signature to a promissory note backed by
your authority as a commissioned officer in the Continental
Army."

Jack's eyes grew wide. "My signature?"

"Yes, that'll be sufficient. Is there anything else?"

Jack stared into his tea for a moment. "Yes, sir. I would request the assistance of Private Coleman for the accounting. May I bring him?"

"Certainly," the captain answered as he stood. "I'll send for him immediately. In the meantime, report to the parade ground. You'll collect your patrol with two wagons at the north end. You may keep the map."

"Yes, sir," Jack answered as he rose.

"One last thing," the captain offered as he placed a hand on Jack's shoulder. "Just a bit of advice, lad. There's a critical difference in this army from the place you came. You've probably already learned that. But just in case – these are free men, here of their own accord and not subjects pressed into service against their will or better judgment. The various regiments have their basis in militias and, as such, their officers are generally elected by the very men they lead. Your commission gives you authority but not necessarily credibility, as the men don't know you personally. When they test you – and they *will* test you – be firm and fair but not abusive. Once you win their trust, they'll follow you anywhere. Remember, they *want* to be led but not to be coerced and you must *earn* the privilege of leading them. This is important."

Jack nodded as he looked in the intent eyes of the captain. "Yes, sir."

"Good lad." Captain Littlefield removed his hand from Jack's shoulder then took his last swallow of tea. He looked toward the three Polish officers casually seated at the far end of the room staring back intently. "How do you say it again? *Thank you?*"

"Dziekuje," Jack murmured softly.

The captain hesitated. His mouth moved awkwardly but no sound emanated. "I can't," he finally muttered.

"Dziekuje," Jack repeated much louder in the direction of the brothers who raised their cups in reply as the captain did the same.

The captain turned back to Jack. "Excellent that was. I need to find a reason to come here again. Now, lad, you must make haste. It won't be long before the weather turns. Good luck. We're depending on you."

"Yes, sir," Jack replied as he straightened. As the captain exited, Jack looked to the end of the cabin where the three brothers stoked the fire and peered back at him. "Dziekuje," he repeated as he swallowed the last of his tea and placed the cup on the table. He donned his coat and shoved the refolded map inside, then followed the captain through the door.

* * *

Jack handed the map back to Custis as he looked at the marbled white cloud pattern that stretched and thickened to the west as far as the eye could see. A *mackerel sky* the Yankees in Boston had called it – one of nature's telltales that portended a coming storm. Well past the zenith of a winter season with no end in sight, every man in camp knew this weather pattern all too well. With the temperature hanging somewhere near freezing, soon the wind would stiffen from the southwest with a grey pall to descend on the world like a giant dark curtain with whatever form of precipitation the heavens could produce. After three days of battering, an increasing wind would veer to the northwest and with it clear blue skies and biting cold temperatures would freeze the countryside solid as it prepared for the cycle to repeat. By now so many layers of alternately melted, packed, and frozen snow covered the road that the ground below lay unaccounted for.

"We've not much farther," Jack turned to his troops. "We must keep moving."

As the young colonial officer once again stepped forward those behind him did the same, thirteen men in all, including include himself, a sergeant, a corporal, and ten privates with two empty horse-drawn cargo wagons on sleds bringing up the rear. Sullen and grumbling, the men trod carefully on the slushy path, none of them having yet eaten that day.

"Just a question if you do not mind there, lieutenant." A voice emanated from behind Jack as a young man vigorously approached, shorter and slighter with a head of thick, dark hair and a wide, toothy grin.

Jack kept his pace as he turned to acknowledge the soldier. "What is it, sergeant?"

"Well, sir," the man hesitated as he drew parallel with Jack, "the men and I were wondering if you knew where you were taking us? You've been looking at that map an awful lot and we've been walking to nowhere for a couple hours now."

Departing Jockey Hollow from the parade ground, the patrol marched to the center of Morristown and then turned right in a southernly direction along the same road upon which Jack and Custis had not long ago travelled to arrive. All of them members of parent units from the middle provinces, each man having been reassigned to Captain Littlefield under a quota system for his composite element. As is typical of the military in such circumstances, the individuals *donated* were inevitably those deemed least useful by their respective commanders.

Jack glanced back at the gaggle, who did little to hide their amusement. "Sergeant Jamieson, you can inform the men that our objective lies not far ahead."

Jamieson nodded. "I see. Sir, can you also tell us why the Negro keeps the map? It would seem quite odd."

"No need for concern, sergeant," Jack answered, his tone somewhat annoyed, "I have appointed Private Coleman as my scribe for the outing as he's quite fitted for that task. In that capacity he is responsible for maintaining our records and paperwork, such as they are, which includes the map."

Jamieson nodded again. "Lieutenant, you have an accent that cannot be placed. May I ask where you come from?"

"I came from Annapolis, as does Private Coleman."

"Annapolis? I'm from Bowie, about twenty miles west from Annapolis. I must say that your tongue is decidedly not that of any other Marylander I've ever heard."

Jack hesitated. "I'm originally from Liverpool in England."

"Liverpool?" Jamieson exclaimed loud enough for all to hear. "In England? I'll say you've wandered a far piece from home."

The chuckles and murmuring now increased from behind. The sergeant now raised his voice to a theatrical pitch. "Seems your navigation skills might be more suspect than first imagined."

Jack raised his hand to stop the column, then turned to face Jamieson. Poking two fingers into the sergeant's chest, he spoke curtly. "Sergeant Jamieson, I won't begrudge you a bit of levity in these hard days of ours. But as you make me the subject of your humor in full view of the patrol, I must consider that as an affront to my authority, a circumstance that can't be tolerated. Now, you've tested my goodwill and I've obliged. You've had yourself a laugh, but this comedy is now finished. You will return to your place in the ranks with no further exchange. Do you understand?"

Jamieson looked at Jack with a toothy smile. "Yes, sir, lieutenant," he chuckled, "you're the officer in charge."

Jack signaled for the column to start forward again as the sergeant dropped back with the others, maintaining a wide grin as he did so. Several minutes later they descended a thickly wooded hill to emerge into the open expanse of a large field whose tree line on the opposite side lay a good quarter mile away. Jack halted the column again as his gaze circled the surrounding area. "May I have the map?" he asked with an outstretched hand as he turned his back to shield the wind. Custis nodded as he retrieved a bundle from inside his coat and handed it to Jack, who opened the thickly folded paper and pointed to the lower center portion. "We're here, on this side of the clearing. Do you recognize this place?"

"Of course," Custis answered. "We were stopped here on our approach to Morristown by a man claiming to be the outer guard. We gave him six pairs of boots. We're practically on the very spot."

"Exactly," Jack nodded as he pointed across the clearing. "We turn at the far end down there. We must move." Jack refolded the map and passed it back to Custis. "Damn it!" he yelled as he took the first step.

"What is it, lieutenant?" Custis asked, his eyes wide.

"Goddamn it! My knee."

"Your knee?"

"My right one. Hurt it some time ago. Seems to have a mind of its own. Hasn't bothered me for some time. But now...."

"Do you want to ride in the wagon? I can...."

Jack cut him off. "No, Custis, I don't," he answered sharply as he glanced back at the remainder of the patrol, who all stared at him in unison. "Let's go," Jack ordered as he started forward with a pronounced limp. "I'll be fine, just not as nimble."

Reaching the opposite side of the field they wheeled left onto what looked to be a path, not quite as flattened as the main road but still discernable in the snow. The trail continued downward as it reentered the woods, leveling out in a section of hardwood trees that lined a brook across which stood another field, this one larger than the one before. Crossing a crude wooden bridge just large enough for the wagons they followed the route to the right along the stream that angled southeast, the water frozen in still places and loudly gurgling in others from the ample runoff. Rounding a bend, they came upon a homestead comprised of several buildings made with logs, not unlike the many cabins that comprised their camp. There lay a small mill with a water wheel along the brook and to the left what looked to be a larger barn and other assorted structures. Jack stopped near the barn in front of what appeared to be the main building, the front yard well-trampled into a small, slushy field. The column behind him fell silent except for the snorting of the horses.

A man emerged from the facing door and strode toward them carrying a musket. He was tall with large shoulders, wearing a long coat and wide-brimmed hat that revealed, as he neared, a beaked nose and a scar that stretched along the left side of his face. He stopped several paces from Jack with the firearm firmly in both hands.

"So, it's you," the man addressed Jack in a low, even tone. "You've returned with numbers to retrieve your boots, have you?"

"Sir," Jack answered, "I am Lieutenant Jack Halliday, in the service of the Continental Army encamped at Morristown. I've been authorized by General Washington to barter with you for provisions as you see fit to trade. I have in my possession a letter signed by the general himself that confirms the same."

Jack motioned to Custis, who reached into his coat.

The man bristled and brought his gun to the ready. "Keep your hands where I can see them," he ordered angrily. "I've no need to see any damn letter, particularly from Washington."

The men behind Jack murmured as Custis removed his hands and showed them palms out.

The man lowered his gun and peered at Jack. "An officer, are you?"

"Yes, sir," Jack answered.

"Here to *barter* for goods?"

"Yes, sir."

"Well, you're not the first band of brigands to come our way to barter under such so-called *authority*."

"We are not brigands, sir. We are Continental Soldiers on a foraging mission sanctioned by General Washington himself."

"Washington," the man scoffed. "Washington is finished. Everyone knows that. He couldn't hold New York and couldn't take Philadelphia. The encampment at Morristown is folly and on the verge of collapse. The Virginian can't fight and now he can't feed himself. Just a matter of time before the entire effort dissolves. Save yourselves the trouble and return home from whence you came."

Jack nodded as he paused in thought. "Far from finished, I'd say. We must but wait out the winter and the arrival of France. There's much cause for hope."

"France?" the man sneered. "I would sooner pin my hopes on the ass of a rented donkey than put one ounce of faith into a government of self-serving whores whose only interest is replacing King George as our master. I served with the Jersey Blue Militia to fight the French. I was there for the capture of Montreal under General Amherst in sixty. That was an honorable war for the defense of this land. This aggression against our own Crown is insanity and will ruin us."

Jack nodded. "I'm not here to argue with you on that account. But you also played the role of a brigand when you claimed to be the outer guard. Yet, we still bartered. Can we not do so now?"

The man spit. "My great-grandfather came here with nothing – an indentured servant with the clothes on his back and a willingness to work. My grandfather built the first house here, which the Lenape burned to the ground. My father added the mill, and I must do what I can to improve on that. This is my land to include the stretch of road into Morristown. And on that land, I won't yield to a damn tobacco planter from Virginia who has proven himself incompetent and now in league with the French."

A young girl of about ten years wearing a dark blue sweater over a long bright blue and white checkered dress appeared from the house doorway behind and approached the man quickly, grabbing onto his left arm. "Was ist das, Papa?" she whispered to him, loud enough for the silent crowd to hear.

"Kein problem," he answered softly as he stooped nearer to her. "Kein problem aber, finde deinen Bruder. Jetz. Schnell." He patted her on the bottom as she ran off toward the barn.

The man straightened again as he addressed Jack. "And just what do you have to barter *with*?"

"I'm authorized to provide you with a promissory note for the amount we agree on to be paid at a time to be determined by the Continental Congress. I'm encouraged to be *generous*."

"A promissory note? In Continental Dollars, I assume?"

"Yes, sir."

The man spit again, this time more in Jack's direction. "Worthless. A promissory note from Washington in Continental Dollars. Absolutely worthless. It's easy to be *generous* when what you offer is of no value."

Jack stared at the man for a moment. "Sir, you seem well aware of our situation. We've only to wait out the winter until conditions permit us to resume the campaign. You have a fine farm here with ample resources. Surely, we can come to terms for something you can spare."

"I have enough to feed my family and even more than that. But I won't bargain for Continental Dollars, promised to me by a commander-in-chief who is a pretender, delivered to me by a man that I won't see again, and underwritten by an illegal *Congress* that will, in all likelihood, soon cease to exist. If you wish to trade, you must present me with something of actual value. I'll take your nigger."

Jack glanced at nearby Custis, whose eyes widened as he looked to Jack. Jack shook his head as he returned his gaze to the man. "His name is *Private Coleman*. He is a freedman and not for trade."

"I'll give you two head of cattle with ample hay. That's more than fair value."

Jack bristled. "And no doubt you'll trade him for twice that worth at first opportunity. Sir, he is a soldier in the Continental Army and therein his value lies. As such he's not for trade."

"Surely your hungry army would value more the milk and beef that ...."

"I said he's not for trade," Jack interrupted as he leaned toward the man, who raised his weapon once again. "We won't speak more of it."

"Lieutenant!" Jack turned to see an approaching Sergeant Jamieson, striding quickly as he reached the pair.

"What's this, lieutenant?" Jamieson asked, seemingly exasperated. "What's taking so long?"

"Sergeant," Jack answered sharply, "return to your place with the men. I'll call you forward when needed."

"We've walked a long way, lieutenant, and not eaten all day. Soon it'll be dark. What need is there for delay? Give this man whatever recompense you see fit, and we'll take what we need."

The man leaned back with a smirk. "Brigands," he muttered.

Jack addressed Jamieson sternly. "We've not yet set a price for recompense, sergeant, and must negotiate first. For this man has no obligation to provide us anything no matter what our circumstances. But that business is my concern, and I'll call you and the others when needed, which is not at this particular moment."

"Yes," the man offered, "I'm willing to trade for the nigger."

"You have chickens," Jamieson answered the man, "we can smell them. We can give you the nigger for two dozen chickens."

"Two dozen chickens?" the man chuckled. "Little wonder you're not in charge. I've already offered two head of cattle."

"Two head of cattle?" Jamieson shrieked, loud enough for all to hear. "We'll give you the nigger for that!"

Jamieson lunged toward Custis, only a few feet away, attempting to grasp the collar of Custis' coat with a free hand as he maintained hold of his firelock. Jack caught the sergeant by the wrist and also grabbed hold of his musket. They struggled for balance with Jack favoring his left leg as he moved to place himself in front of Custis.

"That's enough, sergeant! You'll go to the rear! NOW!"

"We'll fight you, lieutenant!" Jamieson wailed. "There are more of us than you!"

"These vagabonds are no soldiers, lieutenant," the man stated flatly as he shook his head and watched Jack and Jamieson tussle. "Once they've dispatched you, they'll move on to rob *me*. But I count eleven firelocks to our six. I count the nigger on our side along with you and the two pistols in your coat. You do still have those pistols don't you, lieutenant?"

At that moment appeared a plainly dressed woman in the doorway with a musket as did a long barrel aiming down at the group that protruded from an upper window of the barn.

"I don't need your help, sir!" Jack scolded as he continued to hold the sergeant fast.

"But it appears you do, lieutenant" the man answered as he nodded toward the remainder of the patrol, who now made their way forward.

Jack wheeled around to face the group, bringing Jamieson with him, still in his grasp.

"You'll come no further! THAT IS AN ORDER!" Jack bellowed.

"Don't listen to him!" Jamieson admonished, "or we'll leave here with nothing!"

"Brigands!" the man shouted. "As I said."

"Corporal Libby!" Jamieson cried. "Assemble the men! Shoot the lieutenant! We'll dispose of him in the woods and tell the captain he deserted! We'll trade the nigger and take the cattle!"

The troops murmured as they looked from the house to the barn and back at Jack. Corporal Libby, a tall, gangly fellow, stepped forward and nervously brought his weapon with both hands up against his chest.

"Shoot him, Libby!" Jamieson screamed. "Damn it, SHOOT HIM!"

Jack released his grip on Jamieson's wrist and musket and instead grasped the wriggling sergeant by the thick lapels of his coat. In a swift motion he drove his forehead hard into the bridge of Jamieson's nose. Jamieson shrieked as his knees buckled, falling to the slushy ground in a crumpled heap, releasing the musket as he covered his face with both hands, thrashing in the slop as blood streamed between his fingers. Jack kicked the howling sergeant hard in the stomach and picked up his now unsecured firelock. Stepping forward, he placed the barrel of the weapon into Libby's long chest.

"You have me outnumbered," Jack addressed the tall man. "But leave me for dead in the woods and say I deserted? That's a fool's plan. Be assured I'll take at least one of you with me. Will that be you, corporal?" Jack nudged the barrel into Libby as he pulled back the cocking mechanism.

The corporal's eyes went wide as he took a step back.

"You men listen to me!" Jack continued. "We are soldiers – not thieves and murderers. We are *masters of our persons*. Our orders are to trade fairly and, above all, to not harm the citizenry even if that means that we return as empty as we departed. Temperance on this day will be rewarded but misconduct severely punished. None of you have yet erred this day, save for the sergeant."

Jack turned around as he reached into his coat, producing a small leather sack that he handed to the man. All remained silent, save for Jamieson still writhing on the ground clutching his face.

Bewildered, the man slowly extracted a silver coin, then another and another, the purse still bulging.

"Spanish Dollars," Jack offered as he nodded, "given to me by my sponsor so that I wouldn't have want. Take it all. More than enough to account for two cattle, I think you'd agree."

The man nodded in return with wide eyes and mouth open. Quickly replacing the coins, he stuffed the purse in his coat then pointed toward the yard past the house. "Take what you want. Cattle in that barn and hay in that one."

"Corporal!" Jack ordered. "Bind the sergeant. Have the men take the wagons as directed."

In less than half an hour they had loaded both wagons with hay and, in addition, attached a smaller wagon also filled with hay behind each. The man had agreed to fill the larger wagons again upon return of his carts. With the two cattle led in the front, the procession moved off slowly in the direction from where they had come with Jack and Custis now bringing up the rear right behind Sergeant Jamieson, bound by the wrists and drawn by a rope tied to the last cart. The man grinned as the procession passed, arms folded and still gripping his musket. Jack merely nodded as he cinched his coat against the stiffening wind and darkening sky. He moved forward as best he could, his limp now beginning to subside.

15

I am not going to risk my shipping in that damned hole.

Commodore Dudley Saltonstall during the
Battle of the Penobscot

I n June of 1779, exactly four years after the Battle of Bunker
Hill in Charlestown, a British task force of three men-of-war,
four transports and infantry – approximately 900 men in
total – arrived unannounced in the small village of Castine in the
Maine region of the Massachusetts province. Located at the top
of Penobscot Bay midway up the Maine coast, Castine, founded
originally in 1613 by the French, had been a European trading
post with the native peoples for roughly a century before the
Pilgrims landed in Plymouth and was currently a prime location
for England's timber supply of naval masts. The British landed
unopposed and set immediately to build a fort on the 200-foot
hilltop that dominated the peninsula looking down onto the
bay and the mouth of the Majabagaduce River along which the
village lay. In addition to one of the best natural harbors on
the entire Atlantic seaboard, Castine was a natural geographic
demarcation point, above which contained roughly the upper
half of Maine, whose sparse population leaned mainly Loyalist

due to the natural resentment of the provincial seat of government in Boston, where political and economic decision making
never ceased to serve lower coastal Massachusetts' purposes first
and foremost. Beginning here, the British intended to colonize
New Ireland for disaffected Loyalists driven from their homes
further south and also to establish a base closer than Halifax
from which to prosecute the never-ending smuggling operations
in New England.

It did not take long for the powers that be in Boston to learn
of this transgression and, when they did, to set about in a flurry
to raise an amphibious expeditionary force by whatever means
necessary, to include the involuntary impressment of men and
commercial vessels, to eject the invaders. In keeping with the
stubborn and timeless New England penchant to *do it yourself,*
they did not ask for help from Washington's professional army
but instead chose to man and lead the expedition from within
their own resources, however incapable for the task those might
be. About a month later in mid-July such a flotilla of 43 ships
and 2,000 men with a firepower advantage of 350 total cannon
to the British 38 arrived at the mouth of the Majabagaduce led by
both a land force and naval force commander, neither of which
had been given ultimate authority over the entire operation.

After an initial failed assault at the most difficult place on
the peninsula, the rock cliffs below the unfinished fort, the fleet
milled about for three weeks just outside of British cannon range.
The land commander, Brigadier General Solomon Lovell, took
sporadic and ineffective offensive action, constantly demanding
that the navy take out the British ships that guarded the mouth of
the river and approaches to the fort while the naval commander,
Commodore Dudley Saltonstall, insisted that the army first neutralize the fort that protected those ships. Perfectly willing and, in
fact, fully expecting to surrender to the overwhelming American
force should they mount a credible assault on the fort, the delay
gave the British commander time to call for reinforcements back
in New York Harbor, nearly 500 miles away by sea.

By mid-August, on the very morning the New Englanders finally decided to conduct a coordinated amphibious assault on the peninsula, they spotted the sails of British vessels heading up the bay toward them from the south. Bared down upon by three new warships, the Americans, although still possessing a significant military advantage in terms of firepower and men, called off their offensive operation as they scrambled to relocate themselves into a defensive position further north where the bay narrowed into the more constricted Penobscot River. The following day, as General Lovell expected to make a stand, using the high ground along the river – as previously agreed the day before – Commodore Saltonstall instead issued orders that each of his ships should now *fend for itself*. To the utter astonishment of the British and without firing a shot the entire Massachusetts gaggle weighed anchor and fled in a panic farther up the river where every vessel was scuttled, burned, or otherwise abandoned as those who could ran for their lives through the woods back toward Boston. In short, the *Battle of the Penobscot* would become the greatest American naval catastrophe until the attack on Pearl Harbor 162 years later.

As the so-called survivors of the action trickled back south from the Maine hinterland with nothing to show except the clothes on their backs, the Boston citizenry was not impressed. Perhaps the biggest casualty was the reputation of the expedition's leadership, as Commodore Saltonstall along with the senior officer in charge of land artillery, Lieutenant Colonel Paul Revere, were both court-martialed for cowardice due to their actions, or lack thereof, particularly during the final hours. While Saltonstall was found guilty and his reputation ruined, Revere was eventually cleared, no doubt due to his good standing as a trusted messenger for the Sons of Liberty over which current Massachusetts governor John Hancock had presided. At best, a mere footnote in history for his participation in the American Revolution, Revere was lionized nearly a century later by native Maine poet, Henry Wadsworth Longfellow, grandson of Brigadier General Peleg

Wadsworth, second in command of the land forces at Penobscot as well as commander of the militia at the Battle of Bunker Hill.

Notwithstanding and even including the ill-fated but strategically insignificant clash at the northern colonial reaches of Castine and another soon after in the opposite end of the Atlantic seaboard at Savannah, Georgia, the year of 1779 proved of little military consequence in America; however, not so in London as a battle royale raged inside the ministry. After all the blood and treasure the Crown had expended over the better part of a decade to put a small minority of unruly political hotheads back in their place, all they had to show was – *nothing*. In fact, the situation had horrendously worsened as, never mind quelling a simple colonial uprising in some far-flung corner of the empire, Great Britain was once again at war with France. How did the world's greatest political, economic, and military power find itself in such an unquestionable mess that had continued to worsen?

The one unwavering assumption that had underpinned British strategy and resultant policy was that there existed multitudes of loyal subjects in America, a giant silent majority, waiting in the wings to rush to their aid when needed. But while there certainly existed those so-called *Loyalists* that formed militias under the British Army and other individuals willing to provide intelligence and logistic support, there never had materialized nearly the numbers necessary to be of consequence. If anything, more had actively joined the rebel side or chose to not join any side at all, preferring to remain anonymous until the whole affair blew over like just another nor'easter. King George did not understand why those over which he ruled with such wisdom and authority were not falling in line with his policies and actions through which he intended to save them from themselves. It apparently never occurred to the narrow-minded monarch that his whole approach itself was the problem and that his base assumption was wrong even though the still vocal Whig minority, whose voices he had taken great pains to reduce to a mere whisper, continued to murmur as such. Every time he had asked his ministry for advice, he had received precisely the answer he wanted to hear

– that his strategy and policy was sound – undoubtedly because he had formed around himself a support system more akin to an echo chamber rather than a sounding board.

The simmering turbulence in London rose to a boil as finger-pointing for failure across the Atlantic provided the heat. Lords North, Germaine, and Sandwich were skewered by the newspapers. Many inside the ministry did not let such a crisis go to waste as they leveraged the chaos and constant infighting to position themselves for more elevated posts. Not willing to even remotely consider that his heavy-handed policies, to include declaring war on his own subjects, could in any way be the cause for the paucity of colonial support, what King George needed – again – were scapegoats. The Howe brothers, prime targets for the blame, most notably a failure to support Burgoyne, demanded a courts-martial where they fervently defended their honor, mainly with the argument that they themselves were improperly supported with too few resources for such a vast countryside filled with an incorrigible and thankless population – surprisingly similar to what predecessor General Gage had maintained. Unfortunately, such justification ran counter to ministerial conventional wisdom and even the Howes' own past stated beliefs with the general conclusion reached that if the brothers had conducted themselves in America with the same level of vigor as they did the inquiry there would have been no defense needed. The pleas of the Howes did nothing to inform the king and Parliament that America was far too replete with those who would never support the British military effort. Instead, based on all that had transpired to date, the logical conclusion was drawn that the strategic architects' vison remained sound, however, focused in the wrong location.

With New England the political wellspring, New York Harbor the logistical center of gravity, and Philadelphia the de facto political capital, the colonial south had always been considered the *soft underbelly* of the independence movement. With vast tracts of farmable land that produced large crops of, among other things, tobacco, rice, cotton, indigo, and sugar cane that mainly supplied England, these provinces were considerably the most economically tied to the mother country. They were further viewed as having come along on this journey in somewhat of a protest, somehow artfully manipulated by the northern Puritans that had quite skillfully overplayed Britain's economic exploitation and somehow managed to divorce, or at least mask, their severe disdain for slavery and thereby avoid requiring its prohibition as a prerequisite for declaring independence, a condition the southern provinces would never have considered, much less agreed to.

But a southern campaign was not necessarily a new idea. General Howe had dispatched Sir Henry Clinton in June 1776, on a side mission in the lead up to the invasion of New York Harbor, to take control of Charleston, South Carolina, the logistical center of gravity in the south, with the expectation that Loyalist support existed there simply for the asking. This effort failed, mainly because such support did not materialize because the populace sided heavily with rebel forces that defended the city. This should have been an early clue that again expecting otherwise was flawed. Lord Germaine, himself convinced by the wisdom of 3,000 miles of separation that most Americans were Loyalists, continued to prod Howe to consider the south – and the general had remained open to that. But the emergence and stubborn continued survival of George Washington and his army necessitated a concentration of effort in the north, a reality further emphasized by the disastrous defeat of Burgoyne. As 1779 played out and with France now in the war, an imperative emerged that necessitated a bold new strategy – a boldness still colored by the same tired thinking that drove decisions to the only place the British had left to go. With General Clinton now in charge of the entire colonial military operation, Lord Germaine continued to form his southern strategy as a new appetite arose in the ministry to concentrate there in earnest.

The northern colonies had proven far more resilient than expected and the strategy to isolate New England, to *sever the head of the snake*, had failed, a failure punctuated by the defeat of Burgoyne. But this strategy to remove or neutralize the leadership had been born with the goal of quelling a stubborn insurrection, a relatively modest aim when considered on a more global spectrum. With France now in the picture, the stakes had not only grown exponentially but had also changed the context of how the conflict should be prosecuted. If the British could leverage the Loyalist support that they believed existed in the south, from Virginia down, they could control half the colonial seaboard with a huge economic interest and thereby place the northern provinces in a precarious position between them and the French. After all, the ever-scheming Palace of Versailles obviously had designs on controlling, if not outright stealing territory, the threat of which could compel a weakened north to capitulate in favor of maintaining a common culture or face being swallowed by Catholic pope-mongers. In other words, the colonies could no longer be viewed as themselves the end but rather now a means to an end to quash the efforts of France.

Well before, in late December 1778, a relatively small British force had managed to easily capture Savannah, one of the few consequential southern seaports and located in the outpost province of Georgia. This action was not tied to a larger strategic effort so much as rather a low-risk, target of opportunity as the port city was well known to be poorly defended. For little effort and negligent losses, the British now kept a foothold in the southern-most province, where they could stage logistic support until the opportunity presented itself to again move on Charleston, about 100 miles north. Later in September of 1779, Major General Benjamin Lincoln, the commander of American defenses in Charleston, moved a force of 1,500 men south to combine with the newly arrived French Navy with 3,500 soldiers to dislodge the British. This ambitious but disjointed effort failed, in large part due to superior British intelligence, preparation, and defenses. In October the battered Franco-American force withdrew, the French back out to sea and the Americans back to Charleston. Although this stalemate gained no military advantage for either side, it served to inform the British, particularly Lord Germain in London, that the assumption of overwhelming Loyalist support in the south was validated.

Not long after the Battle of Savannah, the day after Christmas 1779, Clinton departed New York Harbor with a sizeable flotilla of 14 warships and 90 transports that held about 8,700 British and Hessian troops. Slowed and battered by the same horrible weather that plagued those in Morristown, Clinton's armada arrived at Savannah five weeks later. Spending a long week to make repairs and take on more men, the invasion force repositioned to South Carolina and went ashore at Simmons Island (Seabrook) on the Edisto Inlet February 11th.

Charleston, a city of approximately 12,000 inhabitants, lay at the tip of a marshy peninsula between two brackish estuaries that set inland several miles from the sea. Not intending to repeat the mistakes of 1776 and now with a larger force not dependent on Loyalist cooperation, Clinton set about to lay siege to the wealthy village. Marching his troops across the marshes from the southeast, he constructed trenches and mounted cannon just north of the town, effectively cutting off land traffic while simultaneously stationing his ships in the harbor to the south to prevent access by sea. All throughout April, in traditional European siege-craft fashion, Clinton inched his trenches and cannon ever closer toward the town, pounding the inadequate colonial defense works that had fallen into disrepair. Defending Charleston were about 5,000 troops split more or less evenly between Continentals and militia, led by Major General Lincoln. A farmer from Massachusetts with little former battle experience but nevertheless considered capable, Lincoln had nonetheless previously contributed to Burgoyne's defeat at Saratoga, sustaining a shattered ankle in that effort. Now placed in charge of the garrison of the most important city in the south he had no experience whatsoever with defending a siege – in fact, no American General did – and had instead expected Clinton to attack by sea, therefore concentrating his defenses along the peninsula shoreline to the south. By the first week of May, Clinton's trench works had moved close enough for his cannon to strike the perimeter of the town as he began to lay waste to the outer wooden houses of the working class. The wealthier citizens of inner Charleston had fully expected their protectors to put up a fight but not at the expense of their handsome village, including their own large brick mansions. The leading gentry consequently implored Lincoln to surrender, which he did on May 12th.

The capture of Charleston had been accomplished in an operationally brilliant manner. However, the subsequent prime strategic effort to bring about *tranquility and order to the country* did not follow that pattern. Ten days after the fall of the city Clinton issued a proclamation declaring that anyone taking up arms or persuading *faithful and peaceable subjects* to rebel would be imprisoned, with their property confiscated. By the end of the month, he granted a pardon to former combatants and anyone else who had strayed from fidelity, but two days later added that all such pardoned or paroled individuals must sign an oath of allegiance to the Crown within 17 days or be considered still in rebellion. The pardon had the effect of angering many Loyalists, who had fully expected such criminals would be punished. Those who accepted parole did so with the understanding that their possessions held most dear – family, property, and livelihood – would remain intact under their control and that they could quietly return to a neutral status outside of scrutiny. Swearing such an oath of allegiance would necessitate assuming the full responsibilities of a British citizen to include mandatory participation in a Loyalist militia, in effect, to take up arms against those like themselves. Many who did take the oath were nonetheless treated as if they had not, with their property and lives destroyed by heavy-handed enforcement by the British military that had no use to begin with for such turncoats, particularly those most prominent.

In the past, the war farther north had always caused certain disgruntled people to take up arms in accordance with their passions, however, the vast majority preferred to remain impartial for a myriad of reasons known only to themselves. By taking such an unprecedented step to formally demand loyalty, an overt threat even if only perceived as such, Clinton had completely removed the relative safety and anonymity of the middle ground and forced the entire province to choose sides, in effect, to cause a provincial civil war. His proclamation suddenly gave top cover to Loyalists who could now disguise their personal grievances with accusations of inadequate fidelity, whether true or not, to justify whatever retribution they pleased. As news of these abusive measures shot through the province with a polarizing effect, the likes of which had never before occurred in the entirety of the colonies, an abundance of organized groups of varying allegiances suddenly emerged, ranging from legitimate militias to loose bands of armed marauders who used this convenient set of circumstances to prey on whomever they could.

Clinton neither realized the severity of the poisonous crop he had just planted, nor did he remain to harvest it, as he departed for New York by sea at the end of June leaving his second in command, Lieutenant General Charles Cornwallis, in charge of the southern campaign with about 3,000 men, a relative pittance that depended heavily on organic Loyalist support. Before leaving, Clinton issued Cornwallis his mission – to pacify South Carolina, subdue North Carolina, and then continue into Virginia to unite with British forces that would join from the north. Although having worked together in America since the Battle of Long Island, the two military officers had fallen out and, for his part, Cornwallis was more than happy to be left on his own. With summer just underway, the British now had a major logistics base from which to conduct the next phase of operation, to split the south from the northern provinces. Although they had not needed Loyalist support to capture the strategic port of Charleston, a follow-on effort to subdue the greater south most certainly would and further require reliance on an assumption that was yet to be proven correct. Once again, the British – and particularly Clinton – demonstrated that they had learned nothing, reaffirming that they could capture territory but not enough of the hearts and minds of their American subjects as they continued to attempt to quash the spread of rebellion with policies that encouraged it. The grand strategy to conquer the south, as derived from the ministry in London, depended chiefly on the ability to leverage a cooperative populace however, the commander of British forces in America in charge of executing this action had just ensured it would never happen.

* * *

MORRISTOWN, NEW JERSEY, MID-APRIL 1780

Jack held the paper in his left hand as he stared at it in silence, gently feeling the thick edges with fingers of his right.

"Why do you look at the letter if you can't read it?" Custis asked quizzically.

"Because *she* wrote it," Jack answered. "I can't read the words, but it's enough to know that she made them. To know that she held this in her hands. That she once looked at this as I do now." Jack handed the letter back to Custis. "Can you read it again?"

"Again?"

"Yes. Please."

Custis nodded as he took the letter and started.

"March 11th, in the year of our Lord, 1780

My Dearest Jack,

It is a bright, sunny day today, a pleasant reprieve from the horrible winter that we are still not sure has passed. Looking out the window I can see two orioles in a nearby tree. They dart and flitter about then return to each other as if lovers that make up from a quarrel. I could watch them all day and I am jealous.

Mister Chase came to visit yesterday and asked about you. We had not seen him for some time as his ship had been in repair. Father told him that you were in Morristown for the winter with General Washington. Mister Chase bade us to wish you well but seemed quite troubled to hear that you had gone for a soldier. He and Father had much to discuss as he remained until just this morning.

There is time for only a short note today as I must go into town to buy a dress. I do not know if my letters reach you, but I will continue to send them as at least it seems that you are with me when I write. Yesterday I found a verse in Father's bible that I must share with you. And Ruth said, 'Intreat me not to leave thee, or to return following after thee: for whither thou goest, I will go; and where thou lodgest, I will lodge: thy people shall be my people, and thy God my God: Where thou diest, will I die, and there I will be buried: the Lord do so to me, and more also, if ought but death part thee and me.'

Return to me soon, Love, as I miss you terribly. Yours always, Priscilla"

Jack hung his head and sighed. "She longs for a reply, but I cannot. She doesn't even know that I can't read."

Custis refolded the letter and handed it back. "If you tell me what to say, I can write it for you."

"You can't, Custis, for she knows all too well your script. Far better that she receives nothing from me than to receive one word and realize what I am."

"I believe we have no choice then, lieutenant, but to teach you to read and write. For you can't continue to hide this once we return."

Jack nodded but did not raise his head. "I believe you're right, Custis. Mister Coleman has offered a place in the family for me, with her, when we return. I'll do anything to earn that."

"I know you will," Custis answered. "It'll be difficult, but we must start. But once we start, we must continue every day – that's most important."

"Now that we've settled in here, I believe we can find the time."

Captain Wadwicz heard the knock first as he hurried from the back of the room past the pair toward the door. Always when Custis visited the cabin, the Polish officers remained far in the rear, never welcoming, or even acknowledging his presence but rather watching intently in expressionless silence. The captain opened the door to find an exasperated Captain Littlefield, who burst through the entry without greetings or even removing his hat.

"Well, lads, I have news," the burly officer exclaimed as he rubbed his hands together. "Clinton has landed in Georgia with a large army and is moving on Charleston by land in the Carolinas. Congress has directed that we move with haste to reinforce General Lincoln's forces that defend the city. Our Maryland and Delaware regiments are to rendezvous with General de Kalb in Philadelphia. You'll accompany them, as they need every man. You must report to Colonel Smallwood immediately."

Captain Wadwicz looked at Jack with a bewildered expression. "Yes, sir," Jack answered Captain Littlefield as he glanced at Custis. "We're ready."

"Good luck, Jack," Captain Littlefield replied as he clasped the junior officer with both hands by the shoulders. "Good luck and godspeed."

As quick as he had entered, the captain now vanished as Jack pushed the door closed and turned to Custis. "Seems those lessons will have to wait."

* * *

NEAR CAMDEN, SOUTH CAROLINA,
AUGUST 16, 1780

"I'll take that glass, lieutenant."

"Yes, sir," Jack replied as he handed the monocular telescope up to Colonel Smallwood.

Straddled atop his horse, the colonel extended the brass piece to its full length of twelve inches and peered in the distance to either side of the Waxhaw Road that led to the small village of Camden just several miles farther south and utilized by the British as a major supply depot. Less than half a mile away against a wall of pine trees stood the British line of 2,200 seasoned soldiers under command of General Cornwallis, their contrasting red uniforms just becoming visible in the pre-dawn light against the dark wooded backdrop. On the verge of sunrise, the summer air hung heavy with a sticky humidity quite normal for the season. Stationed on the north end of a field barely a mile wide and bracketed both east and west by the Gumtree Swamp, more than 4,000 Americans had positioned themselves as well in a line with the Virginia and North Carolina Militia to the left and the 2nd Maryland and Delaware Continental Army Regiments to the right. Colonel Smallwood remained behind in the center with the reserve unit, the 1st Maryland Regiment, who waited in anxious silence. In front of Smallwood between the reserve and line of main units, Major General Horatio Gates, in overall command of the Americans, sat astride his horse near one of several artillery batteries sprinkled throughout the formations on both sides. His adjutant, Colonel Otho Williams, also from Maryland, whispered in the general's ear.

The Maryland and Delaware regiments, 1,400 men in all, had departed Morristown in April, reaching Hillsborough, North Carolina along with Major General Johann de Kalb, two months prior in the latter part of June, already too late to affect the outcome in Charleston. De Kalb was an enormous Bavarian fighting man, formerly of the French Army and more recently an agent of the French Government sent to the colonies in 1768 to report on the growing discontent with Great Britain. He had returned to America in 1777 to join the Continental Army along with numerous French officers to include Washington's favorite, the young Marquis de Lafayette. But with Charleston now in British hands with the ability to use their navy to flow supplies through that portal the stakes had changed from defense of a critical port city to a campaign to prevent the wholesale British control of the south. To that end Congress turned to the one man they could not resist.

Upon learning of the fall of Charleston, Congress appointed Gates to lead the southern campaign. General Washington had recommended Nathaneal Greene however, many of the political class remained enamored with Gates, the *Hero of Saratoga*. In fact, many had lobbied for Gates to replace Washington himself, an initiative that many senior military officers, including Gates, had not only encouraged but actively worked toward. A former major in the British Army who had participated in the French and Indian War with service under General Braddock along with Washington, Gates had become frustrated with his inability to advance in the British system and consequently sold his commission, eventually relocating with his family to America to try his luck as a Virginia planter. As the Continental Congress organized for war in 1775, he was offered a senior commission along with Charles Lee due to their significant prior military experience under the Crown. With a nature oriented more toward the defensive, the typically cautious Gates had taken as much credit as possible for the stunning defeat of Burgoyne and, in truth, deserved at least some of it. But that victory could not have come without the significant efforts of several subordinate commanders such as the Benjamin Lincoln of Massachusetts, John Stark and Enoch Poor of New Hampshire, Daniel Morgan of Virginia, and Benedict Arnold of Connecticut, all of whom remained relatively, and some would say *purposely*, hidden away in Gates' considerable shadow. Of these, Gates had played down Arnold most of all, one of Washington's favorites but whose insolent attitude had pushed his superior to the brink of antagonism during the entire campaign. The feud finally culminated at the second Battle of Bemis Heights, where Gates ordered Arnold to remove himself from the field and relinquish his command. Instead, sensing a moment of glory, the ever-ambitious Arnold blatantly disobeyed and instead rallied his troops to strike the decisive blow that led to victory and, ironically, Gates' trajectory to stardom. With Gates now appointed to lead the Southern Army in the summer of 1780, Arnold continued to chafe at his lack of recognition by Congress and in September would commit treason by joining the British Army from his command at West Point on the Hudson River above New York Harbor.

Of all the senior British military commanders in the conflict, history has judged Lieutenant General Lord Cornwallis as the most capable. A member of the House of Lords and staunch

Whig with an impeccable family pedigree, he had opposed the policies that irritated and provoked the American colonies but nevertheless agreed to serve during the war out of a sense of duty to his country. Following the capture of Charleston and subsequent departure of General Clinton, Cornwallis busily created a logistics network north through South Carolina with posts at Camden, Ninety-Six, Rocky Mount, Hanging Rock, and Cheraw. Using this critical land bridge Cornwallis could push into North Carolina, which he intended to do after the autumn harvest.

Innumerable skirmishes continued between Loyalist and rebellious militia units, the latter of which grew unchecked mainly due to Clinton's ill-advised parting actions that had polarized South Carolina, removing any possibility to remain neutral and forcing citizens to choose sides – overwhelmingly towards the rebels. Capable leaders emerged such as the *Carolina Gamecock*, Thomas Sumter; the *Swamp Fox*, Francis Marion; William Campbell, Isaac Shelby, John Sevier and many others, all of whom without the abusive practices of their British *saviors* may have otherwise sat out the conflict. In the case of Thomas Sumter, the British burned his large estate to the ground even though he had accepted Clinton's parole. These rough but effective leaders directed continued efforts to eliminate dispatch riders and harass baggage trains headed north from Charleston to inform and resupply Cornwallis in the hinterland. Choosing always to fight in an asymmetrical manner on their own terms and places of their choosing, these marauders would appear as if from thin air to capture and destroy what they could before melting virtually unscathed back into the countryside they knew so well. These actions did not stop Cornwallis' progress but rather hampered it significantly as if being crippled by so many paper cuts. London's strategy of leveraging the unclaimed Loyalist support to dominate the south was not working out as envisioned; however, there still existed enough momentum and hope to keep the British Army in operation.

In late July, Gates caught up with his new Southern Army along the Deep River in North Carolina, assuming command from the disappointed de Kalb, whose desire for a major campaign of his own had proved short-lived. Heading for one of the nearest advanced British posts at Camden, South Carolina some 150 miles distant, they picked up along the way militia units from North Carolina and Virginia, swelling their numbers to 4,100 men along with 18 cannon and a small calvary element. By early August Cornwallis learned of Gates' approach and collected a force of half the number to meet him. Sometime during the night of August 15th, advance units from both sides bumped into each other on the road from Rugeley's Mills, several miles north of Camden. After an initial confused but short skirmish, both armies began to organize themselves on either side of a nearby field and waited for daybreak, with the Americans holding slightly higher ground and a two-to-one numerical advantage.

Cornwallis formed his forces in the traditional British military fashion, in a line, with the strongest units in the place of honor to the right; in this case, light infantry and other regulars from the 23rd and 33rd Regiments commanded by Lieutenant Colonel James Webster. On the left stood Loyalist militia and provincial units commanded by Lieutenant Colonel Lord Francis Rawdon and to the rear in reserve were the 71st Regiment and Major Banastre Tarleton's calvary. American General Gates formed his army in a similar manner with his most capable units, the Delaware and Maryland Continentals to his right commanded by de Kalb and to the left, Virginia and North Carolina Militia led by their respective leaders Colonels Stevens and Caswell with overall command by Smallwood with the 1st Maryland Regiment and a small amount of calvary behind in reserve. Gates' alignment had the effect of creating relative parity, or even a slight advantage, for the Continental right facing the provincial Loyalist units but a severe disadvantage to the American left, where the militia, arguably the weakest units on the field, would match up against the professional British regulars, the most disciplined and capable troops.

Several paces to the front of Smallwood, General Gates turned to face him. "Colonel, we have a report that the British right is displaying from their column to a line. Have your troops engage them now while they're vulnerable, before they're set."

"Yes, sir," the colonel responded as he handed the glass down to Jack and relayed the order to the militia commanders.

As the sun peeked through the tall pines to the east on his left Jack peered forward across the expanse and raised the glass again to look. A prelude of cannon from both sides now began to thunder as the two American militia units to his left started forward, the smoke darkening the morning haze that hung over the field as it drifted toward the British.

"FIX BAYONETS!" shouted Colonel Stevens as did Colonel Caswell, their men now reaching to place the spike on the end of their firelocks as they walked.

"They're not displaying," Jack murmured as he lowered the glass. "Colonel, they're not displaying," he repeated louder.

"What is it, lieutenant?"

"Sir, they're not *displaying* but rather their line is set and moving forward to engage us. Those are light infantry and regulars. It wouldn't make sense that they waited so long to position themselves. They're coming now."

"Let me see, lad."

"Please, sir," Jack answered as he handed Colonel Smallwood the glass.

"Damn!" the colonel exclaimed as the cannons increased their fire in earnest.

To the surprise of the Virginia and North Carolina Militia as they approached a low cloud of gun smoke less than a hundred yards distant, a long red line suddenly emerged, their bayonets forward as they fired their weapons and shouted with a great *Huzzah!* To the furthest left toward the swamp, a number of the Virginians fell. A scant few others remained in place to return fire, but the vast majority turned in unison as if a school of fish and began running back in the direction from where they had started, not having even squeezed their triggers. Panicked by the sight of the Virginia herd rushing rearward on the outside, the

North Carolinians did the same, throwing down their loaded muskets to lend more speed.

Colonel Smallwood turned to Colonel Williams to bring the 1st Marylanders up to plug the hole the militia had created but as they started forward their advancement became hampered by the men fleeing headlong back through their ranks. This lack of progress allowed Webster to pivot his professionals onto the left flank of de Kalb's forces now engaged with Rawdon on the American right. For a time, de Kalb held his own, throwing back the Loyalist militia and even counterattacking with vigor. Williams did his best to relieve the pressure on de Kalb's left but arrived too late and became blocked out of position. The British regulars and light infantry, now full onto de Kalb's exposed flank, proved too much as they encircled him in a melee of musket fire, bayonet thrusts, and screams through the choking burnt gunpowder. De Kalb himself was dragged down from his horse by a horde of red as the Americans around him now peeled away to run for their lives, all order and discipline on both sides having ceased.

With Colonel Smallwood suddenly nowhere in sight, having presumably gone to find the suddenly absent General Gates, Jack stepped away from his position to wade down into what looked like a giant brawl. "Goddamn it!" he cried as he grabbed his right knee, nearly falling to the ground. He forced himself forward with a pronounced limp. Grabbing the first discarded musket he came upon; he used it to alternately thrust and butt his way into the fracas where the 2nd Marylanders had been. He found Custis lying on the ground, still alive but pinned under a pile of Continental bodies.

"GET UP, CUSTIS!" he cried as he worked to dislodge the shocked and wide-eyed soldier. "GET UP NOW!" He dropped the musket and pulled one last body off to the side. Grimacing in pain from his knee he grabbed Custis by the collar and hauled him to his feet, placing his left shoulder underneath Custis' right armpit. As best he could, he dragged Custis out of the mayhem, heading in a straight line toward the closest swamp on the right side of the field. Behind them confusion reigned with shrieks and musket fire as a vice grip of Webster's and Rawdon's forces alternately shot and bayonetted what remained of the Maryland and Delaware units with the Virginia and North Carolina militia already long gone. Somehow unscathed and unfollowed, they continued west toward the edge of the field until it quickly gave way to wetlands, thick with hardwoods and shrubs. Now carrying Custis almost on his back Jack waded into alternate muck and knee-deep water until finding a semi-dry patch below a large live oak tree, several hundred yards into the natural cover. He placed Custis against the bottom of the tree and looked him over for wounds.

"Are you hurt?" Jack asked as he continued to inspect the silent Custis, opening his shirt to reveal his chest and stomach. "Can you hear me?" Jack asked as he patted Custis' cheek.

Custis did not respond but rather closed his eyes as he leaned back against the tree to fall asleep. The roar of the fight could still be heard in the distance although now ever-dimming. Jack finished his inspection and nodded. "Just rest now. I'll keep guard. We'll stay here for a short while. Nobody should bother us here. Just rest."

Back on the battlefield the Americans withdrew to the north as if a panicked crowd scattering from a burning building with every man for himself. General Gates, on horseback, led the charge and did not stop until he reached Charlotte, North Carolina some 60 miles away and then further on to Hillsborough another 120 miles by August 19th, an impressive and unprecedented 180 miles in three days with the kind of energy and aggressiveness he had never shown before. General de Kalb was captured on the field with eleven bayonet wounds from which he died three days later in the personal care of Cornwallis. The fight had lasted not even an hour with Gates himself having departed along with the militia in the first 15 minutes. The American right that remained to fight, the Delaware and Maryland Continental units, were devastated with nearly all either killed, wounded, or captured. The militia on the left fled north, pursued by Tarleton's calvary, who caught up with them 22 miles later, butchering many with their sabers even as they tried to surrender. What militia stragglers that remained melted back into the countryside never to fight again. Like a tender dandelion ravaged by the wind, the Continental Southern Army ceased to exist and with it, the American hope to defend the south.

16

For the good that I would I do not: but the evil which I would not, that I do. Now if I do that I would not, it is no more I that do it, but sin that dwelleth in me. I find then a law, that, when I would do good, evil is present with me.

Romans 7:19-25 KJV

GUMTREE SWAMP, SOUTH CAROLINA, AUGUST 16, 1780

"Wake up, lieutenant."

Startled, Jack jolted erect as he remained sitting with his back to the tree. He opened his eyes to find the end of a cutlass blade pressed flat against his throat, held by a thick, wide-shouldered man with a round face, fully blackened with white circles painted around each of his beady brown eyes set abnormally close together with no hair anywhere, not even his eyebrows, or his strangely flattened head. The man wore a vest made of deer hide with a pistol and a hatchet pressed inside his waist belt.

"It's *you!*" The man's face twitched, momentarily contorting before springing back. The cutlass twitched with him. "You're the *scangtreh* – the white man from my visions. Give me your name, son."

"Jack," Jack answered cautiously, "Jack Halliday."

"But you're dressed as an officer in the Continental Army – a lieutenant?"

Jack hesitated before he spoke as the man pressed the blade in harder. "I'm a lieutenant in the 1st Maryland Regiment."

"You're from Maryland, *scangtreh*?"

"From Annapolis."

"Annapolis?" the man shrugged as he twitched again. "I know it not."

"It's the capital of the Maryland province. It's ...." Jack stopped as the man increased the pressure of the blade.

"I don't give a goddamn what it is. What I do care about is a Continental Army officer that does not speak with a Yankee tongue. Now, tell me again, lieutenant, where are you from? It's not *Annapolis*."

Jack swallowed hard as he tried to readjust himself against the tree, the cutlass still pressed hard against his throat. "I'm from Liverpool."

"From England, then?" The man nodded. "And what brings you to possess a Continental Officer's uniform?"

"I'm employed by Mister Arthur Coleman of Annapolis – *Colonel* Arthur Coleman – commanding officer of the Annapolis Militia and leading citizen of that city. Private Coleman and I are both his surrogates for the Continental draft."

"A *private* is he now?" The man turned his attention to Custis as he maintained the blade fast against Jack's neck. "He's but a *yehhoketcheh*. Is he yours?"

"No – he's the property of Colonel Coleman, who's also my sponsor."

"*Colonel Coleman*, you say? Commander of the militia and *leading citizen,* is he? He doesn't participate in person for the cause but rather sends a scangtreh from England and a yehhoketcheh in his stead? Ha! Since the good colonel isn't here himself, I can justly claim his property as a prize of war."

"He is a private in the 2nd Maryland Regiment and as such deserves...."

The bald man twitched again as he pressed the blade harder against Jack's neck. "He may wear a Continental uniform but here he is but a yehhoketcheh – a nigger. As you said yourself, he's but property – a slave. Your Colonel Coleman is obviously a man who cares little for either one of you. As he's seen fit not to represent himself in this matter, he therefore has no say and has, in fact, already bargained away such possessions. I'll now lift my sword and you may stand. I've been expecting you."

Jack rose slowly with his palms raised in plain sight by his shoulders as he looked around. At least two dozen men now encircled the patch of dry ground. Raggedly clothed in filthy, torn shirts and floppy hats, wearing long beards and even longer hair, they stared at Jack with wild eyes, each brandishing large knives and axes in their belts and muskets at the ready in their hands.

Jack slowly lowered his hands to his waist. "I don't understand. You've been *expecting* me?"

The man nodded. "For some time. You've come to me in my dreams beginning when this war started. I hadn't seen you for nearly a year until I saw you again last night. It's the same as always. You walk in a large forest, not hurriedly, but methodically and deliberately, as if you know the path and will not waver from it. You move not in this land but rather one quite strange – that of wooded hills crisscrossed by stone fences and filled with tall, thick pine trees. You wear not a Continental officer's uniform but that of a common British soldier – light infantry, specifically. All around you is death and chaos with musket fire by those unseen further in the woods. Many also dressed in red are felled in the road. But you remain unharmed, simply walking straight ahead, looking for me, it would seem. For this reason, I can't kill you or I already would have and taken the yehhoketcheh. You've been coming for me and now you're here. You're free to go but I know you won't, as we are linked."

Jack stared at the man in silence with his mouth half open as if frozen in place. After a long moment the man raised his right hand with palm facing outward then placed it on his breast. "I am Maurice Sebastian LeClerc, also known as *White Feather* by my people, the Catawba. Here, my men simply call me *Captain*. My father was a trapper from Quebec that made his way south until he came east over the mountains. He traded with my people, and they taught him their ways. He took a wife – my mother – and was taken in to live there. But when the war started with the French in '54 my people sided with the English, as they had always done. They drove my father away, so my mother and I followed him. My father served as a scout for the French Army, but the English captured him and hanged him as a spy. I went with my mother to live with a small band of Cheraw in an area close to here, most of those having relocated to the north many years prior. But the smallpox killed what was left of them, along with my mother. I drifted west over the mountains in the direction from where my father had come and fell in with a Jesuit mission along the Natchez River. They educated me and taught me to pray. But they too were driven away by the English after the war ended. When the rebellion started, I returned here, no longer a refugee in my own land but instead a warrior – an avenger.

"The Catawba now make war on the English, but I won't join them, as they have betrayed me as well. Our association with the English king has brought nothing but hardship, pestilence, and death to this land since the first scangtreh arrived. Like the Romans, who would not accept the new and better ideas of the early Christians but instead chose to persecute them, the English Crown and its malignant *Loyalists* will eventually be swept away by what is just.

"We'd put our hope in the Continentals as they had gathered a large force in North Carolina, and we've been trailing them since they entered the province. But it didn't go well for them today as they were destroyed by an army half their size and, from what I saw, twice their ability. Tell me, lieutenant – how is it that you're neither dead nor fleeing with what remained of your army?"

Jack returned LeClerc's gaze with a hardened expression. "I was assigned to assist with the First Maryland in the reserve. From there I could see the entire field. Our militia on the left flank disappeared on initial contact which caused our regulars on the right to become enveloped and finally collapsed. Private Coleman fell in the melee, but I was able to extricate him. We then withdrew from our battle axis in a perpendicular direction west into the swamp as it afforded our best chance for cover. Nobody followed us."

LeClerc nodded. "You chose then to withdraw when you could have remained to fight. I sense that you're no coward but rather a man with no loyalty to anyone but himself. That instinct will serve you well out here. Your army was destroyed and those few who survived ran north like a pack of scalded dogs." LeClerc pointed his sword toward Custis, who remained seated against the tree just to the other side, staring into the distance as if in a trance. "And what of the yehhoketcheh? Is he fit?"

Jack glanced down at Custis. "I don't believe Private Coleman is wounded."

LeClerc stepped around the tree to face Custis, poking him in the cheek with the flat side of his blade as he chuckled. Custis' expression remained unchanged as his eyes remained fixed ahead. "No wounds on the body at least. But this man isn't a soldier even though he wears the uniform. No matter, as we don't need him to fight. There isn't now and never has been any good reason to arm a yehhoketcheh. We'll see what aptitude he possesses and, depending on that, what value. There are many that would trade for him."

"It's true," Jack quickly implored, "that he doesn't possess an abundance of the temperament necessary for use of arms. But I would request to you most strenuously not to trade or sell him as I must, at some point, return him home."

LeClerc shook his head. "I believe you'll find that task most difficult. As a yehhoketcheh he has value and in this province his home is with whoever owns him. I saw him not in my vision. He and I are not connected, and I may do with him as I please. Your Colonel Coleman cares not for him or else he wouldn't have been cast out."

"But he and I *are* connected," Jack protested, "and...."

"Captain!" a man called as he approached from the direction of the recent battlefield. He was short, stocky and dark, with a scraggly beard and large brown eyes set deep into his face. "Captain, we found these on the field, scavenging the dead."

Behind the man several more raggedly dressed men led a trio of young boys, early in their teenage years, connected by a rope that bound all three together in a line by their hands. Their heads hung low as they kept their eyes fixed to the ground.

"*Scavenging*, you say?" LeClerc answered with apparent interest. "Well, that is our job, isn't it? Tie them to a tree for the time being." LeClerc then motioned his hand in Jack's direction. "Bass, I want you to meet the new additions to our troupe, Lieutenant Jack Halliday and his yehhoketcheh. Fresh from the battle they are from the Continental side, and unscathed at that."

The short man fixed his dark eyes on Jack and simply stared in silence. A large knife lay tucked against his waist, held by a leather belt that secured the rest of his shabby vestments.

"Ha!" LeClerc exclaimed with a wide smile as he slapped Jack on the upper arm near the shoulder. "This is *Bass*, my second in command. It seems he doesn't like you. Don't feel bad – he doesn't like anyone save for me. He came from west of the highlands, much like my father. I think he's actually French but won't admit it. Best damn skinner I know. Make sure not to cross him, son, and do exactly what he tells you for he's the meanest of us all. He'll gut you like a fish and think nothing of it."

"Bass," LeClerc ordered as he turned back toward the dark stocky man who stared at Jack as he clenched his fists, "search them both."

Bass merely nodded in return as his hands quickly found their way inside Jack's coat. He extracted Jack's knife and spoon, handing them to LeClerc, who examined both with curiosity.

"Nice work this knife," LeClerc commented as Bass moved to Custis. "Never seen anything like it. Nice work indeed."

"The nigger is unarmed," Bass growled as he returned to face LeClerc, who pointed now to the young captives nearby, still looking toward the ground.

"Come now, Bass, what of these lads? Scavengers, are they? Did you relieve them of their efforts?"

"We took all they had," Bass answered. "They were assisting to clear the field of the dead and wounded and helping themselves in the process."

"*Loyalists*, they are," LeClerc commented as he moved closer, grabbing the first boy by the hair to jerk his face skyward. "Goddamn Loyalists – I can smell it." He let go of the boy and backhanded him in the face, sending the youth stumbling backwards into the other two. "We'll deal with them accordingly."

LeClerc turned back to Bass. "Gather the men. We're moving. The Yankees are gone for good, and Cornwallis will remain here for a time. We'll take our Loyalists to the *Alter*."

Bass turned to wave one hand in the air as a signal to the others, who began to straggle in the same direction from the dry ground, into the wetlands. Jack lifted Custis from his station at the tree, guiding him by the elbow to fall in with the loose crowd that seemed to know the navigable passage leading further into the swamp. They walked for three days, generally following a northerly direction with the setting sun to their left, stopping before dark on the driest ground to set up a makeshift camp. They moved without speaking and saw no one. Along the way there were stations with traps set for animals that they used to feed themselves. At night many of the men strung ropes between trees and fastened something like sail cloth to fashion a hammock of sorts to keep them off the ground. Jack and Custis simply leaned against an available tree. Pickets continually manned the perimeter even when they walked, posted in a circle well outside of the main group.

In the late morning on the fourth day, they stopped in a small clearing on dry, sandy ground where near the middle of a flat, grassy space sat a large live oak, so matured that several of its long branches bent down into the earth and back out again like a giant permanently attached spider.

LeClerc surveyed the area and nodded. "It's almost noon. They hanged my father here at noon, on this very spot, from this very tree," he hesitated as he pointed to one of the younger and higher protrusions, "from this very branch. They hanged him as not even a criminal but more like a dog, without a trial or evidence or even a chance to defend himself, but simply according to their personal disdain for his heritage and affiliation."

He produced a small book from a haversack he carried – a bible – and opened it, then turned to Jack nearby. "Revelations one: seventeen through nineteen. I like the author, *John of Patmos*, also called *John the Revelator*, as we have much in common. As the last survivor of the original disciples, John had been tried as a criminal for revealing the words of Jesus to the Romans. Emperor Domitian cast him into a cauldron of boiling oil and forced him to drink poison, neither of which caused him harm. He was then banished to Patmos, a barren and rocky isle in the Aegean Sea reserved especially for criminals. It was there that John meditated and received visions of what was and what was to come. And much like Emperor Domitian, and such petty rulers before him and after, King George has neither the wisdom to see the truth nor the power to stop that which has been ordained and revealed by God himself. But today, here on this altar, we'll meter God's justice to the wicked who chose to transgress His will.

"Bass!" LeClerc called toward the group behind. "Prepare them."

Accordingly, the three young boys, now untied from each other but still bound by the wrists at their waist, were marched under the tree and hooded with a noose placed on their necks and the rope secured to a large branch well over ten feet in height. Each were bade to stand on a makeshift stool fashioned from nearby tree branches, about a foot and a half in height.

"These lads have done nothing to deserve this." Jack protested. "They're neither soldiers nor criminal but rather mere civilians."

"But how wrong you are, lieutenant," LeClerc answered, waving his finger in the air. "There's no such thing as a *mere civilian* in this province. Young they may be, these lads are nevertheless *Loyalists* and, as such, own an equal share in the pestilence brought to this land. My father was betrayed by such a man that he had traded with many times, a man he considered a friend. When my father came to that man in confidence for assistance, that man instead delivered him to the English for a sack of coins, much like Judas. When I returned to this land from the Jesuits, I found that man and brought him here. I then hanged him on this very tree on the very same branch in the very same way with no more justification than my desire to do so. I watched him die with righteous joy that I had not before experienced – it was then I knew that I was an instrument of God. And when he was dead, I skinned him like an animal and from his hide I fashioned myself a pair of boots that I wear yet today."

LeClerc pointed down to his boots and waited until Jack had ample time to view them. "But I must tell you," he continued, "that I dreamt of you yet again last night. It wasn't the same dream as so many times before but instead new. We were seated at a long table, each of us at one end facing the other. All around us was commotion, some men dressed in red and others not, running wildly about and struggling with each other. I couldn't see their faces as they brushed past me shrieking. You, on the other hand, were calm, with both of your hands placed on the table in front of you with palms down as you stared at me in silence. You, too, wore a red uniform. I asked you where we were, but you didn't answer. Instead, you plucked a silver spoon from the table and held it in the air before your eyes then carefully placed it inside your coat. It's the same spoon that I took from you along with the knife. What is this spoon? Where was this table?"

Jack hesitated as he stared at LeClerc in stunned silence. "In a land far from here," he finally answered, "to where I can't return."

"And your red uniform? You're a British soldier?"

"I was," Jack answered as he nodded. "But I am no longer. I don't know the meaning of your dreams or how you come to know such circumstances. But I do know that hanging three young lads is wrong. No respectable army would do such a thing."

"You have not the right to judge me, lieutenant, whoever you really are. But hang them I certainly will. You may invade my dreams, but you won't sway me from my purpose in this world.

If I could but rid myself of you I would. My course is quite clear, having been given to me by God Himself, to be His instrument of vengeance against those who would side with the Evil One to steal our inheritance of freedom."

LeClerc raised the book above his head with his left hand as he made the Catholic sign of the cross with his right. Behind him a loose formation of men stood in a semi-circle around him, most leaning on the barrels of the firelocks. "Now, we begin!" he shouted. "Revelations, chapter one, verses seventeen through nineteen." He lowered the book and in a loud voice began to read.

"Je me retournai pour connaître quelle était la voix qui me parlait. Et, apres m'être retourné, je vis sept chandeliers d'or, et, au milie des sept chandeliers, quelqu'un qui ressemblait à un fils d'homme, vêtu d'une longue robe, et ayant une ceinture d'or sur la poitrine. Sa tête et sais cheveux étaient blancs comme de la laine blanche, comme de la neige; ses yeux étaient comme une flamme de feu; ses pieds étaient semblables à de l'airain ardent, comme s'il eût été embrasé dans une fournaise; et sa voix était comme le bruit de grandes eaux. Il avant dans sa main droite sept étoiles. De sa bouche sortait une épée aigue, à deux tranchants; et son visage était comme le soleil lorsqu'il brille dans sa force. Quand je le vis, je tombai à ses oieds comme mort. Il posa sur moi sa main droite en disant: Ne crains point! Je suis le premier et le dernier, et le vivant. J'étais mort; et voici, je suis vivant aux siècles des siècles. Je tiens les clefs de la mort et du séjour des morts. Écris donc les choses que tu as vues, et celles qui doivent arriver aprés elles."

LeClerc again made the sign of the cross then placed the book back in the haversack. He turned to Bass nearby. "You know what to do."

Bass walked behind the youths, methodically kicking the stools out from underneath each. Like puppets on invisible strings, they shook and danced in the air as the men nearby wagered with each other on which would last the longest. After several silent minutes each hung still. They were lifted and removed from their ropes then hung upside down with their feet placed back in the noose and the hoods removed from their black, contorted faces. Jack looked away as Bass slit their throats as calmly and methodically as if buttering a piece of bread.

"We'll bleed them and skin them," LeClerc mentioned, "then leave their carcasses for the creatures of the woods." He then raised his hands high and looked skyward. "And we pray that this sacrifice pleases God."

* * *

NORTHERN CENTRAL SOUTH CAROLINA, LATE AUGUST 1780

"Before we proceed, I must speak to you." LeClerc addressed Jack as Bass raised his arm in a signal for the unit to stop.

They stood just inside the woods at the short edge of a long rectangular field lined on either side of a pathway with cotton. Across the entire expanse, Negro men of various ages, about a dozen in all, worked under floppy straw hats to protect them from the harsh late-summer sun. On the opposite end of the field sat a house, simple in nature; built of wood and red bricks, just as large but plainer than the Coleman home in Annapolis. Behind the house and to the right were several other structures made of logs. Smoke rose from the chimney of the main building.

"This is the former farm of the man that killed my father," LeClerc continued, loud enough for the men behind him to hear. "We're here to speak with the owner. When we arrive, it's important that you do exactly as I'm about to explain. Do you understand?"

Jack said nothing as he shrugged his shoulders in response.

"If you value the life of your yehhoketcheh, you won't say a word. You'll remain as mute as he is. If you utter a sound, Bass will kill him where he stands. Do you understand?"

Jack glanced back at Bass, a few steps to the rear, who moved now to position himself behind Custis.

"I said, *do you understand*, lieutenant?" LeClerc repeated.

Jack moved closer to LeClerc, keeping his back to the men. He spoke softly so they would not be overheard. "No, sir, I don't understand. What's the need for such an agreement? But for the sake of Private Coleman, I'll do as you ask."

LeClerc now lowered his voice so that only Jack could hear. "You came to my dreams once more last night. Again, a dream that I hadn't seen before, but the most disturbing of them. I was on a large vessel on the ocean with no land in sight. There was a cargo of yehhoketchehs, more than a hundred, inside the ship chained to the floor below me. I stood above them up top on the roof. Nearby were several more yehhoketchehs, laying on their backs as they labored to breathe. I saw you at the edge of the vessel near the water, dressed not in a red uniform, but as a common sailor. You held a yehhoketcheh by the feet while a larger man with a red face and crooked leg held him behind the shoulders. The yehhoketcheh said nothing as he stared up at the sky, gasping for breath like the others. He was young, maybe even still a lad. You and the crooked man lifted the yehhoketcheh up over the half-wall and dropped him into the water. He didn't swim but merely floated like a raft past the rear of the vessel where he was set upon and torn to pieces by the sea creatures that lurked there in great numbers."

Visibly disturbed, LeClerc paused to compose himself as Jack waited in silence without expression.

"Then, suddenly, it was me on my back on the floor at the edge where the young yehhoketcheh had been. You held me by my feet and the red, crooked man had me by the shoulders. I tried to wriggle away but couldn't move. I longed to speak, to cry out, but couldn't make a sound. I was powerless, like the yehhoketcheh before. The crooked man behind me bade you in earnest to lift but you did nothing except just to stare at me, as you're doing now. The crooked man pleaded until a tall man with a large, hooked nose appeared – he was angry. The tall man placed a pistol against your head and threatened your life lest you do as he bade. Then, you and the crooked man did lift me to the top of the wall. I saw then many dour faces that watched me with great interest but not an ounce of remorse as if I was nothing more than a sack of refuse. I then fell down into the water, where I landed with a great crash to my ears. Strangely, I felt nothing and to even more of my surprise, I didn't sink even though I cannot swim. Again, I tried to call out but no sound came. I expected at that moment the sea creatures would devour me as they had the yehhoketcheh. Instead, they swam in circles all about but touched me not, seemingly not to even know I lay in their midst. There I floated, not able to move, as I watched the ship continue on. I could see the name of the vessel on the back but couldn't read it. Slowly, it faded away, becoming ever smaller until finally it disappeared, leaving me alone in the ocean, which now turned cold and dark. And then I awoke, shivering and drenched in sweat."

LeClerc looked to Jack for a long, silent moment as if waiting for a reaction, to which Jack offered none, instead simply matching the painted man's stare. "Do you understand what it is I just told you, lieutenant?" LeClerc finally spoke, somewhat exasperated. "Can you offer anything to help make sense?"

Jack looked down at the ground and shook his head. "No, sir," he answered as he looked back up to meet LeClerc's puzzled expression, "but I'll offer you this: I'll remain quiet as you request, but you must also understand that should even the slightest harm come to Private Coleman by the hand of your men, I'll come to you in your dreams in even more terrible ways than that."

LeClerc hesitated, then swallowed hard as he nodded. "Let's both hope it doesn't come to that, lieutenant." He then waved his hand in the air in a forward direction as the men resumed their motion.

They continued through the cotton field, soon arriving at the house. LeClerc bade Jack to remain at the head of the group in the yard as he stepped up onto the large front veranda built with wide wooden boards but not a railing. From the main doorway emerged a black man, about Jack's height but with a thicker, medium build and full head of black, curly hair and beard, somewhat graying on the fringes of his forehead and chin. After greeting each other with familiarity, LeClerc led the man by the elbow toward the opposite end of the veranda. They spoke for several minutes in French, just loud enough for those nearby to hear, as the man alternately nodded and pointed to different parts of the property. They returned to the vicinity of the front door, where LeClerc motioned to Bass, who led Custis up onto the veranda. LeClerc watched Jack intently as the man visually inspected Custis from head to toe, checking even his teeth. LeClerc and the man exchanged nods and a handshake before he and Bass stepped down from the porch, passing Jack in the process, Bass with a hard glare and LeClerc with his forefinger pressed against his lips. Custis and the man stood in silence on the veranda with Jack just below near the front steps as they watched LeClerc and his band disappear back down the road through the cotton fields.

The black man stared down at Jack intently. "Who the hell are you?" he asked with a decided edge in his tone.

Jack looked back to the now empty road and turned to address the man. "My name is Jack Halliday."

"And why do you remain here instead of departing with the captain?"

Jack hesitated as he swallowed. "I don't serve LeClerc." He motioned toward Custis who remained staring in the distance toward the road. "I'm with him."

The man looked to Custis then back down to Jack as he folded his arms. "He's but a slave. Was he yours, then?"

"No. He's the property of Mister Arthur Coleman of Annapolis in the province of Maryland."

"So, what does that make you?"

"I am in the employment of Mister Coleman, who has charged me with the care of this man. *Custis* is his name, and I must return him to the Coleman estate. I can't myself return without him."

The man chuckled as he cocked his head and spit. "I'm afraid that's not possible as he now belongs to *this* estate."

Jack stared up at the man in exasperation. "Under what conditions would he be allowed to leave?"

The man spit again. "He's been fairly purchased and you'd have to purchase him back, at a profit to me, of course. Do you have such resources?"

Jack shook his head. "I've no resources at present except the clothes on my back. But I'm certain that an agreement can somehow be managed. I'm willing to work until his price is met."

The man chuckled again. "There's no business incentive to pay you and there's no amount of labor that you could perform that would accumulate sufficient payment. If you want to remain, you are welcome to work in the fields for sustenance with the others. If that isn't to your liking, you may leave. But you'll not get far in this country dressed as you are in a Continental soldier's uniform."

Jack nodded. "I appreciate your opinion, sir, but, if you don't mind, I'd like to discuss this matter with the master of the estate."

The man chuckled even harder as he spit again. He then leaned down toward Jack with a wide smile. "I *am* the master of this estate."

17

Whereas the enemy have adopted a practice of enrolling
NEGROES among their Troops, I do hereby give notice
That all NEGROES taken in arms, or upon any military Duty,
shall be purchased for the public service at a stated Price; the
money to be paid to the Captors. But I do most strictly forbid any
Person to sell or claim Right over any NEGROE, the property of a
Rebel, who may take Refuge with any part of this Army: And I do
promise to every NEGROE who shall desert the Rebel Standard,
full security to follow within these Lines, any Occupation which
he shall think proper.

Given under my Hand, at Head Quarters, PHILIPSBURGH
the 30th day of June 1779. H CLINTON

The Philipsburgh Proclamation (Philipsburgh, New York),
General Henry Clinton

The unmitigated disaster of what came to be known as
the *Battle of Camden* could not be overstated. With the
Continental Southern Army now obliterated, the British
had a seemingly clear path, unopposed, to push farther north
all the way to Virginia to control the entirety of the southern

provinces. But as the members of Congress wrung their hands at the prospect of a gaping hole in their colonial southern flank, the British kept with their normal pattern of behavior, that is, every time an advantage had presented itself, they failed to leverage it in their favor.

As much as having a major field command pleased him, General Cornwallis carried serious resentment and disgust toward his old friend, General Clinton, who, after masterfully taking Charleston in May, had almost immediately absconded with the majority of the army back to New York in order to pursue a strategy that he himself had formerly criticized – to defeat Washington there – leaving Cornwallis understaffed to do the thankless dirty work in what he now understood to be a province completely devoid of positive value. What evidence existed to suggest that the similarly miscreant population in North Carolina would prove different? Neither they nor even Clinton had provided any intelligence as to the arrival, or much less the very existence, of Gates' army prior to the clash at Camden earlier in the summer.

The entirety of the British strategy in the south had hinged on the assumption that untold minions of Loyalists lay waiting in the wings needing only the prompting of a visible British presence to emerge and join the fight for the Crown. But once again, the exact opposite had occurred. As it was in the north, so it was also in the south – the population, by and large, rejected the very presence of the British. Although culturally different in many ways, the one homogenous thread that connected the north and south was a severe aversion of being controlled by anything other than self-government. Cornwallis was certainly one of those elitists, cut from the same cloth as many of the ministers in London, that never could grasp that concept. But even if he could not understand the reason why, he surely did comprehend the obvious outcome and the realization that just as it had proved further north, no one was coming to help the British in the south, except maybe more British. The American defeat at Camden could not have been more decisive yet it had changed nothing. Cornwallis knew now that he was on his own unless and until he could join forces in Virginia with support from Clinton.

To that end, Cornwallis concocted a plan to establish a magazine for the winter further north in Hillsborough, North Carolina with locally gathered provisions of rum, salt, flour, and meal. Not wanting to move until Clinton created a diversion higher in Chesapeake to prevent the Continentals from sending another army his way, he nevertheless began a march in early September, reaching the waypoint of Charlotte near the end of the month, where he stopped to rest his tired men, more than half of whom were also ill, including the all-important commander of his cavalry, Major Banastre Tarleton, promoted to that rank soon after Camden. This activity did not go unnoticed by nearby partisan factions, who always seemed to know what the British were up to even before they themselves did. Not long after departure a partisan force of 150 attacked and bloodied an advance party of unaware Loyalist militia as they rested at Wahab's Plantation near the Catawba River – just another example of Carolina sentiments.

Although partisan units unceasingly harassed the British throughout South Carolina, they had been nearly eradicated in the western part of the province by British Major Patrick Ferguson, previously appointed Inspector General of the Loyalist Militia by Clinton, forcing many to the other side of the mountainous North Carolina border. An extremely capable officer, Ferguson had invented a breech-loading rifle that was far superior to the musket although inexplicably rejected by the British Army. In mid-September, on the heels of his success, he issued a proclamation that *if the partisans did not desist from their opposition to British arms, he would march his army over the mountains, hang their leaders, and lay their country waste with fire and sword.* Coupled with an extreme hatred for Ferguson, this decree so angered what was left of the western partisans that within two weeks they rose like a phoenix from the ashes, gathering a new army of 800 *Over-the-Mountain Men* to return to South Carolina with renewed vengeance. On October 7th they surrounded him and his Loyalist force on a high point called *King's Mountain* along South Carolina's northern limits. Slowly creeping upwards from tree to tree like a tightening noose toward Ferguson, who led the militia in defense with brave but ineffective linear tactics, the Over-the Mountain Men took great pleasure to blast him out of the saddle from his majestic white horse and then proceeded to massacre anyone still alive, many of whom tried to surrender, citing retribution for previous similar actions of Tarleton.

King's Mountain proved a deciding factor for Cornwallis, as he could not continue his progress north with the chronic instability caused by partisan activity threatening his back, specifically his supply lines from Charleston comprised of several key logistics posts that may not have been adequately defended. Not long after he withdrew from Charlotte and backtracked, repositioning by the end of October in the center of South Carolina at Winnsboro, roughly halfway between Camden and Ninety-Six further west. There, he rested his still ailing force as he pondered his situation and what the new year would bring.

On the American side, Washington again nominated Nathanael Greene to lead what would be a reconstructed Southern Army. The mercurial 38-year-old Rhode Islander was in his third year as Quartermaster General and had excelled in tirelessly and miraculously supplying the colonial war effort by mercilessly squeezing the myriad of provincial politicians and merchants who wanted no part of it. This time, the dithering and panicked Congress was in no mood to oppose their commander-in-chief. In fact, there were many in Congress who detested Greene as he had, over his tenure, doggedly exposed them as disingenuous laggards for not doing enough to support the colonial cause. One of Washington's inner circle, he had begrudgingly taken the senior supply officer position out of humility and loyalty although he yearned for field command. With a new position that well-suited his aggressive and direct nature, most in Congress were glad to see him go — and the farther away, the better.

Greene departed south from West Point, New York in mid-October, with second in command, von Steuben and head of cavalry, *Lighthorse* Harry Lee, in tow. He stopped in

Philadelphia to unsuccessfully petition Congress for assistance and also Virginia, where he left von Steuben to deal with provincial governor, Thomas Jefferson, who would be integral to the reconstitution effort. Greene reached Hillsborough, North Carolina by the end of November, where he encountered about 1,400 Continentals in appallingly poor condition and spirit that in his words, resembled *Indians* – in other words, practically naked. He continued in early December to the American camp in Charlotte, where he presented General Gates with orders from Congress to relieve him of command and a letter of resolution to convene an inquiry into Gates' actions at Camden as a prelude to a potential courts-martial.

The vaunted *Hero of Saratoga*, the former British Army Officer who had worked as tirelessly as he had shamelessly behind Washington's back to lobby Congress to give him control as commander-in-chief and had nearly succeeded, now returned home to Virginia with his military reputation ruined. Gates had always eagerly supported inquiries and courts-martials for questionable conduct of other officers, particularly those competitors who represented a direct threat – such as Benedict Arnold. Now, however, he most strenuously opposed the very thought of that treatment for himself. His supporters from New England later came to his aid in 1782, repealing the call for an inquiry, but he was never placed in field command again.

The first order of business for Greene was to reconstitute an army from the pile of rubble where he presently found it. He leaned heavily on von Steuben in Virginia, the key to recruitment and supply, who dealt with a stubborn Governor Jefferson, who preferred to put the needs of his province above those of the collective effort. He had other problems, such as senior officers like Colonel Smallwood, who may have himself expected to replace Gates, but was upset because with the new chain of command he now ranked below von Steuben. One important adjustment involved cooperating with the myriad of partisan groups instead of discounting them as useless scourges and criminals, as Gates had done prior. Much like Washington, Greene would never possess a force that should seek and risk a decisive battle but rather one better suited to harass, frustrate, and above all, to survive. With the year 1780 nearing a close the exasperated and bewildered Cornwallis rested his worn-out troops in central South Carolina, frustrated at the lack of local support that accounted for his complete absence of progress. To the north across the border some 65 miles away, the newly minted American field commander, General Greene, took similar stock of his situation as he contemplated how to do more with less to accomplish what his disgraced predecessor had not – to rid the south of the British Army.

* * *

North Central South Carolina, December 1780

Jack wiped his brow, replaced his floppy wide-brimmed hat then moved another line of dirt with his hoe. All around him in a long field several black men did the same, methodically working until pausing briefly to rest. With the harvest well past, the soil now needed to be tilled in preparation for the following planting. The farm had prospered under its master, Samuel Cressey, just as it had under his father before him, growing short staple cotton – not quite the same quality as the longer staple *Sea Island* variety found along the coastal areas – but plenty good enough to turn a profit and grow the enterprise. The business model remained quite simple: Clear the forest to plant cotton; when the yields decline, replace the cotton with corn; eventually abandon those used-up fields then clear new land for cotton. Also in the plans were expansion into indigo and tobacco. Rice was lucrative but the relatively high elevation in the northern central part of the province as opposed to the low southern marshes along the coast ruled that crop out due to the relative paucity of water. The major investment was labor – the slaves, of which the Cressey operation now counted nearly two dozen workers, before the arrival of Jack and Custis – nineteen adult men and three women, the latter of which worked mainly in the house.

Samuel Cressey had been true to his word, allowing Jack to work for sustenance, but nothing more. Jack lived with the slaves in their series of shacks on the back end of the property, having found an empty corner in one of the dilapidated structures in which to sleep. He rose when they rose, worked when they worked and ate what they ate. He also wore the same nondescript, loose clothing, having been provided promptly by Cressey, not out of charity but rather because the owner did not want to chance that an outsider would see a military uniform, which he had immediately burned. For all practical purposes, Jack became interchangeable with the rest of the workforce, except that they kept their distance and spoke to him sparingly. Conversely, Custis worked in the main house and was even allowed to sleep in the basement, having made himself useful in repairing and refurbishing many structural issues and other household items that had long experienced neglect and disrepair. As was the case upon their arrival, Custis had yet to utter a word.

The man closest to Jack suddenly stopped his motion and peered ahead as did those around him in succession. Jack did as well, as he followed their unified gaze past the largest of the three barns toward the end of the field to the west, in the opposite direction from where Jack had initially arrived. From the edge of the woods emerged a tall, lanky man in a faded green jacket and equally faded green traditional tricorne hat. He walked with long, purposeful strides followed by about two dozen men similarly attired and armed with muskets. Behind them, horses pulled three empty wagons. The men moved steadily in a loose column of pairs, all holding their firearms against their left shoulder. Jack pushed his own hat down over his forehead as he turned in the other direction toward the main house.

"You there!" called the man in front as they approached the working group. "I said, you there!"

One of the closer slaves approached Jack from behind and gently nudged his elbow. "Excuse me, mister," he uttered almost apologetically. "He wants to talk to *you*."

Jack exhaled deeply, then slowly turned to cover nearly 50 feet to the now halted group of strangers. He adjusted his hat to its normal position and presented himself to the tall man. "Can I help you, sir?"

The man removed his hat, complete with an attached small white feather that the others did not have, to reveal thinning blond hair that ran well down past his shoulders. He had a long, angled face with a large straight nose and piercing blue eyes atop shoulders too narrow for his height. He placed the hat against his breast and made a slight bow. "I am Captain Seamus McIntire of the Second Irish Militia. I hereby serve you notice from Lieutenant Colonel John Cruger, commander of the garrison at Ninety-Six."

The man replaced his hat as he reached into his jacket to produce a document, rolled and tied with a leather strap, handing it to Jack.

Jack accepted the paper but did not untie it, rather, he stared down at it for several moments before handing it back to McIntire. "I believe you have me confused, sir, with the master of this property."

"But you're not the master?" McIntire answered with a puzzled expression.

"No," Jack stated flatly, "but I can take you to him."

McIntire and his band followed Jack several hundred yards to the main residence, where they stopped at the veranda as Jack bade them wait. Jack continued inside the front door and emerged shortly with a much-annoyed Samuel Cressey, who brushed the crumbs from an interrupted meal off his shirt.

"What can I do for you, sir?" Cressey asked as he placed his hands on his hips and leaned slightly forward.

"And who would *you* be?" McIntire answered, his formerly polite tone now hardening with a decided edge.

The black man now leaned back and folded his arms. "Well, I would be Samuel Louis Cressey, owner and master of this establishment."

"*Owner and master?*" McIntire repeated, somewhat caught off guard. Suddenly, also annoyed, he shook his head then spit on the ground toward the porch. "Well, póg mo thóin, you say."

"Oui, monsier, vous pouvez aussi m'embrasser le cul."

McIntire gave Cressey a hard stare and spit again. "I don't know what you said."

"Well, I know quite well what *you* said. Parce que je comprends votre langue païenne."

McIntire bristled again as he paused to study the black man on the porch who smiled widely as he stared back down. "Well, good sir, you have me at quite the disadvantage. But could you be so kind as to do me the courtesy of explaining how a Negro such as yourself would have in his possession an estate such as this?"

Cressey spit as well as he smiled even wider. "Nothing would give me more pleasure. But could you first do *me* the courtesy of explaining who the hell *you* are and what business you have to intrude on my farm and interrupt my lunch?"

McIntire looked to the ground and pawed it with his foot in an obvious attempt to maintain his composure. He looked back up to Cressey, whose grin had not disappeared. "Why yes, sir, how could I forget my manners. I'm Captain Seamus McIntire of the Second Irish Militia under the command of Lieutenant Colonel John Cruger, commander of the garrison at Ninety-Six to the west of here. Being as you claim, the owner, I'm here to serve you notice that is transcribed here."

McIntire handed the rolled document to Cressey, who accepted it tentatively, inspecting it with great care but not untying the leather strap that kept it secure. He looked down at Jack, who quickly turned away. Cressey handed the notice back down to McIntire. "No need for me to open this. I don't know your commander but no doubt he's a Loyalist vassal to the Crown and whatever is written here can't be trusted. In any case, you may save me the trouble and explain it."

McIntire fumed as he accepted the document back. "Take care, sir, that your sharp tongue doesn't serve you poorly. By the same reasoning I must insist that you explain to *me* how it is that a Negro such as yourself would come to possess this estate. For I must be sure I'm dealing with the rightful owner and not a criminal that obtained the property by some nefarious means."

"Of course, captain. Such a reasonable request in these trying times certainly deserves an explanation." Cressey spit as his smile remained. "My father, Louis Cressey, owned this property, having inherited it from his father, Nigel. He was a white man with a white wife and daughter, both of whom died of the smallpox many years ago. Not long afterwards he purchased my mother in Charleston, after she had come up from New Orleans. She was originally from Martinique and a handsome woman. He never took another wife but fathered several children with the Negro women, including my mother. He sold off the other children once they were old enough and would probably have done the same with me. But he was quite fond of my mother, who he brought to live with him in the house. He kept me as a favor to her as she had a way of getting what she wanted. Some said it was the *Voodoo* that she practiced. He placed her in his will, leaving her this property. He was murdered by so-called *militia* when this war began. Soon after my mother transferred ownership in my name. She passed two years ago. This farm legally belongs to me. I have the deed, if you wish to see it."

McIntire stared at the black man, who folded his arms and leaned back. "Well, Mister Cressey, that is a fascinating tale indeed – a shame there's not time to hear more details." McIntire waved his hand. "No need for me to see such a deed. In reality, whether you own this property matters not but a farthing. I have little interest in the operation but rather in those whom you employ." His voice increased in volume as he raised the rolled document above his head. "I have in my hand a declaration from Lieutenant Colonel John Cruger, commander of the garrison at Ninety-Six, approved by General Clinton himself, that authorizes me to requisition, seize, or otherwise free, any Negro that would take up arms in support of the Crown against those in rebellion of this province. I do now require you to present to me all of your Negroes that I may ascertain which are suitable and willing. I trust you'll cooperate, won't you, Mister Cressey?"

"The hell, you say," Cressey rasped as his grin vanished. He unfolded his arms, put his hands on his hips and spit. "And if I don't – *cooperate*?"

"That would be unwise. My men are well-armed and well-trained. I have authorization to use force as necessary to round up your slaves for inspection."

"*Authorization?*" Cressey growled. "Yes, I imagine you do. But let me ask you, if it's bodies that you want, why not purchase them at fair market value? Wouldn't that be the civil thing to do instead of robbing an honest landowner of his livelihood? Without a sufficient workforce, how will I continue to support the British effort with materials and food?"

"I don't think that you understand, Mister Cressey. It's not just mere *bodies* that are needed but rather men willing and capable to fight. In return, they'll be paid, they'll be clothed and most of all, they'll be given their freedom."

Cressey laughed. "*Freedom,* you say? Freedom to do what? Freedom to trade one master for another even more cruel for a mere piece of silver and a shiny uniform? Freedom to be used as fodder when the shooting starts? And when this war is over, then what? I suppose that they'll be rewarded handsome pensions, acres of land, and be treated as equal British subjects? If I have an able-bodied man here that is so foolish as to take your offer, I'll carry him to Ninety-Six myself. No, good captain, there's but one problem. You may certainly have me outgunned to do as you wish here. But that paper that you hold in your hand isn't worth but a farthing, either. We both know that you aren't here on a recruitment mission for your Loyalist cause. No, captain, you and your band of ruffians are here to rob and plunder as you have in these parts for quite some time. So, please take what you came here for and leave. Let's get this over with."

McIntire pointed the paper up at Cressey. "And you, sir – how dare you speak to me as if you're somehow on a higher moral plane. You sell your goods to the rebels as easily as you sell to the Crown. You would sell your goods to Satan himself if he could but produce the correct sum. You may not realize it, but we've provided you security lest the roaming bands of rebel jackals tear you apart and lay this farm waste as is their want to do. And now you would accuse me of the same?"

"If you're here to steal my slaves, what is rightfully mine under the law, then you're no different than any band of jackals, rebel or otherwise."

"What is rightfully *yours*? Allow me to also comment on *that* subject. If your name is *Cressey* then I happen to know on good authority that you did collude with a scoundrel, a man devoid of scruples, a half-breed and a heathen, to murder your so-called father so that you might take possession of this land. Isn't that true?"

Cressey leaned back and folded his arms again. "And how would you know such a thing?"

An obviously dour man, McIntire's stern expression never faltered as he waved the paper in a circle over his head. "The woods have eyes. The fields have ears. And the birds speak of everything. This man's name is Maurice Sebastian LeClerc, isn't it?"

Cressey bristled but said nothing. Jack had been watching intently in silence below the porch nearby. His eyes suddenly widened as he backed up a step.

McIntire turned toward Jack. "And you! You know LeClerc, don't you!"

Jack said nothing as he stared back at McIntire's angry face. The captain withdrew a pistol from his belt, approached Jack and pressed the barrel into Jack's forehead.

"Tell me, goddamn it," McIntire commanded, "before I no longer care to hear the answer and spread your brains on the ground!"

Jack opened his mouth from which emanated no sound. McIntire kept the pistol to Jack's forehead as he turned to

Cressey. "Who's this white man that works in the fields with Negroes?"

"He's nothing," Cressey answered. "He's but a vagrant. Shoot him if you wish. He's nothing to me."

McIntire looked back to Jack. "He fears not to die. But he knows LeClerc. I saw it in his eyes."

Cressey peered forward at the pair as they faced each other, Jack with his hands by his sides and McIntire with his long arm extended. "Of what value is LeClerc to you, captain?"

"*Value?*" McIntire shot Cressey an angry glance, his ire seemingly growing. "The man is fraught with vileness from top to bottom. He's murdered and plundered his way across this province, and he is a scourge to those loyal citizens who support our king. I'd trade my entire fortune to see him dead, and better, to make it so myself. There is a handsome bounty on his painted head."

"Captain," Cressey answered as his smile returned. "You don't have to trade so much as your fortune, as I can deliver him to you for a more reasonable price. You make keep the bounty and I may keep my slaves."

McIntire removed the pistol from Jack's head and lowered his arm, turning toward Cressey, who loomed above him. "Name that price, sir, and then your method."

"First, you will agree that if I can deliver to you LeClerc, alive and well, you will not abscond or even so much as approach one of my slaves to converse." Cressey shook his head and waved his finger. "Not a one."

McIntire slid the pistol back in his belt. "Agreed," he answered eagerly. "But only if you can truly do so. Now, tell me how."

"And further," Cressey continued, "that you or any other agent of General Clinton, your lieutenant colonel, the military or government at large, will not set foot again on this property, my land, for any other purpose except to barter fairly in accordance with the established trade market."

McIntire bowed slightly as he removed his hat, placing it over his heart. "You have my word as a sworn officer of the Crown. I'll make it known."

"Very well, captain. Then what I have to say is for your ears only. Please have your men move themselves into the main barn out of sight." Cressey pointed to a large structure about a hundred yards away. "Then, you may come inside here with me for the details."

McIntire nodded as he replaced his hat then turned to move toward the barn as directed. Cressey watched him without expression for a few moments. Without so much as a glance at Jack, he turned and disappeared back into the house.

* * *

Four days later, Jack watched from the veranda as LeClerc strolled with Cressey along the road in front of the house. LeClerc and his men had entered the property in search of provisions from the same direction as they had with Jack and Custis and several times since. Passing the veranda, LeClerc turned his head to stare at Jack for a long moment then resumed his conversation in French with Cressey. As was the usual routine his men remained within shouting distance away, milling in the front yard save for Bass, who took station on the front veranda, his dark sunken eyes now fixed on Jack nearby with the usual disdain.

Reaching the large front entrance to the barn, the pair stopped. Cressey extended his right hand to LeClerc, who nodded and shook it. Cressey then moved to swing open the large, hinged door. As LeClerc stepped forward toward the darkness a barrage of musket fire greeted him with a force that lifted him as it knocked him backwards, hurling more than a dozen .75-caliber lead balls ripping through his meaty torso. Unlike most of his own victims, he was dead before he hit the ground. McIntire stepped out of the darkness as Cressey emerged from behind the door, bending over to unceremoniously close LeClerc's painted eyes, still fixed wide open. As Cressey stooped McIntire withdrew the pistol from his belt and calmly shot the black man in the back of the head, killing him instantly and sending his body toppling onto that of LeClerc. The remainder of the militia now streamed out from the barn brandishing muskets and howling madly at the top of their lungs as they made for the direction of the main house. LeClerc's men in the front yard turned and ran, streaming past the veranda like a stampede in a race for the woods.

On the veranda itself, an astonished Bass withdrew his knife as he looked wildly at Jack.

"That's not going to do you much good," Jack remarked as the faded green berserkers bore down on them. "If I were you, I'd run."

Turn and run Bass did. Jack watched the short, stocky man flee as his legs and arms moved in a frenzy, his thick thighs rubbing furiously together. But Bass had waited too long as the fastest of the green wave caught up to him in the road not a stone's throw from the house. The first man struck him with the butt end of his firelock hard in the back between his shoulder blades, knocking him forward on his face and dislodging the knife from his hand. A second man buried a hatchet in the back of Bass' head and a third scalped him from the forehead with the skinner's own nearby knife. Unlike the more fortunate LeClerc and Cressey, Bass was left to die slowly in the road where he lay. The green horde continued to chase LeClerc's men as far as the end of the field then stopped to saunter back toward the farm, raising their muskets as they cheered.

McIntire surveyed the scene from the barn entrance as his men filtered back, tossing Bass's scalp to one another in a game of catch. The captain slowly reloaded his pistol then began a deliberate walk toward the house, the weapon dangling by his side as he locked eyes with Jack. Stopping just short of the veranda, he gazed up at the younger man with a curious expression. "Who are you?" he asked in a low, raspy voice.

Jack met the lanky man's hard stare but said nothing.

"Who are you and what are you doing here?" McIntire repeated in a growl. "I shall not ask again. You're certainly not a *vagrant*."

"I am Jack Halliday, from the province of Maryland."

"Maryland?" McIntire scoffed. "A damned Yankee? And how is it that you find yourself in this province, at this farm, as a white man working as a nigger for *sustenance,* such a long way from home?"

"I'm in the company of a Negro who was traded by LeClerc to Cressey in return for provisions."

McIntire paused as he processed that information. "You had a connection to LeClerc, then. I watched him pass this house as he approached. He didn't take his eyes from you. This Negro you speak of, he's yours?"

Jack shook his head. "He's not mine. His name is *Custis.* He's the property of Mister Arthur Coleman of Annapolis, who is also my employer."

"And how is it that you came to be in the company of LeClerc?"

Jack remained silent as he stared back at McIntire.

After a long moment, McIntire removed his hat with his empty hand and wiped his brow with his sleeve. He replaced the cover on his head and raised the pistol with his other hand and pointed it up at Jack's breast. "I've neither time nor patience for this. You'll tell me what you're doing here while I still care, or I'll put a ball through you where you stand."

Jack shifted his gaze to the ground before he raised his head and looked McIntire straight in the eye. "There's no need to shoot me, captain. I'll tell you. You mentioned before that I'm not afraid to die. That isn't true – I'm quite afraid to die but have resigned myself to it, having that possibility before me too many times. But I know that my moment of death is fixed and can't be altered. Above all, I won't die a coward, for that is more distasteful than death itself. You may choose to pull that trigger in return for my explanation, but I'll give it nonetheless. I am Second Lieutenant Jack Halliday of the First Maryland Regiment of the Continental Army. Custis is a private. We fought Cornwallis' army near Camden back in August under General Gates. When our side collapsed, we became scattered. LeClerc found us in the woods nearby a short time later."

"Found you in the woods, did he?" McIntire scoffed. "And how is it that you yet live?"

"LeClerc valued Custis to be used for trade. As for me, LeClerc claimed to have seen me in his dreams and was therefore compelled not to harm me."

What may have passed as a grin emerged on McIntire's face. "Now *that* is a story I can well believe. Your army was thrashed at Camden. You were first ill-served by Gates, then LeClerc – I don't know which is worse. But you have the bearing of a soldier and the luck of an Irishman. In return for your brave conduct, I'll impose no judgment on you but rather will take you to Ninety-Six, where Colonel Cruger may determine your disposition." The captain continued as he lowered his pistol. "I'll maintain possession of your nigger and deposit you both to the safety of our garrison. But you must give me your word as an officer that you won't try to run."

"Run?" Jack asked with a bewildered expression. "To where would I run?"

"Back to your army, of course. Wouldn't you?"

"That army is gone," Jack answered definitively. "They've disintegrated and exist no more. I saw it myself."

"Not so, lieutenant. That army exists as a fact, having been reformed under a General Greene, who is last known to be positioned at Charlotte in North Carolina, organizing his forces. I imagine he'll make the acquaintance of General Cornwallis in good time."

Jack remained silent for several moments, fixed in thought. "Very well, captain," he eventually answered, "I won't run. I give you my word. But I would ask that you not separate me from Custis."

"And where is this Custis?"

Jack motioned behind him. "He's in the house. He worked for Cressey in there."

"Captain. Excuse me, sir." McIntire turned toward another lanky, green-clad man that had approached along the path from the barn.

"Yes, sergeant. Report."

"Sir, we found extra wagons behind the barn and more live-stock further down."

"Good." McIntire answered curtly. "Fit as much as you can into the wagons – Cressey's as well. Anything we can't take we'll burn."

"And I also found this knife and spoon inside LeClerc's vest."

McIntire took possession of both and examined them closely.

Jack took a step forward. "Those are actually mine. LeClerc took them when he found me in the swamp."

"Did he now," McIntire answered casually as he looked away and placed both inside his coat.

"Do we pursue the remainder of LeClerc's men?" the sergeant asked curtly.

"No. They're useless without him and will scatter like dead leaves in the wind. We'll raze this place and take all we can to Ninety-Six. Now move."

Less than two hours later, facing west toward the still high setting sun, Jack found himself bound by the wrists and tied to a rope with Custis just behind him, marching at the head of a line of Cressey's Negroes similarly attached. To the front were McIntire's men, formed in a column similar to how they had entered, laughing as they drank from the numerous flasks they carried. Behind was a row of eight wagons, each stacked full of vegetables, cotton, chickens, pigs, and anything else of value that could be carried. At the end were a half dozen cattle and finally a rear guard of the same number of militia. To the last wagon had been fastened a vertical firelock pointing high with a bayonet that carried the severed head of LeClerc. Jack took one last look behind him as the flames and smoke from what had been Cressey's farm billowed into the air in an angry black cloud.

18

To win one hundred victories in one hundred battles
is not the acme of skill. To subdue the enemy without
fighting is the acme of skill.

The Art of War, Sun Tzu

J ust north of the South Carolina border in December of
1780, as the new commander of the Continental Southern
Army, Major General Nathaneal Greene, took stock of the
terrible condition of the men he had inherited in Charlotte, he
summarized his chances for success quite succinctly – *deplorable.*
But from the moment he accepted the position, Greene had no
illusions as to his severely disadvantaged position, nor would
he waste time lamenting, as that was not his nature. Even with
France's entrance into the conflict, the situation in the north,
where the British held firm control of strategically critical New
York Harbor, had evolved into a stalemate with neither side wanting to risk the kind of major effort necessary to sway the balance.
The arena where the conflict could be affected and therefore
leveraged had moved decidedly to the volatile and messy south,
where it seemed the outcome would be determined. Finally able
to wrestle control from a handwringing and increasingly gun-shy

Congress regarding who would lead his forces, Washington had dispatched Greene from his post as Quartermaster General to the eye of the southern storm. This tall, broad-shouldered natural leader – humble but at the same time audacious – was first and foremost a man of action, cut from the same cloth as the commander-in-chief who selected him. With this appointment, both Greene and Washington had finally gotten what they yearned for – the former, a major command of a fighting army and the latter, a general that could be trusted to save the American cause.

Born in 1742 in the maritime province of Rhode Island, Greene had been raised a Quaker, like his ancestors before him. His lineage had arrived in the Massachusetts Bay Colony not long after the founding of Boston, part of the increasing torrent of religious dissenters from England. Within a year his great-great-grandfather also departed the equally intolerant Puritans to help found the *Providence Plantations* that would become the colony of Rhode Island. Mainly self-educated, as was the Quaker practice, he had inherited his father's business that included a foundry and grist mill, even though he had older brothers. In February 1772, a commercial vessel owned by Greene, the *Fortune*, laden with 1,400 gallons of rum, was seized in Newport Harbor as a suspected smuggler by the British revenue cutter *HMS Gaspee*, for which Greene filed a lawsuit against the *Gaspee's* commanding officer. Later that summer in June when the *Gaspee* serendipitously ran aground in Narragansett Bay, the local sheriff and several dozen hotheads rowed out to the stricken vessel to arrest the commander, regarding Greene's complaint. When the naval officer resisted, the sheriff shot him in the groin and the mob burnt the ship to the waterline. A furious government back in England offered a fortune in bounties for information but never could organize a trial for an acute lack of witnesses. Until this point, Greene had remained ambivalent to the growing political unrest but now became an ardent supporter of those dissatisfied with London. Interpreting the incident as a gross example of tyranny, he wrote that the investigating commission should be *justly alarming to every virtuous mind and lover of liberty in America*.

In October 1774, prompted by the increasing turmoil in New England, Greene provided his own money to establish a militia unit for which he was not given command or even an officer's commission, due to a permanent limp. Instead, he willingly drilled as a mere private. Following the explosive events at Lexington and Concord in April 1775, the unit reorganized and hurried to Boston with Greene now given command as a Brigadier General, the youngest general officer in the collective forces. This Rhode Island unit that participated in the siege quickly gained a reputation, as few others did, as well-equipped, well-disciplined, and well-led. For all of Washington's many sterling leadership qualities, chief among them was his ability to recognize and employ talent. Plucked from the mishmash myriad of New England militias that amalgamated into the makeshift army, Washington immediately identified Greene as a more than capable leader, bringing him into his inner circle and soon entrusting him with command of an entire brigade of seven regiments and eventual employment as garrison commander of Boston when the British evacuated the city. Promoted to major general during the follow-on failed campaign in New York that included Greene's disastrous advice to defend Fort Washington on the Hudson, the protégé nevertheless steadily earned positions of increased responsibility with participation in every major battle, operation, and undertaking. Needing a miracle to salvage a corrupt and failing logistics system upon which the Continental Army's existence depended and with it, the entire American cause, Washington turned to the one man he trusted explicitly, appointing Greene as Quartermaster General to which Greene frustratingly and famously remarked that *nobody heard of a Quartermaster in history.* That Greene dutifully accepted this post when every inch of him yearned for a field command, reflects the immense respect he held for his commander-in-chief as well as the deep commitment to the provincial struggle that put the needs of the collective army before his own. Not every participant in the so-called *glorious cause* had been so virtuous.

As the new commander of the Southern Army, Greene's mission was not only to keep that deplorable and dissipated rabble intact but rather to somehow reconstitute and use it to rid South Carolina of the British. At his disposal were roughly 2,300 ragged men, of which only about two thirds were available and only half adequately equipped, with further supply and provisions nearly non-existent. Neighboring provinces such as Virginia were expected to significantly contribute to force refurbishment but Governor Jefferson's aversion to standing armies slowed those efforts to a trickle. When reinforcements and supplies did arrive, Greene formulated a strategy that closely mirrored Washington's own, that success would be measured in the mere continued existence of his army. Greene could not hope to defeat Cornwallis' main army in a pitched, standup battle; nor should he choose to attempt to without a fastidious examination of the circumstances, but he could certainly wear the British down by forcing them to chase him over a countryside that was not fond of their presence.

Located several days' travel to the south in central South Carolina, General Cornwallis and his force of 3,200 were aware of Greene's arrival and the resultant ramifications of his presence. Only four months prior, Cornwallis had crushed Gates and the Continental Army to the point where any thought of their return seemed incredulous if not ridiculous. Yet here they were, wafting back across the countryside like a bad odor. Under the European conventions to which Cornwallis and his professional military class adhered, such a major defeat of an opponent prompted capitulation of the surrounding citizenry, if for no other reason than their own practical consideration of self-protection. But Camden had changed little as the vast majority of South Carolina provincials continued to show him their backs, providing next to nothing in terms of sustenance and intelligence. The Loyalist militias had proven once again worthless and even worse, the safe transit of his messengers and supply trains was non-existent due to the constant marauding of organized partisans – he was lucky to even know the whereabouts of Greene. With the vision to push north toward Virginia still in play, Cornwallis first needed to rid himself of the unwanted rebel threat that had somehow managed to re-emerge like a stubborn weed.

Before year's end and despite the poor condition of his troops, the ever-aggressive Greene made the first move. Ignoring the conventional wisdom of keeping his entire army intact, he split his forces, sending Brigadier General Daniel Morgan into South Carolina with a contingent of 600 men to include 80 cavalry, to threaten the British logistic network in the western part of the province. Greene understood that the resurgence of the Southern Continental Army, however dilapidated, would necessitate a British response and he wanted to control the play. Cornwallis answered, dispatching Tarleton's Legion with 1,100 men, including three times the number of cavalry, to chase Morgan to ground. Moving like the wolf he was, the aggressive Tarleton caught up with Morgan on January 17th at a place called *Hannah's Cowpens*. Approaching the Broad River and having received reinforcements from Colonel Andrew Pickens' South Carolina Militia that brought him relative numerical parity, Morgan chose to stand and fight rather than risk a less advantageous circumstance such as being overtaken while attempting to ford the river.

A rough-and-tumble, tall and muscular frontiersman from the hard scrabble Virginia backwoods, Morgan was probably the toughest soldier on either side of the war. A wagoner in the French and Indian War hauling supplies for General Braddock during the famed Indian massacre at the Battle of Monongahela, among his many feats of physical prowess was having received 500 lashes for punching a British lieutenant who had struck him with a sword, knocking the officer unconscious. A natural leader with scant education that belied his intelligence, Morgan spoke in a plain and direct manner that resonated with the common soldiers. Morgan had commanded a Virginia rifle company at the Siege of Boston and again under General Benedict Arnold at the failed attempt to take Quebec in 1775, taking overall command of the forces during the battle when Arnold was shot in the leg. Taken as a prisoner of war in Quebec until his exchange in 1777, he rejoined Washington, was promoted to Colonel and given command of a composite regiment of sharpshooters from Virginia, Maryland, and Pennsylvania. Again, with Arnold at Saratoga, his unit distinguished itself with its ability to target and eliminate British officers. Frustrated with Congress and its penchant for promoting those with better political connections than fighting ability and suffering from accumulated physical abuse to his sciatic back, Morgan retired in 1779, returning to his home in Winchester, Virginia. Prompted by the defeat in Camden, he returned to service in 1780 and was promoted to Brigadier General by Gates, just before the arrival of Greene.

With his back to the Broad River several miles to the north and Tarleton about to catch him from the south, Morgan welcomed the fight, knowing full well that the ground he chose defied conventional wisdom. He devised a plan based on three foundational concepts: Tarleton's arrogance and over-aggressiveness; the British absolute disrespect for colonial militias; and the ability of his Virginia riflemen to kill anything. Having hurried his men during the wee hours, Tarleton attacked at first light, charging across a broad field that sloped upward toward the American forces in perfect synchrony with Morgan's plan. With a formation that utilized defense in depth, the first line of militia fired two or three volleys then fled back as ordered. Tarleton's dragoons and light infantry greedily chased the militia over a rise in what they expected would be the usual rout only to be greeted by Morgan's snipers, disciplined Continentals and William Washington's cavalry, all of whom converged on the British and chopped them to pieces. Tarleton managed to rally the few soldiers he could and escape back to the south having lost more than 800 men, a good 500 of them taken prisoner – almost his entire force – along with his vaunted reputation of invincibility.

The *Battle of Cowpens* proved a blow that the British could not let stand without a proper response and from which neither could they fully recover. Tarleton had been decimated, including a major portion of the critical British light infantry now marching away as captives. If Cornwallis was going to eradicate the south of the new Continental Army threat, he needed those shock troops back. Two days later, as the remnants of Tarleton's Legion finished limping back into camp to rejoin the main British force, now reinforced by 2,500 troops who had arrived from New York, Cornwallis set out after Morgan. Due to the usual lack of actionable intelligence, Cornwallis started in the wrong direction, erroneously believing that Morgan had continued south to threaten the supply network. Soon correcting that mistake, and needing more than ever to increase his speed, Cornwallis now forced his men to divest themselves of all unnecessary baggage to include tents, wagons and even the unthinkable – their rum.

Morgan had not continued on to threaten the British supply lines, as was his original intention, for he understood that what had just transpired at Cowpens would prompt Cornwallis to come for him with a vengeance. He must now avoid those superior numbers and find his way back to rejoin Greene. Upon hearing the news, Greene reached a similar conclusion along with the gnawing temptation that, now deficient of cavalry and light infantry, Cornwallis could be vulnerable. To evade British reach, both Green and Morgan independently headed north, the latter with a trove of British prisoners that Cornwallis desperately wanted back. They reunited early February at Guilford Court House outside of Greensboro in north-central North Carolina, where Greene's nagging aggressiveness got the better of him as he proposed to stand and fight Cornwallis, only two days behind them. To a man, his leadership council disagreed, citing an army still too weak, too tired, and too ill-equipped to take that risk. In what became known as the *Race to the Dan*, they continued their press northward through the miserable cold and rain crossing by mid-month the Dan River that snaked its way back and forth across the Virginia and North Carolina borders.

Cornwallis followed as best he could but could never catch up, constantly stymied by lack of resupply and intelligence from the local population as well as the inability to cross the innumerable swollen rivers and tributaries as all suitable watercraft had been removed by Greene's men. Constantly forced in the wrong direction by the need to find shallow crossings and harassed from behind by fast-moving detachments of Continentals designed to slow him down, he arrived at the southern banks of the Dan just mere hours after Greene had crossed, with not so much as a skiff to be found with which to ferry his men. With his army tired, frustrated, nearly starved and now logistically overextended – a full 200 miles from his closest supply depot in Camden – Cornwallis paused, taking stock of his situation, which he now realized had become an exercise in futility. Concluding no need to continue the fruitless chase into Virginia, where Greene's force might be heavily augmented by von Steuben's successful recruiting efforts, Cornwallis headed his dejected army back south to Hillsborough.

As Greene rested his equally weary and hungry men on the north side of the Dan River, Daniel Morgan continued north to return home to Winchester, his ailing back having finally quit for good. Approaching the end of February and bolstered by a stream of new recruits from Virginia as well as North Carolina militia, Greene recrossed the Dan and cautiously followed the redcoats south, using his cavalry to nip at the British heels but keeping his ever-growing main force too far out of reach to give Cornwallis the decisive engagement he wanted. By mid-March, with a superior force of well over 4,000, many of them new militia with six-week enlistments, Greene decided that it was now indeed time to pick a fight. On March 15th he assembled his forces at Guilford Courthouse, the same grounds he had chosen a month earlier, thereby beckoning the British to engage him, a challenge that Cornwallis eagerly accepted. Borrowing Morgan's tactics from Cowpens, utilizing a defense in depth that relied on the unreliable – the unseasoned and ill-disciplined militia to fire an initial volley then cut and run – Greene fought Cornwallis to a stalemate, the latter ultimately choosing to use his cannon to fire grapeshot into what had devolved into a hand-to-hand melee, indiscriminately killing soldiers on both sides. This had the desired effect of chasing the Continentals from the field but at a horrendous cost to the British themselves. In all, Cornwallis lost more than 500 men with Greene only a third of that. It took the British two days to collect their dead and wounded.

The miraculous resurgence of the Continental Southern Army following their complete collapse only months prior and the British inability to eradicate them spoke volumes as to the assumption that the Carolina countryside held vast numbers of Loyalists needing only a slight nudge to rally to the cause. To any rational observer, the idea of vast, untapped Loyalist support, the foundation upon which the entire British southern strategy was constructed, had proven utterly baseless – not that King George and his government of fawning yes-men would ever admit that.

Having got what he wanted at Guilford Courthouse – a general engagement with Greene, and a so-called *victory* at that – a still reeling Cornwallis took stock of his situation. With the Continentals still lurking as a threat, an even bigger threat was the inability to resupply his army with food and ammunition. Desperate to remain intact, he spent the remainder of March limping to Wilmington on the North Carolina coast, where the navy could directly support him, leaving a trail of dying and severely wounded men in his wake. Without Loyalist support the mission to leverage the Carolinas to dominate the eastern seaboard had proved delusional and a fool's errand. However, just to the north lay an opportunity to join with forces recently sent by Clinton to conquer the critical middle colony that had emerged as the clear American economic and political center of gravity. Leaving his deputy, Lord Francis Rawdon, in charge of protecting the patchwork of logistic centers spread across the Carolinas, Cornwallis gathered what remained of his army, approximately 1,500 men, and on April 24th headed to Virginia to salvage both the British cause and his sanity.

* * *

NINETY-SIX, SOUTH CAROLINA, JUNE 18, 1781

Jack stared out the hole in the wall of the tiny shack – a makeshift storehouse with a dirt floor occupied mainly with cannon shot, musket balls, and gunpowder – that served as his current quarters.

Not quite a prisoner, but certainly not a trusted agent, he had been placed inside soon after the arrival of Greene's Continental forces that currently surrounded the star-shaped, earthen-based fort ringed by a ditch fronted by an abatis – piles of tree branches tied together with sharpened ends facing outwards – and upon which supported an encompassing wooden parapet. Not that Jack had indicated even in the slightest that he might somehow seek to find a way to contribute to the Continental siege effort that intensified with each passing day but the fort's commander, Lieutenant Colonel John Cruger, a Loyalist and former mayor of New York City, would take no chances.

The departure in April of Cornwallis to Virginia had left the door open for General Greene and his assortment of partisan allies to threaten the remaining British forces that manned the now obsolete and suddenly vulnerable logistic network spread across South Carolina. Like a pack of foxes inside a suddenly unguarded hen house, Francis Marion, Thomas Sumter, Andrew Pickens, and Greene himself, scoured the countryside in a feeding frenzy to destroy or otherwise force abandonment of every remaining garrison.

Named more than a century prior, and erroneously so, for its estimated distance along the trading path from Charleston to the Cherokee settlement of Keowee (now Greenville) farther to the north, *Ninety-Six* stood as the most remote depot, nearly 200 miles inland from the coast. Now the last holdout of the expansive logistic system that had supplied Cornwallis during his Carolina campaign, the outpost was a small village settlement bracketed by the eight-pointed *Star Fort* – designed such that defense was possible in any direction – less than 1,000 feet to the northeast and a smaller, wooden, oblique-shaped *Stockade Fort* about the same distance to the west, all defended by about 550 Loyalists militia, most from New York and New Jersey, along with minor representation from the local area. Ordered also to evacuate by Lord Rawdon, himself recently forced to relocate to the safety of Charleston, that message had not managed to reach Ninety-Six before the appearance of Greene and his force of more than twice the Loyalist number.

Greene had arrived nearly a month earlier, on May 22nd, with a mix of seasoned Carolina militia and Continental units to include Virginia and Maryland regiments, the latter under which Jack had previously served. With the Star Fort redoubt the obvious stronghold, the Americans immediately began digging siege trenches under the supervision of Polish chief engineer, Colonel Thaddius Kosciuszko, to safely approach and burn the fort. By the third week they had advanced within 30 feet of the walls where they also erected a 30-foot wooden *Maham Tower* built from the plethora of available green pine trees. From the tower, which included a protective barrier on the upper platform, they could fire muskets down into the otherwise strongly defended fort. Cruger answered by piling sandbags on the parapet tops to raise the height of the ramparts that allowed his men to fire at the tower through slits between the bags. The Loyalists also fired heated shot from three 3-pound cannon mounted on the parapets but with limited effect as the munitions could not be made hot enough and the sharpshooters in the tower pinned down the makeshift and inexperienced artillery crews. When the attackers began launching flaming arrows into the fort Cruger ordered the thatched roofs removed from the handful of buildings. As Greene learned that Rawdon was on his way from Charleston with a relief force of 2,000 men, he ordered an all-out assault on both the main and stockade forts.

From a narrow space between the boards of the crudely built door, Jack peered into the yard where men continually edged themselves close to the wall to remain protected from the line of fire from the rebel tower located within view to his left. As movement along the wall suddenly increased in earnest, Captain McIntire appeared, waving his long arms and frantically pointing as he shouted orders to subordinates that included Custis, now strangely clad in a green 2nd Irish Militia uniform. McIntire had marched Jack and Custis all the way from Cressey's farm to Ninety-Six, more than a week's journey, along with the 22 absconded slaves, none of which finished the journey, having been sold along the way piecemeal by McIntire. The captain began organizing small teams along the base of the wall to load muskets and pass them upward to the men on the parapets that now began to fire in earnest, dropping down their spent weapon to retrieve one fully charged.

Suddenly, to the right, the sandbags began to topple down from above the parapets as the rebels had managed to gain access through the outer defensive works and now pounded the make-shift wall extension with the butt ends of their firelocks as well as other tools. The bags crashed down onto the upper platform as a hole opened that allowed a half dozen or so rebels to poke their muskets through, fitted with bayonets, as those behind them continued to beat and push down the wall. The Loyalists countered with bayonets of their own as the platform teamed with men on the inside of the wall that alternately fired then stabbed upward into the ever-increasing crowd of attackers. Punching an entryway large enough for a crowd, the Americans gained access to the platform below as a melee now formed to obscure the opening that began to clog with dead and wounded. Like a strange dance, men on both sides now swung their spent muskets like clubs at each other as they twirled around together atop the inner parapet, stepping over the increasing fallen with many using the bodies to gain height advantage.

"MUNITIONS!" McIntire yelled from the base of the wall below as Custis and another man grabbed nearby hand carts and pushed them across the yard toward Jack. The captain followed, reaching the storage shed first and removing the thick wooden plank that kept it locked.

"HALLIDAY!" He called inside as the door burst open. "Help these men load! I swear by God if you run, I'll shoot you in an instant!"

"You don't have to worry about me, captain," Jack answered loudly as he began to pass wooden crates of musket balls out the doorway, "as there's nowhere else I prefer to be."

Jack and McIntire locked eyes for a moment as the captain peered inside the doorway, quickly removing himself with a gruff exhale.

"But captain," Jack continued, "if I were you, I'd remove that feather from your cap. The Virginia snipers in that tower specialize in killing officers and they can part your hair at that distance."

McIntire leaned back into the entry, pointing his finger at Jack, who continued to hand heavy boxes outside. "Don't waste your breath, lad," McIntire growled, "as I need no counsel from the likes of you. Just load!"

Jack handed another box out the door as McIntire turned to face the wall, standing erect with hands on his hips as he surveyed the scene. Up on the nearby parapet directly across the yard the struggle to protect the opening in the sandbags had grown into a full-fledged brawl as men on both sides alternately thrust their bayonets and swung their muskets as they stepped over bodies that now toppled off the platform along with the sandbags. More Loyalists approached on both sides of the ruckus with fresh muskets and some even tried to fire through the edges of the opening into the rebel side but were cut down by the sharpshooters in the tower as the missing top in the makeshift wall extension now exposed those inside the fort.

With one wagon loaded the first man grabbed its rear handles as he strained to lift it onto the large front wooden wheel. "MOVE!" The captain yelled as he slapped the man on the back then watched him start back across the yard toward the wall, weaving as he slowly labored under the weight of the burdened cart.

"FASTER, HALLIDAY!" McIntire barked as he returned his attention to Jack, who continued to hand boxes outside to Custis at the second wagon. "FASTER, GODDAMN IT, FASTER!"

Not even halfway back across the yard the man with the cart suddenly jerked backwards as he twisted 180 degrees, toppling hard onto his face and stomach. A red stain now formed on his back below the right shoulder where a sniper's round fired from the tower had exited. With the use now of only his left arm he struggled with that elbow to lift himself to his knees and twist back toward the cart to crawl under the small wagon for what semblance of cover it offered. He did not make it as another round hit him between the eyes, completely removing the top half of his head before the exiting projectile skipped past the side of the shed.

Jack dropped a box of lead balls at his feet and stepped outside to push the half-loaded cart from the entryway. He grabbed nearby Custis by the lapels of his uniform jacket and hurriedly pulled him into the shed.

"HALLIDAY!" McIntire shouted as he removed the pistol from his belt, still maintaining his upright posture as he peered toward the tower. "BY GOD, I'LL SHOOT YOU BOTH!"

"Captain, you're a dead man if you don't get in here now.!" Jack answered from just inside the doorway.

McIntire turned around to face the shed as he reached down to point the pistol into the entrance, pinning the door open with his foot. "GODDAMN YOU BOTH!" With a loud thud a musket ball struck him square in the back, the abrupt jolt knocking off his feathered cap and sending his tall frame hurling forward through the doorway. Jack caught McIntire from under the shoulders as he fell into the shed, his body propped up by his knees. A gaping hole formed in the center of the captain's chest, gushing a torrent of blood down his torso past his stomach, staining his faded green jacket to dark red.

"Captain!" Jack exclaimed as he held McIntire off the ground at an angle, his feet still sticking out of the doorway. "Captain!"

McIntire did not answer as he lifted his head with his eyes rolled back. With a loud groan the captain breathed his last as his face fell forward onto Jack's chest.

Jack looked back to Custis, who sat on a short stack of ammunition boxes in the back of the shed, silently staring into nothing. With not a little effort Jack pulled McIntire all the way into the shed and twisted the body to lay him on his back as he reached inside the captain's jacket to retrieve his knife and spoon. Stepping toward the entry he kicked the captain's cap inside as he scanned the barren yard then closed the door and resumed his position to peer out of the hole as he watched the ruckus that continued on the parapet.

Greene's forces captured the stockade and managed to gain access inside the Star Fort by breaking through the sandbags that comprised the heightened wall on the parapet. But their attack ultimately failed, as the Loyalists were able to repulse them in a small but brutal clash that resembled more of a brawl than a military action. In all, the American side suffered more than 150 casualties with the Loyalists about half that number. With Rawdon and his larger force expected within a day, an angry Greene, disgusted with the poor performance of his side, gathered his men and hastily departed. Soon after Rawdon's arrival the Loyalists evacuated Ninety-Six, burning the fort behind them and headed for the safety of Charleston. Greene and his mongrel army that included the partisans, with whom he cooperated but by no means controlled, had not won even a single major confrontation but had nonetheless managed, for all practical purposes, to wrestle control of the Carolinas from the British, who no longer possessed a logistics pipeline leading to Virginia but rather, only two isolated coastal strongholds at Charleston and Savannah. Like the once stalwart defenses at Ninety-Six, now reduced to ashes, so too did London's grand strategy of leveraging untapped Loyalist support in the Carolinas to control the American South.

19

*And in the synagogue there was a man, which had a spirit of
an unclean devil, and cried out with a loud voice, Saying,
"Let us alone; what have we to do with thee, thou Jesus of
Nazareth? Art thou come to destroy us?
I know thee who thou art; the Holy One of God."*

Gospel of Luke 4:33-34; KJV

In the summer of 1781, the British remained unwavering
in the steadfast belief of an inevitable military victory over
what they considered a vastly inferior people just as they
maintained an abject ignorance of why, after six years, they
had not yet obtained it. Nor did King George elect to consider
any honest reflection as to whether the strategy and policy he
had strenuously promoted in America, that is, the resolution
of a political problem with a military solution, was a good idea
executed poorly or just a plain bad idea. As the planet tilted on
its axis, continuing its annual roundtrip in orbit to once again
produce the northern hemisphere's maximum exposure to the
sun, so too did the learned ministers in London leave nothing
on the table during the season in their dogged stubbornness to
maintain the current course of action and habitual penchant to

350

blindly follow a leader who had purchased their loyalty and to whom they owed their lofty positions. Conversely, in America, the planets of this substandard British universe were aligning to produce a set of circumstances so implausible as to be considered as sacrilegious as the discovery by Nicolaus Copernicus, a mere century prior, of the earth's orbit around the sun, that not only challenged but destroyed existing conventions.

Notwithstanding the Crown's substantial holdings in the far-flung northern provinces as well as the Caribbean, the British position along the thirteen American colonies now consisted of a substantial main base of operations in New York Harbor, the remnants in Charleston and Savannah of their failed attempt to conquer the Carolinas, and an ongoing and increasing operation in Virginia to subdue and control that critical colony in an effort to split the Atlantic Seaboard in two and thereby control the lines of communication and commerce in both halves. With no end in sight to the botched domestic struggle that they had managed to escalate into a global war, the British continued to doggedly forge ahead in the quest to militarily defeat their American brethren and their new recent ally, France.

Cornwallis reached Petersburg, Virginia in the latter part of May to take control of about 5,000 men that included those brought with him from Wilmington, an augmentation provided by Clinton up north, and those currently under the command of prize turncoat, Benedict Arnold. One of General Washington's favorites, Arnold had switched allegiances the previous September, influenced by his new young wife from a prominent Loyalist family in Philadelphia and probably more so by his own vanity, mortally wounded by the perception of severe disrespect from Congress, who continued to pass him over for promotion in favor of less worthy individuals that, in his view, took credit for *his* accomplishments. He had also been courts-martialed and publicly reprimanded by Washington for corrupt behavior as military governor of Philadelphia following the British evacuation, those charges brought forth by Arnold's numerous political enemies. To say he held massive resentment for Congress and its many dubious influence brokers would have been an understatement. Given a lucrative lump sum of British Pounds, the rank of Brigadier General, and command of the provincial *American Legion*, he had been dispatched to Virginia that winter by General Clinton to disrupt American activities there, which he did in earnest, slashing and burning farms, mills, and anything that stored supplies as well as capturing the capital city of Richmond. Arnold had not long ago assumed command of the entire Chesapeake forces from recently exchanged prisoner, Major General William Phillips who had been captured at Saratoga, a close friend of Cornwallis that had died of a fever less than a week prior.

Needing to counter the growing threat in his home province, Washington sent young Frenchman, Marquis de Lafayette, south with 1,200 men to cooperate with General von Steuben to do what he could to disturb the British and to hang Arnold if he would be so fortunate to catch his old friend now turned traitor. Only 22 years of age, Marie-Joseph Paul Yves Roch Gilbert du Motier de La Fayette, Marquis de Lafayette, was a French aristocrat and idealist of deep military lineage that had volunteered to serve without pay in the Continental Army. Though only a teenager, he was granted a commission as a major general as part of Washington's staff, initially given no command authority but ultimately earning the commander-in-chief's adoration as if the son the general lacked. Loyal and courageous to a fault, he had participated at Washington's side with increasing responsibilities in many key events starting with the Battle of Brandywine, where he was wounded, as part of the effort to recapture Philadelphia in 1777. As had been the repeated case over the course of the conflict, Lafayette did not have the size force to directly confront Cornwallis but rather shadowed him from the fringes, nipping at the redcoat's heels as best he could and providing valuable intelligence back north to Washington, who remained focused on the British center of gravity, New York Harbor.

With Lafayette's presence over the summer more of a nuisance, Cornwallis' biggest challenge seemed to be a lack of clarity from his superior, Clinton. He turned in circles in southern Virginia as he received a series of confusing and conflicting orders ranging from creating a fortified depot near the entrance to the Chesapeake Bay in Portsmouth to returning his forces wholesale back to New York. By now, more than prone to drink his own bathwater to justify his failure and abandonment of the Carolinas, Cornwallis lobbied strenuously for Clinton to quit New York and shift his forces to Virginia, the obvious point of strategic advantage. The result of this dance was a decision in early August to establish a deep-water naval base at Yorktown, near the mouth of the York River at the end of the southernmost of three peninsulas that extended from the west into the Chesapeake Bay, where supply by both land and open ocean could be easily accessed and where Clinton would reinforce Cornwallis with additional troops.

In a dance of his own farther north with his new allies, an increasingly desperate Washington, his support from both Congress and the people constantly ebbing to new lows, had become frustrated with French land commander, General Rochambeau's inaction that, to this point, had done little to bother the British except for the notion of the French Army's continued presence. With a reluctant French garrison bottled up in Newport, Rhode Island by a British naval blockade and unable, or unwilling, to break out, a second, larger fleet departed France, the product of lobbying by Lafayette and surprisingly unmolested in European waters by the British, who chose instead to guard their homeland island from potential invasion. With twenty-eight ships of the line and a cargo of 3,000 soldiers all commanded by Admiral Comte de Grasse this flotilla headed first to a show of force to the French holdings in the Caribbean before turning up the coast of North America to arrive off the mouth of the Chesapeake in late August. Previously unsure if de Grasse intended to head for New York, the British had no choice but to counter the threat by sending nineteen warships of their own south to Virginia where, in early September the two fleets pummeled each other to a draw. Losing only one ship, the British nevertheless sustained more damage due to the French superior firepower and made the decision to return to New York. Augmented now by the meager fleet that had managed to escape from Rhode Island while the British became distracted by de Grasse, the French now owned the entrance to the Chesapeake Bay with thirty-five ships. A battle that proved tactically insignificant for either side nonetheless would render enormous strategic consequences.

Having been informed in mid-August of de Grasse's intended movements and plans to remain in Virginia, at least temporarily, Washington executed what could have been, except for crossing the Delaware River and resultant capture of Trenton, his most significant action of the war. Having obsessed for years about how to dislodge the British and retake New York Harbor, he suddenly abandoned that prime objective in favor of risking his fortune, and those of the colonies, on the calculation underwritten by the French forces now enroute somewhere on the southern Atlantic seaboard. Using to his advantage his well-known reputation of ineffective positioning he pretended to organize a threat to the British defense of New York Harbor to include the repair of roads and bridges in New Jersey and construction of giant ovens – necessary to feed his army – in plain sight across the Hudson. The professional military criticism of Washington had always been, that as aggressive, courageous, and noble as he might be, such a provincial bumpkin lacked the understanding, experience, and capability possessed by his more sophisticated adversaries in the fine art of large-scale operational movements that defined martial virtuosity and produced military superiority. To the chagrin of his bevy of red-clad detractors, Washington started south on August 21st with 6,000 men to include 4,000 French troops, leaving a smaller detachment behind to hold down the north, and was not detected until September 2nd when his army passed through Philadelphia, too late for Clinton to react.

Washington arrived on the lower Virginia Peninsula in mid-September where, with a combination of Lafayette's men, soldiers from the French ships and those he had just marched down from New York, he now possessed a force of more than

16,000 ground troops at his disposal to include 7,000 of the world's finest infantry and artillery as well as an impenetrable French fleet that guarded the mouth of the Chesapeake Bay. In this complete turn of events, he was suddenly and for the first time no longer at a numerical and qualitative disadvantage. Not far away at Yorktown, just over 7,000 British soldiers continued to dig in, now trapped between a hammer and an anvil with their backs to the York River, unable to escape by sea and nowhere to run on land except through a more than capable army twice their size. Washington and his French allies commenced a siege on September 28th as Cornwallis prayed that Clinton would send reinforcements, which never came. By October 19th, with both the village and British hopes reduced to rubble by the constant bombardment of the heavy allied guns, Cornwallis capitulated. No longer promoting Virginia as the British path to victory and now responsible for ceding roughly a third of the total British forces in the colonies, Cornwallis did not show his face at the formal surrender ceremony.

The defeat at Yorktown did not immediately end the war but it did break King George's government as well as even the king himself, who wrote a self-scathing letter of abdication that was never published. With the hunting of scapegoats back in season – now by the Whigs – the king's hirelings, all of whom had clapped like barking seals over the hardline American policies and were now suddenly devoid of credibility, resigned in droves to include Prime Minister Lord North as the king was forced to accept liberal replacements with polar opposite political bents that he neither liked nor could control. With continued hostilities instantly out of favor, the new ministry forced a shift in policy to negotiate a peace with terms that could even include the previously unthinkable – the formal recognition of the United States of America – an event that did, in fact, occur two years later with the Treaty of Paris. For the more immediate future the British Army in the provinces had no choice but to anxiously wait, holding onto what they still had until London could work out a settlement and provide further instructions. Looming on the horizon was a massive tear-down operation, a humiliating evacuation of their holdings in the thirteen colonies.

* * *

CHARLESTON, SOUTH CAROLINA, EARLY DECEMBER 1782

"Jack Halliday? Is that you, Jack?"

Jack turned in the direction of the voice and looked about. The Charleston waterfront bustled with activity as men moved in all directions, some wheeling carts, some hoisting crates, some carrying nothing at all but in an awful hurry for somewhere. Ships of all types filled the numerous piers along the western banks of the Cooper River and many more lay at anchor to the east and south at the junction of the Ashley River that defined the peninsula where the city began.

"Jack! It *is* you!"

The voice found Jack first as a sturdy young man about the same height with swarthy skin and reddish-blond hair placed a hand on Jack's shoulder as he displayed a toothy smile.

"Jack! It's me – Jacob! Jacob Chase."

Jack stared into a pair of hazel eyes before his own went wide. He placed his own hand on the young man's shoulder. "Jacob!"

Both men stared at each other for a moment with wide grins as a stream of others passed around them.

"Jacob, what are you doing here?" Jack began as he lowered his hand.

"We're here on the *Harriet*," Jacob answered as he pointed off toward the piers. "Isaac too."

"And your grandfather?" Jack asked tentatively.

Jacob's smile disappeared as he lowered his gaze. "Not with us anymore. He left us last year. Worked until the day he died. My grandmother is still alive and doing well enough back in Portsmouth. Isaac and I now run the business. We recently fitted

Harriet with two new masts and are considering a second ship for Isaac."

Jack nodded as a man passed by holding a large chair. "I see."

"I saw you from all the way over there," Jacob continued as he pointed toward the piers. "I knew it was you. I never forgot you, Jack. Neither did Grandfather."

"I'm sorry to hear about your grandfather, Jacob. He was a good man. He did much for me by taking me aboard when he did and not leaving me in New Jersey."

"But what of you, Jack? What are you doing here – in Charleston, of all places? Grandfather told me that he left you with Arthur Coleman in Annapolis. What are you doing *here?*"

"It's a long story, Jacob, and one best not told out here. But what of Mister Coleman? And his family? Have you seen them?"

Jacob shook his head. "No. Not since well before Grandfather passed. It seems the quality of his products began to suffer – and also the need. We've since been trading rice and cotton from here to New York and sometimes Boston. That's proven much more lucrative."

"You're returning north then?"

Jacob nodded. "Today, in fact. We're fully loaded. It's Sunday and normally we'd rest. But the winds are veering west, and the tide will start to ebb this afternoon. There are shallows in the channel that are better passed well before low water, and I want us well clear of the coast by dark. We're lucky to have spotted you before we left."

"Today, you say?" Jack placed his hand back on Jacob's shoulder. "If you're willing, maybe you can help me – again."

"Jack, I'm in your service. I owe you a debt I can never repay. Let's go back to the *Harriet* where we can talk. Isaac is there waiting for me. We can give you something to eat. You look like you could use a meal."

Jack grinned and nodded, clapping Jacob again on the shoulder as the pair started for the piers.

* * *

Jack stood outside the handsome example of contemporary but classic architecture, Saint Michael's Church, located on the corner of Meeting and Broad Streets, and gazed through the four Tuscan columns that supported the portico above the large front door and above that, the tall white steeple that peered out over the city. Originally the site of Saint Philip's Church of England, built a century before but relocated after being badly damaged by a hurricane in 1710, it stood in the center of the port city of Charleston and had been reconstructed as a new house of worship only two decades prior. In both its forms, this physical church along with its theology had been a cornerstone in the founding and growth of the city, and the province as a whole. Unlike the initial Pilgrims of Plymouth and subsequent Puritans that founded the Massachusetts Bay Colony and dominated New England, these later southern settlers held to more traditional Anglican beliefs and sought not to alter or otherwise improve on the Church of England, synonymous with the government itself, but rather to import it wholesale as their governing and moral norms. Equally important to the formation of the *Province of Carolina*, granted charter in 1663 and further parceled in the next century, was the direct relationship with Caribbean Plantation owners, many of whom immigrated to replicate similar growing operations that required large labor pools, thus establishing the deep-water port of Charleston as the premier portal of the slave trade in the south if not the entire colonial seaboard.

Following the battle and subsequent evacuation at Ninety-Six, Jack and Custis had fallen in with Lord Rawdon's forces that marched back through the growing summer heat to the remaining Carolina stronghold of Charleston. Protected and resupplied from sea by the navy and guarded on land by vast marshes and swamps with limited and fortified approaches, several thousand soldiers, citizens and slaves remained out of the grasp of Greene's army and the hordes of rebel militia that roamed outside in the hinterland like packs of angry hyenas. As if from a sponge being squeezed, a steady stream of disaffected Loyalists drained into the city, much as they had in Boston in 1775, with no hope of safety elsewhere and little hope in general. No longer much caring as to his prior affiliations and having more now to concern themselves with than a northern vagabond and his Negro consort, Jack had been left to his own devices, completely unsupervised and, as the days wore on, increasingly unnoticed. To scratch out a means to support himself he had fallen in with the throng of fellow lower sorts who competed daily to service the waterfront to load and offload cargo from the ever-increasing commercial vessels that continually filled the harbor. Custis, on the other hand, had been given *employment* in the service of the church across from which Jack now stood, working with a group of other Negroes in one of the rear buildings that housed the kitchen, his Loyalist militia uniform no longer to be found. On most days Jack managed to scratch out enough wages to feed himself but on many occasions was forced to depend on Custis, who would secretly provide him with scraps from the rectory behind the church.

In the first autumn after Jack's arrival in 1781, news of Yorktown had reached the city like a thunderclap. By the spring of 1782, with the ignominious departure of Lord North, the influence of his bastion of king's men had vanished, scattered to the political winds by vengeful Whigs who, having been relegated to obscurity for the last decade, made it well known that any who espoused the Tory desire for further prosecution of American hostilities were little more than traitors to England. With such a sea change in London and peace negotiations well under-way, British military holdings in the southern colonies became unnecessary, with Savannah the first to evacuate in July. With a provisional treaty agreed on in November 1782, the leadership in Charleston also received instructions to vacate in December. The resident Loyalists, who in their own eyes had committed the noble act of supporting the legitimate government, now faced an excruciating decision, to leave behind with little more than the shirt on their backs what for many had been ancestral grounds for generations, or to remain in the only home they had ever known and risk what would surely rain down on them – a firestorm of hate and violence.

Jack crossed the street and entered the church stepping into a white-painted foyer with a high ceiling and grey stone flooring, then through a second door into the main church filled with brown square wooden pews separated in the middle by a long aisle. At the far end stood a shallow adjacent altar made of wood, like a separate small open room and, just before that, a handsome darker wooden pulpit that rose above and dominated the simple square enclosed pews. Inside this raised lectern stood a frail-looking, middle-aged man with a nearly bald, globe-shaped head that seemed oversized for his small, thin frame. Jack stood in the very back as Reverend Trenton Coombs held up a book in one hand and waved a boney finger toward the congregation with the other.

"So, we read today from the Gospel of Luke," the reverend annunciated clearly with a strong voice that belied his meager stature, "that Jesus drove a demon from a man in a *synagogue.* We can find this passage also in Matthew and Mark with nearly the same text. Except for the events of the final days of Jesus you will not find many instances of Gospel passages that align much less nearly completely but, on this matter, we have three. Listen closely again to the words." He donned a pair of metal-framed spectacles and read from the book. '*Let us alone; what have we to do with thee, thou Jesus of Nazareth?'* The man asked, then said, '*I know thee who thou art.'*" He removed the spectacles, placed them down inside the lectern. "*They* knew who he was. We understand from the Gospels that the world surrounding Jesus did not know who he was or did not believe or want to believe who he said he was and, in fact, he was ultimately put to death simply for stating who he was to the authorities and intelligentsia, those learned men – the high priests and Pharisees – who took it upon themselves to dictate proper thought and behavior to the unwashed masses. Those *learned men,* above all, should have known who he was, yet they did not. Is it not ironic, fascinating, but most importantly, wholly instructional, that those themselves that Jesus came to save could not or would not fathom who he was, even for their own redemption, but those who he came to destroy had not a shred of doubt who he was? Brothers and sisters, the demons above all, *knew who he was.*"

Reverend Coombs paused as he slowly surveyed the congregation. "Brothers and sisters, the demons knew who Jesus was. Let us take this even further. What was a demon doing in the synagogue to begin with?" Reverend Coombs placed his hands in front of him on the lectern and tapped with his finger on the wood as he waited. "Well, if you think about it, it makes perfect sense, does it not? For if I am a demon whose sole purpose is to corrupt good Christians, to turn them away from the ways of God, would I not go to that very place where the word of God is spoken so that I might take measure of the strength of that word and of those who both give and receive it? In this way I might find a flaw, a weakness, an opening in which I could use to advantage to breach the defenses to loot, pillage and murder a soul. Yes, if I am a demon, I make my place in the synagogue.

"Brothers and sisters, look around you. Make no mistake – there are demons among us at this very moment, weaving their evil designs and plots against us just as there are demons outside this good city poised to enter with nothing more than foul intentions, bent on mayhem and destruction. But the lesson here is not the demons, but rather the discovery and recognition of Jesus. For how many of us fail to recognize the hand of God when it is presented to us in plain sight? How many of us act as the Sanhedrin, the high court populated with the Pharisees, to pass harsh judgment on others while ignoring our own sinful behavior? For the Sanhedrin disposed of Jesus not because he spoke *heresy*, as they claimed – no, that was just a convenient excuse. They rid themselves of Jesus because of their jealousy of his ability to influence the people and because he threatened *their* high place in society. Blinded by their own self-importance they could not grasp that the very man they would put to death was he who had come to save them – to actually relieve them of the need to even concern themselves with where they stood in such a flawed earthly society. Brothers and sisters, the lesson here is to be not the Sanhedrin, to be not blinded by yourself, but rather to look continuously for the hand of God. For he hides in plain sight standing before us. Now, let us pray."

Jack stood for the remainder of the service and then also as the pews emptied, careful not to make eye contact as people filed by him out into the foyer, murmuring to each other. When the church grew silent, he moved to his right to a secondary aisle that led down to a simple white door along the wall of the same color adjacent to the altar. Walking slowly past the seating areas and the pulpit to his left he reached the door, finding it just slightly ajar. Pushing the wooden frame open he stepped through the entrance to a small simple room where Reverend Coombs stood facing away, still dressed in his robes. The slight-framed man turned to Jack with a startled expression. "Can I help you, brother?"

Jack hesitated as he cleared his throat. "My name is Jack Halliday. I may not look it, but I'm a second lieutenant in the First Maryland Continental Regiment. Don't worry – for I'm not here for mischief."

The reverend took stock of Jack, methodically eyeing him up and down. "Very well. Why, then, are you here?" he asked softly.

Jack widened his stance and clasped his hands in front of his waist. "I've come for Custis – the silent Negro that works in the rectory kitchen. He is also a private in the Continental Army. More recently, he was more recently a private in the Second Irish Militia when we arrived here over a year ago with Lieutenant Colonel Cruger."

The reverend's eyebrows raised as he stared back at Jack with a look of surprise. He then regained his neutral expression. "So, you say? He is yours?"

"No, sir, he's not. But I must return him home where he belongs, in Maryland."

Reverend Coombs placed his hands behind his back and now paced around Jack in a slow circle, stopping back in his original place. "I do not understand. You wish to take this Negro away, but he is not yours?"

"He was the property of Mister Arthur Coleman of Annapolis. We are both in the service of Mister Coleman and were his surrogates for the Continental Army draft. We were at the battle at Camden two years prior and were separated from our unit. Eventually we landed in the hands of the Second Irish Militia, who brought us to Ninety-Six and then here to Charleston. Custis was enlisted with the militia as a freedman."

The reverend raised his eyebrows again. "A freedman? In the militia? I know nothing of this. He was sold to me fairly – a donation actually – by one of the leading merchants in this city and parishioner in good standing of this church, Doctor Charles Goodwin. Do you know him?"

Jack shook his head. "No, I don't."

"Well, perhaps your business is with him. Now, if you will excuse me, I must...."

"My business is not with *him*," Jack interrupted, his tone now decidedly sterner. "My business is here, right now. I must take Custis with me and I'm not leaving without him."

"Young man, brother, whoever you are, our business here is finished. If you do not leave, I will be forced to sound an alarm."

The reverend moved toward the door, but Jack blocked his way. "An *alarm*? And to whom would you sound an alarm? Don't you see what's happening? There's no one here that would answer such an alarm. Those Loyalists of sound mind are preparing to leave, as it's too dangerous to do otherwise. Custis and the other Negroes here will no longer remain in your custody once the partisans enter. You and this entire church are in danger."

The reverend smiled thinly. "You speak the words of one who has no faith. It is *you*, brother, that is in danger."

"The only faith I need is in myself and no one else. That has served me well and will serve me now."

"I am wed to the Church of England for which I took an oath to serve and serve it I shall," the minister said. "In God's eyes there is no preference for those who remain in this city or those outside who are coming. All are welcome and those in the care of this church will be protected by the Almighty himself, who controls all things."

Jack shook his head again. "Reverend, that is a wager I wouldn't take for I know well the kind of men that are coming. And they care not for this church or any church or any of your high-minded sensitivities but rather only for themselves. They would skin you and think nothing of it, then make from your hide a pair of boots."

Reverend Coombs stepped forward again and reached for the door. Jack grabbed his wrist. "HELP!" the reverend screamed. "HELP!"

Jack pushed the smaller man back, then moved behind him. He cupped his left hand over the reverend's mouth and held him fast to his chest. With his right hand he removed Georgey's knife from inside his coat, holding it in plain view of the reverend's face. "Custis doesn't belong to either you or this church and how you acquired him is of no relevance. To hold a freedman here for your folly makes you no better than the demons you speak of. Now, we're going out back to collect Custis and you'll not utter a word. Then all three of us will make our way down to the waterfront where there's a boat waiting. We'll bring you on board and you'll remain until the boat departs, at which time you'll be returned to land. I'll maintain a hold on you the entire walk to the boat. If you attempt to sound an alarm, I'll gut you where you stand. I could kill you here and now and no one would know better of it but I mean no harm to you unless you oppose me. You said you traded fairly for Custis and so will I – you'll give him to me in exchange for your life." Jack pressed the tip of the blade into the reverend's throat just hard enough not to break the skin. "Do you understand?"

Reverend Coombs nodded nervously as he trembled. Jack then removed the blade and his hand from the reverend's mouth, maintaining hold of the robe in the back. "Not a sound, reverend," Jack spoke into his ear. "Not one sound. You do like I say, reverend and you'll be right as rain."

Jack marched the reverend to the rectory where they quickly retrieved Custis, then continued to the nearby waterfront in silence. All around them the streets bustled with movement as people scurried in haste carrying some type of belonging, none seeming to notice the strange trio as they passed. They soon boarded the *Harriet* as Jacob, Isaac and the crew of six finished the final preparations to depart. In short order Jack marched Reverend Coombs back down to the wharf as the crew readied themselves to pull up the brow. He turned the still-trembling reverend to face him.

"You've kept your part of the bargain, reverend and I'll keep mine." Jack reached inside his coat as the reverend's eyes went wide. Jack withdrew his spoon and raised it up in front of the reverend. "You kept in your possession something that wasn't yours to keep. I also once took something that wasn't mine to take." He handed the spoon to the reverend. "I can't return this piece of silver to its rightful place, but you may have it. Consider it a *donation* to you and your church."

Jack pressed the spoon into Reverend Coombs's palm, then turned and strode back up the brow onto the *Harriet* as the crew hoisted the walkway up behind him. As the wind and tide pushed and pulled the craft well into the Cooper River, Jack helped trim the mainsail as he looked back from the stern at the reverend who grew steadily smaller, standing in place with arms folded and a fixed scowl. As planned, they cleared the mouth of the river well before sunset and continued east toward the deep open ocean, headed for Chesapeake Bay.

Several days later, on December 14th, the British completed the evacuation of Charleston using 130 ships to transport over 14,000 people to include more than 4,000 Loyalists and 5,000 slaves, all with little more than the clothes on their backs, to safer havens such as Barbados in the Caribbean, Halifax in Canada, and even England itself. Of the remaining, those known to have supported the Crown were imprisoned, whipped, tarred and feathered, dragged through ponds, and marked on their bare breasts as *Tories* after being relieved of their possessions and turned out of their houses, which were summarily plundered. A detachment of 400 Continental soldiers led by General *Mad* Anthony Wayne entered the city and cautiously followed the British rear guard as they backed their way to the last departing vessels. To make a concluding point, twenty-four of the most prominent Loyalists were hanged along the waterfront within plain sight of the final evacuees. With the Treaty of Paris and formal end of the war yet another nine months away, the evacuation of Charleston for all practical purposes signaled the end of colonial hostilities in both deed and spirit. Almost a year later in November 1783, more than 50,000 would evacuate New York, the last of the British and Loyalists to do so. The thirteen colonies, now the new *United States of America*, underwritten by an under-manned, under-equipped, and under-organized ragtag collection of guerilla fighters, whose typical calling card was their bloody tracks left from lack of shoes, had nonetheless managed to outlast and defeat the most powerful nation and military in the world.

* * *

ANNAPOLIS, MARYLAND, DECEMBER 25, 1782

Jack and Custis arrived in Annapolis with all the fanfare of the light breeze that had pushed them into the harbor. Continuing on foot through the city unnoticed, they passed under grey overcast skies amid the leafless dormant trees that lined the familiar road to the Coleman estate. A full year later, George Washington would ride down the same path with all the splendor of a new American Caeser to resign his military commission to the sitting Continental Congress as a precursor to their ratification of the Treaty of Paris, which would be signed September 3, 1783, thus formally ending the war. A voluntary abdication of such power proved stunning to the remainder of the world and signaled the birth of a government unlike any before in history. But today, except for the occasional scuffing of their feet on the ground, silence hung heavy with the misty morning air as the weary pair marched together toward what they considered home.

Arriving eventually on the grounds of the Coleman farm, they stopped briefly at the gate to peer down the long drive that led to the main house. As if they had never left, there stood the fine large brick home with an ample field behind where several cattle grazed and in front a circular half-moon driveway that revealed the handsome front door protected beneath a large portico.

Jack placed a hand on the shoulder of his ever-silent companion. "Let's go, Custis." He nodded as he took a step forward toward the house. "Goddamn it!" he cried as his right knee buckled and he lurched forward, catching himself before he fell. He took a few moments to limp in circles before he nodded to Custis again.

They took their final steps down the drive to arrive at the entrance, announcing their presence with the heavy door knocker. A few moments later the door opened to reveal Isum, tall and thin as ever but now with an even whiter head of hair. He stood in the doorway with his eyes wide and mouth open then finally stuttered, "Master Jack. Custis. Is it you? My God, we thought you were both dead."

"We're not dead, Isum," Jack answered as he smiled, "We're very much alive – and we're home."

Isum stepped outside onto the brick porch as he closed the door behind him. He grasped Jack with both hands by the shoulders as if to verify for himself. "Yes...yes you are." He then moved to Custis, hugging the younger man who hung limp and said nothing. Releasing Custis as he eyed him curiously, Isum continued. "Mister Jack, we thought you and Custis had died in a place called *Camden*, far from here. We were told that nearly everyone there had been killed, including you."

"That's mainly accurate," Jack answered. "Camden was a disaster. We were separated and couldn't send word. But we're home now. It's good to see you, Isum. May we come in?"

Isum remained silent with a perplexed expression. "Actually, Master Jack," he eventually answered, "it'd be best if you stayed right here. I must fetch Mister Coleman."

Isum returned inside and closed the door. Jack looked at Custis, who stared blankly into the yard. Jack paced on the porch for several moments before the door opened again. Mister Coleman appeared in the doorway, his brown eyes wide.

"Jack!" Mister Coleman exclaimed. "What's this?"

Jack looked back at Arthur Coleman, straddling the entry but not continuing further to greet them. "We're home, sir. Custis and I are home. May we come in?"

"But how?" Mister Coleman continued. "How is this possible?"

Jack started to answer then stopped, his mouth moving with no sound coming out as he kept his gaze fixed on Mister Coleman.

"Who is it, father?" spoke a soft voice from inside the house. "I thought I heard Jack's voice. Is that Jack?"

Priscilla appeared behind Mister Coleman, peering over her father's right shoulder. "Jack!" she exclaimed. "Is it you?" She tried to push through the doorway, but her father blocked her.

"Stay inside, dear," he ordered sternly.

"But father...."

"I said, stay inside!"

Jack stared past Mister Coleman into the foyer at the beautiful young woman Priscilla had become, her long dark hair spilling down past her shoulders and soft, brown eyes staring back in amazement. She held a baby in her arms, a toddler, who looked silently out past the door as he sucked his thumb. A young man now appeared at Priscilla's side, tall and well-built with blond hair and blue eyes. He stared intently out at Jack.

"Is everything alright, sir?" the young man spoke into Mister Coleman's ear. "Do you need help?"

"No, Rodney," Mister Coleman answered with a glance. "Just stay inside and take Priscilla away."

"What's this?" Jack protested as he moved forward toward the doorway. Mister Coleman blocked his entrance.

"This is my family, Jack," Mister Coleman answered. "I'm sorry, but you can't come in. My daughter is married now with a son."

"Married? To whom? We had an agreement!" Jack complained angrily. "You and I had an agreement! You told me...."

Mister Coleman cut him off. "I know what I told you, lad. But things have changed since then. We thought you dead. I'm truly sorry but there's no place for you here."

A flustered Jack looked at Custis, who now stared intently at his master, who stood in the doorway with both his arms stretched across like a closed gate. Jack began to sweat as he took increasingly deep breaths.

"But I thought *I* was your family!" Jack blurted as tears formed. "You told me!"

"It's good that you are alive, lad, but...."

"No! This isn't right!" Jack rushed forward and pushed Mister Coleman, knocking him backward inside the foyer. The larger young man behind grabbed Jack by the collar as he entered the house, pushing Jack back outside.

"Father!" Priscilla shrieked as Mister Coleman fell onto his back on the floor. She placed her son down and helped her father to his feet as Jack and Rodney wrestled in the doorway. "Custis!" she called outside. "Do something!"

Jack struggled to find purchase, mainly for his good left leg, to push away as Rodney maintained hold of him with both hands by the collar. Jack reached into his coat to produce Georgey's knife.

"No, Master Jack!" Custis spoke sternly as he grabbed Jack's arm. "No, lieutenant!"

"What?" Jack exclaimed. He stopped his struggle and stepped back, allowing Custis to remove the knife from his hand. "Custis?"

Mister Coleman pushed past Rodney in the doorway to step back outside, just in front of the door.

"Master, Jack," Custis spoke slowly and evenly, "you weren't supposed to come back. You weren't supposed to *ever* come back." Custis looked now directly at Mister Coleman, who resumed his position between Jack and the entrance. "I understand, now. I was wrong."

"You may remain, Custis," Mister Coleman offered. "This is your home."

"I won't," Custis answered. "I'm a freedman. And my home is with Master Jack." He then turned to Jack, who still breathed heavily in silent shock. He held Jack by the arm to lead him off the porch. "Let's go, lieutenant."

Jack looked one last time past Arthur Coleman and Rodney into the house then turned to follow Custis back up the drive. He hung his head as he slowly limped and began to weep.

EPILOGUE

Come down off your throne and leave your body alone;
Somebody must change;
You are the reason I've been waiting so long;
Somebody holds the key;
Well, I'm near the end and I just ain't got the time;
and I'm wasted and I can't find my way home.

Can't Find My Way Home, Blind Faith

BLUE HILL, MAINE, NOVEMBER 1829

Jack and Roger stared silently into the fire that began to grow dimmer. Jack reached nearby for another piece of split wood, placing it carefully onto the top of the embers where it would catch quickly. Outside, the rain had quickened, and the wind grown stronger as both whistled past the house.

"What should I call you?" Roger asked gently.

"*Jack* would be appropriate. Just call me *Jack*." The elderly man stood and approached the window at the far end of the house. "Your mare. We should get her under cover. There's a barn here in the back."

Roger stood as well and walked toward the window. "And Custis. What of him?"

371

"He died some years ago. He's buried to the side of the house in the orchid where he preferred to spend his time."

Roger shook his head as he gazed along with Jack out the window at the grey landscape. "All this time. I didn't know. It seems that an entire lifetime has been taken from me."

"The orchid," Jack remarked. "It's because of Custis. I wanted to keep moving. I wanted to keep moving as far away as I could, but Custis knew it would never be far enough. We stopped in many places along the way to work enough to move on, but we stayed here because Custis liked it. The owner, Mister Philip Macomber, took us in and we worked for him many years. He had no family and when he died no one came to assume the farm. He's buried too in the orchid. We still call it *Macomber Orchid*." Jack turned to Roger. "It took much courage to come all this way to find me."

"*Courage?*" Roger scoffed. "I wouldn't call it that. I meant to go back countless times, afraid of what I might find. But I was even more afraid of what I might not. *Fear* drove me here, not *courage*."

Jack grinned. "Fear and courage are two sides of the same coin – both related and inseparable. When you spend that coin, you choose which side to brandish. Courage isn't the absence of fear but instead the mastery of it. Those who don't master their fear are destined to be ruled by it. You must be a *master of your person*, and I see that you are. But grief and regret – that's another coin altogether."

Roger looked at Jack but said nothing.

"I think of your mother often," Jack continued, "every day, in fact. Also, your grandfather. I have mastered fear but not regret. I have withstood battles thicker than you can imagine and not been the worse for it. But one simple memory of your mother breaks me like a twig. Regret gnaws on me like a hungry dog with a bone. An entire lifetime has been taken from me as well. I never used to cry. But now...."

"It doesn't have to stay that way," Roger offered. "You still have much life left." He placed a hand on his father's shoulder as he looked into his watering eyes. "Jack," he continued, "would you come back to Annapolis with me, to remain there for the rest of your days? It would be good to have you home – your home as much as mine. We two are the only family that's left now."

Jack remained silent for a moment as he also clasped Roger by the shoulder. "*Family...home*," he repeated as he nodded. "Yes, I believe I will."

Made in the USA
Las Vegas, NV
11 September 2024